EL PASO SUNRISE

EL PASO SUNRISE

A NOVEL

LOUIS BODNAR

NEW YORK

LONDON • NASHVILLE • MELBOURNE • VANCOUVER

El Paso Sunrise

A Novel

Published in New York, New York, by Morgan James Publishing. Morgan James is a trademark of Morgan James, LLC. www.MorganJamesPublishing.com

ISBN 9781642793253 paperback
ISBN 9781642793260 eBook
Library of Congress Control Number: 2018912493

Cover Design by:
Megan Dillon
megan@creativeninjadesigns.com

Interior Design by:
Chris Treccani
www.3dogcreative.net

Morgan James is a proud partner of Habitat for Humanity Peninsula and Greater Williamsburg. Partners in building since 2006.

Get involved today! Visit
MorganJamesPublishing.com/giving-back

To our Lord and Savior, Jesus Christ,
and to the love of my life, my wife Joan Carol

The farther backward you may look…
the farther forward you are likely to see.
Anonymous

The ultimate of human freedoms is the freedom of choice.
The Author

With God's grace freely given, the completion of the intimacy work in progress
between a man and a woman **depends** *on each, by their own God-given*
choice, coming to know themselves fully and only happens the moment the
woman forgives her own father, lets him go, and lets her son go to another
woman of his own…and the man forgives his own mother, lets her go, and lets
his daughter go to another man of her own.
The Author

"Kill him," the hushed, gravelly, almost hoarse voice said on the speaker to the four assassins slouched around the rough-hewn oak table, three of them sipping Stolichnaya vodka straight, while the fourth drank hot tea. They had all been waiting for the long-distance telephone call and were playing cards in the large kitchen of a rustic log cabin hidden in dense forest near the US-Canadian border in Manitoba, near Melita, Canada, and one hundred miles from Carrington, North Dakota, in the US.

The four said nothing, nodded silently, as Gravelly Voice continued, "You all have your assignments, and this hit must not fail… all understand?"

Four yesses at once, then a click, and the telephone line went dead.

At the same time, the ancient teletype machine sitting on a rusty beat-up file cabinet in the corner came to life with clickety clacks sounding like tank tracks on pavement, and suddenly paper spewed out like toilet paper being unrolled.

An assassin got up from another table in the room, stepped over to the machine, and waited, watching the paper pile up…

The interior of the decrepit five-room lodge was sparsely decorated but well kept. Knotty-pine walls, low ceilings, and shuttered small windows with thick glass panels gave a dark cave-like feel to the old hunting lodge. Kerosene lamps and an immense stone fireplace standing in one corner, fire burning, lent a warm glow to the spacious room yet gave it an acrid aura when mixed with cooking and body odors. A wood-burning stove stood almost majestically in the other corner. One wall had an empty gun cabinet while the other held a massive galvanized-iron sink with two faucets and a narrow hallway leading to four small bedrooms. The oak plank flooring of the cabin was made smooth by a hundred years of wear.

The cabin sat in a small clearing in the dense forest among the tall canopy of pine and oak trees and had several vehicles to the side, all hidden with thick piled brush around them.

It was snowing lightly in the twilight of sunset, gentle flakes fluttering softly, the entire scene like a picture from a Hans Christian Andersen book of fairy tales.

Then the machine stopped. The assassin tore off the last sheet and dropped the pile of papers right in the middle of the table, saying, "We have our assignment. We cannot fail. No excuses." Paused, looked all around the kitchen, and said, "We leave right after our reinforcement and supplies arrive…"

El Paso Herald-Chronicle

Volume 113, Issue 279 Friday, August 14, 2015   35¢

VANDOROL PICKED AS PROSECUTOR FOR TRIAL OF RICARDO ALVARADO AND FATHER ALBERTO ALVARADO

AP EL PASO, TEXAS—Lawyer and Special Judge Steven J. Vandorol was appointed special prosecutor in the fraud and conspiracy case of Ricardo Alvarado and his father, Alberto Alvarado—a prosecution with national implications.

District Attorney Ernesto Martinez said Vandorol, who was appointed last Thursday, will serve as a special assistant deputy district attorney and head the Special Crimes Unit to prosecute this case. The prosecution team includes veteran First Assistant District Attorney North Anderson and Assistant District Attorney Beth Barker.

Anderson is also chief of the White Collar Crime Unit that initially investigated the fraudulent sale of annuities from the Alvarado family's failed insurance companies, which the assigned bankruptcy judge characterized as a giant Ponzi scheme, as well as dealings between the Alvarados, father Alberto and son Ricardo Alvarado; El Paso Power & Electric Company, LLC; El Paso law firm Kemper & Smith, Attorneys; Washington, D.C., law firm Henderson & Lane; and other defendants, both named and unnamed co-conspirators.

The investigations resulted in Texas state indictments last June by a special grand jury called by Chief District Judge Kathy Carbon, at the joint request of the governors of Texas, New Mexico, Arizona and Oklahoma.

Ricardo Alvarado is an El Paso billionaire and, according to *Forbes*, one of the richest men in the United States, listed by *Forbes* as number 27 of the top 100 billionaires. His father, Alberto Alvarado, a Mexican national, is one of the richest men in Mexico, with close ties to the Mexican federal government. Both men are leading contributors to the Democratic Party and were leading contributors to President Barack Obama's election in 2008 and reelection in 2012.

The indictment has national implications, Martinez said, and involves vast corruption at the highest levels of our federal government in Washington, D.C., Denver, New York and Los Angeles.

The indictment alleges 153 separate counts and criminal violations among all defendants named co-conspirators and various unnamed co-conspirators, alleging criminal acts including fraud, money laundering, drug and weapons smuggling and trafficking, white slavery, treason and aiding and abetting Islamic terrorist activities.

North Anderson is the first assistant district attorney and leads both the criminal prosecutions division and White-Collar Crime Unit. For the last 10 years, Anderson has successfully prosecuted and won 28 capital murders and 50 white-collar crime prosecutions. Anderson is a former all-pro linebacker for the Dallas Cowboys, having had to retire after knee injuries destroyed his professional football career.

Beth Barker is chief of the Drug Enforcement Unit and leads the district attorney's office in drug enforcement convictions.

District Attorney Ernesto Martinez said five additional assistant district attorneys and four investigators will be assigned to the criminal trial, now scheduled to begin next February in 168th District Court, Judge Kathy Carbon's court.

A graduate of the University of Oklahoma College of Law, Vandorol first attended the US Military Academy at West Point for two years, where he played football but had to withdraw when he sustained a debilitating knee injury that terminated a probable military career. He later graduated from Oklahoma State University, Stillwater, and University of Oklahoma College of Law, earning a juris doctorate. He also attended Georgetown Law Center in Washington, earning an LLM in international and comparative law while also practicing law in the capital for over five years.

Vandorol arrived in El Paso in summer 2010 and opened a solo legal general practice with emphasis in family, criminal, and military law, also representing Fort Bliss as outside counsel. Vandorol quickly established a reputation in family law and divorce, zealously defending children's rights, so successfully that in 2012 he was appointed special family law judge by Chief Judge Pablo Cortez. He was also appointed assistant municipal judge for the City of El Paso by Chief Municipal Judge Sam Fraxton, District Attorney Ernesto Martinez said.

"His 25 years of legal practice experience, his long and varied experience as a civil and criminal trial lawyer, and his dedication to justice will be extremely beneficial to this complex conspiracy, corruption, drug enforcement, radical Muslim terrorist and weapons violations prosecution," said District Attorney Ernesto Martinez.

Martinez also said that this prosecution had national federal implications as the heads of Homeland Security Administration (HSA), Drug Enforcement Administration (DEA), and Alcohol, Tobacco and Firearms (ATF) are identified as defendants, and the federal agencies they head are further identified as unnamed co-conspirators. Special agent in charge, Jack Reynolds, who heads the El Paso office of the FBI, declined comment on this prosecution.

"While our investigation is far from complete at this time, we have gathered enough documentary evidence and whistleblower witnesses that indicate a conspiracy within our national government more pervasive than the Watergate scandal of the Nixon Administration that ultimately caused the resignation of President Richard Nixon," El Paso Police Chief Edward "Eddie" Egen said.

Martinez has been the 65th district attorney for the last 20 years and is rumored to be considered the next attorney general of the State of Texas. The 65th district encompasses El Paso, Bexar, Dona Ana, and Hudspeth counties in Texas and covers more than 2,500 square miles of the South Texas border with Mexico. The 65th district also encompasses federal installations of Fort Bliss, headquarters for 3rd Armored Cavalry Division, 42nd Ranger Division, 401st Military Police Training Command and Biggs Army Airfield and is the largest military installation in the United States.

Gov. Greg Abbott recently mobilized the Texas National Guard and, along with Arizona Gov. Jan Brewer, closed the border after the administration refused to enforce federal immigration law and tried to flood the southern border with alien children from South America and thousands of Syrian refugees, unvetted and alleged to be fully infiltrated by ISIS. Arizona's National Guard joined Texas and Oklahoma to alleviate the crush of illegal alien immigrants.

Martinez also said that Governor Abbott is closely following this prosecution and its federal government implications by virtue of HSA, DEA and ATF agent heads being identified defendants or as unnamed co-conspirators. The governor, through his press secretary, Glen Beck, had no comment on the prosecution at this time.

El Paso Police Chief Edward "Eddie" Egen, contacted by the *Herald-Chronicle*, said, "Steven Vandorol is an extremely talented lawyer, family law judge, and associate municipal judge with a very clear vision of right and wrong. He has been, in the comparatively short time that he has been in El Paso, a most fair associate municipal judge and friend of the El Paso Police Department. He is my friend as well."

Egen also said that the El Paso Police Department was working closely with both the intelligence and investigative units of the Texas Rangers and that Texas Rangers' Commander Charles Norris will be in El Paso to meet with the prosecution team.

President Obama's press secretary had no comment on either the special prosecution or the Texas indictments.

Attorney General of the United States Loretta Lynn, contacted at a Muslim outreach luncheon by reporters, also had no comment on the Holy Land Foundation, a named defendant in the indictments and on the State Department's list of active worldwide radical Muslim terrorist organizations and the administration's ties to the Muslim Brotherhood.

3

Steven Vandorol, in El Paso now for almost five years, parked his ten-year-old silver Ford Taurus early Monday morning in a reserved space of the courthouse parking garage on San Antonio Street in downtown El Paso. The garage was attached to the fifteen-story El Paso District Courthouse by a third-floor skyway.

The courthouse was built in 1991 on the site of the demolished courthouse built in 1917. A structure of steel and concrete, it featured an Alamo-shaped granite entrance and sky-blue reflective glass that perfectly mirrored the Franklin Mountains, the divider of affluent west and military east El Paso.

Steven got out, stretched, clicked the doors locked, and walked to the garage elevator, then down to the third-floor skywalk and across into the courthouse to the security gate ahead.

"Good morning, judge," the courthouse security officer said as Steven walked up to the security gate and X-ray monitor and conveyor.

"Good morning, Manny." He nodded to the second officer behind the X-ray monitor. "And to you as well, Fernando."

Fernando glanced up. "Morning, judge. Well-armed today as usual?" Smiling, security guard Fernando knew El Paso attorney and municipal judge Steven Vandorol very well and the many death threats a judge usually received.

"As always," Steven answered and reached back, unclipped his holstered Glock 22 from his belt, and handed it to Manny. Reached into his back pocket, pulled out a pearl-handled switchblade five inches long, and handed it to Manny as well.

The ten-inch throwing knife concealed in a leather sheath of his right sea turtle Tony Lama boot stayed right where it was, as it always cleared the X-ray metal detector.

Manny asked, "Well, judge, any threats against your life this week?" As an associate municipal judge, Steven received numerous death threats, sometimes almost daily.

"Not this week, Manny." Steven smiled, handing him the weapons. "But it's just Monday."

"I heard that, judge…"

Manny took the weapons, Steven walked through, reached back and took the holstered pistol and switchblade, clipped the pistol back, and pocketed the switchblade. "You guys have a great day," he said as he walked to the third-floor elevator.

Steven punched the up button on the mirrored panel at the elevators and waited.

He was wearing jeans and cowboy boots shined to a mirror high gloss. He really liked his maroon sea turtle boots. They were the only luxury he had permitted himself since he had arrived in El Paso from Washington almost five years ago. He was also wearing a blue blazer, white cotton short-sleeved shirt for the Texas heat, and blood-red tie, all the standard wear for El Paso lawyers at the courthouse. Since he wasn't going to court, but to see his boss, District Attorney Ernesto Martinez, his tie was loose and collar unbuttoned.

Steven continued waiting.

Staring at his reflection in the mirror, he straightened his shoulders and smiled as his eyes wandered to his face. Clean shaven. Hungarian dark, smooth skin. Wide forehead. Receding hairline. Prominent nose, yet crooked, having been broken many times in childhood brawls. High cheekbones accenting large, dark brown, piercing, sometimes slightly violent, and even cruel eyes. Eyes with just a hint of slant, evident in the race coming from the Mongol and Hun hordes that started the Hungarian bloodlines. His gaze reflected his soul. Previously turbulent, but after recovery from the previous evil of Washington, now reflected a serenity and calm he was proud to have earned. *Free at last from most of my evil ways,* Steven thought and smiled again. "Still a work in progress," he said out loud to no one in particular.

Gold wire-rimmed glasses. Sensual lips which, in pout, matched an elusive sadness and, when unsmiling, a grim, almost ruthless determination and intensity. Hair perfect. Brown, now graying at the temples and sideburns, razor edged. A little over six feet, broad shoulders, and 180, Steven was back to his high school senior football weight. *I feel great,* he thought, *and look okay too.* He winked at himself in the mirror and gave a wry smile.

Steven Vandorol survived Washington with divine guidance and designated angels that the good Lord in His mysterious ways had provided, transformed his soul, managed two overpowering addictions, was narrowing his own circle, and coming to see and know himself as he was, not as others wanted him to be. And after a lifetime of chaos, violence, anguish, and pain, he was finally at peace with himself.

Since I'm not dead, I guess I'm stronger. He thought of that old Friedrich Nietzsche mantra: "That which does not kill me makes me stronger." The elevator opened to his best friend, El Paso Police Chief Edward "Eddie" Egen.

"Hi, judge," Eddie said, stepping out of the elevator. "Can I talk to you for a second?" The elevator was crowded. Steven's usually smiling best friend seemed very serious today.

"Sure, Eddie," Steven said, taking his extended hand as the elevator door closed behind him. "What's up?"

Eddie was huge. Six-foot-five and 260 pounds. Bulging, muscled arms and legs, thick strong neck. An ex-army military police major who, after sixteen years in the army, came to Fort Bliss for his last military assignment, fell in love with Texas in general, El Paso in particular, and married Andi, his fifth wife. At that time, army downsizing had been the order of the day, and when the 3rd Cavalry downsized to ten thousand men, Eddie retired, just in time to apply for the then-open City of El Paso Police Department chief job.

Eddie was a handsome man. Gray hair, intense blue eyes, and a perpetual sly and ironic smile, he reminded Steven of a middle-aged John Wayne in one of his favorite John Wayne movies, *Brannigan.*

Eddie was also a player and womanizer. Glib and a jokester, he had a joke he could tell at every occasion. He could also talk a woman into bed at the drop of a hat. Steven had seen him do just that. Steven accepted his best friend, the big funny Irishman, for what he was, a many-layered individual, many emotional issues, but with a good compassionate heart. And their commonality rested in chaos, violence, aggression, intensity, and personal survival. And there was nothing that either would not do for the other. Chief Egen was probably the best PD chief that El Paso ever had in a department established in 1884 with its violent border town untamed West history, Steven thought.

Then 9/11 changed everything. Fort Bliss again expanded and became one of the centers of the War on Radical Islamic Terror. The United States was now fighting two wars, one on its southern border, the now War on Radical Islamic Terror, and the previous War on Drugs, with the El Paso Police Department and its over one thousand uniformed police officers protecting the very underbelly gateway of the United States.

Steven and Eddie met through Eddie's wife, Andi, who ran a travel agency, Adventure World Travel, where Steven would get airline tickets for his weekend trips to Tulsa to visit his kids, now teenagers, son Josef and daughter Karina. Eddie was the silent partner of the agency, and when a dispute arose with the previous owner, Eddie became one of Steven's first El Paso legal clients.

Steven and Eddie became fast friends that first year Steven was in El Paso. Not only did Steven successfully defend the suit by the previous owner of the travel agency, but he countersued and won a $500,000 judgment for punitive damages for the Egens, which judgment Steven promptly collected by levying on a herd of fine quarter horses. Eddie, a good though oversized horseman himself, agreed to settle by taking the entire herd, some fifty horses, $10,000 each, and release the judgment. Steven was a frequent weekend visitor to the Egen ranch near Canutillo, New Mexico, as Steven had loved horses since his childhood back in Brazil on a *fazenda*, a mega ranch. He purchased one of the quarter horses from Eddie and promptly named Pegasus after his first horse when he was a child on that *fazenda*. A $200,000 collected attorney fee kickstarted his solo law practice.

Eddie touched Steven's shoulder and pulled him over to the fourth-floor window, overlooking downtown El Paso, sparkling in early midmorning sun. Eddie was holding a copy of the *El Paso Herald-Chronicle* newspaper.

"You goin' to see Ernie?" Eddie asked with his usual wide grin.

"Yep, I guess he wants to talk about the Hernandez *Herald-Chronicle* interview. Did you read it?" Steven glanced at the newspaper under Eddie's arm.

"Yep, I did, and yes he does. Ernie called me and wanted me to be here for the meeting."

Steven frowned. "Why?"

Eddie was serious. "There is a real dangerous situation developing. I don't want to upset you, but I have to warn you right now." He hesitated, no longer smiling.

Steven was calmer than his friend. "It's okay, Ed. Just spit it out."

"Steven, there is a contract out on your life."

4

Steven and Eddie silently rode up on the Monday morning crowded elevator to the fifth floor where the entire floor was the offices of 65th District Attorney Ernesto Luis Martinez and his assistants, a total of thirty-five lawyers and more than fifty paralegals and investigators.

Both got off, turned left, and were at a massive wooden double door, encased in bulletproof glass. On the right, in gold-leaf lettering, a sign read:

ERNESTO LUIS MARTINEZ
DISTRICT ATTORNEY
65TH JUDICIAL DISTRICT
EL PASO, TEXAS

On the left side, also in gold-leaf lettering, all assistant district attorneys were listed in order of seniority: North B. Anderson, first assistant; then Elizabeth B. Barker, drug enforcement; and on down the list, thirty-five total assistant district attorneys.

Eddie, with Steven behind, walked right in up to another bulletproof glass enclosure, microphone on front, and a woman behind the glass. She saw Eddie smiling and waving and the door buzzed immediately. Eddie opened the door for Steven, and they walked into a large wood parquet reception area with ten or fifteen massive leather chairs and three leather couches.

Out in front was a receptionist desk with a pretty young Hispanic girl with earphones, maybe twenty, sitting before a huge inset communication system. She smiled brightly at Eddie and blushed visibly, Steven noticed.

The reception desk was flanked by two large wooden doors to either side, both with bulletproof peepholes, the obvious second line of security defense to the inner offices.

Still blushing and stammering just a little, the girl said, "Chief Egen, how are you today?"

"Fine, darlin'. How you been?" Eddie was smiling, all the prior seriousness gone. "Ernie is expecting us." Eddie winked at her. Steven noticed again… and guessed obvious carnal knowledge between them.

"I'll let him know you're here—oh, hi, Judge Vandorol—that you are both here." She was obviously a little flustered, Steven saw. She buzzed Ernie's office, paused, then said, "Chief Egen and Mr. Vandorol are both here." She smiled up at Eddie, locking eyes with him as the door to the right was buzzing. Steven noticed that exchange as well.

This time Steven reached the door first, opened and held it for Eddie, who was still smiling and seemed to be having a hard time breaking eye contact with the beautiful receptionist.

As Eddie passed Steven, he winked at Steven and walked down the long deep-pile luxurious carpeted hallway, Steven following.

The hallway was at least twenty-five yards long, with plush dark-brown carpet, oak paneling, wainscoting, and crown molding down the entire length, large wooden doors on either side, ten feet apart, twenty doors total, ending with a like door at the end with the nameplate "Ernesto Luis Martinez, 65th District Attorney."

Down the hallway on both walls hung the original six flags over Texas, framed behind glass, and between the doors on each side were the offices for the DA himself and his almost fifty assistants, headed by the criminal and civil first assistants, on either side.

As both men approached, the door at the end was opened by Martinez himself, smiling broadly.

The DA was short, as are most Hispanic men—stocky, dark olive skin, black hair combed straight back, with graying temples. Large brown eyes, ample eyebrows, and clean shaven. He was a handsome man, probably in his mid-fifties, and impeccably dressed in a navy-blue tailor-made suit, linen white shirt with French cuffs, and gold nugget cufflinks with monogrammed sleeves, ELM, in old English lettering. He also had on a Bijan silk powder-blue tie, matching silk pocket square, and Gucci loafers.

Ernie smiled at Eddie. "Good morning, chief. Thanks for coming on such short notice." He turned to Steven. "Nice boots, Steven."

"El Paso's best. Tony Lamas." They both walked in.

"Alligator?" Ernie asked as Steven passed by.

"Sea turtle."

"Very cool…and great shine as well. Very, very nice," Ernie said as he closed the door and walked to his mahogany desk. "You guys want anything? Coffee?" Ernie cleared a speck from the corner of his right eye with a manicured finger.

"I never turn down good coffee, thanks," Steven replied, sitting down in a red leather armchair in front of the desk.

"Me too," Eddie said. "And donuts too, if you got 'em." He sat down in the other chair beside Steven, an art deco coffee table in between the two friends.

Ernie grinned. "Cops gotta have donuts. Right, chief?" He picked up his phone. "Marcy, can we get some coffee…and donuts, if we still got 'em from the morning rush? Thanks." Ernie clicked off, still smiling brightly at the two.

Ernie sat down behind his desk piled with neat stacks of files, some eight stacks of ten to twenty files each, and a completely clear red leather desk pad holding only the *El Paso Herald-Chronicle* newspaper and a sterling silver pen and pencil desk set engraved with his name.

Behind his desk was a mahogany credenza, with ornate golden flag stands topped by golden eagles, the state flag of the Lone Star State on the right, the flag of the United States in the middle, and the flag of the Confederacy on the left.

"Hey, Ernie, did you hear about the very gentle Texas lady who was driving across a really high bridge in Austin?" Eddie began.

Ernie looked at his chief of police. "Tell me…"

"Well, as I said, the very gentle Texas lady was driving across that really high bridge in Austin…you know the one I'm talking about, right?"

Ernie nodded as Eddie continued, "…as she neared the top of the bridge, she noticed a young man fixin' to jump." Eddie looked at Steven. "That, for you former Okies, means getting ready to…"

Steven shook his head at his friend in mock disbelief.

"She stopped the car, rolled down the window, and said, 'Please don't jump! Think of your dear mother and father.'"

The young man replied, "My mom and dad are both dead; I'm going to jump!"

She said, "Well, think of your sweet wife and precious children."

He replied, "I'm not married, and I don't have any kids."

She said, "Well, then you just remember the Alamo!"

He replied, "What's the Alamo?"

She replies, "Well, bless your heart! You just go ahead and jump, you little Yankee idiot. You're holding up traffic!"

Ernie was laughing. Steven also, even though he had heard the joke before. Steven really enjoyed his friend's jokes. Eddie had a great timing and talent for telling jokes, and obviously enjoyed telling them.

At a knock on the door, Marcy walked in carrying a tray with two mugs and a plate of donuts, set it down on the coffee table, and walked out.

"Eddie, you should do standup comedy," Steven said, wiping his eyes.

Ernie also did and said, "Good one, Ed! Listen, thanks again for coming." He looked at Steven…

Eddie replied, "Sure thing, boss."

Ernie looked at Eddie again. "Did you tell him?" He was now suddenly serious, his mouth a straight sharp line.

Eddie nodded. "Yeah, just briefly." He paused. "I figured you'd wanna tell him the whole deal."

"Okay, thanks. I did." Ernie sat back in his chair. "Steven, when I appointed you as special prosecutor for the Alvarado fraud and conspiracy cases, I really didn't have the complete picture myself."

Steven said nothing.

"You've been in El Paso for about five years now, but you are still the new kid on the block."

Steven said nothing.

"You built a great little law practice. Ingratiated yourself with absolutely all the district judges, especially the chief judge…"

Eddie interrupted, "Kathy Carbon…she's a real looker, right, Steven?"

Steven said nothing.

Ernie continued, "You did such a great job out at Fort Bliss with all the military family law cases that the Council of Judges thought you'd make a great family law associate judge, and you got that gig as well, which was a real plum for you since it didn't interfere with your private law practice…"

Steven still said nothing.

Eddie again interrupted, "And you did so well out at Bliss with your military background that you became the go-to guy on court martial defense for outside counsel appointments."

Ernie now interrupted Eddie. "And all of a sudden Chief Municipal Judge Sam Fraxton needed to appoint additional associate municipal judges, and you had that job also."

"That was Eddie's doing," Steven said, looking at Eddie. "Thanks again, bud." Eddie smiled and nodded.

Ernie Martinez continued, "So when the initial investigation was done for this case, I found that the corruption ran to the highest levels right here in El Paso, both state and federal." Ernie paused. "So, I had to have a lawyer that was good, real good, but had no ties to local hierarchy, either personally or professionally. Someone that was bulletproof here and could not be bought, influenced, corrupted, or intimidated."

"What's that got to do with a contract out on my life?" Steven asked calmly, sitting up in his chair.

"That's just it, Steven. It's got nothing to do with the Alvarado fraud and conspiracy cases! The information comes straight from the East Coast. From Washington, DC."

5

Steven was stunned. It was as if a ghost from the past had just slapped him hard. Real hard. Ernie and Eddie were watching Steven closely.

Ernie broke the oppressive silence. "Did you read the Raul Hernandez interview in last Sunday's *Herald-Chronicle*?" He handed the newspaper folded to the Hernandez interview across to Steven.

Steven took it and began reading:

El Paso Herald-Chronicle

Volume 113, Issue 282 Sunday, August 30, 2015   35¢

PROSECUTOR SAW OWN FINANCES CRUMBLE - ATTORNEY LOST MILLIONS DURING OIL CRASH OF 2006

El Paso attorney and recently appointed Special Prosecutor and Deputy District Attorney Steven Vandorol knows how quickly financial empires can crumble.

When the oil fields of Oklahoma and Texas were gushing with black gold and real estate mortgage securities were skyrocketing in value in the Sunbelt, Vandorol was a young lawyer and investor riding the crest of the oil and real estate booms.

But then in 2006, when oil prices fell and the derivatives market crashed, banks were left holding worthless energy-related loans and secondary market mortgage securities, Vandorol lost millions on bad financial deals.

His thriving law firm and practice in the Sunbelt were also wiped out.

"I would characterize myself as a beneficiary of the Texas-Oklahoma oil and real estate booms and a casualty of the bust," Vandorol told the *Herald-Chronicle*.

District Attorney Ernesto Martinez recently appointed Vandorol associate family law judge and associate municipal judge as a special prosecutor in the Alvarado corruption and conspiracy case, which has implications that may reach the White House and the current administration in Washington.

Ironically, the Alvarado financial empire also toppled after yet another crash brought on by the excess spending and bailouts of the current administration, which has increased the national debt from $6 trillion under former President George Bush to a present $23 trillion, an increase of over $17 trillion on the last seven years by the Obama administration.

Ricardo Alvarado and his father, Alberto, principal defendants, 25 other people and several corporations and organizations were re-indicted almost one year ago for allegedly engaging in a criminal conspiracy to commit theft stemming from the sale of annuities from Alvarado's failed insurance companies, illegal weapons sales and transfers and border radical Muslim terrorist activities, including white slavery, money laundering and currency manipulation.

The continuing Oklahoma Texas oil and nationwide real estate mortgage crises forced Vandorol to file Chapter 7 bankruptcy—a straight liquidation bankruptcy— early 2006 or 2007.

Vandorol listed $750 million in debt and $650 million in property, all transferred to bankruptcy creditors, wearing apparel and personal possessions as assets. The banks also foreclosed on his home, fleet of exotic sports cars, Oklahoma lake home, Colorado ski lodge, five Crested Butte condominiums and Wyoming cattle ranch.

At the peak of the oil and real estate booms, Vandorol said, his law firm represented 27 Southwest banks. After the bust, he could not support his family but moved eastward from the Sunbelt and became employed by a law firm in Washington, D.C.

"My law practice was devastated. My law partners left like rats from a sinking ship. My practice was gone," said Vandorol, a graduate of the University of Oklahoma College of Law.

Vandorol said he had to file for Chapter 7 bankruptcy because he was left holding the bag as the chief executive officer and guarantor of a venture capital and bank holding company for several Oklahoma and Southwest businesses, including a Florida intrastate airline.

When business deals—including one involving a major international airline—went sour, Vandorol said, creditors went after him personally along with several other defendants, former Vandorol clients, as guarantor of massive corporate debt in a class-action federal civil fraud lawsuit, the plaintiffs seeking nearly a half a billion dollars of monetary damages from all the defendants.

He listed the Federal Deposit Insurance Corporation (FDIC) as a major creditor in the bankruptcy. The FDIC took over the bank consortiums that financed the airline venture, he said.

When First Continental Bank & Trust collapsed as a result of "reckless" loans made by bank officials, according to the FDIC, to start the oil bust, which then led to the costliest bank failures in U.S. history, the Wall Street Journal reported. It continued on and fueled the further crash of the derivatives marked in 2006.

The FDIC became the receiver for the failed First Continental Bank and sued Vandorol and others to recover $25 million in overdrawn bank accounts. The company had $30 million as working capital when the bank was seized by the government, Vandorol said.

The FDIC suit resulted in a judgment against the company and Vandorol individually but was dismissed as a part of the bankruptcy agreement, he said. Vandorol showed the *Herald-Chronicle* documents that released him from the bankruptcy.

Vandorol said his malpractice carrier, which represented him in the bankruptcy proceedings and federal lawsuits, did not contribute a penny to a $100 million settlement fund, thus absolving him personally from any wrongdoing whatsoever.

Vandorol said the First Continental closure caused other banks nationwide to close as well—including First Continental Bank that Vandorol represented. He said he also represented that the owner of the bank, Joseph Ross, and other bank officials.

First Continental was shut down by state and federal officials and criminal corruption allegations involving bank officials; however, Ross committed suicide before he could be arrested and prosecuted.

Vandorol cooperated with an FBI probe of the bank and helped authorities locate $36 million in certificates of deposit from the failed bank.

The failure of First Continental resulted in the failure of Continental Illinois Bank of Chicago as the single largest bank failure in US history, the failure of Seafirst Bank of Seattle and the near failure of Bank of America, N.A.

Then the freezing of financial markets and collapse of financial institutions like Washington Mutual Bank, Goldman Sachs and Bear Sterns, among others, sparked the worst economic decline since the Great Depression and led directly to the election of Barrack Hussein Obama as the "historic" first black president, defeating Republican Senator John McCain.

"I first represented the bank officials themselves and consulted with the FBI about various insider transactions that had happened after those clients countersued me alleging wrongdoing, which lifted the attorney-client privilege and allowed me to defend myself,"

Vandorol said. "I told them everything I knew. I was completely candid with them."

Barry O'Donald, FBI spokesman and head of the FBI Southwest office, said, "Mr. Vandorol's help was invaluable to our investigation."

In a *Daily Oklahoman* news article, Vandorol's attorney, Robert Bailey, stressed in a court hearing arising from the liquidation of First Continental that Vandorol wasn't engaged in "any wrongdoing but was a witness to investor fraud and various crimes."

Vandorol was named in a half-billion-dollar securities fraud and racketeering suit filed as a class-action of investors. The suit alleged that Vandorol was part of the "insider" group at the bank.

"At that time, there was a cycle of disgruntled investors suing everybody they could to try and recoup their money, and I was a part of those lawsuits which were then settled," Vandorol said. "With all the lawsuits and my bankruptcy, I was through in Oklahoma City. My Sunbelt law practice was gone, and I couldn't even support my family. So, I left for Washington, D.C., and became Of Counsel at Henderson & Lane on K Street, with the help of my good friend, Martin L. King, a Washington lobbyist."

In retrospect, Vandorol says the financial woes have made him a lot wiser.

"Our past experiences can only make us better in our profession," he said. "I like to think that I learned much and what happened took a long time for me to heal from the devastation. To quote my favorite philosopher, Nietzsche, 'That, which does not kill me, makes me stronger.' "

Vandorol said District Attorney Ernesto Martinez was aware of his prior legal and business affairs. "There are no secrets," he said. Martinez couldn't be reached for comment last Friday.

Steven finished reading the article and looked up, directly into the district attorney's eyes. "It was an okay interview. So what? I told you all that stuff, all that Sunbelt rest-of-world stuff, Ernie, when you were getting ready to appoint me, didn't I, Ernie?" Steven's eyebrows lifted as he looked at his boss.

"You did." Ernie raised his eyebrows also, locking his eyes with Steven's, paused a beat, and continued, "Steven, this is not about the Sunbelt rest-of-world crap that you told me about. It's about your five years after, while you were in Washington, that you didn't! I found all that out from my source at the FBI."

Steven flushed, closed his eyes. Beads of sweat surfaced on his expansive reddening forehead. He was stunned yet again. Very tense suddenly. Nervous, legs trembling as well.

The horror—all the slime, evil, and corruption—of Steven's time in Washington before his coming to El Paso flashed before his eyes like a movie, each frame going past lightning fast. The calm, serenity, and newfound purpose of El Paso had calmed his soul after he had survived that particular horror and evil of Washington in his near past, before arriving in El Paso five years ago.

The ultimate survivor had survived one more time.

Ernie and Eddie sat quietly, respecting Steven's silence.

Steven finally opened his eyes. "The farther backward you can look the farther forward you're likely to see." He paused and continued, "My DC friend, Courtney Wellington, told me that. I'm bulletproof. What happened in DC doesn't matter."

Ernie looked directly into Steven's open eyes. "It was your good friend Courtney Wellington who told the FBI in DC, who then contacted our FBI friends here in El Paso, that your former clients in Washington, the Alvarados, father Alberto and son Ricardo, were the ones behind the contract to kill you!"

Steven took a deep breath, exhaled, remembered his old DC friends Courtney Wellington and his wife, Arlene, and told his new El Paso friends, Eddie and Ernie everything…

Steven's new El Paso friends, Eddie and Ernie, listened…

Steven told them that once he finally realized that the ultimate of human freedoms was the freedom of choice, his spiritual awakening, coupled with the power of prayer, and the help of angels that the good Lord designates, Steven figured out that he had been set up and betrayed by those closest to him. With whispers of divine guidance, his plan for ultimate survival and to defeat the evil corruption that swirled around him both emerged. All that was left was to carry it out with full conviction and righteous anger.

Steven then told Eddie and Ernie about Project Triple X.

Initially Project Triple X started out as a benign yet massive technology transfer and exchange transaction between the United States and the Republic of South Korea involving almost half a trillion dollars of private and taxpayer capital. Steven was both counsel and dupe. Project Triple X ended as a vast conspiracy orchestrated by communist China, led by Steven's then best friend, Dr. Martin L. King, and enabled and abetted by the corrupt Washington establishment which not only threatened the survival of America as a nation but also Steven's personal survival as well.

Steven, manipulated by those he trusted most preying on his addiction and weakness, was set up as the stooge. A stooge to be easily betrayed. They would be wrong. Dead wrong.

Project Triple X as a transaction and conspiracy was meaningless, irrelevant, and meant nothing to the present, Steven told Eddie and Ernie. That Steven had survived meant everything to him. His own life and the lives of his loved ones were in jeopardy and imminent danger. Steven had to save them and save himself. And at that time in DC, Steven did just that.

In an evil and corrupt world, Steven had twice amassed wealth, prestige, and power. In his awakening he realized that all of it had been meaningless excess, Steven told his two new friends.

In goodness, Steven would protect the ones he cared the most about.

As the stooge, Steven was to infect the constitutional republic with a virus carried into its heart by Steven himself, planted in his Gucci briefcase, a gift from Dr. King, his then best friend in the world who would ultimately betray him, and to be unleashed that fateful day when the cherry blossoms were in full bloom in the capital.

Secrecy had been the key to his plans of personal survival. All outward appearances had to remain the same. Steven told Eddie and Ernie of his then plan for the survival of the nation, his loved ones, and himself.

Most important things first…

Steven had called his two friends, Robert Bailey, attorney, and Officer Smitty Dixon back in the Sunbelt. Robert Bailey almost immediately became trustee of his two children, his son, Josef, and his daughter, Karina, with $500,000 wired into Robert's trust account, thus guaranteeing his children's college education and future. Another $500,000 was wired to Robert's trust account for child support and maintenance to the mother of his children, Marianne.

Smitty Dixon, now a captain in the Tulsa police department, became the children's and their mother's bodyguard. Marianne, Josef, and Karina would be watched and guarded twenty-four hours a day, seven days a week. All without their knowledge.

With Marianne, Josef, and Karina now fully protected, both financially and physically, Steven secretly met with Courtney and Arlene Wellington, told them everything, and asked for help. They gave it.

Soon Courtney made arrangements with his friends in high places in Florida, and Steven's beloved Aunt Helena too had around-the-clock physical protection, all without her knowledge.

While Courtney and Arlene's daughter, practicing law in Austin, Texas, filed Steven's application for admission to the Texas Bar, Courtney and Arlene, through their movie theater business, rented a small house and some office space in El Paso, Texas.

Steven then secretly met with his friend and mentor in the cesspool of DC, Senator Griffin, and told him everything and asked him for help. The senator gave as well.

Steven and Senator Ron Griffin immediately met with the FBI and CIA, and Steven told them everything. "Gucci secret agents and CIA real secret agents carefully took the briefcase apart, piece by piece, and found all the virus and parasitic microbe software that had fooled X-ray detection," Steven told his two friends, now both smiling broadly.

Steven's plan was in full bloom like the cherry blossoms in Washington.

Once the CIA knew what they faced, sophisticated homing devices were implanted in all the software. Then the CIA and Gucci agents went back to work and carefully put the briefcase back together so that by all outward appearances nothing had changed.

In the meantime, Steven told the Justice Department and the FBI everything again, this time under oath and on the record. The basis for federal warrants for documents and people.

Steven told them everything. No one would be shown any favoritism.

All the documentation and usual suspects would be rounded up. All would be invited to the Big Party immediately after the Triple X Big Show, as Steven would call the conspiracy and the arrests in its aftermath.

The FBI then arranged round-the-clock secret protection for Steven's Aunt Helena in Florida, his family in Tulsa, the Wellington's and Steven in DC, yet they would keep all outward appearances the same.

Before the Big Show, scanners of the homing devices and surveillance equipment were secretly installed at the Pentagon, the Federal Comptroller's building, and the State Department building by the CIA. Now Steven's Gucci briefcase, with the software viruses inside, could be watched every moment.

Before the Big Show, three teams of agents became full-time residents at the Pentagon, the Federal Comptroller's building, the State Department building, and at the complicit and corrupt William Jefferson Clinton White House.

Before the Big Show, since Steven told the FBI everything, all the usual suspects were now under 24/7 secret surveillance. The watchers became the watched. The hunters became the hunted. Yet all outward appearances remained the same.

At the Big Show, after Steven took the Gucci briefcase into the heart of the Federal Government, all federal warrants were issued, and all the usual suspects and accompanying documentation were marked for easy pickup, as the poison was now in place.

After the Big Show, still with round-the-clock protection, Steven told Eddie and Ernie he faced both of his own two ultimate evils, beautiful Glee Robinson and believed best friend Martin King, cut all tentacles, and drove the stakes into their hearts, figuratively.

"From Martin's condo, picked up by the FBI, I was whisked to the Wellington's home. Courtney and Arlene, still with full FBI protection, took me to the airport in their Suburban."

Steven paused, took a deep breath, and continued. "At Ronald Reagan Airport, in an emotional farewell, Courtney and Arlene both hugged me, and we cried together. At the very last moment, Courtney opened the back of the Suburban and pulled out a pet carrier with a door. Courtney and Arlene's present to me. An awkward yet still small Great Dane puppy, with a collar on that gave the puppy's name, Rommel." Steven was crying, tears running down his face as he finished.

Steven wiped his eyes, swallowed again. "I, now on the side of angels and armed with their weapons, and a Great Dane puppy named Rommel, arrived in El Paso five years ago."

6

Steven wiped his eyes again. "And that's that." He wiped his eyes a third time and looked directly into his friend's eyes. "You still want me as your special prosecutor?"

Ernesto Martinez, locking eyes with Steven, said, "Before I answer that, I have a statement and two questions." Ernie paused, gathering his thoughts. "I knew all that from our FBI friends here and in DC. You made some powerful enemies both in and out of the federal government. It's not going to be an easy deal."

"'Life's a bitch and then you die,' to quote an old cliché," Steven said flippantly, but immediately regretted it. *Still some old evil left in me*, he thought. "Sorry about that…sometimes the old poisonous hubris rears its ugly head." Steven smiled at his boss and friend. "I have to be careful and vigilant."

Police chief Eddie Egen had teared up at Steven's narrative as well but now was smiling and nodding. He reached across and squeezed Steven's right shoulder.

"First question, you represented the Alvarados in DC and here in El Paso. Is that going to be a problem for you?" Ernesto asked. "The Alvarados, father and son, have some very deep tentacles in every aspect of El Paso life. Business interests, the Kemper & Smith law firm, El Paso Power & Electric, and city and federal government, judges, district, municipal, and federal." Ernie paused and with contempt dripping from his voice continued. "They're both a couple of real pirates!" Ernie first looked at Eddie, then right at Steven. "The chief will bear me out…but El Paso PD, AFT, and ICE suspect that the Juarez Cartel, formerly with the Sinaloa Cartel, is led by none other than Ricardo Alvarado, nicknamed "El Chapo!"

Steven was solemn. "No, not at all. That was bank and real estate work, and Ricardo was mostly a delivery boy." He paused. "Oh, they may claim attorney-client privilege, but the timing of that work will make any request that I be disqualified total crap. I can't see any El Paso judges, especially Chief Judge Carbon, granting it."

Both Ernie and Eddie were nodding.

Steven continued, "As far as Henderson Lane is concerned, I was never a partner…they always were very clear that I was in an 'of counsel' capacity, which is legalese for 'bull crap capacity,' and they made millions, paying me at the rate of $100 an hour and charged clients at my 'experienced' attorney rate of $1,000 per hour on billings to that particular client. Typical corrupt snake-in-the-grass DC attorneys. So, no, I don't think they'll be a problem." Steven was gathering strength again as he squared his shoulders and sat up in his chair.

"I don't either," Ernie said. "Second question, do you realize the magnitude of this special prosecution? It's just the tip of the iceberg."

"What's the iceberg?" a now grinning Steven asked, relaxing back in his chair again.

"A second American Civil War."

Steven swallowed. Looked at his friend Eddie, who nodded, and said, "You up for it, Steven?"

Steven looked back at Ernie. "Tell me."

Ernie took a deep breath. "Steven, I'm sure you know the current political climate. You've always been, from what I can tell, a solid conservative, and from what you told me about DC today, you also know that our republic is hanging by a thread."

Ernie stood up. "We got a Manchurian candidate Muslim puppet in the White House! He's in bed with the Chinese communists, the *Chicoms* as Rush Limbaugh calls them, Raul Castro, and all the radical Muslim terrorists…and the Muslim Brotherhood…"

"The president is a Muslim nut job himself. He follows all Muslim precepts, especially the one about covering your true intentions; you lie like a dog to all the infidels."

"Tell us how you really feel, Ernie," Eddie said, laughing out loud. Steven was smiling also.

Ernie continued, still animated, his face reddened with anger. "Okay, I will. Marxists and Muslims permeate every level of his corrupt administration. His czars are a bunch of Solinsky hippie radicals and Chicago thugs. He is engaged in massive Ponzi schemes to benefit his cronies a la Solyndra, labor unions, and General Electric, which is also completely in bed with the Chicoms."

Ernie looked at Steven directly. "Your own Triple X project, which you effectively killed back in DC five years ago, was all a part of that usurpation of power that had been ongoing for a long, long time. That time under Billy Clinton, this time under the current president himself!"

Steven nodded in agreement. He understood the evil now more clearly. He had just not seen the cancer multiplying exponentially and spreading in the United States, the Americas, and worldwide...

Ernie was getting even angrier. "And now we come to the southern border. On one side of this border war, we got Texas, Arizona, and Oklahoma. California has already turned to crap. Our governor here in Texas, the governors of Arizona, Oklahoma, and New Mexico, and the various state National Guards, the Texas Rangers, the local FBI, and lots of our friends in ATF, ICE, Homeland Security, DC FBI, and the CIA...except for Muslim Brennan that the president put in charge." He relaxed a bit but was still standing. "That's our side! On the other side, you have the Department of Justice that's run by that cockroach—"

Eddie interrupted, "That cockroach just resigned."

Ernie looked at Eddie. "Yeah, I know! But the president appointed another cockroach..." Ernie paused, thinking. "What's her name...like the country and western singer..."

"Loretta," Eddie finished.

Ernie, nodding, said, "Right! Her!"

Ernie continued, "Also on the other side, the whole shadow federal government appointed by the president and riddled with Muslim Brotherhood plants, and radical Muslim sympathizers, DC establishment Democrats and Republicans, progressives, coffee lounge elites, socialists, communists, a 'deep state' only concerned with maintaining their own power and wealth…"

Now broadly grinning, Steven interrupted his boss. "Like my old law partner and mentor used to say, 'It all depends on whose ox is getting gored.'"

Ernie pointed at Steven. "Exactly! Enlightened self-interest…"

Steven finished, "It's what makes R.O.W., rest of world, go around." Steven had discussed his R.O.W. bias with Ernie and Eddie many times.

Eddie laughed. "Reminds me of a joke about two Muslims on a camel—"

"We heard it!" Ernie and Steven both said in unison

All three were laughing now as Ernie continued. "Now, as to the illegal immigration cancer, which, prior to the great fake recession of 2008 saw almost thirty thousand illegals crossing into Texas per month, but is now again a flood of illegals, since the current Washington Democrat progressive administration turned the Texas-Mexico border into a porous sieve by the president's unconstitutional executive orders…

"The radical Muslim cancer on three fronts is fulfilling the promise of the intentional transformation of America by the George Soros Muslim puppet president himself."

Ernie paused and frowned. "Do you know that we've had fifty-four incidents of sex trafficking of minors that were completely covered up at the DOJ. We have two FBI agents in hiding. The deal is that the radical Muslim nut jobs are so castrated by their religion that when the Mullahs are not looking, pedophilia and sex slavery are the norm."

That one got Eddie's attention. Now he was really listening. It was like Ernie had hit a chord with Eddie, Steven guessed.

"And I'm sure you've heard about Fast and Furious, where ATF, the administration's lead agency in the War on Drugs, is supplying the drug cartels with automatic weapons so the president and his Muslim cronies can assault our Second Amendment."

Steven nodded. Called "Fast and Furious" by the conservative media, the White House and the attorney general conspired in a scheme to encourage the Mexican drug cartels to purchase automatic weapons in the United

States that backfired in their faces when a border patrol agent was killed with a gun traced directly to the White House.

Ernie, serious again, continued, "Like during our First American Civil War, our country is deeply divided. During the First Civil War it was the South wanting slavery and the North wanting freedom for slaves. This time it's the federal government wanting slavery for all, while Texas and most Americans want freedom from a cancer of big government that's being totally infiltrated by evil." Ernie stopped. Took a deep breath. Wiped his forehead. Calmed, sat down, and looked out on the El Paso skyline, the majestic Franklin Mountains in the background.

Steven and Eddie said nothing and sat quietly, almost reverently, looking out the window as well. Even from the fifth floor the view of downtown El Paso into Juarez, Mexico, was breathtaking.

After a long pause, Ernie spun back around and said, "I love this country. I love Texas and I love El Paso. But you're from Oklahoma and this doesn't have to be your fight. So, yes, I want you as the tip of our spear, but only if that's what you want." Ernie looked directly into Steven's eyes.

Steven grinned. "I love a good fight. Always have. I am an American first and now a Texan! Count me in. And thank you."

"Welcome home, partner." Eddie pumped a closed fist in the air.

7

The three men sat in silence, deep in their own thoughts.

Steven was first to speak. "Let's talk strategy. I need thirty to sixty days before I can take full charge of the Special Crimes Unit and this case, okay, Ernie?"

"I understand. You've got it. What can we do to help?" Ernie paused, looked at Eddie and asked, "Eddie, how about protection for Steven?"

"I don't want it, Ernie," Steven interrupted. "It's not a macho deal, but I'm pretty clear with who I am and know that I'm in the good Lord's hands."

"I'll take care of the good Lord's hands," Eddie said, winking at Ernie, who nodded silently. Steven knew it was futile to argue and smiled at Eddie.

Steven, now relaxed and peaceful again, said, "I'll talk to the chief judge about reassigning my docket of family law cases and talk to Judge Fraxon about leaving me out of the municipal court docket rotation until next year."

Steven paused, looked back at Ernie, and continued, "Then I've got to hire some help, someone, maybe a good younger lawyer that I can trust, to work at my direction, me looking over their shoulder, so my law practice, especially the Fort Bliss stuff, won't turn to crap." He paused. "And administrative help. Christmas is coming up and then New Year's, so I'm thinking mid or late February. In the meantime, Eddie and I will be reading files and flyspecking, to use an old real estate title examiner's term, all the investigation stuff, all witnesses, and all documentary evidence. That sound okay, Ernie?"

Ernie had been listening, nodding his head. He got up. "You bet, Steven! Anything else?"

Steven had the DA's attention. "Also, I need for you…the county…to put Ray Ortega, my investigator and good friend, on the payroll for fifty hours per week at a hundred per hour, or five G's per month, if that's okay with you…and hire a legal assistant typist for my law office, half of that salary paid by me and half again by the county. Also, if that's okay with you, Ernie?" Steven rose to meet Ernie, extended his hand.

Ernie shook Steven's hand firmly, warmly, and said, "All that's okay with me, and my office is open to you 24/7, Steven." Ernie looked at Eddie, said, "Chief, please watch his back!" as Eddie nodded, smiling broadly as well.

Eddie shook Ernie's hand as well.

As they left the DA's office, Steven turned to his friend and said, "Eddie, all this talk made me hungry. Let's go get some breakfast, especially menudo."

———

As Eddie and Steven walked out to the elevator, breezing by the cute receptionist again, Steven looked at his best friend. "Eddie, I meant what I said about no protection required." Steven said, as the two entered the elevator.

Inside the empty elevator, Eddie pressed the button and the elevator started down.

As the elevator descended, Steven continued, "I've got Ray Ortega, my investigator. And he offices with me."

"Yeah, I know. He's a former army military police and retired from the army as a major, right?"

"Right," Steven answered. "And he then spent five years' civil service with Army Criminal Investigative Division out of Fort Bliss. His daughter, Chris, is my legal assistant and receptionist."

Eddie's eyes widened. "Chris is Ray's daughter?" He seemed really surprised. Eddie had been in Steven's office many times, both as a client and as Steven's friend.

When Steven came to El Paso five years ago, he had $1,500 in his pocket and his dog Rommel, who was now a 180-pound giant that consumed 50 pounds of dog chow a month in addition to his weekly T-bone steak.

Steven immediately hung out his shingle over a small four-room office, previously leased by his DC friends for Steven in secret, met all the judges personally, requested court appointments to represent indigent criminals, and offered his services to Fort Bliss. Steven also offered to help his El Paso lawyer friends Don Stewart and Jim Maxwell, whom Steven met years earlier, having engaged Don to help on a shopping center real estate deal for the Alvarados while Steven was practicing law with Henderson Lane in DC. Slowly client referrals came that first year, and his law practice grew.

Steven's social life that first year consisted mainly of monthly weekend trips to Tulsa to visit with his kids, airline tickets purchased though Adventure World Travel, owned by Eddie and his wife, Andi. In addition to selling the agency, Eddie was now thinking divorce again—Andi was his fifth wife.

The elevator door opened, and the two men stepped out onto the first floor of the courthouse and walked out to the street. The morning sun was brilliant yet the air cool and dry, especially in the shade. El Pasoans always liked to brag about this fact regardless of the blazing heat anytime during the day, even when the temperature was over 100 degrees.

"The usual place for menudo?" Eddie asked. Like Steven, he loved menudo, the thick and hearty Mexican soup made with tripe, pork intestines, both a holiday and hangover favorite.

Walking side by side, Steven continued, "Yessir, Chris is just nineteen years old, but she is a great secretary, blazing speed typist, and hard worker." Steven thought he was finished with that subject.

Eddie wasn't. "She's just nineteen? Oh boy, she looks just like Selena Gomez…she'd be a really great lay!"

Steven stopped abruptly, taken aback at that comment. He frowned and looked at his friend intently.

Eddie stopped also. "What?"

Steven put his arm around Ed's shoulder. "Not here. Let's talk at lunch."

———

Steven and Eddie sat face-to-face at a small table at Hernando's, a small mom-and-pop restaurant on Mesa Street, two blocks from the courthouse, on the ground floor of the Phillips Building, eating menudo, fried eggs, and chorizo, the delicious Mexican sausage, and buttered flour tortillas. Steven had been silent until they had their food.

Eddie was trying to deflect from his perceived mistake. "Steven, did you hear about what happened in Houston?"

"No, what happened?" Steven was serious as he ate.

"Last Thursday night around midnight, a woman from Houston was arrested, jailed, and charged with manslaughter for shooting a man six times in the back as he was running away with her purse. The following Monday morning, the woman was called in front of the arraignment judge, sworn in, and asked to explain her actions. The woman said she was standing at the corner bus stop for about fifteen minutes, waiting for the bus to take her home after work. She's a waitress at a local cafe. She was there alone, so she had her right hand on her pistol in her purse. All of a sudden, she said, she was spun around hard to her left. As she caught her balance, she saw a man running away with her purse. She said she looked down at her right hand and saw that her fingers were wrapped tightly around the pistol. The next thing she remembered was saying out loud, "No way, punk! You're not stealing my paycheck and tips." She raised her right hand, pointed her pistol at the man running away with her purse, and squeezed the trigger."

Eddie paused. "When asked by the arraignment judge, 'Why did you shoot the man six times?' the woman replied under oath, 'Because when I pulled the trigger the seventh time, it only went click.' The woman was acquitted of all charges. She was back at work the next day! That's gun-control, Texas-style." Eddie giggled nervously.

Steven was silent, though a small smile was surfacing.

"Steven, did I step in it with you, my friend?" Eddie asked.

Steven smiled, swallowed. "You're okay, Ed. You just caught me by surprise about Chris. She works for me, and she's just a kid." Steven shook his head. "You gotta quit thinking with what's between your legs!" Steven took a bite of his tortilla.

"I know, I know. You've said that before. I just can't help it!"

"Ed, we've gotten to be good friends. You are my best friend here in El Paso. I'm not here to judge you or analyze you. I ain't your shrink. It's your deal." Steven paused, then continued, "You've asked me about divorcing Andi. What is she, your fifth wife, right?"

"Yeah," Eddie said sheepishly, his broad shoulders slumping slightly.

"So, you surprised me with your "lay" comment about my nineteen-year-old receptionist. You think there is a problem here?"

Eddie was embarrassed. "What's wrong with me, Steven?" Eddie looked directly at his best friend, forehead wrinkling, his eyes tearing up.

"Ed, you really want me to tell you honestly?" Steven paused. "It's your choice. But if you do, I'm gonna tell you the truth." Steven continued eating.

"I know that! You already told me that your favorite saying is that the ultimate of human freedoms is the freedom of choice, and yes, I want you to tell me. You've become my best friend and are probably the only one here that I can really trust." Eddie paused and wiped his mouth. "You've achieved a certain serenity that I wish I had. So yes, I do want you to tell me the truth. I need your help, my friend." Eddie was sincere. He looked at Steven with tears forming in his eyes.

Steven continued to eat his menudo.

Several minutes passed.

Steven finished, wiped his mouth, and put his napkin by his plate.

"What are you doing Saturday?" Steven asked.

Eddie looked directly at Steven. A small tear emerged from the corner of his eye. "I'll be at the ranch...by myself." Eddie paused. "Andi moved out and got herself an apartment on Stanton Street." The tear eased down his face and dropped into his menudo.

"Oh yeah?" It was Steven's turn to be surprised. "And probably a lawyer as well, right?"

"Probably. Why don't you come out to the ranch?" Eddie was smiling again. He loved his ranch and his horses probably more than his wife, Steven guessed. "We can ride, talk, and drink. Why don't ya spend the whole weekend? We have to meet…the whole prosecution team…anyway. I'll even try to have a surprise guest Saturday morning…"

Steven really enjoyed the ranch as well. He had spent many weekends there with Eddie and Andi, drawing, riding, playing gin rummy. Eddie allowed him to keep Pegasus, his snow-white Arabian, on the ranch. Steven loved both Rommel and Pegasus, his two four-legged friends. "Okay, I'll bring Rommel," he said. "I need you to get me up to speed on the special prosecution anyway. I need the complete story, all the truth and no crap. In return, I'll tell you the truth also. Do we have a deal?"

"Deal, Steven." A new hope was shining in Ed's moist blue eyes.

Steven finally smiled. "Ed, you know how you can tell a lot about a woman's mood just by her hands?"

"How's that?" Eddie managed.

"If they're holding a gun, she's probably pissed off…"

8

The six-vehicle convoy slowly snaked its way along a well-worn and well-kept graveled dirt road, heavy tires crunching and shooting rocks into the dense forest tree curtain amassed on both sides. The brilliant setting sun sent slivers of blinding sunshine onto the vehicles as rays of red laser lights, dancing, blinking, and jumping on gleaming metal like a thousand fireflies as the vehicles moved along through light and shade.

The six vehicles were two GMC 2.5-ton trucks, one with Stylex Painting Contractor marked on the side, the other unmarked, but both totally nondescript older, well-used vehicles. Also, one black Ram crew cab pickup with oversized monster tires and oversized front bumper with two large decals, one that read "Texas: Love it or Leave it" and a Confederate flag on the other. Also, a white Toyota Tundra pickup, used but clean, no markings whatsoever. All the vehicles were led by a white unmarked Jeep Cherokee, while a silver steel Humvee took up the rear. All six vehicles had thick smoked-glass bulletproof windshields.

As the lead Jeep Cherokee came over the low-rise in the road, lights became visible two hundred yards ahead in a clearing that held a rustic log cabin in its center and six vehicles off to the side, all well hidden among the tall canopy of pine and oak trees, with thick piled brush around them.

"Well, we made it! Colonels Lemev and Liang…sounds like an American law firm… will be pleased!" said Ward Powell in perfect English, sitting in the passenger front seat, two-way radio in his right hand and black Uzi in his left, to the driver, Uri Gagarin. "I'll call so they won't be surprised when we arrive."

The driver nodded but said nothing.

Ward Powell was tall, dark, and handsome. At over six feet and 200 pounds, he looked like a middle linebacker, which he had been when he played college football. He had also been an honorable mention All-American as a senior at Stanford University. Deep-set, ice-blue eyes, perfect nose, mouth in a perpetual and somewhat cruel smile, Ward Powell was extremely handsome. A young Clint Eastwood lookalike, he would brag to his driver and friend.

Powell was also a thoroughly indoctrinated communist.

Powell was adopted as a child of ten from Hungary by two childless American college professors at Catholic University in Washington, DC, where they taught constitutional law and political science, respectively.

Powell was a classic product of the Cold War, that time after World War II when the Russians had enslaved most of Eastern Europe. Ward Powell's adoptive parents were liberal American college professors and avowed communists, Hungarian immigrants who had taken advantage of America's benevolent and compassionate immigration policies after the devastation and rebuilding of Europe. They were true Russian-planted fifth columnists and spies.

Though Hungarian by nationality, Powell was an orphan and trained by the Russian communist government from birth. Though furthered by the communist Hungarian government, his father had been a tank colonel in the Red Army and a hero of the Soviet Union who was subsequently executed by Hungarian revolutionaries when the Russians quelled the 1958 Hungarian Revolution. His mother was a beautiful Hungarian girl, just nineteen years old, raped by Powell's father after the recapture of Budapest by the Russian tank forces. Powell's ravaged mother thankfully died in childbirth and the Russian government became his parents and Uri, like an older brother, another Hungarian war orphan unrelated to Ward Powell by blood was also adopted along with Ward Powell at the same time.

During the first ten years of life, Powell received the very best schooling that the victorious Soviet Union could well provide as one of the two emerging superpowers. The Hungarian communist professors were the perfect foster parents to further his education, mentally and physically, to take his place in American society and prepare for his destiny and role as his Russian slave masters later determined.

Further educated in Washington, DC, prep schools reserved for elite American politicians and top-level bureaucrats, Powell excelled in scholastics and football. A National Honor Society and merit scholar, he was a Virginia High School All State linebacker, becoming an honorable mention All-American in his senior year at Stanford, where he earned a PhD in both political science and psychology and a Masters in the Russian language. After Stanford, Powell graduated from Catholic University Law School at the top of his class and went to work in the Justice Department in the Carter Administration, just to be fired when President Ronald Reagan cleaned out the vestiges of President Jimmy Carter's failed administration. Powell hated Americans in general and American political conservatives with a passion in particular.

Ward Powell was a womanizer and a sex addict, and his Russian handlers provided him with the very best to keep him enslaved and under their complete control. For appearances only, Powell was to be attached to the assassination team as an advisor, familiar with American language, customs and ways, politics, and government bureaucracies.

Powell had also spent three years in Washington and remembered Steven Vandorol very well… He hated Vandorol but had no idea as to why.

The driver, Uri Gagarin, was Powell's confidant, bodyguard, best friend, butler, handler, pimp, and shadow designated by Powell's superiors to report any deviations from the ultimate goal, such plan completely unknown to Powell himself, but very well known to Uri, who had memorized Powell's secret dossier and knew just as much about their top-secret mission as Powell did himself.

Uri, like Powell, was an extremely handsome man as well. Tall and muscular, he could have been Powell's twin brother, though almost five years older. Uri was a highly trained Spetznaз commando with a penchant for young boys. Uri knew Powell's history all the way from his birth in Hungary to his later adoption in America.

Uri, Powell's designated handler, knew Ward's complete history very well, knew how to control Powell's addiction as well and had since the two were teenagers.

In the back seat, behind Powell and Uri, and taking up the whole bench seat from window to window, lay a huge Russian Caucasian Ovcharka dog, sleeping soundly, his massive head larger than a medicine ball, and slobbering snout lying on his two front paws.

This was Powell's protector and personal dog he had named Ubiytsa, in Russian meaning "killer."

The Ovcharka was the most brutal of Russian dog breeds—a large, very bad-tempered dog with a powerful and muscular body, bear-like face, deeply set oval dark eyes, round-shaped cropped ears, and low-carried bushy tail. Known as the Russian bear dog, the strength and dedication of this dog had made it a popular working, police, and guard dog throughout Europe and the former Soviet Union states. They were the largest dogs in the world, as Powell liked to brag to Uri.

The sleeping killer loudly passed gas in the back seat and groaned in satisfaction.

"Hey, Ward," Uri asked. "How old is Killer, anyway?"

"Oh, he's still just a pup," Ward Powell answered, smiling broadly. "No, I'm joking. He's three years old and meaner than Satan himself. Don't stick any bodily appendages near him because that will just be a snack for him." Powell laughed. "Killer eats sixty pounds of food in a week…in addition to his weekly goat!" Now he was laughing so hard he had to wipe his eyes. "Plus, after he tears your arm off, he'll probably eat it as well."

"Did you train him to kill?" Uri asked, laughing along for the benefit of his ward.

"No, I didn't. He had professional KGB trainers. I just went along so he would only follow my commands. So, Uri, you better not mess with me!" Ward was laughing again. "They were also our prison dogs. During the communist era, Ward rambled on to his driver, these dogs guarded prisoners of the Soviet Gulag camps and served as border patrol dogs along the Berlin Wall. They were widely used by the Russian army's kennels to develop new Soviet dog breeds. Being a fearless fighting dog, the Caucasian Ovcharka was still employed in some former Soviet republics for dog fighting. He'd die for me, Uri!" Ward finally finished.

"Is Killer hard to handle?" Uri was getting bored with all of Ward's sanctimonious ramblings, but he had his separate orders—handle Powell, keep him distracted and addicted and enslaved, and report all to his superiors. Uri would gladly do so as he was enjoying Powell's many addictions as well…

"Not really," Ward answered. "Owning a Caucasian Ovcharka is not an easy task. This independent and strong-willed dog will obey only a dominating and equally strong-willed owner that it respects. Obedience training and early socialization are mandatory for this breed…"

Powell couldn't contain himself. "You should see Killer screwing the bitches! I put him out to stud every month. He's multiplying faster than the Muslims," he laughed.

Uri was laughing also. "Well, does Killer get laid more than you do, Ward?"

"Well, I'll tell you, Uri," Ward answered. "It's a real close race, but I think I win…as I always do!" Ward was smirking, cruel eyes shining. *Powell looks like Satan himself*, Uri thought.

Uri was getting annoyed with his charge. "I now know everything I want to know about your stupid dog, Ward!" Uri paused a beat then changed the subject. "How do we handle these guys we're hooking up with?"

Powell held up a middle finger of one hand, the American high sign, as he hit the call button on the two-way radio, which beeped and crackled.

Powell talked into the two-way: "Killer Two calling Killer One…over…"

No answer, so Powell tried again. "Killer Two calling Killer One…do you read me? Over."

Crackling static, pause, then, "This is Killer One, Killer Two! Read you loud and clear…over."

"Killer Two, this is Major Powell and assassination team reinforcements and supplies arriving from killing fields headquarters, over!"

"About time, Major Powell! Where are you?" It was Colonel Stanislav Lemev talking; Powell recognized his voice and heavy Russian accent.

"Look out your window, Killer One! I see the clearing and cabin…we're ten minutes out…out!" Powell clicked off the two-way radio.

"Who was that, Ward?" Uri asked.

"That was Colonel Stanislav Lemev," Powell answered. "Colonel Lemev is one of the leaders of the assassination team to kill that piece of garbage Vandorol and his whole prosecution team—or he's to think so!" Powell laughed out loud. "I'm going to just let him think so…you and me know different, right, my friend? And the only ones that do!" Powell paused, thinking, then continued, "He is a real dangerous and really ugly dude that likes to pretend his English is bad, but is almost better than mine…and the muscle in Vladimir's inner circle!"

"No way!" Uri said and asked again, "So how do we handle these guys, Ward?"

"*We* don't, Uri," Ward answered. "*You* do nothing. Nothing at all. You're just my chauffeur. *You* listen, observe…and in private tell me everything, okay?"

"I got it, Ward," Uri answered, then paused, scowling. "What about the other colonel you told me about that's with the assassination team?"

Powell laughed. "You mean the ninja author and assassin?"

"He is an author as well?" Uri was smirking.

"Yeah, and is one ugly *mat' ublyudka*, as they say in Russian, as well," Ward answered, laughing. "But be careful! The ninja and his co-author are in charge of the takeover of America. They are at the top of communist China's military as a result of that book!"

"What's the book, Ward?" Uri asked.

"It's *Unrestricted Warfare: Communist China's Master Plan to Destroy America.*" Ward paused several beats thinking, then continued, "Let me tell you about these two."

Uri was listening…

"Colonel Qiao Liang is a cultured man," Ward said, rolling his eyes in disdain, "who along with General Wang Xiangsui, on his way from communist China to join the strike team in El Paso, within the next week, together authored the book which vaulted both men to the highest level of communist Chinese military leadership and to the forefront of the coming communist Chinese and Russian takeover of America…"

Uri just listened, driving and looking straight ahead as Ward continued. "Colonel Liang is just supposed to be an observer, and he is an egocentric jerk, but General Xiangsui is much more dangerous. General Xiangsui is the organ grinder behind the whole Chinese takeover of America, and he knows it, Uri! General Xiangsui knows he has the power of life and death over all of America, and he definitely acts like it…all the while reluctantly tolerating the alliance with us Russians."

Uri interrupted, "Well, did you read the book?"

Ward smiled sardonically. "Yes, I've read it several times. And I'm going to beat the co-authors to death with it! Or better yet, I'm gonna stuff it down their throats."

Uri stopped laughing. "How are you going to handle Colonel Liang, Ward?"

"I'm not," Ward answered. "I'm just going to bide my time…then kill him…and his no-good co-author as well!"

"How you gonna do it?" Uri asked.

Powell smiled again. "I've got a designated killer right inside the assassination team itself, Uri."

"Who is it?" Uri asked.

"My secret!" Ward answered. "I'll let you know at the right time." Ward paused, thinking, pulled out his cell phone, tapped a number, waited…said, "You gone?"

Ward listened, started to smile, swallowed, his Adam's apple bobbing. "Great! I'll meet you there for some real fun…keep your motor hot…" He laughed and clicked off.

"Who did you just call?" Uri asked.

"We all have secrets, my friend," Ward answered, pocketing his cell phone then going silent.

Finally, Uri thought as the vehicles approached the clearing in the dense, dark forest. *I'm really getting tired of his blah, blah, blah bull crap.*

9

Steven was driving straight up North Mesa Street going to his law office after Eddie dropped him by his car parked in the courthouse garage.

He felt peaceful again. Recalling the agony of DC more than five years ago hadn't been much fun. It had been very painful and unsettling and brought back all the anguish, horror, and emotional pain of that terrible time he had survived.

Steven had much to do to get ready for the special prosecution. He had accepted the special prosecution but hadn't quite understood its magnitude and national political implications. But Steven was committed now and accepted it completely. *No turning back now*, he thought. He was all in. And he well understood the implications now as well.

Steven was thinking…

First and foremost, he needed help in his private law office. Especially in the last few years since arriving in El Paso, his practice had grown substantially. Slowly at first, then much quicker since he met Eddie and became good friends.

Initially, his early move to get acquainted with all the judges resulted in a few appointments to defend indigents charged with various crimes.

Steven's sense of right and wrong and good and evil had sharpened as he had survived the pain of the Sunbelt, and of DC thereafter, to really see himself. Having unlayered partially to see himself fully, his sense of justice clarified as well. Having cured his need for violence, he nevertheless enjoyed the channeled violence of courtroom conflict.

The few appointments in lower-level misdemeanor crimes of petty theft, drunk driving, and assault soon turned to representation in the more serious felonies: rape, assault and battery, kidnapping, and even murder. Steven never wavered from his oath as an attorney to provide the very best representation and defense to his clients, all in accordance with the Constitution of the United States and the Bill of Rights, in both of which he ardently believed. Steven also fervently believed in the presumption of innocence until proven guilty by a jury of one's peers. Then, if guilty, he also believed in the guilty being punished accordingly.

As Steven's defense skills, aggressive trial tactics, and especially his win record became known among the criminal element, his new reputation drew more cases, including several capital murders, all of which Steven handled in the same thorough and professional manner.

Then Steven met Eddie Egen. The superficial commonality had been right there at the start. Both had a strong sense of justice and both loved horses. As they got to know each other, they found that initial commonality especially in horses, both from their childhoods—Ed having grown up on a ranch in Texas, Steven having spent his early childhood in Brazil on a *fazenda*, a large cattle ranch. Both had experienced abject violence and both were survivors.

Eddie, as El Paso police chief, was in a very good position to refer clients, both civil and criminal, and very soon Steven needed secretarial help. With only a criminal practice, Steven's typing skills were adequate, but with several new civil clients with civil lawsuits, it wasn't good enough. So, Steven prayed again for divine guidance and placed an ad in the *El Paso Herald-Chronicle*, once more relying on the good Lord's mysterious ways.

The good Lord answered with nineteen-year-old Christina Ortega.

Chris was short, dark, and very attractive with big brown innocent eyes, long black eyelashes, jet-black hair down to her waist and scorched the keyboard with blazing speed.

And she loved her father, Ray Ortega, very, very much.

So, then Steven met Ramon "Ray" Ortega, a former military policeman who retired from the army as a major, then spent five years' civil service in the army's Criminal Investigative Division, CID, as an investigator at Fort Bliss. Steven's law practice exploded. Ray Ortega became Steven's full-time contract investigator and good friend.

In the third year in El Paso, with Ray as contract investigator at Fort Bliss and all his contacts at Fort Bliss, up and down the entire chain of command, Steven became the "go-to" lawyer for courts martial, as civilian outside counsel.

Soon fairness and zealous defense of the underdog spread Steven's reputation in the military ranks. Being concerned about fairness and justice to the real victims, children, Steven surprised even himself and began a family law, child custody, and divorce practice.

Ray and Steven became good friends. Ray also helped Steven as an investigator on his criminal cases, in most cases doing a better job than the city and county investigators. Steven had represented some ten criminal cases, including three capital murder cases, where Ray's investigative skills were the difference between his clients' guilt and innocence.

In the short time since they had become friends, each had gained the other's absolute trust, especially exemplified by a certain night in a Juarez bar, where the two had gone for a few beers after work—a few too many beers for both but especially for Ray. A burly Mexican called Steven a "stupid gringo." Before Steven could confront the guy, Ray was in his face, screaming at him to apologize, and when he refused landed a swift uppercut to the much larger man, floored him, and caused a barroom brawl in which Steven and Ray, standing back-to-back with pool cues in their hands, closed the premises for the night, both bloody but laughing.

Driving up North Mesa Street, he thought, *Yes, I've got much to do now.* He remembered another one of his favorite sayings: The farther backward you can look, the farther forward you are likely to see. *I've looked back all the way to my birth,* Steven thought. "I've seen myself completely as a result. Now, with my God and Jesus Christ in my heart and with divine guidance, I can look forward to the future, and farther forward I'm likely to see," Steven said out loud. Anxiety about the contract on his life now gone, Steven relaxed at the wheel. He had faced much worse threats in his life before than the rehash of the Washington horror.

As he passed the University of Texas at El Paso on University and North Mesa streets, he was reminded that he did have much to do. *I've got to be careful. I can't backslide into replacing my lifelong search for emotional intimacy with escapes of various types, like becoming a workaholic in the Sunbelt, or a sex addict in DC.*

Steven remembered both horrors, his meteoric rise and cataclysmic fall in the Sunbelt, where only his children's lives saved him, and the survival of the Washington horror of evil, corruption, and betrayal, where his lifelong survival skills saved him. Now Steven knew better, realizing that the grace of the Lord had been with him all his life. *I've got to remain absolutely vigilant and not to fall back into any of my own self-destructive patterns of the past!*

Steven glanced in the rearview mirror, smiled, and said out loud, "I'll be at Eddie's ranch this weekend with Pegasus and Rommel," as he pulled into the parking lot of his office on Sun Bowl Drive.

10

Steven parked his Taurus but stayed in his car. Looked around at the cars, wary. *After all, I've got a contract out on me,* he thought, but smiled ruefully to himself in the rearview mirror.

The small parking lot was on a bluff facing I-10 and was concealed from the highway below by acacia and mesquite trees and six-foot shrubs. There were six cars, all familiar office building tenant cars. Ray's four-wheel drive Ford SUV with smoked windshields and Chris's small red Toyota pickup were both conspicuously absent, Steven noticed. *All clear*, he thought and then said out loud, "No bad guys lurking about!" Steven had learned the situational awareness lesson, as he called it, over a lifetime of vigilance, awareness, and observation.

He got out, locked the door on the front door inside, not using his key fob as he had heard somewhere that bad guys could override the flicker by using their own from another car, warily looked around again, and went up the concrete stairs on the north to the street-level stone walkway to the building entrance. The midday late August sun was still brilliant, and Steven could feel its warmth on his shoulders as the temperature was rising.

The building was a neat two-story art deco, Frank Lloyd Wright-style garden office building with sparkling mirror-glass windows nestled among the trees on a bluff overlooking the Rio Grande. The Juarez slums sat across the Rio Grande River in the distance. Steven could smell the aroma of the trees mixed with the exhaust fumes from Interstate I-25 right below.

Steven walked into the lobby with the elevator straight ahead and staircase to the left. A lobby building directory next to the elevator had six or seven names and showed "Steven J. Vandorol, Esq. Lawyer…Suite 205." He walked past the elevator and up the stairs to a deep-pile carpeted second floor.

Steven walked down the subdued, oak-paneled hallway past two other office doors on each side and down to Suite 205 at the end, the fifth suite on the second floor. He unlocked the door, flicked on the suite lights, and locked the deadbolt from the inside.

Steven was alone in the reception area waiting room.

Steven paused and looked around the now familiar austere yet elegant reception room. He was a firm believer in the KISS doctrine, "Keep it simple, stupid!," and he wryly told clients, jurors, and litigants, "That's me, and that's what you should be—keep it simple. The truth is always the simplest." Now Steven really believed that; before he had not.

The front door led right to a sliding glass opening for reception, and the whole left side inside wall was mirror glass that, unbeknownst to clients and persons coming into the reception area, was two-way glass into Ray Ortega's office. That was Steven's accommodation to his friend and investigator, who was also a student and observer of humanity and human behavior, not unlike Steven himself. Steven respected Ray's instincts about people in general and his clients in particular, both in the office and especially during jury selection.

Steven unlocked the inside door to the offices, entered, and closed and locked the door behind him. Double security to the inside offices. To his left, a glass divider to the receptionist area contained built-in reception bank with fax machine, telephone, and credit card machine. *I'm gonna have to talk to Ray about getting a teletype,* Steven thought. *We're gonna need it in this prosecution. It's probably still the most secure form of private communication in this internet age...*

Steven walked down the hallway, Ray's office to his right, also with glass divider for Ray's office, desk chair, desk, computer desk, gun rack with his in-office arsenal, and one-way glass out to the reception area. *Perfect open office for an investigator and student of human nature,* Steven thought, and kept walking.

I'm gonna also need another legal assistant typist for the increased workload, Steven thought as he opened his own office door. Glanced into a smaller empty office to his right...*and put another lawyer in there, or in mine, which is bigger. I can work out of the smaller one.*

Inside his own office, he left the door open and hung up his sport coat. He didn't turn on the light as the sun of Sun City, still high in the western horizon, shone brightly and made his small simple office sparkle.

Steven sat down in his desk chair, smiled for no reason at all except that it had been an interesting Monday so far and he was now feeling really good. *Very good indeed,* he thought. *In spite of regurgitating all that Washington, DC, rest of world stuff! I guess I have worked it through my own psyche and have to remain vigilant that it not affect me at all.*

Steven glanced around his own office: built-in oak credenza with doors below a full plate-glass window to the outside, the view magnificent. He looked down to Interstate I-25, also Paisano Drive right below and the Rio Grande River ambling by. The river was the designated Texas-Mexico border, and the Juarez slums were barely visible in the distance. Those slums always reminded Steven of the Sao Paulo slums of his own Brazilian childhood. Another open door led to a small conference room and two wingback client chairs sat in front of his desk. To his right was a low cabinet with an ornate bronze statuette of the blindfolded messenger archangel Gabriel holding the sword of righteousness in his right hand and the scales of justice and reason in the other hand. The bronze statuette was the only remnant from Steven's law practice in the Sunbelt and then in Washington that he cared anything about and brought to El Paso with him to adorn his law office once opened.

On the other side, opposite the statue, was the now famous Gucci briefcase he told Ernie and Eddie about that served as an abject reminder of the Triple X project and Steven's agony and survival and recovery of Washington, DC.

The only decoration on the wall opposite was the "Hungarian Village" original oil painting by Hungarian artist Verace that Steven purchased in Annapolis, Maryland, during his previous rise to superficial wealth in the Sunbelt, a prior agony all its own. Steven shuddered slightly at that particular agony, now just a bad memory, where images of his children, he thought, had saved his life in an almost successful suicide attempt when everything he had built was toppling into chaos all around him.

Steven picked up his phone to check messages as Christina was due in at 4 pm after classes at UTEP, listened, saved all for Christina to handle then turned toward the magnificent view—it had a calming effect all its own.

Steven glanced down to the parking lot below, just in time to see a strange car that he had never seen before in this parking area pull into a space right next to his own car.

He picked up his cell, punched in a number, and waited for his friend and investigator Ray to answer. "Steven, what's up?"

"Where are you right now?" Steven asked.

"Just leaving the courthouse garage. Why?"

"You coming to the office? I'm here already."

"Yep," Ray answered. "What's up?" Ray repeated.

"Got through with the DA, Ernie Martinez; Eddie Egen was there as well. I've got a lot to tell you." Steven paused. "I got back to the office and our parking lot was clear. But when I got to my own office, there was a strange car in the lot below...smoked windows...I can't see if there is anyone in it...or how many. It's a 2009 white Silverado pickup, tinted windows, Texas license number XYZ666."

"Got it," Ray answered. "Why are you interested?"

"I'll tell you when you get here. We got a lot to talk about and a lot to do. Is Christina coming in?"

"She is. It'll be four o'clock or so, after her Monday afternoon class." Ray paused; he was writing. "I'll call my Texas Ranger bud and get a make on the Silverado." He clicked off.

Steven opened the doors below the plate glass of the built-in oak credenza, revealing the Persuader shotgun Ray had given him as a present last Christmas. "I think I'll take it home. Ray's got his arsenal here," Steven said to himself.

He glanced down into the parking lot. The Silverado pickup was still there, stationary but idling.

Steven spun around to the rolodex on the top of his desk. Remembered the ten-inch, double-edged, razor-sharp, German tungsten carbide steel throwing knife concealed in his right boot, slipped it out of the sheath where it was concealed, and put it on his desk. Unclipped the holstered Glock 22 and put it right beside the knife. "I'm ready for an office invasion!" he said out loud and smiled at both his own over-caution and because his friends Eddie and Ray, the only ones in El Paso who knew about the concealed throwing knife, would affectionately kid Steven about his precise description of the knife, mimicking him mercilessly, both knowing that it had been a part of him since his childhood.

Steven was a bit unnerved about the contract on his life, but his faith was strong. He no longer was a slave to R.O.W. Steven truly believed in faith, family, and friends being the only important things in life. He also fully believed in the ultimate of human freedoms being the freedom of choice and that the good Lord worked in mysterious ways. Finally, he still hadn't resolved himself with cynically believing that while there was no survival for humanity as a whole, there was for the individual. *R.O.W., the rest of world, was going to hell,* he thought ruefully. *As is America. I hope and pray our country can survive a civil war, but I don't bet on it,* Steven thought. *I can only do what I can do*—words his very practical old law partner and mentor, George Miller, had said.

Steven had survived the agony and pain of Washington and found himself and his serenity in El Paso. *And I've got my dog with me,* he thought as he again saw his own reflection in the glass covering the license to practice law issued by the Supreme Court of the State of Texas above the cabinet.

Steven had learned much about himself and R.O.W. in Washington. He had looked all the way to his childhood, paused when the circle had closed—partially at least for it never really closes until one meets his maker—and arrived in El Paso to look forward to his future in R.O.W. And Courtney and Arlene Wellington had been the angels the good Lord designated to help, and their gift of Rommel was the added bonus.

Since Steven's arrival in El Paso, Steven and Courtney had stayed in touch, talking once or twice a month. Steven considered Courtney and Arlene his surrogate parents.

Steven sat back in his chair and thought back to the train trip when he met for the first time, Courtney Wellington and his wife, Arlene, a time in which Steven, in retrospect, now believed that the good Lord had designated them as His angels to help him in a time of personal agony and need.

He shuddered again at the memory of the jump from the frying pan of the Sunbelt he had just left, jumping right into the hellfire of Washington, DC.

Steven remembered the train trip that had saved him from a nervous breakdown…

Steven walked into the dining car of the train he had taken after the devastation in the Sunbelt, when his entire world had crumbled, and was met by the smiling old gentleman, Mr. Ruppert, the black waiter. Steven had befriended him the night before and the old waiter, in turn had taken a liking to Steven., a somber and exhausted white man. The snow white haired and wrinkled waiter had even noticed Steven's seriousness and utter exhaustion.

This time Mr. Ruppert had been looking for Steven come into the dining coach, "Well, Mr. Attorney at Law, have a good evenin' with your lovely dinner companion last night?" He was grinning ear-to-ear, sparkling white teeth shinning.

Steven had just spent the night with Glee Robinson, a dazzlingly beautiful and exotic black woman he had met on the train the day before and who had been his dinner companion the evening before.

Steven's face sparkled. "I can't tell you anything, Mr. Ruppert. You already know."

A knowing smile. Mr. Ruppert led Steven to a table. An elderly black couple were already seated there…

"This okay, Mr. Vandorol?"

Steven looked at the couple. They were smiling brightly at Steven. He smiled back. "Sure, Mr. Ruppert. This is fine." Steven sat down. Mr. Ruppert stood by.

"I'll have four eggs poached…" Steven began.

Mr. Ruppert's eyes twinkled. "How about the biggest steak on the train, to go along with your eggs?" Steven had dined on a big steak dinner with Glee the evening before.

"Great idea. And a large glass of orange juice. Some of those great rolls. And coffee... black."

Mr. Ruppert stifled a laugh. "Comin' right up!" he said, and hurried to the kitchen.

Steven looked at the couple. "How are you folks doing?"

They said in unison, "Very nice." They looked at each other and smiled. They were one. A couple, together forever. Steven felt a tinge of sadness...

The old man was dressed in a suit. Out of style but still tailored. It fit him well, and he looked good in it. Life had not been easy, yet Steven saw peace. A gentle, wrinkled face. Shining, dark peaceful eyes. Mirrors to a gentle, good soul. Snow-white hair, hairline receding.

The old woman, still beautiful, sat calmly with her arms locked into his. Well dressed. Neat as a flawless page of a well-typed contract. Also, snow-white hair. And her eyes, the same shining, brilliant, peaceful eyes of her husband. Young eyes always.

"You folks on vacation?" Steven asked.

The old man replied, "Oh, yes. We just love to ride the train."

The old lady, proud of her husband, said, "Courtney and I met on a train fifty-four years ago."

Steven extended his hand to the old man. "I'm Steven Vandorol."

The old man took it. "Glad to meet you, young fellah. I'm Courtney Wellington, and this is my wife, Arlene." Courtney was also proud of Arlene. She was beaming.

"Are you folks retired?" Steven asked.

"Oh, no," Courtney exclaimed. "We own some movie theaters, and we both work in the business."

Steven heard but didn't listen to the word 'some' or the plural 'theaters.' "So, you work hard and play hard too. Right?" Steven was not yet listening...

"That's right," Arlene answered. "Our oldest son, he's about your age, keeps things running while we go and ride the train." She and her husband were still beaming.

Steven liked these people. Their enthusiasm, pride, and serenity were marvelous. He wanted to know more. "How many children?"

Courtney and the children were Arlene's department. "Five. Robert, he's the oldest." Robert was obviously the apple of her eye. "Eddie, he's thirty-eight. He also works in our family business. Courtney Junior. He's thirty-five. And Gloria, she's married and got three little ones."

Courtney was grinning from ear to ear.

"Gloria's husband is a lawyer like you, Mr. Vandorol," Arlene said.

Steven wondered how she knew as Arlene continued, "He's a partner at Sullivan & Mercer."

Steven again thought, That's one of the biggest firms in Chicago, and best...

"That's the law firm that does all our law business," Courtney interrupted. Steven thought, Courtney Wellington's business?

"And Sissy," Arlene continued, "is our youngest. She is our baby. She's twenty-five. She's going to law school at the University of Texas."

Steven swallowed. "What a nice family. That's just great. Just three grandchildren?" Steven really liked these people.

Arlene's department again, "Oh, no. Robert and his wife got two. Eddie's got four, and Gloria three. Courtney Junior is a bachelor. So that's nine."

Steven had the distinct feeling that the buttons were going to pop from Courtney's shirt. "What a nice family," Steven repeated. "You both are very proud. I can tell."

The breakfast was served to all three. They ate in silence and enjoyed it.

Steven swallowed, said, "Mr. Wellington, is the theater you own in Chicago?"

Courtney said, "Please, Courtney and Arlene. Yes, some of them are," he added matter-of-factly.

Steven was surprised. "Some of them? How many do you folks own?"

Courtney put his fork down. "Well, let's see, we just bought a chain of 58 theaters in New York, Washington, DC, and Pennsylvania. That's a total of 280."

"Wow." Steven asked the right question: "The two of you built it up together?"

"That's right!" they again replied in unison. Looked at each other. Both smiled. Courtney put his arm around Arlene, drew her close, and they kissed.

Steven saddened. He glanced out the window and focused into the distance.

Arlene said, "What's the matter, son?" A loving, gentle voice.

Steven looked at her tender face. "Oh, nothing, ma'am. I was just thinking how much I've missed by not having parents like the two of you." That thought struck his heart and his eyes misted.

That was Arlene's department too. "You are a good person, Steven. May I call you Steven?" Steven nodded. Her voice was gentle. "It'll come. You just be patient. Patience. The young are so impatient. You'll be all right. It'll be there for you. You've got yourself. And you are good...as God made you that way."

"Thank you, Arlene." Steven swallowed the lump. Her words struck another chord.

Courtney was watching Steven. It was his turn. "You just be careful, son." Steven looked at Courtney. He knew he better listen. Kept eating.

"I can see this is a bad time in your life." Courtney, the voice of experience, continued, "Just be careful and patient. Remember that God plus one equals a majority."

Steven continued eating slowly. He was now really listening.

Courtney leaned across the table, "You got acquainted with Glee Robinson last night?"

Steven shifted uncomfortably in his seat. "You all know Glee?"

"Yes, we do." Courtney's tone was slightly sharp. "Son, just be careful. Glee could be trouble for you."

Steven looked away. Glee's address and telephone number, in Washington on a piece of paper in Steven's pocket, seemed to have a life of its own.

The three sat in silence, eating. Courtney and Arlene gave Steven the right to think. They understood patience. Steven still had so much to learn.

Steven finished eating. Finished his coffee. Slowly wiped his mouth with a napkin and stared at two beautiful smiling people. Steven finally spoke, "Thank you both. Your children are very fortunate." Steven rose. Courtney did as well.

Steven leaned over to Arlene and kissed her on the cheek. She was beaming again.

Steven extended his hand to Courtney. The old man grasped it. They both lingered. Steven smiled as the old man said, "Take care of yourself, young man." The old man knew he had to say no more.

Steven swallowed another lump. "Thank you."

Two hands parted slowly. Steven turned and walked down the aisle, returning to his train compartment.

11

Steven spun back around to see if the white Silverado pickup was still in the parking lot below. It was, the engine still running and the windows still closed. Steven glanced at his watch. It had been in the same place now for almost forty minutes. He reached for the rolodex and Courtney's Chevy Chase, Maryland, home telephone number. Steven had it in his cell phone index but noticed that it needed charging. Plugged in and relaxed…Steven picked up the office phone, dialed the Wellington's private residence number, and waited. Long distance clicks…paused…ringing.

"Hello." It was Arlene's sweet and tender voice that Steven remembered so well and always made him smile.

"Hello, Arlene! This is your surrogate son. How are you?"

"Well, hi, Steven. How is my fourth son?" Steven could feel Arlene's bright smile in her tender voice. "I'm doing just great. But I'm sure you wanna talk to Courtney. He's been grinning like a kid since he's heard me mention your name. Here he is…"

Pause…

Courtney was on. "Hello, Steven. Glad to hear from you! We haven't talked in almost a month. You haven't forgotten about your late life parents, have you?" Steven could feel his smile in Courtney's voice as well and heard the tenderness in his voice.

Steven said right away, "Absolutely not! It's my bad. Your fourth son has been really busy, especially these last two weeks. I've got some news here in El Paso to share, that's the main reason I'm calling today."

"I figured you'd be calling. Both the *Washington Examiner* and the *Washington Post* picked up the Associated Press story about your appointment as special prosecutor in El Paso for the Alvarado prosecution…"

It was Steven's turn to interrupt surprised. "Even the *Washington Post* ran it? I am surprised that liberal rag would run anything from Texas…"

"Even Reuters ran it, Steven, so I bet the *New York Times* probably ran it as well. But as you know, I quit reading that garbage during the Kennedy years." Courtney paused and then continued, "You shouldn't be surprised; you were pretty visible here in DC during those five years."

"Yeah, but it was on uncontroversial stuff. I thought I stayed well under the radar on Project Triple X, don't ya think?"

Courtney answered, "You did, but still, the legal work was highly visible big bucks R.O.W., like you say…legal work that got you a pretty significant reputation and media coverage."

"Yeah, well…all that R.O.W. superficial crap's emphasis is on stuff… and money and power…the government's cocaine addiction." Steven remembered his own addiction and survival. "So, what did you think when you read about me, Courtney?"

"Honestly?" Courtney had always been direct with his surrogate son.

"As always, Courtney." Steven paused then continued, "You and Arlene made the difference in my DC catharsis and survival." Steven was serious. But for Courtney and Arlene, his DC guardian angels, and their guidance and help, he may not have survived that recent pain of his lifetime. "For which I'm grateful to you both and to the good Lord and His mysterious ways."

"Good, it's all a part of *our* intimacy, Steven." Courtney paused. "Arlene and I talked about it and we…" Courtney and Arlene, married for fifty-four years, were always together in their own intimacy. "…We both thought, 'We hope Steven is not backsliding into old escapism patterns,'" Courtney finished.

Steven was thoughtful. He had become a very good listener, having been cured of his many past demons. "You know, Courtney, I'm glad you said that. I have thought about the old workaholic escapism of the past. Just today, as a matter of fact, I thought I've got to be careful. I'm still in the practice, practice, practice phase of the therapeutic cycle we discussed many times."

"I remember it well. Good answer, Steven. You certainly went through the awareness phase in DC, which took you, what? Four and a half years, plus the Sunbelt agony…" Courtney chuckled good-naturedly and continued, "in your therapy of seeing the goodness in your own heart. Also, the understanding phase of the therapeutic cycle, through which you came to understand your own layers of evil, a phrase you yourself coined. Then you finally followed your favorite saying…"

Steven interrupted. "Which you said to me first: the ultimate of human freedoms is the freedom of choice…"

"That's right," Courtney said. "You made a clear choice, a clear decision, to shear those layers of evil, drive a sword with all righteous indignation and anger, and cut the tentacles that were robbing you of your freedom of choice…and made the main decision to leave DC and go to El Paso, which was Brazil-like, and in your psyche…so it's still 'practice, practice, practice phase,' huh?"

"Yeah, Courtney, it's like daily I have to be diligent and vigilant so that the old patterns don't return."

"Especially the sexual, right?" Courtney and Steven had also discussed Steven's primary demon many times.

"Correct, Courtney. When those old urges come into my mind, whether by some free association like seeing a pretty girl…or reading some sex scene in a John Grisham novel…I have to consciously think about something else and pray for the good Lord's grace for guidance." Steven paused a moment, swallowed, then continued. "It's like an alcoholic or drug addict, getting up before an Alcoholics Anonymous meeting and admitting to the alcoholism, and taking responsibility for my prior addiction. So, yes, I've been here five years and am still in the practice, practice, practice phase…yep, and still in the 'One' part of the 'One, Two, Three, Four' theory of relationships, which we together developed in DC, the 'one' being surviving with the good Lord in my heart!" It was Steven's turn to chuckle in wry amusement.

"The old part one, huh? So, you've got serenity in the now. Good, I'm glad we're talking about it. It would be so easy for you to slip into the old escapism of workaholism or…sexual addiction. Especially you, Steven! You've always been so passionate about what you're doing. That's the passionate artist in you, passionate about your work and sex…"

Steven answered, "That's right, Courtney. That's one of the reasons why I took this special prosecution. Like you said, life is really simple if you have the good Lord in your heart. One needs only three other things: someone to love, something to do, and something to look forward to. You said that to me first also!"

"To which *you* said that the only three important things in R.O.W. is faith, family, and friends," Courtney countered. "So how are your kids?"

"They are doing great. I'm taking a whole week off at Thanksgiving to spend time with them in Tulsa. I won't be able to see them during Christmas. They're going skiing with the Baileys."

"Oh yeah, how is Bobbie doing anyway?" Courtney and Arlene knew all about Bob Bailey, Steven's lawyer friend in Oklahoma, who was the trustee of the trust Steven had established for his two children, Josef and Karina, and their guardian, Steven's ex-wife, Marianne, as he left DC for El Paso. "Bobbie just got appointed to the Federal Bench, the first African-American federal judge in Oklahoma."

Courtney was laughing. "Oh, that's just great. Our historic Marxist president just appointed a conservative black attorney to the Federal Bench without even knowing his politics."

Steven chimed in. "Yeah, a real Manchurian Candidate judge. Bobbie has always been a registered Democrat, so I guess the party label and his race fooled that incompetent twit." Steven paused, heard the office door rattling. "Hold on, Courtney, I'm the only one here. There's someone at the front door…"

Steven put Courtney on hold and pulled his 9mm Glock 22 from its holster on his desk by the throwing knife and walked out to the hallway.

Almost to the door, he heard it being unlocked, and Ray Ortega opened the door. "You're not going to shoot me, are ya, Steven?" Ray was smiling broadly at him.

Ramon Ortega, Ray to his friends, was short, maybe five-foot-five, with stocky build like a wrestler, which he had been in Bowie High School in South El Paso. Barrel-chested, dark olive skin, handsome with a long scar running from his right eye to his chin, a memory of a knife fight in the slums of Juarez, where his parents had lived before emigrating to the United States and El Paso. Bowie High School had socialized but did not conquer Ray. He was about Steven's age, had the same street smarts, and had been just as aggressive and violent in his younger days. Age, time, faith, family, friends, and sports had matured them both. Football for Steven, wrestling for Ray, sports had been the teenage angst outlets for both. Both were realists regarding R.O.W., and neither suffered fools. Ray had a remarkable resemblance to a young John Travolta, Steven always said to him.

Steven laughed. "No, no! I've got Courtney on the phone. I just didn't want someone coming in to shoot me!" Steven winked at Ray. "I'll go finish with Courtney and then we'll talk, okay?"

Ray raised his eyebrow at Steven's comment. "Okay, Steven, tell Courtney I said hi," he said as he walked into his own office.

Back in his office, Steven looked out the window. The strange white Silverado pickup was gone. Sat down, picked up the phone, punched the blinking button: "Courtney, I'm back. That was just Ray. He says hi."

"Old Ray is a good man, from what you told me about him. I'd like to meet him sometime. Anyway, where were we?"

"We were talking about Bobbie Bailey." Steven paused. "What I wanted to talk about was the other reason for calling you…"

Courtney was perceptive. "The FBI and the contract out on your life?"

"Yeah, the district attorney, Ernie Martinez, heard from his FBI contacts here in El Paso, who in turn heard from the FBI in DC, that there was a contract out on my life, that the Alvarados were behind it, and that they had heard from you, after my appointment news was out."

"Steven, the FBI here in Washington contacted *me* the very day the article came out in the *Post*. They told *me* that there was a contract out on your life, and did I know where you could be located. I didn't tell them anything. I said you might be back to Oklahoma somewhere; they remembered that when you left DC, Arlene and I had taken you to the airport. They even remembered that we gave you a Great Dane puppy as you were leaving at the airport."

"So we don't know how the FBI knows about the contract on my life?" Steven asked.

Courtney sighed. "Steven, with your involvement in killing Project Triple X, you can't trust anything coming out of DC, especially now with the corrupt Chicago Marxist thugs, or the imbedded Muslim Brotherhood zealots of this administration."

"District Attorney Ernie Martinez heard from FBI contacts in DC that the Alvarados were involved behind the contract," Steven said. "They got lots of crap here in El Paso and Juarez. You remember I represented those Alvarado snakes in DC? They were clients at Henderson Lane way before I even got there."

Courtney agreed. "Yeah, I remember. But it could be the Chinese, the Russians, or even the Muslim nut jobs. Did you know that your old best former friend, Dr. Martin King, had converted to Islam right under your nose?"

Steven was shocked. "Really? He was once a lay Baptist minister. Boy, I really had my head up my butt during that time, didn't I?"

"Bless your heart, Steven. You just hadn't unlayered yet. Martin King was evil, and you did cut that tentacle without killing him. You didn't have to; Martin killed himself. Like evil people always do…shoot themselves right in the foot!"

"Thanks to you and Arlene and the good Lord." Steven's eyes teared up.

Courtney sensed it. "You always did have a good heart. You've just now been recognizing that over the last few years, since you left DC and found some peace in El Paso." Courtney changed the subject. "Steven, my surrogate son, now I have a confession to make to you."

Steven was listening. "Go on, Courtney."

Courtney paused for a second. "You are like a son to me. You know that. So I'm going to tell you something." Another pause. "I've worked undercover for the CIA for a long time…"

"Really?" is all Steven could manage. "Tell me…"

"Well, when the Muslim president initially got elected to the presidency, a lot of black Americans knew about his ties to Saudi Arabia…"

Steven interrupted. "Weren't the Saudis the financing behind the 9/11 terrorist attack that brought down the twin towers in New York City?"

"They sure were! And now the administration is desperately trying to keep that intel from the 9/11 survivors suing the Saudi government," Courtney answered. "Plus the Muslim Brotherhood, ousted in Egypt, has now permeated the entire administration."

"Wow" is all Steven could say. "How is it being done, Courtney?"

"Well, not only is the White House run by the president's chief of staff, who is a longtime Muslim Brotherhood slave, but she also leads the first lady around by her nose." Courtney paused then continued. "Steven, don't trust anyone. Trust only your gut and your heart, okay? There is a lot of evil here in DC."

"I will, Courtney. Thank you. Who is the master puppeteer?" Steven asked.

"Probably another Hungarian, just like you…George Soros. He's been jerking the president's chain since his Chicago community organizer days!" Courtney was ready to change the subject. "Any young ladies out there in El Paso?" He knew about Steven's prior addiction very well and about Steven's DC girlfriend, Glee Robinson—both topics that made Steven shudder slightly.

"No, Courtney, and I'm not even looking. Thankfully, no more girls in the grass, or their substitutes, or pseudo mommies needed anymore. I also got some really good counseling from a Christian therapist, Doc Bill I call him, and he's helped me a lot." Steven paused, took a deep breath. "Abstinence has been my cure, or the practice on that issue going through the therapeutic cycle. And it's working well." Steven wiped his eyes and continued. "I've got Rommel and Pegasus, my horse, here in El Paso and my El Paso friends, Eddie and Ray, you and Arlene in DC, and my kids in Tulsa and Oklahoma friends. I'm good to go with my hard-earned El Paso peace and serenity. I'm truly in the good Lord's hands! And most grateful for all His blessings and grace…"

"Steven, my son, you've really got it." Courtney paused. "But a slight correction; you do have other friends here in Washington, DC, other than just Arlene and me."

– 12 –

Steven hung up after saying goodbye to Courtney. He felt good, as he always did, sharing intimacies with Courtney and Arlene. He grinned and thought, *I wonder who Courtney was talking about when he said that I had friends in DC other than just him and Arlene?*

Steven sat back in his chair and sighed. Talking with Courtney about Martin King and Glee Robinson had unnerved him even further. Even though he felt peaceful now, he still couldn't help thinking back to Glee, the woman who ultimately betrayed him in DC almost six years ago.

Glee was a beautiful woman. Steven inhaled deeply and let it out.

Glee had controlled Steven in DC. She had been a large part of his addiction in DC. Steven thought he was in love at the first sight of Glee Robinson back in that train ride when he was escaping from the Sunbelt. But he would be wrong—almost dead wrong!

"God, what a woman." He thought back to Glee as his tired mind projected the train trip that had been his first, yet therapeutic, escape from the Sunbelt horror and devastation where he had almost killed himself. On the way to Seattle escaping from the Sunbelt, Steven had met Glee Robinson. *Her betrayal also saved my life,* Steven thought. It seemed as if it had happened yesterday…

"You look great, young fellah!" The old black dining car waiter with snow-white hair was grinning broadly at Steven Vandorol. "Haven't seen ya for a while. How are ya?"

Steven had spent the last two days in his compartment, recovering, sleeping.

Steven grinned at him. "I feel better"—he glanced at his name plate—"Mr. Ruppert."

"Nothing like sleep, right?" Mr. Ruppert led Steven to a table. "This is a good table. It's over the train car's wheels. That's the smoothest ride. Yes, siree. Well, what can I get fer ya?"

Steven was starved. "The biggest steak you got on the train, medium rare."

70

"Comin' right up! I'll really getcha fixed up. All the trimmings." Mr. Ruppert *had been watching this sad, exhausted white man since he got on the train in Chicago and liked him, yet he felt the sadness and an unknown intangible kinship. Mr. Ruppert was a wise old man.*

"Thank you." Steven smiled as Mr. Ruppert winked and hurried away. *Steven looked around. The dining car was almost full. Eight, nine seats, still empty. People being seated. At Steven's table, three empty spaces. Outside, dusk, purple, electric blue and pink hues, darkness setting in. Beautiful. Inside, a warm glow. Food smells. Delicious. This is great, he thought as he saw his own reflection in the window.* Still look like hell…still really exhausted.

Another waiter came walking toward Steven, a woman following behind him.

The waiter stopped. "Is this okay, ma'am?" He was pointing at the seat opposite Steven and by the window.

"Yes," the woman said. She smiled down at Steven. "Hello."

"Er…hi," Steven managed.

She sat down. "Can you get me a vodka on the rocks, Stolichnaya vodka, please?" she asked the waiter, her profile to Steven.

Steven looked at her…

She was beautiful. One of the most beautiful women he had ever seen. She was black. Gorgeous.

Steven stared…

Her profile was perfect. Jet-black, short tight-curl afro. Soft and silky. Shining. Chocolate brown skin. Flawless. High cheekbones. Broad forehead. Small nose, just a hint of flatness, and slightly flaring nostrils. Wide eyes. Huge black marbles in an expanse of white. Long black eyelashes, curling at the corners. And her mouth, small silk pillows. Lipstick perfect. Blood red.

The waiter left. An Egyptian princess looked at Steven and smiled again. Steven smiled also. Continued to stare…

Half-moon face. Long neck. Strong chin. She was wearing a red silk dress, which fit her like a glove. She was between thirty-five and forty, Steven guessed. A model stepping out from the pages of a fashion magazine. He glanced at her ears. Dangling, shimmering earrings decorated the already beautiful. And then Steven looked into her eyes and saw pain.

"You like my earrings?" A smile was dancing on her lips.

"Uh…yes. I like your earrings." Steven smiled. "I'm sorry. I was staring. You are beautiful." He meant it.

She took it exactly as Steven meant it. "Thank you. A woman likes to hear that, especially when it's sincere, rather than flattery for a piece of…you know." Her smile was dazzling.

Steven laughed. The waiter came back with her drink. "I'll take one of those as well, please," Steven said to the waiter.

"Certainly, I'll tell Mr. Ruppert. Ma'am, what'll you have for dinner?"

She was looking at Steven. "Whatever this gentleman is having." Even her voice was beautiful. Strong and resonant.

The waiter nodded. "I'll ask Mr. Ruppert and bring you the same thing."

"What am I having for dinner?" she asked Steven.

"The biggest steak on the train, medium rare."

"Good. Exactly what I wanted. If you like Stolichnaya vodka, I thought I'd probably like what you are eating." The sadness he had seen in her eyes was no longer there. She was more beautiful now than a few minutes earlier.

Steven looked directly into her beautiful brown eyes. "Since we're drinking and eating the same thing together, I guess we're having dinner. I'm Steven Vandorol." He slid his right hand across the white linen tablecloth.

"Glee Robinson." She slid her dark left hand across into Steven's and squeezed. He squeezed back. Warm, soft hand. Fingernails, sculptured. Each almost an inch and bright red. Shining. A wedding ring. Five-carat diamond, probably. Steven paused at the wedding ring. Her hand outshone the diamond.

The waiter was back and set her drink before her.

"Glee? That's an unusual name," Steven said, eyebrows raising, as the waiter again left.

She pulled her hand back, picked up her drink, and took a sip.

She smiled a dazzling smile again. This woman was truly an Egyptian princess, Steven thought.

"That's right, Glee is my name. My granddaddy, a part of the "Greatest Generation" went to Grambling University after World War II on the GI bill. He didn't like sports. But, oh, did he love to sing. He was a member of the University Glee Club. You know, those were popular in the late forties. So, when PawPaw and NaNa had my Momma, they just had to name her Glee. And that's just what she named me as well! I'm Glee two!"

"That's great. I like it. You're thirty-seven years old, aren't you?" He flashed her a smile.

Glee Robinson was surprised. "How did you know? A girl, especially one thirty-seven, doesn't like everyone to know. Do I look it?"

"Glee, may I call you Glee?" She smiled and nodded. "Glee, I already told you how you look. The age, I guessed. A lucky guess."

Glee smiled. "Let's toast to lucky guesses!"

"The two biggest steaks on the train," announced Mr. Ruppert as if Steven Vandorol and Glee Robinson were the only ones in the dining car. Mr. Ruppert, wise old Mr. Ruppert, knew that Steven's fortunes had just turned for the better.

"Those look great," Steven said as Mr. Ruppert and the other waiter placed a feast before them. Steaks, fried potatoes, corn on the cob, and huge salads oozing with Roquefort dressing. Steaming hot dinner rolls.

"Can I get you another drink, ma'am?" Mr. Ruppert was proud of his efforts. These two obviously appreciated it.

"Yes, please. And bring Mr. Vandorol another one too." A mischievous smile danced on the corners of her beautiful mouth. "Can I call you Steven?" She was imitating.

Steven nodded, smiling at Glee.

Mr. Ruppert smiled. He was old. But he had been there long ago. He knew what would happen later, although Steven and Glee still didn't. He looked at the two, who were staring at each other, and briskly went to get more drinks.

They both prepared their feast and dug into the juicy steaks.

Glee spoke first. "You are a lawyer, aren't you, Steven?"

It was Steven's turn to be surprised. "How did you know?"

"You've got the gift of gab." She smiled that dazzling smile again. "And I know lawyers, Steven. I'm also married to one."

Steven was busy with his steak. He didn't look up.

"Disappointed?"

He looked at her. "Yes. A little." She looked away. He looked back at his steak.

"Well, I am too. Disappointed," Glee said. He looked at her again as she continued. "I noticed your wedding ring also."

Steven looked at his own left hand, wedding ring on his finger. "We separated last November."

"Me too, in January."

Steven looked into her eyes and saw pain again. She looked away, eyes clouding.

Back to the steaks. They sat in silence. Both eating slowly.

Steven spoke first. "I'm just chilling."

Glee didn't look up. "Me too."

Both looked up again.

She's so beautiful, *he thought,* but said, *"Tell me."*

"Congressman Robinson."

Steven was again surprised. "Congressman Melvin Robinson? From Cook County? Chicago?"

"Yes," Glee said. "That's my husband..." Her voice trailed off.

Steven had met the congressman once. A rising star in Washington politics. Head of the Black Caucus. Steven's very best friend in the world, Martin King, had introduced Steven to the rising star. A congressman from Chicago. A black Republican congressman. Steven felt Glee Robinson's pain. He thought he knew. He thought he understood. Steven's hand inched across and gently squeezed Glee's hand. She squeezed back and quickly withdrew.

The sadness again, as she spoke: "The Great Congressman Robinson found another. I'm expendable, like they say in DC." Glee continued on her steak, her knife tearing into it.

"What are you going to do?"

"I don't know. Maybe I'll find out on this trip," Glee said, tears forming in her eyes.

"Hey, no tears at this dinner. I've had enough tears to last me a lifetime." Steven tried to sound flippant. He didn't succeed.

Now Glee was looking at him. "Steven Vandorol...you're a good person."

Steven stared again. "Glee Robinson... you are too."

"Er...er...folks? Can I get you anything else?" Mr. Ruppert stood straight, like a tall oak tree. He was particularly proud of his work today. It was a little game he often played. Seating the right people together, he would tell Steven later.

Glee and Steven looked at Mr. Ruppert. Both had distant looks in their eyes. Mr. Ruppert smiled. He had really done a good job tonight…

"No, thank you," the two said in unison. Looked at each other. Both smiled.

"Little something for after dinner?" Mr. Ruppert asked

Steven didn't want dinner to be over. He looked at Glee. "Would you like something?"

"No, thank you."

Steven was disappointed. He looked at Mr. Ruppert., "I guess not. Thank you very much. That was wonderful."

"I'll get your checks." Mr. Ruppert walked away. He knew that the evening wasn't over just yet for these two.

Steven slowly looked back at Glee Robinson. She was looking directly at him. He was a bit nervous.

Glee smiled. "I didn't want to have a nightcap here."

Steven's attention riveted. His eyes widened.

"Thought you might like to have a nightcap in my compartment." Her smile was once again dazzling. Her perfect white teeth were brilliant. "Would you? It's next to the last car, Compartment D."

Steven smiled. "Is it over the train car's wheels?" Picked out the small yellow rose from the silver bud vase on the table by the window and handed it to her.

Steven gently knocked on the compartment's sliding door. The curtain on the door was closed.

"Come in." The soft, now familiar voice inside said. Stephen pulled the door open and stepped in.

Glee Robinson sat by the window. She had kicked off her shoes. Black spike heels lay on the floor. Her crossed feet were on the seat across. Small tiny feet. Cute little toes. The red silk dress was tight against her legs. She had a drink in her hand.

She said softly, "You just gonna stand there staring?" Her face had a dazzling smile. "Irish Crème?"

"I was just memorizing. Irish Crème sounds good." Steven looked around. An open bottle of Bailey's Irish Crème was on the ledge by the sink. Small yellow rose Steven had given her was in a paper cup with water by another glass, ready. Steven poured himself a drink. He could feel her eyes and smile. He sat down across from Glee, at a proper distance from her beautifully small feet.

Steven took a sip. "I thought about not coming."

"I know. I thought about not inviting. I'm glad you came."

He was nervous but tried not to show it.

Glee said, "This is kinda awkward and tense. Isn't it?"

They both smiled.

Steven broke the silence. "Are you going back to Chicago from Seattle, Glee?"

"Maybe back to Washington. I need to know for sure."

"I understand. I'm not sure either."

Both sat immersed in their own thoughts.

Glee broke the silence this time. "You've been through hell, haven't you?"

"It's the past. Thanks for understanding. You know, the Great Congressman Robinson is a fool."

Glee looked out into the black night. "I don't want to talk about the congressman anymore."

Steven's hand slowly inched to her foot and held it. His grip tightened. She kept looking out the window at her own reflection.

Steven stared at Glee, looking out, for a long time. Neither spoke.

Very slowly, Glee turned toward Steven and their eyes met and held. Steven squeezed her left foot again.

They both rose. Glee and Steven stood facing each other, only inches apart, in the middle of the compartment. Steven wrapped his arms around her waist. Her arms did the same around him. Two bodies met. Tightened. Two lips met. Two tongues intertwined. Steven and Glee would become one at the start of Steven's rampant sexual addiction...

13

Steven got up from his desk, stretched, shook off his reverie, and stepped down the hall to the open reception area on his right.

Christina Ortega sat at the reception desk taking down messages. He looked at his watch. It was almost 6 pm. He had been on the phone with Courtney Wellington for over two hours.

Looking at his receptionist, Steven thought, *she does look exactly like Selena Gomez, as Eddie said.* He waved at Christina, who acknowledged. Christina adored her father, Ray Ortega, sitting in the next office across from her. And her father adored his daughter.

Steven smiled at Christina as he stepped into Ray's office. He was on the phone. Steven sat down in the armchair, the gun rack right behind him.

"Okay, I've got it, Juan. Hey, thanks a bunch. I owe ya, padnah." Ray hung up, looked at Steven. "That was my Texas Ranger bud. The white Silverado pickup is registered to a Nevada corporation with a nationwide service agent, CT Corporation, and the local El Paso service agent is a representative of the Kemper & Smith law firm, and you know what a snake pit that is."

"Yeah, the firm itself is an unindicted co-conspirator in this prosecution." Steven paused. "So, the Silverado pickup was scoping us out."

"I guess," Ray mused. "What's up, Steven?"

Steven summarized the morning's conversations with DA Ernesto Martinez, referring to him as "our boss," and Eddie, everything but the personal stuff about Ray's daughter, but including the contract on his life and ending with his long conversation with Courtney and his FBI and CIA contacts.

Ray was perceptive. "I would bet there are contracts also on the FBI guys and Muslim radicals in hiding, and maybe even on the other announced lawyers on your prosecution team, North Anderson and Beth Barker."

"I agree, Ray," Steven answered. "We'll keep that between just me and you for right now. Ernie and Eddie are the only ones, other than you, me, and Courtney, that know about the contract out on me. I'm not going to do anything different. I'm just going to be that much more vigilant than I already am and was about R.O.W. in general."

Ray also knew about Steven's R.O.W. contempt and cynicism and agreed with it. Both used their street smarts, learned early in life, to their best advantage. Both had been street warriors long ago as teenagers, Ray on the streets of Juarez and South El Paso and Steven on the slum streets of Sao Paulo, Brazil, and South Bronx, New York City.

"Need any more weapons?" Ray was smiling. Both were what the leftist parasites in the mainstream American media and the liberals mockingly called "gun nuts," and both were proud of the moniker. "I know you're pretty well-armed right down to your really cool, concealed, ten-inch, perfectly balanced, double-edged, razor-sharp, fine German Tungsten carbide steel, very thin throwing knife…but you need any more?" Ray laughed, kidding Steven affectionately about Steven's own description of the knife he always carried in his boot.

"In answer to your questions, no, I really don't," Steven said. "I carry my Glock on my belt, sometimes a 22mm North American Five Shot Derringer in my back pocket, and all the time my trusty pearl-handled switchblade in the other, as you know!" Steven paused.

He had discussed his Brazil and South Bronx childhood "layers of evil" with Ray many times, and that was a part of their commonality. Ray himself carried a shorter-barrel 9mm Beretta 19 in a shoulder holster. "I'll take the Persuader you gave me last Christmas home, where I got a 357 Magnum, 9mm Marlin Carbine, and two vintage 9mm German World War II Lugers that Captain Reacher gave me after I handled his divorce." Steven was finished.

"Oh, he's the tank company commander at 3rd Cavalry, right?" Ray had even more contacts at Fort Bliss than Steven had accumulated at Bliss in the over five years he had been in El Paso. "You know he is a West Point grad?"

"Yes, I did," Steven answered. "We've become good friends since I handled his divorce. Did I tell you that he let me drive an Abrams M1A1 main battle tank one Saturday on the Bliss North Range?"

"No…I bet that was really cool." Ray was impressed. "I heard it was like driving a big old Harley motorcycle."

"It was…exactly." Steven grinned. "Captain G. Jack, that's my nickname for him. G. Jack is a good guy and has a really good heart."

"I know and agree," Ray said. "They have any kids?"

"No, they didn't." Steven paused thoughtfully then continued. "G. Jack and Joan just grew apart, they said, so I'm trying to get them back together. They are both as sweet as they can be."

"Jack, really sweet?" Ray laughed. "That's not what I would call him! You know he was a Ranger and paratrooper and led an Abrams M1A1 tank company in Iraq when we decimated Saddam's Republican Guard at 73 Easting…"

"I know," Steven answered. "G. Jack's tank company of five tanks took out thirty Russian-made T-58s…pretty amazing!"

"Wow!" was all Ray could say. "What's his current assignment at Bliss?"

Steven knew. "Captain Reacher, soon to be a Major G. Jack Reacher, by the way, now commands a full company of AH-64 Apaches…"

"Wow," Ray said again. "That's twelve of those killers!"

"Do you know anything about those babies, Ray?" Steven asked.

"Yes, I do!" Ray answered. "The Boeing AH-64 Apache is an American four-blade, twin-turbo-shaft attack helicopter armed with a 30 mm M230 chain gun carried between the main landing gear, under the aircraft's forward fuselage. The AH-64 has a large amount of systems redundancy to improve combat survivability."

It was Steven's turn to say "Wow." He blinked. "How did you learn all that?"

Ray smiled broadly. "When I was CID at Bliss, they prosecuted a ground-crew mechanic for selling Apache secrets to the Ruskies!"

"No kidding?" Steven frowned. "What did he get?"

Ray smiled even wider. "Twenty-five years at Leavenworth moving rocks from one place to another...a hundred yards or so away." Ray laughed at his own humor. "Anyway, the US Army is the primary operator of the AH-64; it has also become the primary attack helicopter of multiple nations, including Greece, Japan, Israel, the Netherlands, Singapore, and the United Arab Emirates, as well as being produced under license in the United Kingdom as the AgustaWestland Apache."

Steven was really surprised at all Ray knew about the AH-64 attack helicopter, "Wow, Ray...did the Ruskies get any top-secret information?"

Ray answered, "Naw, they didn't get crap!" He laughed. "It was a sting and the Ruskies got a great recipe for guacamole, in top secret code, of course!" Ray laughed, paused and continued, "American AH-64s have served in conflicts in Panama, the Persian Gulf, Kosovo, Afghanistan, and Iraq. Israel used the Apache in its military conflicts in Lebanon and the Gaza Strip; British and Dutch Apaches have seen deployments in wars in Afghanistan and Iraq." Ray was finished with his seminar.

"Israel have a bunch of them?" Steven asked, always interested in the Jewish State of Israel.

Ray answered immediately, "Yeah, we sold Israel about five hundred of them!" Ray paused a beat, frowning, "Unfortunately, the ISIS nut jobs got about fifty Apaches when the President abandoned Iraq..."

"Yeah, that's what Reacher told me as well!" Steven paused. "Reacher served three tours of duty in Iraq during Desert Storm," Steven paused, then continued, "What's the Apache's range, do you know, Ray?"

Ray knew that as well, "About five hundred miles..." Ray paused, thinking, then continued, "But completely stripped down, armaments and all, and two extra tanks of fuel, it can triple that..."

"Boy, that's fifteen hundred miles!" Steven said, eyes widening. "I think Reacher flew the AH-64 Apache in Iraq...I'll have to ask him..."

"Was he wounded in Iraq?" Ray asked.

"No, but he was in Afghanistan, God bless him," Steven answered. "I think he also got PTSD, post-traumatic stress disorder…" Steven paused. "I think that was the problem in their marriage…and the long absences."

"I bet!" Ray answered. "And then our veterans got back and the corrupt and chaotic Veterans Administration under the Muslim puppet President treated them like they had leprosy."

"Well, he's doing a lot better now. G. Jack leads a company of Bradley fighting vehicles, right now that is, until the Apache command takeover in January, in view of the more downsizing by the corrupt Pentagon, decimated by the President as well." Steven was finished with that subject, "I'm going to try and help G. Jack and Joan reconcile…"

"Well, anyway, Steven, you should get Reacher to take you up in his lead Apache, and let you fly the thing, just as he let you drive the Abrams…and see El Paso from fifteen thousand feet."

"Maybe I will! That would be really cool," Steven answered, thinking out loud, "That would be…" Steven paused, then continued, "Anyways, back to your question, I don't need any more guns…and there is plenty of them around here…" Steven finished, smiling broadly at Ray who was smiling back at him and looking at the MP5/10 submachine gun, Colt M 4 Carbine, M 1911 A1 Custom 45 ACP pistol, SIG Sauer 9/10mm, Remington 12-gauge shotgun and Remington 700 Sniper rifle, all in Ray's gun rack in his office.

Ray wasn't quite finished with talking about Captain Reacher. "Steven, you said Reacher's full name was G. Jack Reacher and your nickname for him was G. Jack. Do you know what the G stands for?"

Steven shook his head. "I sure don't. I'll have to ask him sometime." He paused, thought a second, then said, "All his uniform name tapes just say 'G. Reacher'"—and saw that Ray was looking at his own arsenal, thinking…

"You know the three most important rules in a gunfight, Steven, don't ya?" Ray was smiling ear to ear, an impish John Travolta.

"I know some rules, tell me yours…"

"Okay, here are mine." Ray cleared his throat. "One, always win—there is no such thing as a fair gunfight. Two—always win, cheat if necessary, and…"

Steven interrupted, laughing. "Three—always win—second place doesn't count."

"And make your attacker advance through a wall of bullets…you may get killed with your own gun, but they'll have to beat you to death with it because it will be empty," Ray added.

Steven was laughing out loud. "You can say stop or use any other word, but a large-bore muzzle pointed at someone's head is pretty much a universal language."

"And you won't have to press one for Spanish or two for Chinese or three for Arabic…"

Steven said, "Never leave an enemy behind. If you have to shoot, shoot to kill. In court, yours will be the only testimony!"

The two men could hear Christina next door, laughing as well.

Steven stopped laughing, wiped his eyes. "We'll have to go shooting on the Bliss gun range with G. Jack, okay?"

"You got it," Ray answered. He was relaxed yet tired after a long day as well.

Steven yawned. "We better stop jacking around, Ray. We could do Saturday Night Live skits…together."

"Much to the dismay of the leftist liberal media!" Ray finished.

Steven got up and closed the door to the hallway. "First things first. I need you on the special prosecution part time, Ray. So, I got authorization from the DA to put you on the county payroll. It'll be contract work with the county on a timesheet signed off by yours truly." Steven smiled, raised his eyebrows, and continued. "At the rate of a hundred per hour for fifty hours per month."

"Wow, Steven, that's five grand a month. Thanks a lot, bud." He wiped his eyes.

"You're welcome. So first we need to get up to speed totally on the special prosecution. You and I are meeting with Eddie on his ranch Saturday. His Texas Ranger guys will be there also, as will his police department investigators. It's all top secret. Don't even tell your wife, okay? Jessie doesn't need to know."

"You got it." Ray leaned his head to the left toward his daughter. "We won't tell her either."

Steven nodded, glanced toward Christina's area. "We'll just be available to her by cell phone, okay?"

Ray nodded. He was real protective of his daughter. Sometimes too much, Steven thought.

"We're riding early Saturday morning…just the three of us…as usual," Steven said. "Sunday, we're riding also, so come back out Sunday again and ride with us, okay?"

"You bet, Steven, that'll be great." Ray also loved horses and dogs. "What time Sunday?"

"Probably at sunset. Even in August, it can get too hot for the horses." Steven smiled. "Rommel loves the horses and will be with us as well." Ray was nodding as Steven continued. "In the meantime, Ray, please hire another legal assistant for the legal work and part time for the special prosecution. As close to your daughter's twin as possible. Christina may have some good suggestions."

"I'll do it right away, Steven." Ray would do the right thing. Steven trusted him on that. "I'll start at UTEP." The University of Texas at El Paso had a wonderful business college. Steven himself taught business law in their management department in the evening for three semesters. "Then I've got to get busy and hire an eager and aggressive young lawyer. One that's had several years in actual practice experience so I don't have to spoon-feed him…or her," Steven mused.

"I'll keep my eyes open for a good one, okay?" Ray said.

"Thank you, Ray. I appreciate the help."

The telephone buzzed. Ray picked it up. "Yes?" It was his daughter, Christina. Ray held the phone out. "Steven, it's for you. Emergency." Steven took the phone.

"This is Steven Vandorol. Who is this?"

"Judge, this is Lieutenant Samson." Steven remembered Lieutenant Samson as a very able police officer, Eddie Egen's second in command at El Paso police department. "We've got an emergency. Chief Egen is in the emergency room at Providence Hospital." Lieutenant Samson was very excited, almost stuttering.

"What happened?" Steven asked.

"He's been in an automobile accident..."

14

Steven was driving south on North Mesa Street again heading toward Providence Hospital. It was about five minutes from his office on North Stanton Street, which ran parallel to North Mesa Street two blocks away.

Lieutenant Samson told Steven that the chief had been returning from Pecos, some sixty miles from El Paso, on Interstate 10 in his personal cruiser, a Dodge Charger, when outside of Van Horn and a hundred miles from El Paso a white Silverado pickup, tinted glass, came up behind him fast, and forced him off the interstate, which was under construction with a sharp drop-off shoulder. When his front wheels jammed in the soft sand, his cruiser did a one and a half gainer, landing on the roof. Eddie was at Providence Emergency being evaluated, the lieutenant had said. Chief Egen was badly shaken up but otherwise unharmed, he added.

Steven pulled into the Providence Hospital lot, parked in a visitor space, got out, adjusted his Glock in back on his belt, and realized he should have worn his sport coat. Slamming the door shut, he looked around carefully. Enhanced situational awareness. Didn't notice anything unusual except for three police cruisers parked by the emergency room entrance, two officers standing by.

Steven walked across the lot to the entrance. As he neared, one of the officers saw him and waved. "Hi, judge…"

Steven kept walking. "Hi, guys. The chief okay?"

The other officer, who Steven also knew, answered, smiling broadly, "Just real grumpy, still in bed, but he's all right." The officer chuckled as Steven walked into the emergency room and stopped; the nurse behind the desk looked up.

"Chief Egen? I'm Judge Vandorol to see him."

"Judge, he's down the hall, then to your right in 115."

Steven went down the daylight bright hallway, turned down to the right, took in the antiseptic aura, and headed down the hall where he saw two more officers standing at the door, hanging around.

"Hey, guys, how's the big Irish?"

"Still grumpy," an officer laughed as Steven entered the room.

Eddie was dozing in bed, wrapped in and bulging out of a skimpy blue hospital gown. The TV was muted, and a plump nurse stood over him straightening the sheets. Steven glanced at her name plate, Nurse Warren. Eddie looked up as Steven drew near. Eddie was still very groggy and a little incoherent.

"This is my nurse, Jillian." Eddie may have been groggy, but he still couldn't resist the urge to flirt. "I'm gonna get her to give me a full-body bath and massage, right Ms. Jillian?" Eddie was smiling up broadly as was Nurse Jillian Warren.

Steven looked at the nurse, smiled at her himself, and said, "Let Ralph do it…with all the lights on!"

Nurse Jillian laughed out loud. She was a dumpy, obese, short woman with plump but strong arms who probably was a petite and very attractive woman 150 pounds ago, Steven thought. She was blushing, however, and preening to Chief Egen and Steven both, straightening her shoulders displaying her very large breasts.

"Chief Egen is such a wag! I'm really enjoying taking care of him," she said, looking at Steven, her wide face in a big smile.

Steven interrupted: "Nurse, would you give us some privacy?"

She flushed, feelings hurt. "Fine!" she said, turned away, and walked out of the room in a huff.

Steven thought, *I guess she took it personally, which is the maximum expression of selfishness because she made the assumption that everything is about her*, as Eddie, now smiling, said, "I guess no full-body massage."

"Oh, Chief Egen, you're such a wag!" Steven said in a falsetto voice. "Do you know why the good Lord invented whiskey?"

Grumpy Eddie answered, "No, but I'm sure you're gonna tell me." He was still scowling.

"So the Irish won't take over the world."

Eddie finally smiled again and chuckled, "Hey, Steven, get me outta here. They're driving me nuts with all that medical crap!"

Steven bent down and hugged his friend. "I'm really glad you're okay…"

"Hey, did you hear about the new *Survivor* series set in Texas?"

"No, but I'm sure you're going to tell me," Steven said, imitating his friend.

Eddie finally smiled. "Due to the popularity of the *Survivor* shows, Texas is planning one entitled *Survivor: Texas-Style*! The lucky contestants will all start in Dallas, drive to Waco, Austin, San Antonio, then over to Houston and down to Brownsville. They will then proceed up to Del Rio, El Paso, Odessa, Midland, Lubbock, and Amarillo. From there they will go on to Abilene and Fort Worth…"

Steven was already laughing at the Texas geography lesson, wondering where this joke was going, as Eddie continued. "Finally, back to Dallas." Eddie paused for dramatic effect and said, "Each contestant will be driving a pink Prius with thirteen bumper stickers that will read…"

Eddie recited the numbers in order, as if he had written the joke himself: "I'm a Democrat, Amnesty for illegals, I Love the Dixie Chicks, Boycott Beef, I Voted for Obama, George Strait Sucks, Re-elect the President in 2012, Vote Eric Holder for Texas Governor, Rosie O'Donnell is Texas-born, I Love Obamacare and Chuck Schumer, Barney Frank is My Hero, I Side with Jane Fonda," Eddie paused, took a deep breath, and dramatically continued, "and the last sticker is…I'm Here to Confiscate Your Guns." Eddie finished with the punch line: "The first contestant to make it back to Dallas alive wins."

Steven laughed so hard he was almost crying. He was relieved that his friend was well enough to crack jokes. "So, you're okay?" Steven stepped up and held the bed bar with both hands.

"Yeah, I'm fine. My arms are a little scratched up." He lifted his arms. Both forearms were heavily bandaged. "It took me half an hour to crawl out of the darn car…and my butt is bare in this open-air gown!"

Steven was now serious. "Tell me what happened. Samson said you were forced off the road by a white Silverado pickup with tinted windows…"

"Yeah, well, I was right outside Van Horn, you know, where they got construction going?"

"Yeah, for about twenty-five miles outside of Van Horn." Steven had driven past that construction many times in going to court in Van Horn and Pecos.

"Well, it's all concrete dividers everywhere, one lane only both ways, and nasty concrete pavement shoulder drop-offs, almost a foot deep…" Ed paused and swallowed. "I was driving back from Pecos, so I wasn't in any hurry. Had Rush Limbaugh on talk radio…was going about sixty when outta nowhere this big white Silverado pickup pulls up on my left…the windows were tinted…black…and whoever's timing was perfect…turns sharply into me…" Ed swallowed again, the memory distressing. "I swerved sharply to the right, hit a drop-off, my front wheels went into soft sand, left front wheel jammed in, and up and over I went." He indicated a flip with his hands. "Did a one and a half gainer and landed on the roof with a thud." Ed paused again, shivered, and took a couple of deep breaths. Swallowed hard. Beads of perspiration were showing on his forehead.

Steven said nothing. He kept listening to his distressed best friend.

"Steven, I gotta tell you," Eddie continued. "One of the few times in my life that I was really scared."

Steven still said nothing.

"Here I was lying upside-down, strapped in, stunned, about an 18-inch gap to my left to the outside desert beside me, when suddenly I smelled gas. Looked up, the engine was still on…Steven, I tell you, this incredible calm descended on me and I clearly heard like a whisper…I reached up, turned off the engine, and thought…the car could very well have exploded." Eddie paused a couple of beats. "After a couple of minutes, I didn't smell any more gas, so I unbuckled my seatbelt and crumpled into the car roof upside-down. Man, it took me…I think almost half an hour to crawl out. I took out my cell, it was okay. Called the department…and here I am. So whatcha think?"

Steven was still very serious. "First, do you know what happened to you?"

Ed was puzzled. "What?"

"Ed, you landed in the good Lord's palms. He works in mysterious ways. I know." Steven was looking straight into his friend's eyes, remembering his own brush with death in the Sunbelt years ago. "It's God's grace, Eddie!"

Eddie said nothing. He was thoughtful. His eyes glistened.

"Eddie, my friend, the good Lord was trying to catch the attention of a goodhearted but flawed human being…"

———————————

Steven Vandorol was exhausted. It had been a very long and most trying emotional day. The sun was setting on beautiful downtown El Paso and Juarez in the distance and was almost behind the Santo Cristo Mountains of Mexico to the west. The sky was a cloudless violet and pink and red palette as he drove up Scenic Drive, the winding street on the south side of the Franklin Mountain toward Sierra Medical Center.

Curving up on Scenic Drive as he drove up the mountain, the entire El Paso downtown and Juarez opened to his right. Steven glanced out the window and marveled at the scenic view and especially at the shining silver ribbon of the Rio Grande River dividing Texas and Mexico far down below, thinking for the thousandth time how much he loved that calming and serene view. With the coming sunset, the panorama was already a sea of sparkling fireflies as a million lights came on, lighting all below rolling into the eternity of the expansive horizon.

Steven drove on up, past Sierra Medical Center on his left, a massive crowd of three-story buildings, all six modern glass buildings connected with landscaped and covered canopies.

The landscaping on Scenic Drive was mostly decorative stone covering with a wide array of cacti and multicolored flowers blooming, the most common landscaping in the El Paso desert environment. Further up, about fifty yards later, Steven was on a residential street, Golden Hill Terrace, with the rocky mountain terrain and wildflowers everywhere to the left and residential houses to the right. All the houses to the right of Scenic Drive would have panoramic views into that eternity from their own backyards.

As he turned onto his street, his home and oasis in El Paso came into view on the right, ten houses up. Number 4444 Golden Hill Terrace was a one-story grayish white stucco with large paneled glass windows protected by wrought-iron bars and grates with spear-point ends. Steven liked the security of those window bars on the street side and the iron screen door with deadbolt outside lock covering a large double front door. The double front door had sidelights on both sides and opened to a narrow concrete walk bordered by a ten-foot brick wall.

Steven felt secure in his oasis, especially since on the other side there was a 200-foot drop cliff. Even if someone broke in, they still would have to contend with a very angry, snarling, well-trained Rommel immediately going for their jugular. Steven smiled at that thought and was surprised by raindrops suddenly hitting the windshield as he approached his driveway. He turned on the wipers as the rain got heavier. Then a deluge fell all at once, most unusual for El Paso in late August. *But a nice quick rain is always good*, he thought as he drove up and into his own driveway, touched the garage door opener, and the door rose to his own two-car garage.

One side of the garage, nearest to the kitchen entry, was for his car. The other was for his dog, the entire garage sparkling clean except for a huge dog house with a stenciled plaque that read "Rommel" in old-styled German lettering. Inside the dog house was a plush doggie bed of imported Australian sheep wool. Gallon-sized water and food bowls, both with like lettering of "Rommel" on each, sat beside the dog house. Various chew toys littered the rest of the garage space on that side.

Steven's Great Dane was named after the famous World War II German general who defied Hitler and was part of the conspiracy to assassinate him. Steven's friends who gave him Rommel knew about Steven's Hungarian and World War II background and interest in history when naming the puppy, as he left DC for El Paso.

Steven opened the car door, and huge Rommel came bounding to the car nearly knocking him backward, long tail wagging excitedly. He jumped up, putting his huge paws on Steven's shoulders and immediately slurped his face.

"I guess you're glad to see me," Steven said, laughing and trying to dodge the dog's tongue.

The huge dog seemed to be actually smiling, and his tail kept wagging as they stood together like two dancing partners. Steven was six-foot-two but Rommel was taller as they stood hugging and holding each other. At 180 pounds, Rommel was a formidable "partner." Steven hugged his huge dog affectionately.

"I bet you're hungry. I'm sorry I'm late. It's been a really long day."

The dog's face was a foot away from Steven's, and Rommel cocked his head to one side as if he understood his master perfectly.

Steven chuckled as he lowered Rommel to the floor by his front legs. "Let's get you some food." Rommel's long tail was still wagging feverishly, like a whip snapping back and forth.

Steven grabbed the dog's food bowl, went into the big bag of dog chow in the large cabinet by the side, ladled out several scoops, and took it back, Rommel following closely. He quickly scarfed the food. Steven filled the other pan with distilled water and said, "Bon Appetit, big guy," and walked into the hallway. On into the kitchen, Steven yawned, took out a bottle of Aziano Chianti, his favorite, and sank into his favorite leather easy chair in the living room. He pulled off his boots and pulled the cord next to him on the dupioni drapes that opened across the picture window, revealing the breathtaking panorama of downtown El Paso and Juarez right below.

The rain had stopped, leaving the outside shining, sparkling. The sun had set completely, revealing a black ocean illuminated by a million jewels, diamonds, rubies, silver, and gold, a palette of a billion lights all upon plush black velvet. Steven was always awed by the nightly light show of sparkling brilliance outside on an immense outdoor movie screen in sharp and bright technicolor, an IMAX theater of God's very own nighttime creation as he inhaled and smelled the recent rain permeating the mountain air.

This was Steven's oasis in the calm desert of magnificent Texas and neighboring Mexico, both uncorrupted and clean in the dark night sky.

It's been a real long day, Steven thought as he let out a long sigh. *I've got to remain focused and keep my hard-earned peace and serenity and not backslide on any of my past anguish…* Sighed again, deeper this time, and took another sip of wine…smelled the fresh rain outside again, still thinking…finished the glass and yawned.

Steven walked back into the kitchen and poured another glass of Chianti. Rommel sauntered past Steven into the living room, cocked his head as if thanking his master for supper, and went out to the backyard through his large doggie door.

"You're welcome," Steven called after him. "Bathroom break, buddy?" Steven smiled and sat back down still thinking about his very emotional and exhausting day.

He remembered his conversation with Courtney Wellington about his former best friend, Martin L. King, who had committed suicide, and Glee Robinson, who had not, the two former DC friends that embodied Steven's own evil. *Dr. Martin L. King. He sure turned out to be one of the two key players that taught me much about the evil in my own soul.* Steven inhaled again and closed his eyes…and dozed off into a deep slumber…

Steven awoke with a start. The view into Mexico looked the same, with the vast dark sky lit by a billion sparkling stars and shimmering lights of El Paso and Juarez. The view always brought a smile to his face.

Sitting straight up before him, mere inches away, Rommel looked right into his face, head cocked slightly to the side and large black eyes shining in the brilliance of lights streaming into the dark room. His dog was smiling right back at him.

"I guess I fell asleep, boy," Steven said out loud. Rommel wagged his tail, wiggled his rump, and licked Steven's face. "I love you too." Steven wiped his face with both hands and looked at his luminous-face wristwatch. It was 12:30 am. Yawning, he got up and turned down the hallway to his right, Rommel following right behind.

15

Jason Warren was bathing his sweet little eight-year-old daughter Michelle, washing her tiny little feet with a soapy washcloth as she lay back in the bubble bath.

She smiled at her daddy. "Tickle my feet, Daddy."

Jason complied and lightly ran his index finger along the soft pad of her foot. "Tickle, tickle…." he said smiling, as she laughed in glee.

He loved his little girl Michelle with all his heart and soul. She was his life, and he really enjoyed their nightly ritual of bath, bedtime reading her old fairy tale stories, which Jason loved from his own childhood, prayer, and tuck-in. Jason's wife, Jillian, chided Jason about their routine incessantly, saying that she was not a baby anymore, that a father bathing a beautiful little eight-year-old girl was totally inappropriate, blah, blah, blah, as Jason would mutter under his breath.

Jason Warren didn't care. It was a daily routine that he looked forward to all day, gave him immense pleasure and the feeling of intimacy with his little girl that he surely didn't get from his wife, and gave his mundane life some real meaning and joy. Jason would take a bullet for his little girl! For his wife, Jillian, not so much…

He looked at Michelle and smiled at her again, noticing for the thousandth time her cute dimples when she grinned at him. "Tickle, tickle…" Jason did it again and she giggled more. "I love you sooo much, Daddy!" she said. "I love you more," Jason finished.

Jason Warren was a computer engineer, a very good computer engineer, sitting all day before banks of computer terminals, monitors, closed circuit TV screens, and keyboards outside his own office in the "Star Wars" computer control room of El Paso Power & Electric Corporation that ran the electrical power grid supplying electricity to more than 2,500 square miles—and three million people—of East Texas, southern New Mexico, and across the border into Mexico. Homes, businesses, and factories all benefited from the electrical power the company provided.

Jason was a brilliant computer engineer and took great pride in doing it well, although Jillian really couldn't care less about anything Jason did or was doing...ever.

As an early seventies graduate of Texas Tech University, he played NCAA basketball and obtained dual PhDs in computer science and philosophy. Jason met Jillian as a junior at the local watering hole while she was attending the nursing school at the university. The two fell into lust immediately, married two weeks later, and after graduation moved from Lubbock to El Paso for Jason's first job with El Paso Power & Electric over twenty years ago. Jillian went to work for Providence Hospital in the trauma unit and was a well-experienced emergency room registered nurse. Jason and Jillian were both workaholics living separate emotional lives in a big ostentatious home on the west side of El Paso.

In his middle age, Jason still worked out regularly, enjoyed WWII computer war gaming, and spent weekend late evenings in his study before his monitor, only occasionally switching to pornography, especially bondage, to which he would stimulate himself obsessively. Jason Warren was despondent, depressed, and very lonely in his own house, escaping from the lack of emotional intimacy in his life through pornography and workaholism. His father died when Jason was a teenager, and his mother then provided Jason with a revolving door of lovers and stepfathers.

It was an important job. It was a very responsible and meaningful job. It was an agonizingly boring and mind-numbing job. Jason longed for something...anything... more meaningful in his life.

"Daddy, Daddy...tickle my feet some more," Michelle giggled. "Can you read me the Princess and the Pea again tonight?"

"Sure can, sweetheart, Michelle my belle," Jason said. He was a Beatles fanatic as well. He beamed at his innocent baby girl. "You really love that old Hans Christian Andersen fairy tale, don't you?" he said as he continued to wash her little feet.

"I sure do, Daddy!" she giggled. "Especially when you read it to me in bed, before I go to sleep…" She blew some soap bubbles she had in her hand right at her daddy, and he in turn chuckled with pure joy.

The father and daughter were interrupted by Jillian watching them by the open bathroom door. "Let's get out of there!" she exclaimed. "You two have been in here long enough…it's a school night." Jillian kept looking in with her hands on her hips and a sour expression on her face.

Jillian was once an attractive woman. Brunette, hair cut short, almost five-five. She was now a full-bodied obese woman with large breasts, big buttocks, and thick fat arms and legs. She was a nurse, a very good one, and had been one for over twenty years. She was a good caretaker of others, leaving her own family wanting. Jason and Jillian were living separate lives emotionally, craving intimacy yet not knowing how to find it. Her father was just a hazy figure in her past and her mother, who she couldn't stand, was always sick with some ailment, real or imagined. Her life continued to be governed by her finding her older sister one day with her throat cut in an apparent suicide. But she loved her baby boy Jacob dearly. Jacob, now eighteen years old, was enrolling at University of Texas-El Paso in the fall to major in computer science and wanted to be just like his dad.

Jason looked at Jillian almost with disgust and rolled his eyes in disdain, which Michelle noticed. "Just leave us the hell alone," he said, paused, and then continued, "and do your own crap, Facebook, with fifteen hundred of your nearest and dearest girlfriends." Jason stopped short. His little sweetheart was watching and listening, sadness passing across her sweet face.

Jason perked up. "Come on, my little angel. I'll dry you off."

As the naked eight-year-old slipped out of the bathtub, Jason wrapped her in the plush bath towel and rubbed her vigorously, which brought the beautiful smile back. She was happy again. "I love you, Daddy" she said and hugged him tight, her arms wrapped around his neck.

"I love you too, my little angel!" he said. "Go get your jam-jams on, okay?"

Jillian, still standing by the door, shook her head in disgust, turned away with a sigh, and walked into her study, slamming the door behind her.

16

The sun had set, and it was pitch black except for the bright light on the front porch of the log cabin in the forest that was twenty miles from the US-Canada border in Manitoba, Canada. Two huge men stood straight and at attention, flashlights shining down on gravel at their feet. Both wore heavy fur-lined parkas and all-weather combat boots.

Ward Powell jumped out of the white Jeep Cherokee, shouldered the Uzi, adjusted his sidearm, a Glock 22, and walked toward the two sour-faced colonels, Lemev and Liang, who both started walking toward him. "Gentlemen, are we on time?" Again Ward's English was flawless. He wore cowboy boots, jeans, and a fur-lined, fur-collar Russian pilot's flight jacket.

Ward was smiling. He had met his superior KGB officer, the Russian Colonel Stanislav Lemev, knew him well and barely tolerated him. Ward had never met the Chinese communist Colonel Qiao Liang but had met his co-author, General Wang Xiangsui, who was arriving in El Paso from California within the next ten days, and knew all about both men very well. He hated all the "slant-eye bastards," as he called them, but only behind their backs. Ward Powell knew that the later arriving Xiangsui was ultimately in charge of all their destinies.

Colonel Lemev was nodding, a sour look on his deeply scarred face. "Yes, you're fine. Show us what you brought!" Lemev was strictly business as he scowled at Powell and spoke haltingly with a heavy Russian accent.

The colonel was a huge bear of a man. Powell knew him very well. A veteran of the Russian fiasco in Afghanistan, the Russian Vietnam, he had a deep hatred for the United States, whose stinger missiles, shoulder-fired, and CIA-supplied to Afghan freedom fighters, brought the Russian bear to its knees. Over 270 pounds and six-four, Lemev was as strong as an ox. In his prime a heavyweight Olympic weightlifter and gold medalist, he was an ugly man—proud of his disfigured face and dour countenance. He had a heavy scar running diagonally across his face, a trophy from a Muslim woman trying to decapitate him in Kurtz Valley that the colonel later disemboweled.

The scar turned his lips into a permanent sneer. He hated Muslims just a bit less than he hated Americans. That hatred he religiously kept to himself, but especially in the present company of his own assassination team. His ruddy, pock-marked face with deep-set gray eyes was topped by a shock of gray hair.

The colonel also knew Powell very well and didn't even tolerate him. Thought he was a womanizing egomaniacal pretty boy. *But apparently has handlers that ordered me to kiss his butt... But if he crosses me, I'll remove his kidneys and won't even sell them on the black market*, he thought to myself and sneered at his own private joke as he approached a smiling, jovial Powell.

Colonel Liang remained silent.

Colonel Lemev said again, "Show us what you brought, Powell." Lemev was still scowling, eyes narrowing, right eyelid twitching.

Powell thought, *what an ugly mat' ublyudka* but said, "Here's your reinforcements..." and swept his arms dramatically toward the five vehicles and trucks now bumper to bumper behind the Jeep Cherokee still idling in the lead. All the vehicles still had their headlights on.

Powell, tour guide, silently proceeded to show the two colonels all six vehicles, rolling up the backs of the two trucks to reveal enough supplies and weapons to equip and sustain the now twenty-four-man assassination team and advance guard of the forthcoming invasion of the United States of America from Canada.

Uri, Powell's driver, and twelve other Spetznaɜ commandos remained in their vehicles, all behind smoked-glass bulletproof windows and dark windshields.

Both colonels remained silent. Both absorbed everything, especially the supplies and weapons as if they had photographic memories, walking and shining flashlights into the trucks and pickups. Enough weapons and supplies to equip a small army in the field for at least six months. Colonel Lemev grunted in satisfaction, ugly sneer relaxing just a bit.

Powell walked with the colonels leading the way, feeling awkward and silly. *Like talking to a couple of big ugly robots*, he thought to himself, but kept talking.

"Lemev and Liang…I was just telling Uri that Lemev and Liang sounds like a multicultural American law firm!" Powell laughed at his own joke.

Neither Lemev nor Liang did. Neither said anything. Both continued scowling.

Powell, feeling even more awkward, and a little nervous especially in front of Liang, whom he had never met, continued nervously, "As I'm sure you both know what Comrade Lenin said about peace, that it's that brief glorious moment in history when everybody stands around reloading…" and laughed again.

Liang's eyes narrowed to a dark slit.

Lemev, sensing Powell's discomfort, finally managed an ugly sneer that almost looked like a smile as Powell continued to talk when he shouldn't have. "Hey, you guys, lighten up, okay?" Powell said. "It's been a long trip. A nice *spacibo* would be nice!" Powell continued laughing. A *spacibo* was thank you in Russian.

Colonel Liang finally spoke, almost in perfect English. "You are amused, Mr. Powell?" His voice was ice as he looked directly at Powell, his tongue flicking out like that of a cobra, his slanted eyes so narrow they almost disappeared from view.

Colonel Qiao Liang of the People's Liberation Army of Communist China was also huge by Asian standards. At six feet and 250 pounds, he was a fully trained ninja assassin. Hunched shoulders. Stooped and gnome-like, he was a huge effeminate monster. He had entered Canada under false documents as an oil and gas engineer and had worked on the Keystone Pipeline.

The question startled Powell like he was hit in the forehead with a hammer. He recovered quickly. "Why, yes, I am, Colonel Liang," Powell said. "At your silence…and your lack of any sense of humor." Powell snickered. He was approaching dangerous territory.

Colonel Liang started toward Powell; Lemev restrained him. "You are not here for spring break as the Americans say, Mr. Powell," not giving him the respect of his Russian rank. "You are not here to party, drink, philander, or do standup comedy." Liang was almost growling, menacing.

Powell immediately fought back. "Screw you, Liang. I am a Russian officer with the rank of a major in the Russian army, and you're not my superior." Powell paused a beat, then continued, "I have my mission, colonel, and I certainly don't need your wrath or criticism." And to underline his emphasis, Powell let out a high-pitched whistle as the rear door of the Jeep popped open and a huge bear of a dog came bounding and loping to Powell's side, sat down on his haunches, and growled, thunderous and menacing, with his tail tucked between his hind legs.

Both colonels tensed, went for their sidearms, and held.

Powell smiled and patted Killer on the head. The huge dog relaxed immediately. Both colonels relaxed as well, shoulders slumping noticeably.

Colonel Lemev broke the tense confrontation by speaking first. "We're not here to argue, fight, or joke. We have a mission, and all of us have our orders. Mayor Powell has a most important mission, Polkovnik...er... Colonel Liang, that is to first and primarily to find weaknesses in Steven Vandorol, as he has studied and memorized his entire dossier, and then to infiltrate the El Paso local government, ingratiate himself with the legal, political, and military establishment, and to help our team accomplish its mission as ruthlessly and savagely as possible, so that we will set an example for all the masses of American sheep to follow. We are the guard dogs." Lemev wasn't finished. "Mayor Powell has spent the last two weeks studying and learning everything possible about Steven Vandorol to find his Achilles heel." He paused, the fight diffused, even his heavy Russian accent gone.

All three relaxed. Colonel Liang finally exhaled as his shoulders slumped further.

The huge dog also relaxed even further, lay down, and closed his eyes, bored.

Behind them, Uri got out of the Jeep Cherokee, waved his arm in a circle, and all the others started out of their vehicles and were soon following Uri toward the cabin in the dark, exhausted and hungry.

"Tell us, Powell, have you found any weaknesses?" Colonel Lemev looked directly at Powell, then shifted his gaze to Colonel Liang, walked over to Powell, and put his arm around his shoulders as all three started walking toward the cabin as gentle snowflakes fell.

"Yes, I have!" Powell paused, swallowed, and looked directly into Colonel Liang's eyes. "Steven Vandorol is completely bulletproof with but two exceptions. But first I'm starving! It's been a long trip..."

———————

Exactly twenty-six miles away, Canadian Mounted Police Sergeant Trevor Collington and Constable Jack Ryan, both of the D Division-Manitoba, had just replaced the day shift of the Manitoba-United States border checkpoint that was on Canada Highway 83 South turning into US Interstate 83, some 150 miles from Carrington, North Dakota.

Mountie Sergeant Collington was manning the glassed-in booth at the median while Constable Ryan slept inside the border checkpoint house to the right of the median booth. The entire checkpoint, the road just two lanes heading north and south, was brightly lit by numerous sodium-vapor lights to almost daylight. The border crossing checkpoint was located in a two-acre clearing in the dense forest among a tall canopy of Jack pine and blue spruce trees. A light snow was just starting to fall, the air cool and crisp. He would be relieved by Constable Ryan promptly at 4 am.

It was 1:50 am, Thursday, September 3, 2015.

Snow is a little unusual for early September, thought Collington as he poured himself another cup of coffee from his multicolored thermos his daughter had given him last Christmas and said out loud, "Just love the Jack pine smell," as it reminded him of Christmastime with his family. He had light classical music playing on his cell phone and was reading a David Morrell thriller. He was really looking forward to going home to be with his family as he had just been reassigned and promoted from border checkpoint duty to his all-time dream job of fully horse-mounted border patrol work at an over 100-square-mile area of horse trails in dense forest.

Tonight, and in honor of his promotion, he was wearing full horse-mounted uniform rather than his usual boring everyday gray shirt and dark blue tie. He glanced at his own reflection in the bulletproof glass and thought, *I look rather smart this eve in my brand-new uniform!* He admired his flat-brimmed Stetson hat with dark brown leather band, red Serge tunic with epaulettes, and Sam Browne cross belts and gun belt with his Smith & Wesson Model 5946 service pistol with Hogue grip. He especially liked the rest of his riding outfit with dark blue riding jodhpurs with yellow stripes down both legs after British cavalry tradition, completed by high riding boots and long-shank nickel spurs. He thought of his dear wife and said out loud, "She thinks I'm very handsome in my tunic and especially likes the epaulettes," and smiled at his own reflection.

"Hello!" Sergeant Collington said looking out into the night as he took a sip of his coffee. Bright headlights on the road coming from America about two miles away, he guessed. He looked at his cell: 1:30 am. "What's this?" It was most unusual for cars to come through this late at night in this very lightly traveled border checkpoint.

The headlights dimmed as the vehicle approached about a mile out and slowed to ease into the checkpoint lane yards away from his booth as Collington watched the car approaching.

It was a four-door white Honda Civic, Nevada license plate UZ 3242, which he jotted down in his day logbook, and had tinted windows so he couldn't see the driver, or passengers, as it came into the brightly lit clearing and slowly rolled to his window.

Sergeant Collington raised his left side window to the outside just as the driver's side window was lowering.

"May I help…er…you, ma'am," Sergeant Collington stammered and thought, *she is absolutely gorgeous,* as he looked down to a woman driving.

She had long shining blonde hair, large blue eyes, long eyelashes, perfect eyebrows, and a very bright smile as she looked up at him. She was wearing a low-cut blouse, open at the neck revealing marvelous cleavage of ample breasts.

"I'm on the way to visit my mom in Melita," she said, turning serious. "She's really sick and I've been driving from Las Vegas airport for the last twenty hours." She was tearing up and shivered.

"Would you like some hot coffee, ma'am?" Sergeant Collington asked, staring at this gorgeous woman. "I'll make some fresh if you would just park over by the house." He pointed to the house on her right.

"Why, that's so sweet of you, Officer..." She was smiling again.

"Sergeant Collington, ma'am," he stammered again, smitten by this very beautiful creature.

"Okay," she said and started in reverse. Sergeant Collington was looking down at her breasts smiling when, in a sudden flowing move, the woman pointed a 9mm silenced Beretta and—pop, pop—shot him in the face.

She calmly put the car in park, left the engine on, stepped through the glass booth's door, and shot him in the back of his head again...stepped over Sergeant Collington's body and pressed a button on the panel, ducked down, and waited.

In a few minutes, the lights in the house went on and the door opened. "Hey, Trevor, it's not four o'clock yet...what's up?" said the man coming out.

The woman raised up, fired twice again—pop, pop—and hit him right in the forehead. He was dead before he crumpled to the ground.

She closed the window and locked it. Stepped over dead Sergeant Collington again, opened the door, flicked the lock, and slammed the door shut behind her. Calmly walked over to the dead man outside. Pop, pop... fired two more shots into his heart, put the gun in the back waist of her jeans, and with some effort dragged the dead man back into the house. Again locked the door from the inside, slamming the door behind her, and walked back to her car. Pulled out the Beretta again, aimed, and pop, pop, pop, pop...shot out all four camera monitors, emptying the gun. She backed the Civic out of the checkpoint, turned around, and went back to the United States, leaving a previously manned US-Canada border checkpoint completely unmanned.

17

Back at the old rustic cabin, it was almost dawn.

All the vehicles outside had been serviced, gassed, and camouflaged among the Jack pine and black spruce, with all the supplies and munitions stowed; all were ready for the trip to El Paso, Texas.

The entire contingent was well fed, billeted, and sleeping in the four bedrooms of the cabin. Inside, the smoldering coals in the fireplace radiated warmth to the entire cabin. Outside a light snow was falling, unusual for early September in Canada.

All except for Powell, Uri, and Colonels Lemev and Liang. The foursome sat at the worn oak table in the kitchen area, three of the men drinking coffee while Colonel Liang held a delicate china saucer and daintily sipped hot tea from an even more delicate gold-inlaid china cup.

Colonel Lemev asked in precise English, "You were going to tell us the two exceptions to Vandorol being completely bulletproof…" Even his heavy Russian accent was almost gone.

Colonel Liang was silent. He had not said a word since the confrontation at Powell's arrival the evening before. Uri was quietly oiling his sidearm, a Russian PK42.

"You got it, Lemev," Powell answered in a far more familiar term, by his last name, in addressing a Russian Spetznaz intelligence colonel. He wiped his mouth with a napkin and continued, "Gentlemen, let me summarize his dossier. Steven Vandorol is the ultimate survivor. He was born in Germany to parents who survived our takeover of most of Europe, at least all we could grab from our very stupid and benevolent allies, including Nazi Hungary." He paused, looked around the table. "Steven Vandorol is a Hungarian. Steven's family, his brother, his mother and father, were all Hungarians. In 1958, during the Hungarian Revolution we Russians remember so well, Hungarian college students with Molotov cocktails almost kicked our butts when they torched an entire armored division!

Lemev interrupted, looking directly at Colonel Liang, who remained impassive and silent. "Just like the Muslim radicals have infiltrated the United States government in Washington, DC, and the White House, with the head Muslim himself." Colonel Lemev smiled, proud of his own contribution to Powell's narrative.

Undaunted by the interruption, Powell continued, "Then Steven's mother, Karina Vandorol, jerked Steven and his older brother, Josef, through a keyhole, to use a good old American expression, and dragged them to, of all places, Brazil, in Sao Paulo to join her lover before the war, Bach Vandorol, the boys' father's older brother.

Ward glanced at Uri and then continued. "In Germany, young Steven apparently developed an extremely strong attachment to Karina's sister Helena." Powell paused again. Cleared his throat and said, "I think that's Steven's number one weakness. He has been searching for his own intimate relationship his entire life, without success. He survived Brazil, but I think only because of his brother, Josef, who taught him all the survival skills and street smarts he had himself learned from their father, the elder Vandorol, an Austro-Hungarian cavalry brigadier general in World War I. The elder Vandorol was the Hungarian minister of the interior and led the Nazi Party in Hungary after the Nazis took over Hungary. We killed the bastard, executed him in Germany after we turned his mistress…"

"He had a mistress?" Lemev asked, surprised.

"Yes, he sure did. While Karina was having sex with the elder Vandorol's younger brother, Bach, who by the way was also a World War II Hungarian hero, kicking our butts on the Eastern front and then chief of the Hungarian secret police, the elder Vandorol was copulating with Admiral Horthy's daughter, who escaped our armies, swooping in from the east to Germany as a refugee. Admiral Horthy was the figurehead Hungarian regent…"

"So what happened in Brazil?" Lemev asked, getting a bit impatient.

"Well, we chased Bach and his buddies from Europe all the way to Sao Paulo, but they pulled out and we lost them for about three years…finally found them. Comrade Trotski did…on a Brazilian *fazenda*, the owner of which had been supplying the Nazis during World War II. The Patron, boss in Portuguese, had been providing sanctuary to the Hungarians…we lost many agents when we finally cornered them there on the *fazenda*, but they escaped again."

"Those oily Hungarians" was all Lemev could say as he continued. "What about the two brothers, Steven and Josef?"

"They both grew up—Josef teaching his little brother. But they all escaped again…we didn't know where." Ward was using the word "we" a lot, Lemev thought.

"Were they found?" Lemev asked.

"Yes, back in Sao Paulo, Villa Anastacio, where they all started out," Powell continued.

"What happened there?" Lemev asked.

"They killed Trotski!" Ward answered. "Comrade Trotski was our main Nazi death squad hunter and a hero of the Soviet Union."

"And the boys?"

"Their Uncle Ted, an American soldier originally from New York City, who married Helena in Germany after the war as a war bride, arranged for Karina and the boys to immigrate to the United States, New York City…"

"Both boys?"

"No, just Steven," Ward answered. "Young Josef stayed and married a Brazilian girl he met on the *fazenda*, one of the Patron's gorgeous daughters."

"So Steven Vandorol was saved again…" Colonel Lemev was understanding Vandorol much better now—and disliked him that much more.

"Yes, he survived Brazil only to be put back into chaos on the streets of South Bronx," Powell answered. "And there, teenager Vandorol almost didn't survive!"

Lemev finished, "But I guess he did!"

Powell smirked. "Obviously. No joke, Lemev. Look at the brains on the colonel!" Ward laughed out loud. Big mistake.

Lemev hit back viciously, his now again halting English as cold as steel. He pointed his massive index finger at Powell's handsome face. "I've had just about enough…Mayor Pow'…ell!" Uri swallowed hard and Liang's squint narrowed to a thin line as Lemev continued, "I am your superior officer and you dis'…respect me again and I will kill you Mayor Pow'…ell!" Lemev paused a beat but held his finger two inches from Powell's nose. "*Vy ponimayete*, Mayor Pow'…ell?"

Powell's Adam's apple bobbed as he answered, "I understand, Polko'vnik Lemev."

Colonel Lemev unscrewed the top of the vodka bottle, splashed some in his coffee, very deliberately screwed the top back, and said, "And Mayor…I am also berry…berry tired of your using…*syroy seksual nyy*, crude sexual language." He paused, took another sip of his coffee, and continued, "We do not use such language in our Mother Russia…I do not use such language ever…and I have never allowed any of my soldiers to use such obscene and *pornograpficheskly* language." He paused again. "Do you understand that as well?"

"*Da ser,* Polko'vnik Lemev," a humbled Powell answered in Russian.

Lemev relaxed. "Allow the stupid Americans to use such obscenities as their culture continues to…*ukhudshat*." He looked at Uri.

Uri translated, "deteriorate," as Lemev continued, "Ya, deteriorate!" He glanced at Colonel Liang, who was nodding slightly, looked back at Powell, and said, "Continue, Ward."

A completely deflated Ward Powell looked at Lemev and thought, *Vy mat' ublyuka!*, paused, swallowed again, and continued, "He was saved again by his Uncle Ted taking him to Japan on a tour of duty. So that's his second Achilles heel. He's been pining after the loss of his brother…who was everything to him." Powell was finished. "So, I'm going to become his substitute brother and then betray him if you guys don't kill him first." He cocked his head toward the sleeping Muslims and said, "Let's not tell the Muslim idiots anything, okay? Sometimes the enemy of our enemy is definitely not…I emphasize…*not* our friend. The Muslims will ultimately be nuked back into the dark ages where they belong."

Powell was laughing again, a little nervously, Colonel Lemev noticed, and thought, *I got the vy mat' ublyuka's attention.*

"Gentlemen," Powell said, "I've studied Vandorol's entire dossier, compiled since the news release and the Raul Hernandez interview in the *El Paso Herald-Chronicle* articles that went national two weeks ago." He looked at Colonel Lemev and respectfully asked, "You got the news release and the Hernandez interview, didn't you, Polko'vnik Lemev? It was teletyped to your team? Correct?"

Colonel Lemev nodded. "Yes, we got it."

Powel nodded too and continued. "I consulted with KGB psychologists and psychiatrists and other healthcare professionals and now know Vandorol even better than his brother, mother, or even his Aunt Helena, his lifetime dream woman, obsession, and addiction."

"Does Steven really have an addiction?" Colonel Lemev asked.

Colonel Liang was watching Powell intently, waiting for his answer.

"Yes, he absolutely does," Powell answered. "Our Washington intelligence revealed that in the five years Steven was in Washington, he was close to a black man, Martin King, and together the two were having sex with anything that moved." Ward almost giggled. "A couple of real whore dogs." Powell looked at Colonel Lemev and reddened.

The previously silent Colonel Liang finally spoke. "Vandorol spoiled our first attempt to take over the US government."

Powell was stunned. He managed to stammer, "So…Project Triple X was not a North Korean conspiracy?"

Colonel Lemev was equally astonished.

Uri continued to quietly clean his sidearm.

Liang laughed. "Gentlemen," he said, mimicking Powell in flawless English. "Who do you think wrote *Unrestricted Warfare, Communist China's Master Plan to Destroy America*? I did, along with my colleague, the now

General Wang Xiangsui…who is on his way to El Paso by Amtrak, as we speak."

All three were now laughing, the two Russians nervously, the communist Chinese most heartily, as Colonel Liang had just taken control not only of the conversation but of the leadership of this assassination group as well.

Broad-smiling Colonel Qiao Liang was finished. "Like the old *Chinese*"— he looked directly at Powell as he emphasized the word—"proverb states: the enemy of my enemy is my friend. The North Koreans are nothing but our stooges."

Powell glanced at Uri again. "Gentlemen, our mission is three-fold: one, the immediate elimination of Steven Vandorol and his entire prosecution team; two, the elimination of key El Paso and Fort Bliss civilian and military leadership; and three, to prepare the underbelly of the United States from the south through El Paso and from Canada from the north as a launching pad for the takeover of America by communist Chinese and Russian ground forces already assembling in Mexico and Canada."

Powell looked directly at Colonel Liang and continued. "*General* Wang Xiangsui, on the way to El Paso by train from California as we speak, and with whom I've had extensive discussions, will be overall commander-in-chief of all combined Chinese and Russian forces." He had personally received all that as a direct order from Comrade Putin himself.

Suddenly, the ancient teletype machine on the rusty file cabinet in the corner of the kitchen area came to life with clickety clacks sounding like a train riding on old rails, and paper started rolling out again like crepe paper on New Year's Eve party…

Colonel Lemev looked over at the noise and said, "Looks like Gravelly Voice has more *der'mo*, crap, for our team." He walked over to the machine and waited, watching the paper unroll on the floor by his feet.

"What is all that?" Powell asked.

Colonel Lemev, waiting at the teletype spewing paper from the machine, said, "That's how we got the Vandorol appointment as special prosecutor press release and his interview after, both of which went nationwide in the

American media a few days ago. It was the signal for one of our members to leave immediately for El Paso and make contact there in advance of the rest of our team's arrival."

"Okay," Powell answered, shifted his eyes to Uri, and smiled. Looking back at Lemev, he said, "So what's the *der'mo* you're getting now, Polko'vnik Lemev?"

Uri continued to clean his weapon with an oily rag.

The colonel tore off the last sheet, folded it all together, and read, "It's more media *der'mo* on Vandorol! He sure is getting a lot of attention from the media. This is from the Amerikanskiy *Washington Post* about how the Texas-El Paso prosecution could influence the fall nationwide elections"— Lemev kept reading—"and derail, *krusit*, wreck the present administration and the entire Amerikanskiy Democratic Party!" Lemev continued to read. "Oh, the last sheet has a message…"

All turned and looked at Lemev, even Colonel Liang, who set down his teacup and listened as Lemev continued. "Once we are all in El Paso, we're to contact a Juarez, Mexico, antiques dealer and give a Ciudad Juarez telephone number." He walked back to the table, sat down, and tossed the papers in the middle of the table. "I'm sure Gravelly Voice will be calling again…the stupid Amerikanskiy *mat' ublyudka*…" Colonel Lemev sneered and rolled his eyes in disgust, having violated his own warning to Ward regarding the use of obscene language.

Powell noticed but asked, "Did our advance team member make it down to El Paso already?"

"Yep" is all Lemev said.

A noise from the bedrooms… The two Sunni Muslim assassins, Mohammed Abu Dabi and Mustafa Dobe, were up and came walking out from the bedrooms, stretching and yawning.

Dobe spoke first. "What was that noise?"

Colonel Lemev answered, "Just some more instructions for our assassination team. Don't worry about it."

All four at the table were silent, eating their breakfasts.

And my mission, Powell thought to himself. *I'm going to enjoy killing Steven Vandorol, but first I'm going to make it really painful.* He sure hated Steven with a passion yet wasn't quite sure why. *And, Lemev, you're a dead man as well.*

Ward suddenly laughed uncontrollably. Both Lemev and Liang looked at him very strangely. Even the Muslims were staring. Uri just shook his head and continued to clean his weapon.

The huge dog, Killer, sleeping and snoring by the warmth of the fire, moaned and passed gas again, startling the two Muslims walking by.

18

Steven opened his eyes. It was still dark outside, the view into Mexico the same, the vast dark sky still lit by a billion sparkling firefly stars and another billion on the carpet of black velvet below, spread with yet another billion diamonds and kernels of gold and silver.

Steven glanced at his digital clock; it showed 5:50. *Almost six o'clock. Up and at 'em*, he thought. *I've got another long day ahead.* His own digital clock in his mind was still sharp, honed by his long history of light sleeping and situational awareness learned by his past experience of turmoil, *or by the thousand years of Hungarian history my brother Joey used to lecture me about, or better yet, the "Thousand Years of Hungarian Crap" as my thirteen-year-old daughter Karina called it, really putting it into perspective for me*, Steven thought.

Beside the bed, on his hind legs and looking right into Steven's face, mere inches from his nose, Rommel sat patiently waiting for his master to open his eyes.

"I guess you're up, big boy?"

Rommel nodded his massive head up and down, licked his chops, and wagged his tail, gently putting his huge paw on Steven's arm.

"I guess you're hungry too?" Steven smiled at the huge dog, who actually seemed to be smiling back. Said out loud, "Okay, okay, I'm getting up." He swung his legs out and, still sitting on the bed, yawned, stretched, arms extended. "Good sleep, Rommel! How about you?" Rommel barked, answering him.

Steven got up, stretched again, and walked barefoot out to the garage, Rommel following right behind.

In the garage, Steven scooped dog chow and filled Rommel's dog food bowl. "Okay, boy, go for it!" he said as the dog dove into his food, chomping a mile a minute.

Steven walked back to the kitchen to prepare his regular breakfast, a mixture of whole milk, protein powder, three raw eggs, vanilla, and a dash of cinnamon.

By the time he was done blending the concoction, Rommel was standing at the door waiting patiently to be let out. Steven unlocked the doggie door and Rommel went outside.

Steven drank his breakfast in several swallows, made a cup of very strong coffee imported from Brazil, and walked back into his bedroom.

He made the bed and put on running shorts, a light gray T-shirt, and fluorescent orange running shoes. Although the shoes were less than a month old, they had already carried him almost a hundred miles and were broken in enough to be very comfortable.

Back out to the living room where Rommel was already waiting patiently by the door to the street, Steven locked the doggie door on the inside and walked into the entryway; he put one foot against the outside window ledge to start his warmups. Bending at the waist and bouncing slightly several times until the tightness in his calf receded, he switched legs and performed the maneuver again.

When his stretching was done, he did a hundred sit-ups.

Then a hundred pushups.

Despite the intensity of his warmup routine, Steven was not bulky or muscular. Instead he had the lean, sinewy build of a gymnast. His 180 pounds was the weight he had returned to in Washington at the urging of his friend Vanessa Moore, and the original weight he'd had when playing football as a freshman at West Point, where he blew out his knee, ending his football and probable military career.

At forty-six, having survived the DC ugliness, and now having the serenity of El Paso for the last five years, Steven looked and felt ten years younger and had the energy to match. He shuddered at the thought of the DC horror, dredged up as if from the depths of an open sewer this past week by his appointment as special prosecutor to lead the prosecution team in the Alvarado fraud and conspiracy prosecution.

Steven was a peaceful man. He was now in control of his own destiny. He had followed his favorite black pearl of wisdom, that the ultimate of God-given freedoms is the freedom of choice. With divine guidance and by earnest prayers, Steven had survived DC; he had also followed and was still following his other favorite black pearl of wisdom, that the farther backward you can look, the farther forward you are likely to see.

He was secure, serene, and peaceful. All that was about to change. Change with a vengeance.

Warmup completed, Steven put on his belt with his holstered Derringer hooked on, pulled the T-shirt over the belt, and called Rommel.

It was time to run, and Rommel loved to run. "Let's go, Rommel!"

Hearing his name, the dog trotted to Steven's side and waited as the lead was snapped into place on his collar. The leash wasn't really needed as Rommel was well trained by the K-9-unit officer of the El Paso police department for both security and attack by the order and voice of his master. The leash was more for the master than the well-trained dog. Especially in the newly required extra vigilance, Steven felt very secure with his weapon on his belt and dog at his side.

Out the front, Steven locked the door and screen grate, put the key and cell phone in his wristband holder, and started up Scenic Drive, Rommel trotting easily at his side.

The usual morning course would be to run up Franklin Mountain on Scenic Drive, past the scenic lookout above at 653-foot elevation, 4,222 feet above sea level, and around Rim Road to then return, all a five-mile run that Steven covered in less than an hour.

The morning air was still cool, and dew had settled over lawns and rock gardens, giving them an almost aluminum sheen. The air smelled fresh and clean as Steven inhaled deeply and started his run. To the east, over the crest beyond downtown El Paso and Juarez, a warm purple hue illuminated the horizon as the sun began its ascent. It wouldn't be long before it broke the horizon for an always wonderful El Paso sunrise.

The neighborhood was still quiet at this hour, which made for a peaceful run. Only the pounding of Steven's feet, his own even breathing, and the jingle of Rommel's tags broke the silence. It was a comforting time with which Steven was familiar for the last five years since coming to El Paso with his gift puppy, and it provided him with a sense of stability that only the familiar can. Steven now reveled in that stability of structure and routine, after a lifetime of abject instability, horror, and pain. This was now his well-deserved serene structure and personal routine, he had thought many times before.

As he ran, Steven thought about Martin King, as he had the night before, his prior best friend, the former king of his DC life, and Glee Robinson, the sexual betrayer, as both were again brought to the forefront of his mind by the last two days' events, along with memories five years past. Steven kept running...

"Yes, I thought Martin was my brother Joey!" Steven said out loud. "But Martin sure wasn't. My brother Joey never betrayed me...but Joey's loss when I was so young made me vulnerable to the Martin Kings, Joseph Rosses, and Roy Williamses of the world..."

Rommel, trotting beside Steven, was looking up at his master with a big question mark.

Steven looked down at him and smiled. "You understand me, don't you, my true little buddy?"

And a smiling dog woofed out loud in clear understanding. Steven had to laugh...

———

The two runners approached Fort Boulevard, the halfway point of the five-mile run. To their left and high up on the Franklin Mountains on Ranger Peak was the Wyler Observatory, to which the only access was the

Wyler Aerial Tramway. To their right, the housetops of the businesses along Piedras Street. They both knew the route well.

Steven had taken the tram up to Wyler Observatory many times alone. He had even taken Rommel with him many times as well. The peace, tranquility, and freedom at the top really fit well into his newfound El Paso serenity, and he would spend entire evenings and afternoons up there, thinking, reading, and enjoying the magnificent view below.

The tram took a 946-foot vertical rise up to Wyler Observatory on top of Ranger Peak, which, at 5,600+ feet above sea level, more than a mile high, afforded amazing views of the Hueco Mountains over Juarez, Mexico; New Mexico's White Sands Missile Range; Fort Bliss Military Reservation; and Biggs Army Airfield.

The view along the route was the most beautiful Steven had ever seen in his lifetime, and he had been in Europe, Brazil, Japan, and several states in the US. He didn't wish for any other than right here, right now, in El Paso, Texas.

Steven knew the Wyler Tramway was a Swiss-made aerial gondola that traveled along a thick steel cable and rose straight up to the top of Ranger Peak. The four-minute ride included a voiced descriptive tour of the local flora and fauna that one passed along the way. The station at the top provided accessible ramps and paved grounds leading to an observation deck with a 360-degree view. Steven loved the view and had been up there many times himself on weekends. The pay-per-view high-power binoculars located along the observation deck enhanced the viewing experience.

He breathed deeply as he continued to run. The arid El Paso air was invigorating and renewed him daily in ways that made him feel lighter, as unbound by earthly constraints as the freedom that came with unchecked flight. He felt he could leave the earth and return at will.

I remember in Washington when the crap was really hitting the fan, Steven thought, *and my only real friend there, Vanessa Moore, Dudley's wife and my co-worker friend at Henderson Lane, advised me to take up running again.* It had been good advice. Running always helped him think better and was a terrific help in his self-discovery and recognizing his own addictions, the evil in his own soul. Running was helping him now and had helped him over the last few years in controlling his addictions to finally find serenity and peace of mind. Steven fondly remembered all those times during the chaos and hell of DC when he and Vanessa would meet in the morning at the small coffee shop in the lobby of their office building on K Street for coffee and warm bagels with cream cheese and lots of bacon…

Thinking about Vanessa, Steven remembered the last woman he'd had a relationship with, Glee Robinson. *I thought I found the love of my life in Glee.* "Boy, was I wrong again, big-time," Steven said out loud. He shook his head, and Rommel looked up at him quizzically. Rommel was perceptive when it came to his master, and probably had a sixth sense about evil as well, Steven thought.

"Just thinking, boy! I'm fine," Steven said and smiled at his dog. Rather than being the love of his life, Glee Robinson turned out to be the evil betrayer. Martin King and Glee Robinson were inseparable in the evil that was once in Steven's soul…

Steven and his dog continued running. Steven looked up into the still dark sky and quietly thanked the good Lord again for the courage to have defeated the evil that time in DC, the evil that had gripped his soul for a very long time, and with his dog looking up at him, remembered John 14:6 and silently said the Lord's Prayer.

19

As dog and master turned back at Fort Boulevard, Rommel tugged at his leash, pulling Steven—a clear and familiar sign that it was time to separate the men from the dogs.

"Ready to run, huh?"

Rommel barked and pulled harder.

Steven stepped up the pace, slowly at first, but then faster as Rommel maintained the cadence effortlessly.

"Show-off," Steven said, and the dog barked again, and the two, man and dog, were almost flying.

Steven thanked the Lord every day for Courtney and Arlene's surprise gift of Rommel, one of God's creatures to help him recover from the pain and anguish that he had survived while in DC.

Rommel was now fully in Steven's heart. They were best friends. Loved each other dearly. They ran together, ate together, and slept together. Rommel also eased the personal loneliness wrought by the lack of intimacy between a man and a woman, a void that was self-imposed by complete abstinence in this, his period of practice, practice, practice—of Steven trying to cure his past sexual and codependency relationship addictions.

The two continued to run on Alabama Street, two miles left to go…

Steven loved running and thinking and letting his mind go into flights of thought and spirit and looking forward to the future…and the special prosecution…

I've got a lot to do before the holidays, he thought. He was looking forward to the weekend at Eddie's ranch, the Chico Gringo, especially riding Pegasus, his beloved horse, in the mornings or at sunsets.

Eddie had said that Saturday they would be working on the special prosecution and that all law enforcement would be well represented by the El Paso police department leadership and Texas Rangers, El Paso Headquarters Company being the primary investigative and intelligence arms of the special prosecution, would both be there Saturday. Eddie had also mysteriously promised Steven that a very special guest would be there as well.

Eddie said that the primary reason he had been to Pecos when an attempt on his life had been made by a white Silverado pickup was that he had once again met with the Texas Rangers assigned to protect the five key witnesses, all under Texas Ranger witness protection. Even Steven was kept in the dark. Eddie said it would be better that way. Eddie had a knack for big drama and suspense, Steven thought and smiled, but he knew above all that Eddie was deadly serious.

They did have to be very careful, Steven thought as he ran, keeping pace with his dog. While the El Paso and Dallas offices of the FBI were friendly to Texas, the Washington, DC, headquarters and the snakes in the Justice Department were definitely not. So, the FBI locally was on a very sensitive tightrope in the coming civil war that Ernie had described. The same was probably true with the CIA. Steven would stay in touch with his friends, the Wellingtons, and Courtney's CIA contacts for intelligence, *and I'll keep all that information to myself,* he thought. This was truly the Second American Civil War, and no one could really be trusted. Steven remembered President Ronald Reagan's admonition, "Trust but verify."

During the First Civil War it had been the abolitionist North against the slaveholder South. Brother against brother. Right against wrong. This time the Civil War was a war of ideas. A war of philosophies. A war between good and evil. Truth against lies. Freedom against the new slavery, government control and Islamic slavery and Caliphate. Yet a conventional and physical war of Fifth Column radicals that had insidiously infected America. The Islamist radicals, the children of the hippie radicals of the sixties, the president being one, the communists, Russian and Chinese, the worldwide corruption of socialism and progressive leftist cancer. All stiflers and enemies of our God-given freedoms, Steven kept thinking.

This Civil War, or a World War III, was exactly like the war against Nazi Germany in World War II, Steven thought. That time Nazi Germany tried to control the world and by their grandiose Third Reich was ruthlessly killing first the political opposition, then the intellectuals, homosexuals, priests, pastors, and ending with Hitler's Oedipal enemies, the Jews, whose absolute extermination would have been his ultimate obsessive orgasm… killing his mother's Jewish abuser. Steven shuddered at the thought, but continued the stream.

This current American Civil War, a potential World War III with worldwide implications, where Islamic Arab terrorists by way of proxies of Russian, Iran, communist Chinese, and North Korean governments, were now indiscriminately killing their opposition at home and in the Middle East. They were killing Jews in Gaza and persecuting and killing Christians in the entire Arab world. All the killing was not unlike the killing of thirty million by Stalin or the extermination of some ninety million by communist Chinese Mao Tse Tung, or the extermination of eleven million Jews by Adolf Hitler during the Holocaust.

Not unlike what was happening in the United States right now, Steven was still thinking, where the George Soros Muslim puppet, that liar in the White House, was a leading proponent of amnesty, illegal immigration, open-border Muslim terrorist entrance, and outright war by the Democrats and the American left and progressives on Christians, tea party conservatives, and libertarians hungering for freedom of choice and freedom from oppression of all kinds. The lying president of the United States was intentionally transforming America, as he himself had promised, Steven kept thinking, and was not only completely covered by a corrupt leftist media, the Democratic Party, and timid establishment Republicans afraid to oppose him for fear of being called racist by the media and Democrats…

Suddenly Rommel picked up the pace even more, sensing the end of their morning run.

It's gonna be interesting times, Steven thought, still running near Scenic Drive. *I'll need some help on the special prosecution. North Anderson, I know and think is a good man. Beth Barker, though I've seen her around the courthouse, is an unknown quantity, and Ernie assigned her to the team. I wonder why?*

Steven now judged people by the quality of their hearts. North Anderson was a good man with a good heart, Steven knew, and could be trusted.

The jury was still out on Beth Barker…Steven didn't trust her at all. *I've got to be careful with women in general and beautiful women like Beth in particular,* he thought as the two continued to run on Scenic Drive, nearing a side street, Cortland Street, and turning down the mountain toward Piedras Street.

Then Steven saw it again.

The white Silverado pickup with the tinted windows was parked curbside off Cortland Street, which opened onto Scenic and was about ten yards away. Steven slowed to a jog, restraining and slowing Rommel as well, then stopped short and held Rommel. The dog looked up at Steven, sensed that something was wrong, cocked his handsome head and snout at his master, and started barking. A loud, resonating bark, echoing loud enough to wake up the dead. So loud that lights started going on up and down the street on the left and right like a pinball game, blinking, flashing, and glowing.

Rommel continued barking, fierce and loud, Steven straining to hold him back from attack and lunging forward at the white Silverado pickup parked on the curb of the downslope of Cortland Street.

Windows on the second floor of the residences opened and heads popped out at the barking and commotion in the street below.

A burly guy from a second-floor window, deep-voiced, yelled in Spanish at Steven and Rommel, "¿Que paso, señor?" In Spanish, "What's going on, sir?"

"No se, señor," Steven answered. "No se que excita mi perro, señor." Steven paused, restraining Rommel, and continued in Spanish, "¿Usted conoce de quien es el blanco Silverado?" ("I don't know what excited my dog. Do you know whose white Silverado that is?")

The man answered, "¡No, señor! No es mio. Yo no conoce de quien es. Tienes un perro muy guapo!" ("You really have a beautiful dog!")

"Gracias, señor," Steven said. "Lo siento mucho que mi perro dispensa usted tan temprano." ("I'm really sorry that my dog woke you…")

"No problema, señor," the man answered as Steven was quieting Rommel.

"It's okay, boy, calm down," he said as Rommel sat down on his haunches and shook his regal head. "Ya voy a llamar la policia…" Steven called as the guy waved and closed his window.

Steven took out his cell phone, punched speed dial for Ray. "Hey, Ray. You up?"

Ray mumbled, "Barely."

"Okay, sorry to wake you…I was running with Rommel this morning… early…and came on the same white Silverado pickup you checked on for me, parked on Cortland Street…yeah, the four hundred block…two-story residences…yeah, the street that goes down the hill toward Piedras …yes, you got it…Rommel woke the whole neighborhood barking…"

Steven listened.

"Yes, you got it. Call Eddie and get a cruiser out here. Rommel and I will wait for it right here…on the intersection of Cortland Street and Scenic Drive…okay?"

Steven listened again, then, "Yes, I'm armed…as always…okay, I'll talk to you later." He clicked off and kneeled down beside Rommel, saying, "Good boy, Rommel, we'll wait…"

Five minutes. Ten. Steven heard the siren wailing from Interstate 10 below and up on Texas Avenue, and in seconds he saw the flashing red light pulsating, the car screeching to the intersection by Steven, the siren cutting off abruptly with a loud *whoop*…

The officer jumped out. "Judge, which one is it?"

"Hey, Louie, good morning! It's the white Silverado pickup." Steven was pointing. "It's the same license plate as the one that derailed Ed on his way back from Pecos."

"Thanks, judge. I'll call for a wrecker to impound. Thanks again, judge. I've got this covered." The officer was on his phone.

Rommel tugged at his collar again, pulling Steven along.

"Okay, okay. You're ready for home?"

Rommel woofed, answering his master.

The pair jogged back to Scenic Drive, turned, and jogged home as the morning that had started when they left the house blossomed into a brand-new day…

And just like that, in the brilliant El Paso sunrise, Steven saw the future, knew what he had to do…they, including the president and his attorney general, were just common evil criminals, conspirators in national corruption, criminal traitors, and fellow conspirators in the international war against Islamic terrorists, and criminal abettors of leftist progressive Fifth Columnists eating away at the fabric of the American way of life he cherished and loved, *as a Hungarian immigrant to America myself,* Steven thought.

He realized that he was at the forefront of the only way the evil could be slowed…the criminals all had to be indicted and state warrants issued for their arrest by the State of Texas and enforced by arrest by the Texas National Guard, treating them as simple criminal fugitives in the five-state area, and then enforced by a five-state sovereignty over the corrupt leftist progressive federal government which, like an evil octopus, had its oily tentacles in all states and was the clear and present danger and enemy of the people within those states.

Steven knew that he was in the fight of his life and hoped by the grace of God that he was destined to lead…

– 20 –

Steven was eating his favorite at Cafe Central, green chile soup, glancing between spoonfuls at Beth Barker talking shop with North Anderson sitting right beside her. Steven had invited both for lunch.

North Anderson asked Beth, "So how was Vegas? Didn't you and Francisco just get back yesterday?"

"Sure did. I'm still a little tired." Beth paused and rolled her eyes. "Lost about a grand…Francisco lost about ten…the loser, my husband!"

Beth Barker was District Attorney Ernesto Luis Martinez's second assistant district attorney and chief of the Drug Enforcement Unit. Beth led the district attorney office in drug convictions and was very proud of that record. She took every criticism or slight personally, *which was the ultimate in selfishness,* Steven thought, *as she made everything in the world just about her.*

Beth was not only a tall, statuesque woman with what some might call a handsome face, but she was also a fireball in the courtroom. Not gorgeous, but pretty in a way. She had short red hair showing gray strands and bright blue eyes. Her designer dress, a beautiful shade of blue, made her eyes sparkle. Her only real flaw, if you could say that, was a small scar on the side of her straight nose. Extremely aggressive, she took no prisoners and opponents were immediately executed…verbally. Steven had seen her in action. She could be manipulative, ruthless, and sometimes downright vicious.

Steven liked her anyway but did not trust her in the least. Still, there was something about her that appealed to Steven that he didn't quite understand…

Despite her imperfections, Beth could have been the tall twin sister of the actress Susan Sarandon, Steven thought as he continued to eat. She had a high forehead, soft perfect eyebrows, long eyelashes, and high cheekbones. With a dazzling yet haughty smile, a strong chin and long neck, *Beth Barker is a ball buster,* Steven thought. *Especially in the courtroom.*

Steven Vandorol and Beth Barker had crossed swords in the courtroom before. Neither had drawn blood. Steven defended three border mules getting "not guilty" jury verdicts, one "not guilty" by the judge, when Steven's client waived a jury and elected to go to the judge for sentencing as was his right under Texas law. In another major drug case, Steven's drug dealer client was facing 30 years but only got five because the judge and Steven were friends. Beth still resented Steven for that particular win, Steven thought, although she got convictions and sentences totaling 150 years on three of Steven's client's co-defendants. She probably never forgave Steven for the perceived "undue influence," Steven thought.

Steven really liked to look at Beth. After all, he liked women in general and Beth in particular. Steven had always been very visual and always had enjoyed pretty women. Steven knew his own weaknesses much better these days...

He still had a bad feeling about Beth. *I don't trust her at all*, Steven thought again, as she always looked away when he tried to look her right in the eyes as they talked. Steven was now judging people, especially women, not through the prism of his past sexual addiction as he had done for a lifetime, but by looking into the quality of their hearts, a wonderful skill he had learned since the past horror of Washington, DC, especially with selecting clients, picking juries, and making friends.

Steven, North Anderson, and Beth Barker, all of whom had been assigned to the special prosecution by the boss, the DA, were sitting in an art deco booth and having lunch at Cafe Central, an upscale restaurant two blocks from the courthouse. One of El Paso's most upscale restaurant, Cafe Central opened in 1918 in Juarez, Mexico, and quickly developed a clientele of gamblers and cabaret-goers who grew to expect an excellent culinary experience in the region of this chic nightspot. After Prohibition ended, Cafe Central migrated closer to the border and finally crossed into downtown El Paso, at which time it became known as Miguel's Central Cafe. Finally, in 1991, V. Trae Apodaca III noticed the need for a chic bistro downtown and opened Cafe Central in its current location. With a chic black-and-cream art deco interior that set off Apodaca's collection of original art, the restaurant was truly elegant, its centerpiece an ornately gated New Orleans-style courtyard.

He really liked North, both professionally and personally. As DA Ernesto Martinez's first assistant district attorney, North was head of the criminal division and Ernie's top trial prosecutor. Steven had also crossed swords with North many times. Steven was three and two in the loss column, but respected North even more for the *butt-kicking* he got, as he told Eddie Egen the other day. North was always well-prepared, stuck to the facts, and like Steven well knew the difference between good and evil, truth and lies, facts and fiction, Steven thought. North was also fair and compassionate when the case required mercy.

Steven had tried several cases against North, winning some and losing some. North was an excellent prosecutor, and though they were not close friends, they had developed a mutual respect as professionals.

North was big, black, tall, and muscular. Over six-feet-five, 220 pounds, he had played professional football as an outside linebacker, first in college with the Texas Longhorns and then with the Dallas Cowboys for three years, when a third knee injury finally ended that career. He then picked himself up, pulled himself out of depression, went to law school, graduating at the top of his law class at Baylor, and was hired by Ernie Martinez straight out of law school. North had been in the DA's office for twelve years, advancing to the DA's first assistant trial attorney. North was enjoying his green chile soup as well. Steven understood the DA's reasoning for assigning North to the special prosecution. North was Ernie's most able trial prosecutor, but Steven wondered why Beth had been assigned as well.

"Did Ernie share his big dramatic Second American Civil War speech with you, Steven?" Beth was smiling mischievously at him.

Steven ate some of his soup, wiped his mouth, and looked directly into her Prussian-blue eyes, sparkling with light. Just enough makeup on a face to make it seem like she didn't need any. A long delicate neck. She was slim, almost too thin, yet had ample breasts and a toned body.

Around six feet, Steven guessed, maybe 140 pounds, and about his age, maybe a few years younger. She was in an elegant and tailored professional dress that hung on her well, revealing perfect cleavage. Steven thought, *probably bought and paid for!*

She set her spoon down and focused on Steven, looking right past him, but feigning attention. *The Ernie reference was a bit too familiar,* Steven thought.

"Yes, he sure did. To Eddie Egen and me when we saw him together on Monday morning," Steven answered. "What did you think? You buy it?" Steven smiled and went back to his soup.

"Oh, Ernie can be a bit macho dramatic at times." Beth was still smiling but crossed her arms defensively, revealing a Cartier watch on one arm and a David Yurman bracelet on the other. "He can be really good at throwing the bull around *too* sometimes." Again, a little too much familiarity with the boss, Steven noticed, the "too" reference probably referring to himself as well, as their previous dealings in court had been less than amicable, though both respectful and cordial.

North, sitting beside Steven to his right, cringed imperceptibly. Steven noticed that as well.

Steven looked at North directly. "What do you think, North? Great football player name, by the way." Before North could answer, he said, "How long did you play for the Dallas Cowboys?"

"Just a couple of years…before blowing my knee out a third time!"

"So what do you think about all those NFL players signing for multimillion-dollar contracts?"

North answered quickly. "Way overpaid! Just feeds their big egos!"

Steven smiled. "I agree, North. Anyway, great name! What did *you* think about Ernie's rant?"

North looked up. "Thanks, Steven. I'm on board completely. Ernie is spot on!" Steven glanced at Beth. She was frowning. "It's probably much worse than any of us know." North continued eating.

Steven was calm but serious. "I agree completely as well." He glanced at Beth then continued. "We got a lot to do, guys. We're out at Eddie's ranch this Saturday—"

Beth interrupted. "This just a guy thing?" She was smirking.

Steven looked directly into her eyes. "No, it's for you, North, and I to get an evidentiary overview of the case. North, Ernie said we could have some help. So, would *you* pick two assistant DAs to help our special prosecution? They need to be young, aggressive, disciplined, and especially hardworking, and know how to keep their mouths completely shut, okay?" Steven finished by glancing at Beth again as he felt her bare feet under the table gently touch his calf.

North understood. He was second in command to Steven. "Got it! Want them at Eddie's ranch tomorrow as well?"

Steven flushed slightly from the touch of Beth's bare feet, but covering, answered, "No, that's just for the three of us. It's top-secret. That's why I wanted to have lunch with you guys first. Everything in this case is top-secret. At my office, only Ray Ortega, my investigator, you both know Ray, knows everything I know...or will learn...I trust him implicitly." Steven paused. "North, please make sure the lawyers you pick swear a blood oath of silence...and sign a confidentiality agreement, putting their jobs on the line."

Beth was frowning. "Aren't *you* being a bit dramatic, Steven?"

Steven looked into her eyes. "No, Beth. I'm not. This is serious." His own eyes blazed with intensity.

Beth recoiled, taken aback by Steven's gaze.

North got it. "I will Steven. It'll be done by next week."

Steven continued, looking directly at Beth, "This isn't a Saturday walk in the park...or some routine felony prosecution. It may in fact be a prelude to the Second American Civil War." He paused, put his spoon down, and said, "And there's a contract out on my life and may be out on both of your lives as well."

21

Jason Warren sat in his office outside the glass-enclosed electrical power grid control center, the "Star Wars" center as all called it, before his own triple side-by-side monitors and an Ergotron Neo Flux keyboard.

The entire inside wall of his office was non-reflective one-way mirror glass where Jason, from his desk could always be aware of everything that was happening. He could also look directly into the control center across a hallway and see directly into the control center with dozens of drone cubicles. Heavy curtains could be drawn to encase his office to a tomb if Jason wanted complete privacy, which allowed him to conduct his business without all the noise of the busy, and noisy, control center. The control center completely controlled all of El Paso Power & Electric's electrical power grids over the 2,500-square-mile service area of East Texas and southern New Mexico.

El Paso Power & Electric Company was a regional public utility company, engaged in providing the generation, transmission, and distribution of electricity in west Texas and southern New Mexico founded in 1901, was based in El Paso, Texas and was headquartered at the Stanton Tower in Downtown El Paso. Its energy sources consisted of nuclear fuel, natural gas, purchased power and solar and wind turbines. The company owned ten electrical generating facilities with a net dependable generating capability of approximately 2,010 megawatts and provided line voltage to approximately 400,000 residential, commercial, retail, industrial, public authority, and wholesale customers in a 10,000 square mile area of the Rio Grande Valley in west Texas, southern New Mexico and northern State of Chihuahua, Federal Republic of Mexico, of which Ciudad Juarez was the capital and largest city on the entire Texas-Mexico international border with a population of 2.5 million.

The company distributed electricity to retail customer principally in El Paso, Texas and Las Cruces, New Mexico; and resold electricity to electric utilities and power marketers, in a service territory extending from Hatch, New Mexico to Van Horn, Texas.

El Paso Power and Electric's transmission system of line voltages ranged from 115,000 volts to 345,000 volts and has two 115kV interconnections with Mexico to the south and its ownership in power generating plants included a 15.8 percent interest in the Palo Verde Nuclear Generating Station in Wintersburg, Arizona; the Rio Grande Power Station in Sunland Park, New Mexico; the Newman Power Station, the Copper Power Station, and the Montana Power Station in El Paso; and Hueco Mountain Wind Ranch in Hudspeth County, Texas.

Jason Warren's latest major accomplishment for the company was entering into an agreement with Colorado-based Juwi Solar Inc. to build a 10-megawatt solar energy facility in Northeast El Paso right next to the company's Newman Power Station. He would be responsible for developing, designing, building, and operating the computer systems of the Newman Solar project. Construction and completion of the project were tentatively scheduled for the end of the year. The construction of the new solar facility will help power over 3,800 homes throughout the year. The facility will be built on approximately 100 acres and the company will sublease the land in partnership with the El Paso Water Utilities Company that it currently leased for the Newman Generation Station currently has 47 MWs of solar power in its generation mix and recently secured an additional 50 MWs of solar power that will be online by the summer. In total, 5 percent of the company's dedicated generation, which included long-term purchase power agreements, would come from solar energy. As a result of the transaction, Jason was appointed to the company's board of directors.

He was very proud of this achievement and loved it when all the Kemper & Smith lawyers representing El Paso Power complimented Jason on a job well done.

As the company's top IT software specialist and computer engineer with a title of executive vice president, Jason was responsible for all computer systems that controlled the transmission of electricity in East Texas, southern New Mexico, and, with joint venture partner, most of northern State Chihuahua, Federal Republic of Mexico.

Jason's office was on the ground floor of the Montana Street main generating station on the mountain where the downtown El Paso skyline opened below. A spacious corner office with large sun-protected windows on two sides, it had the best views of downtown El Paso and Juarez, Mexico. From his desk, Jason could see the Rio Grande's two bridges linking Juarez to El Paso, one in the far distance and the other, the main international bridge linking downtown El Paso to downtown Ciudad Juarez. Both downtowns were separated by the silver ribbon of the Rio Grande. The main international bridge was almost two miles long spanning the Rio Grande, which in turn was the international border between the United States of America and the Federal Republic of Mexico.

Jason loved the view from his office, especially after dusk when the billion sparking lights illuminated his office and his now numbingly boring work. The brilliant lights provided Jason the feeling of power and control as he knew his computers controlled all the lights and power which made up the nightly light show. During the day, heavy drapes protected Jason from the bright and burning El Paso sun blazing through the large plate-glass windows.

From his office, Jason could also see the five-story United Bank of El Paso del Norte Tower. The bank was best known for its magnificent light display of a giant Christmas tree during the Christmas holidays and a giant American flag during all nights of the rest of the year, beginning on the day after Christmas. It always welcomed in every New Year like a bright beacon that could be seen almost fifty miles away.

The control center had fifty operator employees that he supervised on a daily basis, each sitting in small cubicles like a honeycomb of compartments before their own separate computer monitors of the system that made up a giant dynamic map wallboard. The dynamic map showed the electrical power distribution through El Paso Power's electrical power supply grids, its myriad multicolored lights—red, green, orange, and yellow—all frantically blinking, and covered the entire north wall of the control center.

Jason was proud of the system he himself had initially designed, then over the years perfected and now almost ran and maintained itself. He controlled the system entirely and had designed and inserted a "back door" that was his own personal secret and enhanced his power and control over the whole system.

While the office itself was spacious and airy, it was also simple and austere. During the day when the drapes were drawn, it was illuminated by three Tiffany lamps purchased at Tiffany's in the Houston Galleria when Jason had been there for a Texas Power and Energy conference. It also had a $25,000 authentic ship architect's model of the French frigate *Le Fleur*, a French ship that fought alongside the colonial navy during the American Revolutionary War, all preserved in a massive acrylic case. Jason loved old ships, especially old four masters, yet he had no idea why…

As Jason stared out the window into the expanse of El Paso and Juarez, his private line beeped and rang.

He was startled out of his reverie and almost knocked over his coffee cup as he picked up the phone. "Yes?"

"Mr. Warren," a voice asked in very precise and clipped English, although Jason detected a faint Far Eastern accent. "Is this Mr. Jason Warren, chief engineer and executive vice president?"

Jason answered, "Yes, who is this?" He was most surprised at the call as the private line in his office was only available to his wife, Jillian, and children Jacob and little Michelle. "And how did you get this number?"

"That is not important, Mr. Warren," the voice said. "What is important is that when you leave work today at precisely 3:30 pm from the building's parking garage and turn down on Kansas Street headed north, at the intersection of Kansas Street and Rio Grande Avenue, a courier will hand you a small package which should be of great interest to you, if you follow the instructions contained in it."

"What's in the package?" Jason asked, intrigued.

"You will just have to see, Mr. Warren!" The voice paused then continued, "Just follow the instructions given in the letter…have a most pleasant evening." The line went dead.

———————

Jason Warren pulled out of the garage in his snow-white Porsche Carrera into the still burning heat of the midafternoon El Paso sun onto Kansas Street, turned right onto Missouri Street, and headed north. Traffic was still light heading north at 3:30. The blazing sun was still high up in the sky as he drove slowly, looking on ahead at the previously designated intersection, air conditioner blowing full blast.

Up ahead by the traffic light and crosswalk, Jason saw a young Asian man, about twenty, standing by the traffic light with a brown package under his arm looking straight at him. He was clean cut, well dressed, and had a Fu Manchu mustache and narrow slanted eyes that gave him a most sinister look.

As Jason approached, the young man smiled in recognition, although Jason had never seen this young man before in his life. The light was red as Jason drove slowly to the intersection, stopped, and lowered the passenger window down.

The young man stepped to the window and looked in. "Good afternoon, Mr. Warren, this is for you," he said, and set the brown paper package in the passenger seat, turned, and just disappeared from Jason's sight, almost by magic. Jason involuntarily shivered in the blistering heat as he raised the window back up.

He looked down at the package on the seat. It was about the size of a small shoebox. Brown wrapping. Totally blank and innocuous, it reminded Jason of the sex toy packages that he had mail ordered secretly one time. Nothing on the package except tan masking tape.

Jason heard an impatient honk right behind him. Looked up at the light. It was green. He accelerated abruptly, drove north, and turned into a gas station at the next corner. Drove to an end space, parked, left the car running, and looked around. There was no one in sight. He picked up the package; it felt like it weighed just a few ounces. Turning it over, there were no markings anywhere. Set it back down. Looked all around again. No change.

Jason slowly pulled out from the station and drove north again on Kansas, down Myrtle, right on Mesa, and headed north on Stanton Street. He kept looking in the rearview mirror and all around. Nothing suspicious. Traffic was still light as he headed north on Stanton. He turned into the fitness center, Gold's Gym on North Mesa, and parked. There were just a few cars in the parking lot.

He tore open the wrapping leaving a small box, four inches by three, two inches thick. Removed the top and took out a white folded piece of paper, unfolded it, and read:

"Mr. Warren, the burner cell phone is our link. You will receive a call with instructions. The cash is for you to use right now. It is unmarked and completely sanitary."

Jason laid the note aside and lifted crumpled tissue out revealing three shrink-wrapped stacks of currency. From his glove compartment, he took out a small Swiss army knife, slit the plastic wrap off, looked all around— still no one—and started counting the currency.

In $20 bills, the first stack had exactly $5,000. Jason put the stack back into the plastic sheath, put it back in the box with the burner cell phone, wrapped it back in the brown paper, put two rubber bands around it, placed all in the glove compartment, and locked it. Setting the car alarm, he went inside the gym to work out.

22

"Let's roll!" Ward Powell said to his driver Uri Gagarin, getting into the passenger side of a silver Humvee that was bringing up the rear of a now twelve-vehicle convoy of two Suburbans, two panel trucks, two pickups, two 2.5-ton trucks, and two Jeep Cherokees descending from the north on El Paso, like a pack of hungry wolves bent on destruction and evil. The assassination team now totaled twenty-four men.

Uri laughed out loud, stepping on the accelerator, as the Humvee lurched forward. "Ward, you're such a wag! Isn't that what that guy said when the Muslim retards had taken over Flight 93 on September 11th on its way to fly right into the American White House?"

Ahead of them eleven other engines roared to life in the dawn mist hanging over the dense forest. The light snow falling during the night, unusual for early September, had stopped but still covered the clearing among the tall canopy of Jack pines and spruce trees and the log cabin.

"Yeah, a true American hero, the stupid idiot." Ward was chuckling. "Though I gotta admit the guy had a pair, for sure!"

The convoy was to separate leaving Canada and take separate routes to meet in Farmington, near the Four Corners Monument in New Mexico for rest, then on again for separate entry right into El Paso three days later by September 11, 2015. That day marked the fourteenth anniversary of the attack on the twin World Trade Towers in New York City by Islamist terrorists that killed 3,274 Americans including 400 police officers and firefighters and was the first attack of American soil since the Japanese attack on Pearl Harbor, Hawaii, on December 7, 1942.

"Hey Ward," Uri said. "What's really our mission here?"

Ward answered, "What Colonel Lemev has never shared with 'Gravelly Voice,' his Washington, DC, contact… and the administration's stooge that ordered the assassination hit on Vandorol and the entire El Paso special prosecution bunch in the first place was our Anchorage headquarters in North America of our Russian Spetznaz commando regiments that already numbered in the thousands. We Russians and our friends and partners for this gig, our communist Chinese buds, have been infiltrating North America through the Bering Strait for years and now probably number over fifty thousand communist Chinese and fifty thousand Russian commandos. It's the spear point in the takeover of America from the north through Canada."

Ward paused, smirked, and continued. "All that is totally unknown to Gravelly Voice and his DC handlers, whoever the hell they are. They, whoever *they* are, only know that Colonel Lemev and his team of contract assassins had been hired at mega bucks, millions of US dollars now probably in unnumbered or hidden Swiss or Cayman Island accounts, to kill that bastard Vandorol and his whole prosecution team…"

Uri, already again tiring of Ward's rantings, interrupted, "Why all that to kill a bunch of lying lawyers…just like you, Ward?"

"Up yours, Uri!" Ward answered. "Again, you didn't let me finish!" Ward punched him on the arm. "That bunch of lying lawyers *are* the spear point of their own…" Ward paused for dramatic effect, trying to impress his older friend. "…that could bring down the current administration, the whole Democratic Party, and unite the American people at the next presidential election to stop the transformation of America started in earnest by America's first Muslim president…the historic first black president…another crock…" Ward said, laughing.

Uri had been privy to some of what Ward described, but now he had the complete picture, he thought, *and probably the only one of the whole bunch that does.* Uri filed all the information away for later use and just said, "I've got it, Ward. Thanks."

"You betcha, old buddy! I guess the odds-on America's complete demise just went up, right, Uri?" Ward was again laughing.

Lying on the back seat behind Ward and Uri, again sleeping soundly, the huge Ubiytsa, almost as big as a bale of rolled hay, snorted every few seconds.

"Hey, Ward, I think the colonels are more scared of Ubiytsa than you," Uri laughed. "But old Colonel Lemev sure singed your pretty little nose with a really hot iron this morning!"

Ward was embarrassed. "Yeah, he sure did, the ugly *mat' ublyudka*." He paused. "He's a dead man…the first one I kill or have killed…but he means what he says! I'm sure not going to antagonize the vicious *mat' ublyudka* anymore. Yeah, about Ubiytsa…that's exactly what I want, especially with that ninja Liang!" He smiled now. "I think the Chinese are aligned with the Muslims, but I don't know for sure. Colonel Lemev can't stand the Muslims either, but he won't confront Liang. I think he's a little naïve. All this observer crap. The Commie Chinese are the kings of the East coming across the Euphrates River twenty million strong during the end times as mentioned in the Bible, in the Book of Revelation."

Ward paused again thinking. "Yeah, with that other stupid Chinaman we are meeting in El Paso, the fat General Wang Xiangsui…" He grimaced at Uri, like he was about to throw up. "You know he's an author, don't you, Uri, my best bud?" The contempt in Ward's voice was palpable.

"Yeah, you already told me several times."

"Oh, I did, didn't I?" Ward said, eyebrows raised. "Well, excuuuuse meeeee…"

Both men laughed.

"And is now a big general in the People's Democratic Army…what a crock, another American expression," Ward added, laughing and repeating himself again, Uri noticed.

Colonels Lemev and Liang were in the black Suburban, the first vehicle in the convoy, driven by the scowling Russian Sergeant Vladimir Gorki, the silent killer.

Vladimir Gorki, a grizzled Spetznaʒ sergeant, had been Colonel Lemev's adjutant in Afghanistan where he survived the incursion, though got wounded three times. He was a well-decorated soldier, having received two Hero of the Soviet Union medals for leading the mass murder of hundreds of Afghan freedom fighters and civilian women and children.

Gorki was also massive and grizzled. While Colonel Lemev gained fame as an Olympic weightlifter, Vladimir was an Olympic gold medalist in boxing. A Russian Muslim by birth, he cared not who he killed. He just enjoyed the killings.

Colonel Lemev and Vladimir Gorki were also active KGB officers with ties to Vladimir Putin's innermost circle and had their own cherished reputations as the fixers and muscle of that very powerful governing circle, and both were masters of deception, lies, and falsehoods as well. Vladimir Gorki remained silent, just listening to everything all the time.

"Ward Powell is such a *mu'dak*, as we say in Russian!" Colonel Lemev said to Liang and crossed his arms again, reverting to flawless English, Liang noticed. "But I have my orders, and he has a lot of friends high up in our government and our KGB."

"I know," Liang said, frowning. "I know him very well." Liang paused, smiled for the first time, Lemev noticed, as Liang continued, "Powell was in Washington, DC, when we communist Chinese almost succeeded in the takeover of the American government five years ago by our Project Triple X that Steven Vandorol killed…"

Lemev was stunned. "Really?"

Liang smiled again, this time looking like a huge cat who just swallowed a rat. "Yes, Colonel Lemev, my colleague, really! Colonel Wang Xiangsui, my co-author of *Unrestricted Warfare—China's Master Plan to Destroy America*, was actually in charge of Project Triple X. He's a four-star general now in our army…just as Powell said."

Colonel Lemev interrupted, "But how was Ward involved?"

Liang soured. "Let me finish, will you?"

Lemev nodded as Liang continued. "Then Colonel Wang needed help in Washington and needed to find an agent that was in the lobbying community, so Wang contacted your KGB at the Russian Embassy, and he got Mr. Ward Powell, then a DC lawyer and lobbyist who had been subverting the American political system all his life."

Lemev, now at a distinct disadvantage, managed, "Really?"

"Yes again, really, colonel, really." Liang paused again for effect. He knew he had gained an advantage. Information, good information, and good intelligence was power. "Ward Powell also knew Martin King, Steven Vandorol's buddy in Washington intimately, most intimately. Let me tell you about Mr. Martin L. King, an American negro and lobbyist extraordinaire…"

Colonel Lemev thought, *African-American*, but he wasn't about to correct or interrupt Liang again, as he continued, "And Ward became involved sexually…"

"As homosexuals?" Lemev blurted out.

"Of course," Colonel Liang said. "How better to corrupt than sexually!"

"So Ward Powell swings both ways, does he?" Colonel Lemev had to agree. "That's so true, politicians and lobbyists are like overactive rabbits. No self-discipline whatsoever. They truly just think with what's between their legs…"

"How politically correct, colonel! I'm impressed!" Liang said, then continued, "So Martin King was corrupted by Ward Powell just as Martin was trying to corrupt Steven Vandorol and make him the dupe in our takeover of America by the unsuccessful Project Triple X." Liang paused. "I made it my priority to get Vandorol for messing it all up for us, Lemev!" Liang grimaced like a toad. "Vandorol made us Chinese look really bad to our allies in general, and myself and General Xiangsui to our chairman in particular."

"Everyone trying to corrupt everyone else…it's the way of the world," Lemev said, waxing philosophical. "Did he do that just having sex with him?"

"Mainly that." Liang was still also scowling, looking more like a Buddha statue. "But also, philosophically, with religion."

"How is that?" Lemev wondered.

"Ward Powell corrupted him further by converting a Baptist minister, which he was, to Islam!"

Lemev was surprised again. "No. I can't believe that…not doubting you, but he really did suck him in? After all, colonel, you know what *our* Karl

Marx said about organized religion, that it's the opiate of the masses…so what happened to Martin King?"

"After Vandorol killed the Project Triple X, the jig was up…pardon the most racist American expression." Liang smiled again. *He did have a sense of humor after all*, Lemev thought as Liang continued, "Steven Vandorol disappeared and Martin King committed suicide by jumping off the balcony of his condo at the Watergate Towers in Washington, DC." Liang finished with a flourish.

"So, is Ward Powell a Muslim?" Colonel Lemev asked.

"No, Ward Powell is not anything. He is absolutely just about himself…a classic case of a man who thinks only with what's between his legs and is therefore completely controlled by it!" Liang also knew all about Powell's sexual addiction. Colonel Liang had all the psychological profile of the Clint Eastwood lookalike and knew it well. "Ward Powell is the consummate womanizer," Liang said. "Sex is his addiction. His cocaine, escape, habit, aphrodisiac, heroin all rolled into one…"

"With men and women?" Lemev interrupted.

"I think so," Liang answered. "Our contacts and agents in DC have some great movies of Powell with both men and women." Liang paused for a beat, then continued. "As we have great films on a vast number of American politicians, all thinking with their genitalia!" Colonel Liang smirked. "All of them so easily bribed and controlled." He was actually smiling, eyes squinting to a thin line.

Lemev thought to himself, *I better change the subject. Liang might suspect something more than just innocent addiction questions,* and said, "What about his driver, Uri Gagarin?"

Liang noticed the change in subject as well. "I don't know anything about him. What do *you* know about him, Colonel Lemev?"

Lemev took back the advantage. He knew about Uri's secret role as Ward Powell's handler. "Not much, Colonel Liang," he lied. "I think he is just a Spetznaᴣ sergeant…but other than that, I don't know."

The driver, silent killer Vladimir Gorki, kept looking straight forward and absorbed it all. "I'm really going to enjoy the killing fields," he muttered to himself. He would remain silent and continue to absorb.

"And what happened to Ward Powell?" Lemev was fascinated with the story Liang was telling.

"Powell simply went back to corrupt some more Washington, DC, politicians. After all, that's what lobbyists in DC do…to use another American expression…sex, drugs, and rock and roll…and of course money!" Liang paused again, now smiling like a Cheshire cat.

Lemev thought to himself, *The American Big Four…sex, drugs, rock and roll, and especially money*, and smiled. Lemev was proud of his own wit, though he was just repeating what Colonel Liang had said. "That's true… it was our great Comrade Lenin who said 'sell the Capitalists the rope with which they hang themselves.' So, I think our KGB did very well in having Powell as part of our assassination team and spear point for the takeover of America."

Liang said, "If you're a politician, and if you can't take the lobbyists' money and bribes, drink their whiskey, use the prostitutes they provide, and vote against them, you have no business being a politician."

Colonel Lemev thought, *I guess our communist Chinese friends will not be ultimately voting for Major Ward Powell,* and laughed.

They were both laughing when Sergeant Vladimir Gorki interrupted, "Gentlemen, we are now entering the United States of America and on the way to El Paso, Texas." Sergeant Gorki looked around the completely deserted US-Canada border checkpoint as they flew by, smiled into the rearview mirror, and said, "Looks like the border checkpoint is totally unmanned."

Colonel Lemev looked at Liang. "Thank you, *Sershan's* Gorki! I knew our colleague and leader would do her job very well!" Lemev paused a second thinking of their leader…and their tryst…then continued the Muslim conversation with Liang. "So, what's going to happen to all the Muslim radicals that are running the current American administration?"

Colonel Liang, noticing the slight pause, smiled his crooked enigmatic smile. "We're going to do some mass killing just as Hitler did with the Jews and Comrade Mao did with eighty million." Liang was smiling broadly again as Lemev thought to himself, *and then we Russians will ultimately wipe out the Chinese*, but he said, "And just as Comrade Stalin wiped out fifty million of our peasants." Colonel Lemev was laughing and looking at Liang with eyes widened in anticipation of an answer to his Muslim cancer question...

Colonel Liang again: "As far as the Islamists are concerned, the old Chinese proverb 'the enemy of my enemy is my friend' definitely does *not* apply!"

In the silver Humvee bringing up the rear of the convoy, Uri asked his ward, "So what happens to the Muslim radicals once you're in like Flynn, another good American expression." Uri looked at Powell sitting beside him.

Ward was ready. "They're like cockroaches spreading their cancer in all levels of the American administration and coming across the southern border like flying locusts. There are a few thousand in El Paso already. They all think we're their allies in stamping out the little Satan, Israel, and then the big Satan, America, but all those Muslims are in for a rude awakening right before we turn them to burnt toast." Powell was giggling almost like a teenager.

And Uri thought, *just like you, Ward, just a sex addict yourself,* but he said, changing the subject again, "I think you're really turning Lemev over to your side, Ward! Did you notice how he starts drooling every time you go into your sex stories?"

Ward smiled. "Yeah, I'm going to turn him into my little fornicating friend." Ward paused then continued, "And once I have him controlled, I will personally kill him!"

Ubiytsa, snoring in the back seat, farted...a real stinker.

"Looks like that goat you fed him is not agreeing with Ubiytsa," Uri laughed.

Ward sniffed the air and burst out laughing himself.

"So, you got some pros waiting for us in El Paso?" Uri asked, smiling, and thought, *Ward is just great in lining up the women...*

"It's a surprise, Uri!" Ward winked. "Guaranteed fun."

"I can't wait," Uri said as the Humvee passed an empty and unmanned US-Canada border checkpoint heading south on US Interstate 28 toward Carrington, North Dakota.

23

Rommel and Pegasus were racing toward the sunrise in the vast East Texas horizon. Only the sliver of violet and orange sun separated land from sky in the dark haze of the Texas sunrise, the full moon still visible in the early September sky. Beyond lay dark, brooding mountains, their peaks lit lavender by the rising sun.

The two beautiful animals were neck and neck, Rommel loping gracefully and Pegasus staying right with him, Steven high in the stirrups of the horse rocking under him.

Steven loved his horse as well as his dog. Pegasus, about fifteen hands tall, was a bit shorter than the other two horses, but with a strong back and distinct chrome star on his forehead, snip on the muzzle, and pure white stockings. Both his mane and lush white tail waved in the cool desert air as he strained toward the sunrise and home.

Not far behind, Eddie was on his favorite horse, Mijo, a chestnut Morgan, small for its oversized rider but a very strong work animal that was gaining on the swift white Arabian ahead.

Ray was on his favorite loaner at the Egen ranch, a paint named Gringo that was the tallest of the three horses at almost seventeen hands. Ray was leaning forward as his horse strained to catch up to the frontrunners.

All three were racing the last mile toward sunrise in the eastern Texas sky just starting to show brilliant yellow, crimson, and orange of a rising sun.

It was a cool morning in the open desert outside Egen's Rancho Gringo, a 2,500-acre ranch with grasslands and tundra a mere ten miles north of El Paso, the ranch being in both Texas and New Mexico.

Steven lowered himself in the saddle and gently pulled the rein back, trying to slow Pegasus to a trot. The horse didn't want to slow down. Steven whistled his shrill and very loud whistle to slow Rommel as well, who immediately slowed to a trot. Pegasus slowed down too.

"Whoa, boys," Steven said, smiling. "I guess you could both run until you dropped dead." He was having a wonderful time with all his friends.

Steven turned the horse toward Eddie and Ray trotting up behind him. "So, who won?" Eddie was laughing.

"Looks to me like Rommel did, by at least three lengths," Ray answered.

"I think it was a definite tie," Steven said. "I don't play favorites, right, boys?" He patted the flank of his wet horse affectionately; Pegasus raised his handsome snout, nodding and snorting.

Rommel, a smug look on his face, knew better.

The riders and dog were now in a cluster as the sun rose on the horizon. It was a spectacular sunrise over Sun City, the dawn cool and warming all at the same time. The cloudless sky was a gorgeous violet and pink, the sun a brilliant orange and yellow. God's palette of divine colors again.

Eddie Egen, staring into the dawn, was first to speak. "Thank you, Lord, for saving my life." Eddie had tears in his eyes, Steven noticed.

Steven did also, awed by the brilliant sunrise as he bowed his head. "I am also grateful for saving mine, Lord. Please continue to bless my family, my friends…and Rommel and Pegasus…" He smiled down at Rommel, who looking up at Steven adoringly, as if he knew what his master was saying.

Ray, who had bowed his head as well, looked up. "Gracias a Dios." He paused and said, "We better stop or we'll all have a good cry right out here in the desert."

Eddie smiled. "Yeah, it wouldn't look good to the good Lord for the three amigos to be boo-hooing in cowboy country, right?"

"The three amigos and a dog," Steven corrected, chuckling. "Well, I guess we better get back. When are the guests coming for our top-secret meeting, Ed?"

"Around eleven," Eddie answered. "Let's go get breakfast. Ray, you up for some great menudo? Conchita's been cooking some since early yesterday, I saw!"

"Nah, I'd rather do huevos rancheros. I just do menudo for hangovers," Ray answered, laughing. Ray's horse was a bit skittish around Rommel. He drew his reins tight. "Whoa, boy."

Steven loved breakfast on Saturdays, deviating from his weekday morning regimen. "I think I'll have both. I'm starving," he said as all three turned their horses home and made clicking sounds; the horses knew right where to go without further nudges.

Rommel took the lead. He also knew the drill. He took off in a lope.

"So who's coming?" Steven asked, relaxing and riding easily between his two friends.

"Well, your people," Eddie said, meaning North Anderson, Beth Barker, and Ray. "My lead investigator, Detective Milo Sturgis; his partner, Alex Delaware, these guys affectionately referred to as 'Sherlock and Watson'; my intelligence chief Detective Lucas Davenport, who is also my Texas Rangers liaison; Johnnie Paulsen, who is handling our informants and witness protection." He paused. "We've got the five well-hidden and secure…"

"Those the ones in and around Pecos?" Steven asked.

Ray was listening, riding easily, his horse getting used to Rommel.

Eddie answered, "Yep. But I don't want you guys to know where. It's better that way, okay?"

"Gotcha. Who else?" Steven again.

Ed was thinking. "The FBI will *not* be there. They have *no* comment." Ed was smirking and winking.

Steven got it. "Okay, but who from the FBI will *not* be there and will have *no* comment?"

Eddie again: "If it got out, he could lose his job. It's Jack Reynolds."

Steven knew Jack. "Man, he's really taking a chance. He's the agent in charge and a rising star with the FBI." Pegasus was tiring and slowing. "What's Jack's pulse, Eddie? Is he on our side?"

"Yeah, but he can't stand all those Washington thugs either, especially his boss, the former Muslim AG Holder." Eddie paused. "Jack is a patriot and will be our mole in the FBI. And last but not least, our surprise guest…"

Steven looked at Ed in anticipation as they neared the ranch compound. He already knew.

"Ta-da. The Texas Sate adjutant general…"

146

Ray was surprised. "General John F. Nicholas, himself? Wow. That guy has some real pull. Why's he coming, Ed?"

"He's representing our governor. He's coming but also on the QT. We don't want the press to know anything—especially the biased leftist media!"

They were back at the ranch entrance, the range and desert behind them and a long and sandy gravel roadway ahead. The back entrance to Eddie's ranch was two hundred yards ahead. Before them, the ranch compound itself.

It was a large ranch compound: forty acres, surrounded by several hundred tall oak trees, neatly spaced and wind rowed. Straight ahead, left and right, two huge barns. One for the horses, the other for the cattle, both enclosed by seven-foot wood fences. Both barns were already busy, with several persons working in each area. The rest of the 2,500 acres spread to the north, west, and south, Fort Bliss military reserve to the east and vast Texas desert.

The three riders veered to the left. One of the workers was already petting Rommel as the three horses approached the horse barn. Three cowboys had the herd out to the left in exercise, the herd milling about.

Eddie pulled up and dismounted. "Thanks, Jesús. We had a good early ride."

Jesús Chavez was a third-generation Hispanic in the Egen employ; his grandfather had worked for the Texas Rangers at the turn of the century, as did his father. Jesús had been working for Eddie for almost ten years, Steven knew.

"Mr. Ortega's horse was okay, boss?" Jesús asked as he walked over to Eddie's horse as he dismounted. He seemed to be avoiding Ray.

Ray, dismounting as well, answered Jesús. "Good horse, Jesús. Gracias." He handed Jesús the reins and looked at him, not smiling, Steven noticed, making a mental note to talk to Ray later about Jesús and the change in Ray's expression.

Steven, still on Pegasus, surveyed the back of the compound, the huge mansion and outlying buildings in the midst of hundreds of trees that reminded him of the Patron's compound on the Brazilian *fazenda* of his childhood. "Eddie, you have so much to be grateful for," Steven said, dismounting. "Your ranch always reminds me of the happiest time of my life."

"I know it, Steven. I am." Eddie paused then continued. "Let's get some breakfast.

24

On the way to El Paso in northern New Mexico, Colonel Lemev was on his burner cell phone to the El Paso recon and assassination team. "What's going on in the Sun City?" He was fondling his pistol with one hand and had his cell phone in the other, a half bottle of Stolichnaya and empty glass before him.

Muhammed Abu was listening intently, while Vladimir Gorki slept in a drunken haze on the bed.

It was Saturday morning, September 5, 2015.

Colonel Liang sat silently nearby, again daintily sipping tea out of his personal gold-inlaid china cup. Ward Powell and Uri sat together on the couch.

The twenty-four-man assassination team and advance guard in the coming takeover of America had arrived in Farmington, near the Four Corners Monument in northern New Mexico, all separately, in pairs, so as not to attract any attention whatsoever.

All reservations were made under assumed names with matching false documents. The twenty-four men were spread across seven hotels, which had been picked several days ago in preparation for their arrival, the La Quinta, Hampton, Fairfield and Region Inns, Holiday Inn Express, Motel 6, and the Courtyard by Marriott right at the Four Corners Regional Airport. The two colonels, Lemev and Liang, Syrian Muslim intelligence officer Muhammad Abu, Ward Powell, and Uri Gagarin were all together at the Courtyard by Marriott, all in separate but adjoining rooms. Ward Powell and driver Uri Gagarin had a separate room adjoining the two colonels, both with separate rooms as well. Sunni Muslims Abu and Mustafa Dobe had a separate room to themselves, as Colonel Lemev privately and personally demanded.

The twelve vehicles were concealed at various 24-hour high-traffic parking lots, all guarded by various team members.

Colonel Liang was appalled by the Muslims in their midst, he told Colonel Lemev. They were all filthy throwbacks to the Middle Ages in their habits, customs, and especially their pedophilia and homosexuality with young boys. Colonel Liang couldn't stand any of them, whether Sunni or Shiites. *They are all scum thinking just with their genitals*, he thought, especially of Colonel Lemev, *who is doing the very same with our team leader already in El Paso,* Colonel Liang thought as he knew of Lemev's little liaison in one of the bedrooms of the hunting lodge.

Colonel Liang was really looking forward to the arrival of his co-author, now Major General Wang Xiangsui and star of the People's Liberation Army of Communist China, due to arrive in El Paso by Amtrak almost at the same time they all would be arriving in El Paso. *I can't wait for us to rid the world of all the Islamists…and Russian cockroaches as well,* he thought as he listened to Colonel Lemev talking on the burner cell Lemev had placed on speaker and put on top of the round table in the middle of the room.

"There's some big deal happening on the Egen ranch," the Arab man said on the speaker. The Arab speaking, whom KGB Colonel Lemev himself had recruited months ago, was a wiry Middle Eastern who could easily pass for a Mexican. Colonel Lemev knew the Muslim well, having met him in Afghanistan and personally trained him for covert operations as well. Dark-skinned, barrel-chested, and stout and hard, he had hooded, dark dead eyes. He was Muhammed Atta, Hezbollah operative, now in the United States for three years and leader of the Muslim terrorist cell operating in Juarez and El Paso. He had crossed the porous southern border of the US from Mexico into Texas along with illegal aliens under the president's executive order that effectively granted amnesty to thousands of illegal aliens, Lemev knew. Hyperactive, knees bouncing at all times as he sat, Colonel Lemev remembered. He was a coiled cobra, a flicking tongue added to the picture in his mind's eye.

The colonel put his gun down, downed his drink.

"You still there?" Atta asked on the phone.

"…yeah, hold on." The colonel filled his glass with vodka again. "What's going on?" he repeated.

"Our plant on the ranch says some kind of meeting is happening," Atta answered. "The housekeeper and maid are getting ready…and Vandorol and his investigator, Ray Ortega, were out riding with Chief Egen before sunrise."

"Oh yeah?" The colonel wanted to know more.

"Steven came last night, and it looks like he's staying for the whole weekend."

"Who is your plant?"

"Just a stupid Mexican in the Egen employ."

"What did it take?"

"To bend him?" Atta said. "Big dollars for his drug habit."

"Do you think you can take Steven out this weekend?"

"No way." Atta sounded despondent. "The security on the ranch is incredible, I'm told. Motion detectors all around the fenced main compound, five police officers on patrol on the grounds 24/7. Armed house staff and virtual arsenals in the big house and staff quarters and bunkhouse, both impenetrable." Atta paused, took a deep breath, and continued, "I think they know." Atta didn't want to incur the colonel's wrath for the failed attempts on Chief Egen and Steven Vandorol.

"Tell me, Atta."

"Well, our men from Juarez…" Atta started.

The colonel interrupted, "The cartel killers?"

"Yeah," Atta answered. "Well, they had been following Steven and Chief Egen for days. Anyway, they got to the chief and ran him off the road, but he came out of it unscathed. I think they spotted the white Silverado pickup several times now." Atta hesitated, really didn't want to get into the screw-up on the Vandorol hit. He swallowed and hesitated.

Lemev noticed. "And what about Vandorol? Were they following him also?"

Atta hesitated. "You might as well know. They screwed up big-time. They were all set to ambush Steven when he was running…"

"So, what happened?" Lemev interrupted angrily.

"Steven was running with a big dog. I mean, this dog was huge…a Great Dane, I think…"

Lemev was stunned. "Vandorol has a dog?"

"Yeah, he is a giant!" Atta paused then continued, "I think the fricking dog weighs more than Vandorol."

Colonel Lemev calmed. "So, what happened?" He looked at Colonel Liang and frowned. Colonel Liang rolled his eyes but said nothing, frowning also.

"Long story short, the dog woke up the whole neighborhood…with our two guys getting stuck next door to some Mexican, who raised his window and got into a nice conversation with Vandorol…in Spanish. It's like they were bosom buddies…the guy even complimented Steven's dog…"

"Long story short," Lemev reminded Atta.

"Okay, okay." Atta hesitated and continued, "…the white Silverado pickup got impounded by the cops."

"*Chert!*" Lemev said again, reverting to Russian. "That's a major screw-up. I can't believe the idiocy…idiots used the same vehicle for both attempts. Has it been sanitized?"

"No…it hasn't."

"Well, you gotta get to it…and blow it sky high…do you understand me, Atta?"

"Will do," Atta said. "What about new surveillance vehicles?"

Lemev was abrupt. "Retire them and get some new ones." Lemev paused, thinking, then continued, "Just leave it in Juarez. It will be stripped and gone in minutes." He laughed, relaxing just a little. "Did you contact that antique dealer in Juarez whose number I gave you yesterday?"

"I sure did, colonel…and wow," Atta said, seemingly beside himself. "You're not gonna believe this, but that dealer was the go-between for probably the richest family in Mexico…the Alvarados…" Atta was almost stammering. "And get this…rumor has it that Ricardo Alvarado is suspected to be the Patron of the Juarez Cartel."

The colonel already knew but matter-of-factly answered, "Are they going to help…moneywise?"

"Yes, those guys got big money from all kinds of stuff," Atta said. "Slavery, drugs, illegal aliens, gun running…the Alvarados are into it all, especially Ricardo Alvarado, who lives right here in El Paso, in the country club addition on the west side." Atta paused. "Did you know, colonel, that it was the Alvarados that put the hit on Steven Vandorol?"

"Yeah, I knew," Lemev answered, deflecting. "But it's been expanded." Lemev paused and abruptly changed the subject. "We could sure use three or four of those pretty girls around when we get there," the colonel finished.

"Just that great vodka is not enough?" Atta asked.

Colonel Lemev was irritated. "We'll be in El Paso on September 11, 2015."

"Who is coming?" Atta wanted to know.

"Our ten-man strike team…er, assassination team…with eight men in five vehicles," the colonel lied and said nothing about the additional ten-man reinforcement group that had just arrived and was in the Four Corners area with them right now. *There's no point in telling the insolent Muslim everything, even though the enemy of my enemy is also my friend,* Lemev thought to himself. "Is Bliss under surveillance also?"

"Why does it need to be?" Atta asked.

Lemev answered quickly, "Because Vandorol represents a bunch of militaries and is out at Bliss all the time…"

"Okay, okay, I'll get a guy on it," Atta answered.

"That's good!" Lemev was finished with that subject. Again, he didn't want to tell the Muslim anymore and thought, *we should provide the Americans another big surprise on September 11, 2016. Right before the 2016 election, we should be in control.* Lemev was thinking as he continued, "Do you have the full layout of the compound?" He looked directly at Colonel Liang, sitting near him, still sipping tea.

Atta replied immediately, "I sure do; we have good information, insider information!"

"How about Vandorol's residence? Got that covered? We have someone special for that part, got it?" Lemev continued, still looking at Colonel Liang. "You guys screwing up the Eddie Egen hit is just going to make it that much tougher to get Vandorol!"

"Yeah, I know," Atta answered, paused a beat, then continued. "We'll get you the layout from Vandorol's house on the mountain from another source hopefully. It was unfortunate about not getting Egen when he was alone on the highway."

Powell signaled Lemev, holding a finger up. Lemev put the phone on silent and looked directly at Powell.

Ward said, "Ask him where Egen was on the highway."

Lemev clicked off silent, asked, "Atta, where was Egen on the highway?"

Atta replied, "He was outside Van Horn…coming from Pecos."

Ward motioned to end the conversation by drawing his index finger across his throat.

Lemev again: "You guys don't screw up again! We have other morons to take your place if you screw up again…we'll keep in touch. We'll be in El Paso on the 11th of September. Be ready to plan." He clicked off the cell phone and looked at Ward. "What do you think?"

Ward answered, "I think the witnesses are under guard in Pecos, probably. I also think we should strike Vandorol's residence right before Thanksgiving. Colonel Liang, would you lead the strike? That's right down your alley as a ninja professional, right?

"The cartel killers didn't do so good trying to hit Vandorol," Lemev said to Liang, frowning at the conversation. "I agree with you, Ward…"

Colonel Liang slowly sipped his tea, gently sat his china cup on the ornate saucer, and said, "I will lead the team and kill Vandorol…and his dog! My partner and good friend General Xiangsui will not be pleased, I assure you, Colonel Lemev." He took another sip of tea. "General Xiangsui will deal with all the offenders…and the El Paso covert team…most harshly, I assure you." Colonel Liang paused then continued, "General Xiangsui should be arriving in El Paso by train day after tomorrow and will be expecting a full report."

Ward and Uri got up and left the room without saying another word.

The meeting was over.

———

Powell was on his burner cell phone talking to his own El Paso contact. "Have you missed me, gorgeous?" He winked at Uri, who was driving and listening to the conversation as the two drove the silver Humvee to their hotel in Farmington, several miles from the airport Marriott in which the colonels and the Muslims were staying—a change Ward made himself after they all arrived in Farmington, New Mexico.

Uri Gagarin motioned a click with his index finger for Ward to hit the speaker button on his cell phone, and Ward did, winking again.

A sultry, throaty woman's voice said, "I sure do, my stallion. Can't wait to see you! So, when are you getting into El Paso, stud?"

Ward, grinning like a teenager, put the phone back on listen then placed it to his ear. "Day after tomorrow," he lied. "We are just leaving Canada." He paused, listening, then said, "That's fine; get a suite at the Artesian for a weekend and we won't get out of bed, okay?" Ward listened for almost a full minute, Uri glancing at him two or three times until Ward talked again.

"That's good! You did well," Ward said, again listening, then said, "Did anybody find out where you were?" Ward glanced at Uri and said, "What a moron mijo," and laughed. "Have fun...but be careful...and call me when you get done, okay? I'll be waiting right here in Farmington for you"—he swallowed—"at the Quality Inn Farmington. Get this...1901 East Broadway, Farmington...right off Interstate 64, room 344." He paused again, kept smiling, then said, "I'll keep *my* motor running...really hot!" Ward clicked off, still grinning. He winked at Uri.

Uri giggled like a schoolgirl. "You stallion, you! Why the Artesian, Ward?"

"Because the Artesian reminds me of the Shoreham Hotel on upper Connecticut Avenue in DC, and that was fun too," he said simply.

- 25 -

The train slowly pulled into a sparkling new train station, Union Depot in El Paso on San Francisco Avenue, near the El Paso convention center and the Rio Grande River not far away.

Major General Wang Xiangsui of the People's Liberation Army of Communist China, standing at the door of the train car, was wide awake. The station sign read: "El Paso, Texas/Juarez, Mexico." It was Saturday morning, September 5, 2015.

The Amtrak train stopped with a lurch, the uniformed porter hopped off, placed the stair step down on the platform, and allowed the general to step down, saying, "Watch your step…have a good stay in El Paso, Mr. Hayakawa."

"Thank you, Mr. Washington," General Xiangsui said in flawless but clipped English, handing the porter a hundred-dollar tip.

The general had introduced himself to the porter as a Japanese businessman, based in Los Angeles, for Toyota Motors, Japan, and was headed to El Paso and Juarez on Toyota business. He had a fake passport, driver's license, and other credentials and credit cards to prove just that. He had told the porter he had a lifetime aversion to flying and loved to ride trains anyway.

Xiangsui was a very large, very fat man by both Chinese and American standards, fitting in well with an obese American nation. At five and a half feet tall and almost 300 pounds, he resembled a Chinese Jabba the Hutt. He was dressed in an oversized tan linen suit, tailored to hide the obesity, white cotton custom-made shirt, monogrammed French cuffs with gold American flag links, and pink Christian Lacroix silk paisley tie. Real Gucci shoes, very expensive, and not just cheap Chinese knockoffs. He was already sweating profusely as he was hit by the blazing El Paso midday sun, 110 degrees today, Mr. Washington had said. The perpetual scowl on his fat face made him look like he had indigestion from swallowing a large lizard.

The book *Unrestricted Warfare, China's Master Plan to Destroy America,* co-authored by then Colonels Wang Xiangsui and Qiao Liang, vaulted both men to communist China's top military leadership, Xiangsui to a higher level than his colleague, a generalship, as he was a master manipulator and corruptor not unlike his idol and mentor, Mao Tse Tung, the killer of seventy million Chinese during and after World War II, and still had taken full credit though his co-author was the actual writer.

General Xiangsui was the designated dictator of America, and in complete charge of the sword point of all the ground forces amassing on the Canadian and Mexican borders of the United States, all such forces unknown to most of the assassination team and totally unknown to all their Washington, DC contacts within the current administration. Once his job was done and America was subdued and neutralized as a power, the general would foreclose on the United States' massive debt of $121 trillion, and communist China as the lone remaining world power, and the general personally as dictator, would in effect own all public American lands. *We Chinese will then truly be the Kings from the East as their nonsense Christian Bible foretells in the Book of Revelation,* the general thought.

General Xiangsui was first going to discipline the assassination team for their various failures and make way for further reinforcements standing by and already waiting in areas outlying Ciudad Juarez, a stone's throw away from downtown El Paso.

He was not a believer in the old adage about the enemy of my enemy being my friend; he would kill all enemies regardless of any alliances and had been in daily contact by cell phones far more advanced than any in America with Colonel Liang, his partner and co-author, and claimed to be just an observer on the assassination team but actually was the leader of the advance guard already on the way to El Paso. He had to smile to himself as he thought again about how he managed to insert his co-author into Putin's inner circle so that Colonel Liang would then join the assassination team merely as an observer. *Liang would be the cobra in the henhouse, as the ancient proverb said,* General Xiangsui thought as he looked around the shaded platform in the dry heat.

He was livid that the attempt on both Egen and Vandorol had failed, that Vandorol was still alive and continued to be a factor in this prosecution with national implications. General Xiangsui would make sure that Vandorol was destroyed this time! He hated Vandorol and knew exactly why.

Not only had Steven Vandorol thwarted the kings of the East from the takeover of the United States government by blowing up the failed Project Triple X several years ago, but Vandorol represented everything about America that communists and the American left hated most.

As for hated America, the general had already turned a local El Pasoan to carry out his plan, already authorized by the chairman himself, to neutralize American armed ground forces and pave the way for the invasion of America. He was going to test his plan first before the end of the year, the year of the horse on the Chinese calendar.

General Xiangsui hailed another porter for his two bags and walked from the tracks in the oppressive El Paso heat to the air-conditioned terminal.

The station was brand new, granite and marble, and was an art deco masterpiece that appealed to a sophisticated connoisseur like himself, he thought, and smiled, very pleased with himself.

"Would you please get me a cab," the general said to the porter carrying his two Louis Vuitton large travel bags. "I'll be in the snack bar getting some refreshments. I'll be checking into the Camino Real Hotel."

"Yessir," the porter replied. "I'll come and get you."

"Thank you so much." The general walked into the cool snack bar sweating like a pig and shuffled to the serving line counter where a young couple, both with trays, were just being served. He got right behind them and took out a monogrammed Belgian linen handkerchief, unfolded it carefully, and mopped his face.

The two ahead were served and in unison glanced back at him. The general smiled at them, his eyes almost disappearing into his face with his fat jowls rising. "Sure is hot today," he said to the couple.

The young man smiled back. "Welcome to El Paso, sir," and followed the young woman to the cashier.

"What can I get'cha, señor?" the man behind the counter asked, his dark eyebrows raised.

The general wiped his face again, folded the handkerchief, very deliberately put it in his pocket, and said, "Large Coca-Cola with a straw and two bottles of Perrier, if you please."

"Coming right up, señor." He turned to the fountain behind him, filled a large cup with Coke, put it on the counter, opened the cooler, took out two bottles of Perrier, and put them on the counter as well. "Something to eat?" he asked.

"No thank you, but would you carry these to a table for me?" The general went to the cashier just ahead, took out folded currency with a Tiffany money clip, and paid with a twenty. "The change is for him," he said to the cashier, nodding toward the cook, walked to a table in a secluded corner right under the air conditioning vent, and plopped down in a chair. The man following behind set his drinks on the table, said, "Muchas gracias, señor!" and went back to the counter.

The general was alone on one side; the young couple was at another table eating and talking, almost out of earshot. He took a long drink, sighed, and enjoyed the cold air blowing down on him. He took out his cell phone, speed dialed, and in clipped English said, "Mr. Warren, are you ready to conduct our business?" Waited, listening, then: "Are all our arrangements satisfactory?" He listened again then said, "Good, good." The general paused. "Is the New Year's surprise going to be ready?" He listened a few seconds more and ended the call thinking, *the year of the Horse approaches...*, and finished his drink still smiling.

The Texas leadership of the special prosecution was in Eddie Egen's large den, waiting for their surprise guest. All the windows were blackened, shut tight, and the security on the perimeter of the ranch compound was extremely tight, Steven knew. Eddie told him security was well disguised so that all would seem like a normal day on the ranch to not arouse any suspicion in case of outside surveillance.

Steven looked around the warm and spacious room. The large den, Eddie's "man cave" as he called it, was a huge combination living and recreation room. The walls were covered with prints of the American Revolutionary War, the Constitution of the United States, the Bill of Rights, and the Declaration of Independence, all in sterling silver frames.

Steven and Eddie sat together on the large leather couch drinking coffee. Eddie was a bit solemn and very distracted. Andi had left the ranch and was staying with her parents in Anthony, New Mexico, Eddie had said.

North Anderson and Beth Barker, the only woman present, sat at a table nearby, North drinking coffee and Beth tea. She was scowling, not happy to be there. Steven glanced at her and thought, *I still sure have this bad gut feeling about her, but she's not bad to look at,* and wondered whether it was her or just his own old layers of evil, or neurosis, he had fought and thought handled.

Ray Ortega and Milo Sturgis, Eddie's lead investigator, sat in the well of the huge fireplace also drinking coffee. Ray and Milo were old friends and had been for years of working together, Ray in Army Criminal Investigation Division, and Milo at the El Paso police department. Milo was a big man, over six foot and 200 pounds, with a Marine Corps buzz haircut. He had served three tours in Afghanistan. He was a brawler and a womanizer, just like his boss. Milo could easily have been mistaken for Vin Diesel of *The Fast and the Furious* fame, Steven thought.

At another table to the right of the fireplace, Lucas Davenport and Johnnie Paulsen were chatting. Both wore casual jeans, leather jackets, boots, cowboy shirts, and discreet shoulder holsters. Proven and able leaders, Lucas and Johnnie were Texas Rangers. Today neither wore their unmistakable Texas Ranger Stetsons. They were the top two men in the entire Texas Rangers command structure. Steven was impressed. He knew and respected both as very good men and very able leaders.

Eddie got up and casually walked to the closed door by the bar, opened it, and motioned. "Come on in, gentlemen." He ushered in District Attorney Ernie Martinez, who was followed by two men, the first one a tall man wearing a Texas Ranger Stetson, jeans, cowboy shirt, jacket, and alligator boots, and the other wearing a windbreaker, T-shirt, jeans, and boots as well. All three walked to the table and, still standing, Ernesto said, "Gents, let me introduce Major General John A. Nicholas, Texas adjutant general, in disguise of course with borrowed Texas Ranger hat. General, you know everyone here…" The district attorney walked over and sat down by his two assistants, North Anderson and Beth Barker.

General Nicholas was tall, about six-five, Steven thought, lean and on the thin side, maybe 220. The general was a handsome, distinguished-looking older man, probably in his mid-sixties. He had previously commanded all ground forces in Afghanistan, successfully implementing President George Bush's now famous "surge" in defeating the Muslim Taliban, before being replaced by the president as he plundered the military, infiltrating it with Muslim Brotherhood plants and Sharia Law sympathizers.

Steven had to smile when he remembered the now famous story Eddie told him about the exchange the general and the president had when the general was resigning in the Oval Office, and the president remarked, "General Nicholas, I bet that when I die you'll be peeing on my grave," and the general smiled, saluted, and solemnly replied, "Mr. President, I always told myself that after leaving the army, I'd never stand in line again."

Steven had met the general on a previous visit to Fort Bliss where then Captain G. Jack Reacher had been his guide to Fort Bliss and El Paso for three days and observed a court martial Steven had handled and Ray investigated.

Captain G. Jack Reacher, the general, Steven and Ray, Eddie, and the DA had then all become acquainted over dinner at the Dome Grill at the Camino Real Hotel. The general and his adjutant were staying at the hotel on an official visit from Washington. Steven could tell back then that Captain Reacher, as their local guide, was one of the general's favorite young officers at Fort Bliss. Obviously, Captain Reacher was the general's guide and security at Ft. Bliss and El Paso on this current visit as well.

The general cleared his throat. "Let me first introduce Captain G. Jack Reacher. Doesn't he look nice in his civilian clothes?" The general paused a beat then continued. "Captain Reacher was under my command in Afghanistan, and it would not have been good for my guide to El Paso on an incognito mission to be seen in his Army Ranger uniform, right, gentlemen?" He nodded toward a muscular young guy in a leather jacket, polo shirt, jeans and boots who looked like he could have been a running back for the Dallas Cowboys.

Tall, six-foot-four, 230 pounds, handsome, with piercing ice blue eyes, Captain Reacher looked like a young Roger Staubach, the Heisman Trophy winner at the Naval Academy and later all-time most prolific quarterback with the Dallas Cowboys.

Reacher had played football at West Point, where he had been a middle linebacker All-American, and remembered Steven as a freshman cadet running back whose knee injury ended his football playing days.

Captain Reacher waved at the group, adjusted his shoulder holster, smiled at the general, and gave a thumbs-up to Steven, Eddie, and Ray, all three saluting him back immediately. He walked over to the large leather couch and sat down next to Steven. The general remained standing by the bar.

"Thank you, Mr. Martinez," the general began, "and thank you for inviting me to this momentous meeting...and your hospitality here in the Sun City of El Paso. Gentlemen... ma'am"—the general glanced at Beth, who nodded slightly—"Chief Egen, Rangers, detectives, Steven and Ray, how are you guys?" All were nodding as the general began with a broad smile.

"Maybe I should be wearing a hood as no one is supposed to know I'm here today," the adjutant general of the State of Texas said. "But I'm here not only representing the governor, our Texas attorney general, and all our ground and air forces in Texas, but also as a patriot among the patriots in this room, especially Captain Egen and you, Steven…" The general looked toward Eddie and Steven, nodding.

Both Steven and Eddie nodded and smiled as the general continued. "Not only is another American Civil War beginning but also World War III may just be starting as well, as in the late 1930s. History is repeating itself… as it's been said: those who cannot remember the past are condemned to repeat it…well, our nation is repeating it, but as the Bible tells us and shows: if the good Lord brings you to it, He will take you through it. To get out of a difficulty, one usually must go through it. Our country is now facing the most serious threat to its existence, as we know it, that we have faced in your lifetime and mine, which includes World War II."

The general paused a beat, looked around the room, and continued. "The deadly seriousness is greatly compounded by the fact that there are very few of us who think we can possibly lose this war and even fewer who realize what losing really means. First, let's examine a few basics: When did the threat to us start? Many will say September 11, 2001. The answer, as far as the United States is concerned, is 1979, twenty-two years prior to September 2001, with all the attacks made by Muslim men in their twenties or thirties."

The general paused again, getting angry as he continued. "During the period from 1981 to 2001 there were 7,581 Muslim terrorist attacks worldwide. Why were we attacked? Envy of our position and our freedoms." He looked around the room and asked, "Who were the attackers? In each case, the attacks on America were carried out by Muslim men in their twenties and thirties…every one of those attacks." The general frowned. "The Muslim population of the world is 25 percent, that's almost two billion. Isn't the Muslim religion peaceful, you ask? Hopefully, but that is really not material. There is no doubt that the predominately Christian population of Germany was peaceful, but under the dictatorial leadership of Hitler, who was a Catholic, that made no difference. You either went along with the Nazi administration or you were eliminated. There were five to six million Christians killed by the Nazis for political reasons, and seven thousand Polish priests as well.

"Thus, almost the same number of Christians were killed by the Nazis as the six million Holocaust Jews who were killed by them, but we seldom hear of anything other than the Jewish atrocities. Although Hitler kept the world focused on the Jews, he had no hesitancy in killing anyone who got in the way of the extermination of the Jews or of trying to take over the world—German, Christian, or any others.

"Hitler's main reason for hate, and hate of the Jews specifically, was because his mother had been a housekeeper for a rich old Jew who raped her, or Hitler thought he did. Mother was probably intimate with the old Jew from day one!"

General Nicholas paused again, took a deep breath, and continued. "Same with the Muslim terrorists. They focus the world on the Jews and Israel, and on the US, but kill all in their way, even their own people, or the Spanish, British, French, or anyone else. The point here is that, just as the peaceful Germans had no protection from the Nazis, no matter how many peaceful Muslims there may be, they are of no protection for us from the terrorist Muslim leaders and what they are fanatically bent on doing—by their own pronouncements—killing all of us 'infidels.' I don't blame the peaceful Muslims. What would you do if the choice were to remain silent or be killed? They continue to give lip service to terrorism for religious reasons, while just a bunch of adolescents continue the killing."

The general was finished with that subject. "So, who are we at war with? There is no way we can honestly respond that it is anyone other than the Muslim terrorists. Trying to be politically correct and avoid verbalizing this conclusion can well be fatal. There is no way to win if you don't clearly recognize and articulate who you are fighting…who the enemy really is.

"So, with that background, now to the two major questions: Can we lose this war? Yes, we can! Our treasonous president just released five of the worst Muslim terrorists and is threatening to close Guantanamo in Cuba, and letting Iran have nuclear weapons by giving them $500 billion to continue financing worldwide terrorism and the Shiite Caliphate.

"Gentlemen…and ma'am…" The general smiled at Beth Barker, who nodded in acknowledgment but was still scowling, a sour look on her face. "…We now have a Muslim government. John Brennan, current head of the CIA, converted to Islam while stationed in Saudi Arabia. The president's top advisor is a Muslim who was born in Iran where her parents still live. Hillary Clinton's top advisory, Huma Abedin, is a Muslim, whose mother and brother are involved in the now outlawed Muslim Brotherhood in Egypt. The assistant secretary for policy development for Homeland Security is a Muslim. The Homeland Security advisor is a Muslim. A presidential advisor and founder of the Muslim Public Affairs Council, Salam al-Marayati, is a Muslim. The president's Sharia czar, Imam Mohamed Magid, of the Islamic Society of North America, is a Muslim. The Advisory Council on Faith-Based Neighborhood Partnerships, Chairman Eboo Patel, is a Muslim.

"And, last but not least, our closet Muslim himself, Barack Hussein Obama. It's questionable if Obama ever officially took the oath of office when he was sworn in. He didn't repeat the oath properly to defend our nation and our Constitution. Later the Democrats claimed he was given the oath again in private!

"Considering all these appointments, it would explain why the president and his minions are systematically destroying our nation, supporting radical Muslim groups worldwide, opening our southern border, and turning a blind eye to the genocide being perpetrated on Christians all over Africa and the Middle East.

"Our nation and our government have been infiltrated by people who want to destroy us. It can only get worse! I hope all of you have this firmly in your minds." The general paused and again looked around the room. "We must know our enemy in this coming civil war, and it is a civil war; we're going to have to fight against our own government."

Steven also looked around the room. North and Ray were both nodding. Beth, with her arms crossed, was completely still. Steven again felt queasy in the pit of his stomach. Beth locked eyes with Steven for an instant then quickly looked away.

"What does losing really mean?" the general continued. "If we are to win, we must clearly answer these two pivotal questions: The first one, what does losing mean? We would no longer be the premier country in the world. The Russians and Chinese communists are already kicking our butts economically and technologically. The attacks by Muslim terrorist radicals will not subside but rather steadily increase. Remember, they want us dead, not just quiet. If they had just wanted us quiet, they would not have produced an increasing series of attacks against us over the past eighteen years. The plan was clearly for terrorists to attack us until we were neutered and submissive to them."

Steven couldn't help thinking back to Project Triple X, which had almost succeeded in an attempted North Korean or communist Chinese takeover that challenged his own personal survival. Steven shuddered at the recent developments of the last few days. He locked eyes with Eddie, who seemed really depressed and hurting, completely distracted, his thoughts seemingly miles away.

General Nicholas continued, "We would, of course, have no future support from other nations for fear of reprisals and because they would see that we are impotent and cannot help them. Spain, Denmark, Sweden, Germany, and France are all history. They are being overwhelmed by Muslims and Syrian refugees, many thousands of Muslim men in their twenties and thirties. If we lose the war, our production, income, exports, and way of life will all vanish as we know it. After losing, who would trade or deal with us if they were threatened by the Muslims? If we can't stop the Muslim terrorists, how could anyone else?

"The radical Muslims fully know what is riding on this war, and therefore are completely committed to winning, at any cost. We'd better know it too and should be likewise committed to winning at any cost.

"Why do I go on at such lengths about the results of losing? Simple. Until we recognize the costs of losing, we cannot unite and really put 100 percent of our thoughts and efforts into winning. And it is going to take that 100 percent effort to win.

"And the second question, how can we lose the war?" the general asked. "Again, the answer is simple. We can lose the war by 'imploding.' That is, defeating ourselves by refusing to recognize the enemy and their purpose and failing to dig in and lend full support to the war effort. If we are united, there is no way we can lose. If we continue to be divided, there is no way that we can win.

"I don't say this lightly, but the current administration would literally like to see us lose. The president promised a radical transformation of America. The current administration is doing it on purpose. Lie to the infidels when you can. It is because they just don't recognize what losing means. Nevertheless, that conduct gives the impression to the enemy that we are divided and weakening. It concerns our friends and it does great damage to our cause. This is TREASON."

The general took a deep breath, his eyes on the gathering. "Remember, the Muslim terrorists' stated goal is to kill all infidels. That translates into ALL non-Muslims—not just in the United States but throughout the world. We are the last bastion of defense. If we don't recognize this, our nation as we know it will not survive, and no other free country in the world will survive if we are defeated.

"And, finally, name any Muslim country in the world that allows freedom of speech, freedom of thought, freedom of religion, freedom of the press, equal rights for anyone—let alone everyone—equal status or any status for women, or that have been productive in one single way that contributes to the good of the world.

"This has been a long way of saying that we must be united on this war or we will be equated in the history books to the self-inflicted fall of the Roman Empire. If, that is, the Muslim leaders allow history books to be written or read.

"The fact is that the fanatics rule Islam in this moment in history. It is the fanatics who march. It is the fanatics who wage any one of fifty shooting wars worldwide. It is the fanatics who systematically slaughter Christian or tribal groups throughout Africa and are gradually taking over the entire continent in an Islamic wave. It is the fanatics who bomb, behead, murder, or honor-kill. It is the fanatics who take over mosque after mosque. It is the fanatics who zealously spread the stoning and hanging of rape victims and homosexuals. It is the fanatics who teach their young to kill and to become suicide bombers. The Islamic way is only peaceful until the fanatics move in.

"As for we who watch it all unfold, we must pay attention to the only group that counts—the fanatics who threaten our way of life, Islamic terrorists and ISIS…or ISIL, to which the administration stubbornly clings, the radical Muslim cancer…"

The general concluded: "So now we come to our own beloved constitutional republic…you all know our choice politically in November… on the one hand we have billionaire Donald Trump, a political outsider who promises to build a wall to secure our borders, deport as many Muslim terrorists as possible, close all Muslim radical terrorist mosques, clear the government and military of all Muslim Brotherhood implants or sympathizers, repeal Obamacare, all in his first term in office by executive order, proceed to rebuild the military, drain the Washington, DC, slime and corruption swamp, and indict the current administration—including the president himself and his Muslim plants, and the current Democratic presidential candidate Hillary and her Muslim advisor—for treason, and jail thereafter for all the usual subjects."

He paused and looked around again. Steven did as well and noticed Beth with her head down. Steven decided to question her later about her political views more closely.

The general now looked directly at Steven and Eddie. "And on our side at this momentous time in the history of our beloved United States of America, we have the states of Texas, Oklahoma, New Mexico, and Arizona in general, and Steven Vandorol and Eddie Egen in particular, and we also have this special prosecution indictment to gain the popular support of the American people as the sword points in the coming and impending civil war."

Steven and Eddie were both nodding as the general finished. "Eddie will first review our evidence and witnesses and then Steven will give us the summary of this historic criminal indictment that's in the works. Eddie?" The general walked to an easy chair beside the couch and sat down.

Eddie rose and approached the bar where the general had stood. He took off his hat, laid it on the desk, and cleared his throat.

"This morning, around 7 am, I went for my stroll around the docks. I noticed a man shouting at the top of his voice, 'Allah be praised!' and 'Death to the infidels,' when he suddenly tripped and fell into the water.

"He was struggling to stay afloat because of all the explosives he was carrying. If he didn't get help, he would surely drown. Being a responsible citizen and abiding by the law of the land that requires you to help those in distress, I contacted the police, the Coast Guard, Homeland Security, and even the fire department." Eddie paused, looked all around the room, and continued. "Well, it's now 11 am, the Muslim terrorist has drowned, and none of the authorities have responded." Eddie paused again, looked directly at Steven, and said, "I'm starting to think I just wasted four good stamps!"

All gave low snickers as Eddie continued, "There are only three types in this world: sheep, wolves, and sheepdogs. We are the world's sheepdogs. If the government wants to prevent stable, law-abiding citizens from owning gun magazines that hold more than ten rounds, but gives twenty F-16 fighter jets and M1A1 Abrams tank brigades to the crazy new Muslim Brotherhood leaders in Egypt—you might live in a nation that was founded by geniuses but is run by idiots."

Snickers now turned into waves of laughter.

Captain Reacher, who commanded an M1A1 Abrams Battle Tank Company in Iraq, was nodding and laughing as well, Steven noticed. Captain G. Jack winked at Steven, who gave him a thumbs-up, as Eddie continued, "If being stripped of your constitutional right to defend yourself makes you 'safer' according to the government—you might live in a nation that was founded by geniuses but is run by idiots."

Eddie paused; the laughter was drowning him out. He paused as his audience wiped their eyes, then continued. "Seriously, everyone...one of our main witnesses, well hidden away, is Major Ernest Hemingway of Border Patrol-El Paso/Juarez, not his real name, thanks to one of Steven's favorite authors, who was fired by the administration after going public with the swap of assault rifles bought in the US in Arizona and smuggled to Juarez to Mexican cartel hit squads. His testimony alone could destroy the attorney general and assistant attorney general for border security and convict them of fifteen counts of conspiracy and treason, resulting in Texas death penalties for both. Major Hemingway is backed up by Arizona Border Control Captain Somerset Maugham, another of Steven's favorite authors, on medical leave, thought by the Washington, DC, border patrol establishment to be in Florida, convalescing after knee replacement surgery in June, but is well hidden and under guard in parts unknown."

Eddie looked around the room, smiled knowingly at everyone, and continued, "Both are key witnesses to the administration's treason and conspiracy in the open border jeopardy to our national security and Muslim terrorist entry in the Southern United States."

He looked at Steven. "Then there is Abu Ali Babba, not his real name either. He was caught crossing the border back to Mexico by local FBI and not reported to Washington by our friends in the local FBI office, all sympathetic patriots. We have given him full immunity and will give him a whole new identity physically. He's gonna become a real cowboy...might even start rooting for Texas in the annual Texas-Oklahoma football game."

Laughter again as Eddie continued, "This Muslim turned on his Muslim Brotherhood pals big-time and is connected to our other two witnesses, another Muslim Brotherhood plant, who's been to the White House forty-seven times along with another Hamas Muslim who was captured last August. We've named him Muhammad the Pedophile. Hamas, by the way, is the acronym for the Islamic Resistance Movement in Arabic, sometimes referred to by its followers as 'the Movement,' based in the West Bank and Gaza Strip and totally dedicated to the elimination of Israel. He's been living the good life on Texas Ranger hosting and is not aware of a rude awakening after he testifies to the grand jury and his testimony is videotaped when he is then turned loose right back to ISIL for decapitation."

Eddie paused a moment and focused on Steven. "Muhammad the Pedophile, obviously not his real name, is going to be one of Steven's key witnesses as he was a very influential Palestinian businessman and in charge of Hamas's Zakat, which is millions that are collected externally under humanitarian banners and routed to military and operational use, in addition to freeing up other funds for specific terrorist acts. Such uses include the provision of weapons, explosives, transportation services, safe houses, and job salaries for operatives. This guy is a major player in global Muslim terror and has direct links to Iran on the nuclear capability granted to them by the president, and he visited the White House almost thirty times."

He took a drink of water, a deep breath, and continued, "And then there are our initial and primary defendants, the Alvarado boys, father Alberto and sonny boy, Ricardo Alvarado, both like George Soros, Muslim financier, and Muhammad the Pedophile—all are scum and no better than the Muslim terrorists themselves."

They all chuckled. Beth was laughing along, but decidedly embarrassed, Steven noticed, and thought, *I wonder if she's a team player?*

"Plus, we have the Canadian Mounted Police, person unnamed and high in government in Quebec, as part of our Texas witness protection as well." Eddie Egen paused and looked around the room. He smiled at Steven and winked. "And having saved the best for last, and to make Steven's job in this special prosecution what the legal profession calls a slam dunk, we have one witness I called a Judas in the White House, now on extended leave from his White House staff position, who knows all the inner workings and is under Texas Ranger full protection."

Applause interrupted Eddie, who put up both hands. "All our special prosecution witnesses are well hidden and under twenty-four-hour protection somewhere in Texas. That's all I can say." Eddie looked directly at the two Texas Ranger leaders, Lucas Davenport and Johnnie Paulsen, and continued. "And I want to especially thank Lucas and Johnnie for all their work and leadership in the investigation of this case for the last four months since the initial indictment was filed before Steven was appointed by Mr. Martinez to file an amended indictment and lead this special prosecution. Thank you, Lucas and Johnnie. The Rangers know how to deal with these Muslim terrorists."

After the laughter died down, Major General John Nicholas again stood before all, looked at Steven, and asked the all-important question, "On what basis can the president be tied to an arrest warrant?"

Steven was ready. He had researched and given that question the most thought. "It will be for treason under Article 3, Section 3 of the Constitution of the United States which provides, 'Treason against the United States, shall consist only in levying War against them, or in adhering to their Enemies, giving them Aid and Comfort. No Person shall be convicted of Treason unless on the Testimony of two Witnesses to the same overt Act, or on Confession in open Court.'"

Steven continued, "In this special prosecution, we will enforce the Constitution of the United States of America and indict all defendants, including the president, for treason as defined in our Constitution, the ultimate law of our land. All defendants, especially the president, have as the Constitution provides 'adhered to our sworn enemies, giving our sworn enemies aid and comfort…and financing…money…as the Alvarado family, father Alberto and son Ricardo, have done…" Steven paused again. "And can prove to the grand jury by secret testimony of the Judas in the White House alone."

There was complete silence in the room for a full minute.

Breaking the silence, Eddie got up and walked over to the bar and picked up his Stetson, put it on. He was smiling as he looked at all gathered.

He had one final joke. "US presidential candidate Donald Trump and Canadian Prime Minister Stephen Harper are sitting in a bar. A guy walks in, sees the two sitting at the other end of the bar, so he asks the bartender, 'Isn't that Trump and Harper sitting over there?'

"The bartender answers, 'Yep, that's them alright!'

"So, the guy walks over and says, 'Wow, this is a real honor! What are you guys doing in here?'

"Donald Trump says, 'We're planning World War III, after I'm elected!'

"The guy says, 'Really? What's going to happen?'

"Stephen Harper says, 'Well, we're going to kill 140 million Muslims and one beautiful blonde!'

"The guy exclaimed, 'A beautiful blonde? Why kill a beautiful blonde?'

"Prime Minister Harper turns to President Trump and says, 'See, I told you, no one gives a crap about 140 million Muslims.'"

Only Beth was not laughing, Steven noticed.

– 27 –

Five good friends, two human and three animals, strolled toward the spectacular sunset, two leading their horses, the third exploring the vast desert, running around sniffing for God only knew what. Rommel was totally at ease, enjoying the cool sunset, only occasionally noticing desert life with detached interest as the dog roamed ahead, his master and horse Pegasus ambling along behind.

The daylong strategy meeting now over, Steven and Ed had been on a Saturday evening ride and were walking their horses to let them cool off. The setting sun painted a brilliant palette of colors in the vast Texas infinity. The two friends and their animals were completely alone in the enormity of the El Paso desert.

Eddie, walking beside Steven, had his reins on his shoulders as his favorite horse, Mijo, walked and followed with instinctive familiarity.

"Steven, why can't I have the same intimacy with Andi that I have with my horse?" Eddie was serious and sad. "You promised you would tell me the truth about what's wrong with me and why I don't have your serenity in my relationships, particularly with all my man-woman relationships and especially now with my wife."

"And I said that I would tell you the truth." Steven, still awed by the colors of the spectacular sunset, smiled. "But I might hurt your feelings."

"The truth will set you free, but first it will piss you off," Eddie intoned. "Another one of your favorite sayings."

"Yes, it is. But I value your friendship, and I'm not your shrink. So, I'll ask you again: Do you really want me to tell you, and it won't affect our friendship?"

"Yes, I do, and no, it won't," Eddie answered. "It seems like I'm on this lifelong fantasy to find a soul mate…that doesn't really exist. Steven, help me understand what's wrong with me."

"I was just waiting for you to ask. I wasn't going to bring it up unless you asked again." Steven paused. "My very favorite saying is, the ultimate of human freedoms…"

Eddie finished for Steven, "…is the God-given freedom of choice. I'm asking again. I'm really serious; I want to know."

"So, the good Lord really caught your attention?"

"As I lay there in the desert, upside-down, strapped into my seat, in that calm that descended on me, it was as if the good Lord was asking, 'What are you doing, Ed?' I couldn't answer. I need help. So yes, again, tell me!"

Steven was thoughtful. He would be talking to his friend, but he would also be talking about himself. Rommel trotted back to his side. Steven patted the dog's side and continued, "As I said, Eddie, let me tell you about the Oedipal complex, my friend!" Steven paused a beat. "Have you ever heard the old song 'I Want a Girl Just Like the Girl That Married Dear Old Dad'?" Steven looked directly at his friend walking beside him.

"I sure have!" Eddie replied. "It's an Irish barbershop quartet standard I've sung myself before." Eddie grinned. "Want me to sing it to you?"

Steven smiled as well. "No thanks, I don't want Rommel to start howling." Eddie chuckled as Steven continued, "Seriously, Eddie, as a result of our early relationship with our parents, and for us guys with our mothers, we youngsters have intimate feelings for our mothers especially." Steven *knew* he had his friend's attention now. "And on the other side, as youngsters we have a main competitor for Momma's affection, dear old Dad!"

Eddie was nodding as Steven continued. "It's that early tension we young boys feel that's the basis of the Oedipal complex. The affection and feeling for Momma, on the one hand, and the anger and jealousy against dear old Dad, our main competitor, on the other, who gets to sleep with Momma all the time. The feeling is more important than the act; I heard that somewhere."

"Gosh, Steven," Eddie interrupted. "I remember those exact feelings when I was a kid." Eddie swallowed. "Sometimes I would get so pissed off at my dad that I just wanted to kill him!"

Steven looked at his friend. "Eddie, you just broke the code on the Oedipal complex!" Steven knew that Eddie was really listening, so he continued, "In most cases, and if Mom and Dad are tight in their marriage, sonny boy grows up, lets that tension go, and finds a woman of his own, probably a lot like dear old Mom, get it?"

"I sure do," Eddie answered. "But what if that doesn't happen, the letting go?"

"Ed, you've asked the right question," Steven answered. "In many, many cases in this world, that does not happen for one reason or another, and we guys go through life looking for a soul mate or a 'pearl and only girl that Daddy ever had' and 'one who loves nobody else but you,' as the song goes, chasing an impossible dream, a sexually impossible dream that's enslaving. That's the feeling and emotion that we guys have to release before we can really be free." Steven looked at his friend directly. "Just remember, Eddie, the feeling is more important than the sexual act itself," he emphasized.

Steven paused, kept walking. Ed did also. He was listening. Frowning but still listening. Eddie was puzzled.

"That's exactly what I had to do, Eddie." Steven paused for full effect. "And it has taken me almost a lifetime to do it." Steven swallowed. "By the good Lord's guidance and with His grace freely given, and with the good Lord firmly and by choice in my heart, I was saved. First by the love of my children, and then by my own choice, with the grace of the good Lord. By sincere prayer, asking the Lord for help, I saved myself and saw who *I* am, not who I had been for others, but who I am! There is no one-upmanship in pain. It's all relative, but you had a stable upbringing and not nearly the dysfunctional family I had. You can do it, Eddie, keeping the good Lord in your heart now that you've asked Him to come in…"

Steven looked over at his friend and noticed that his eye was glistening. Eddie kept looking straight ahead as Steven continued, "Look at all that you have to be grateful for, Eddie, my friend."

Ed nodded his head slowly.

"You are a very good guy, Ed. Professionally, you're a true American hero and a true patriot. A great and honorable military career and now a real Texas leader in a war that's gripping our country. A drug, illegal immigration, and Muslim war, but I digress…you have a wonderful home and ranch and, last but not least, you have a wonderful wife, Andi…"

Eddie looked at Steven. "She's the one who filed for divorce."

"Ed, old buddy." Steven raised his eyebrows. "I've got another good wise saying for you, 'the buildup and breakdown of every relationship is always fifty-fifty.' My old mentor used to tell me that all the time. So, spare me, and yourself, the whining. What was *your* role in this breakdown?"

Eddie Egen said nothing. He was tearing up again, Steven noticed.

"Ed, I'm your friend, and I say this with all the love and kindness possible: you just are looking for love obsessively and in all the wrong places." Steven swallowed hard then continued. "I know…because I had…still have such an addiction. I'll work on it for a lifetime…the old saying goes: once an addict, always an addict."

Eddie was stunned. He stopped; his horse didn't. It nudged him from behind and stopped also. "Tell me, Steven. I'm listening. Please…" Tears glistened in Eddie's dark eyes.

"You're not a coward, Ed. You can beat it just like I did…control it really…and have some peace, serenity…and with Andi, happiness and joy. But *you* got to do it!"

"How do I do that, Steven?" Eddie resumed the walk, his horse again following.

Steven already knew. "I'm glad you asked again. You've been thinking about it for a while, haven't you? Of course, in your heart and mind, you already know it well because you have lived it. Going from woman to woman, without peace or satisfaction. Just like I have. Let's put it this way; you are already aware, but you don't understand it. It's going to take me, your friend, to lovingly and respectfully enlighten you so that you can really get it, make your own decision about this, and stop, and then do the hardest part, practice it, so you can be free once and for all. You have a choice, Ed! It's up to you."

Steven paused a few beats. "Only you can free yourself from that enslavement, just like I did, Ed, by making choices and taking your addiction through the therapeutic cycle, all with fervent prayer and the grace of the Lord, a gift that's freely given to us all." Steven put his arm around his friend and smiled again.

Eddie frowned. "The therapeutic cycle? What in the hell is that?"

Steven smiled. "One thing at a time, my friend! I'll tell you about that later…over a couple of six packs, okay?"

Eddie finally smiled. "Okay, my friend." He was feeling much better, Steven could tell.

"The main deal is that the two complexes are the basis of all the neurosis and evil on this planet and will lead to humanity's destruction," Steven said. "That's it for us guys, Eddie, it's the same for the ladies with their daddies, the Electra Complex it's called in psychoanalysis by the shrinks…"

"So, what do we do, Steven?" Eddie asked. "Who can we trust?"

Steven was ready. "Some trust in chariots, and some in horses, but we will remember the name of the Lord, our God! That's Psalm 20:7, Eddie. I was just reading it yesterday, trying to get guidance in my task ahead." He paused a moment and then continued, "And I have to be careful with that as I've had a tendency to trust my own abilities, street smarts, aggression, and survival rather than turning it over to the Lord, and as long as we continue to trust in our own abilities and activities, we gain nothing!"

"That's just like me," Ed said. "And my activities especially with sex and women got me nowhere but grief, hurt, and pain."

"Just like any other addiction," Steven finished.

Eddie could hardly speak. "I know what you're saying is true, but we all don't have to continue in it…there's got to be an alternative."

"Yes," Steven interjected. "But only to a point. It happened to me, so I know it can happen, but I also feel that there's salvation for the individual, regardless of humanity as a whole."

Eddie again looked a little quizzical, so Steven continued, "The best example of that in our contaminated pop culture is the movie *Pulp Fiction*. Did you see it, Eddie?"

Eddie nodded. "Yeah, it was great!"

"Yes, it was," Steven agreed. "It sure showed all the filth, corruption, and evil of a downward cycle that neurosis brings to humanity, but then one man, the Samuel Jackson character, the hitman Jules Winfield and his partner, the John Travolta character..." Steven was thinking.

"Vincent Vega," Eddie interrupted.

"Right!" Steven answered. "When the two were fired on by the fourth drug dealer coming out of the bathroom with a 44 Magnum, a real hand cannon, four shots...all of them missing the two...! Why did that happen, one may ask?" Steven raised his eyebrows.

"One guy said it was just chance," Eddie answered.

"Right again, Eddie!" Steven said. "But Jules, on the other hand, said it was a miracle. And that was the right answer...it was the grace of the Lord!"

Eddie was beginning to understand. "The Vincent Vega character was the doubter who thought it was only luck that they survived..."

Steven finished, "And Jules knew that it was a miracle and grace of the Lord, and it changed him just like grace changed me when Martin was trying to destroy and enslave me."

"Do you remember Jules quoting the Bible, Ezekiel 25:17?" Steven asked. "I've memorized it: 'The path of the righteous man is beset on all sides by the inequities of the selfish and the tyranny of evil man. Blessed is he, who in the name of charity and good will, shepherds the weak through the valley of darkness, for he is truly his brother's keeper and the finder of lost children. And I will strike down upon thee with great vengeance and furious anger those who would attempt to poison and destroy my brothers. And you will know my name is the Lord when I lay my vengeance upon thee.'"

"Wow" was all Eddie could say.

"And that's how you need to handle your addiction…the evil in your heart and soul. It's how I did with Martin and Glee …it's what I have said about dealing with the rest of the world, R.O.W. That sometimes with righteous anger…you have to drive the archangel's sword of righteousness into evil so it comes out on the other side…bloody and showing steel… bloody steel!" Eddie was looking at Steven, eyes wide open by Steven's intensity, as he continued, "And that's exactly how it is in R.O.W.! To a Vincent Vega, the sleazy, corrupt, evil in R.O.W. it all happens by chance, but to Jules, the good in R.O.W., everything happens by choice, the ultimate of human freedoms, and by grace and miracles of faith."

Eddie took a deep breath. "I understand now, my friend. Thank you! I understand the concept…but how do I do that, make the change in my heart, mind, and soul?" Eddie paused. "How?" he repeated, chilled by Steven's tone.

Steven replied, now smiling, "Both Martin King and Glee Robinson tried to destroy me, Eddie, but I was saved by grace and had been all my life…I just didn't know grace. I do know it now! Martin's neurosis and addiction ultimately destroyed him and Glee continued her own enslavement. Martin committed suicide after Project Triple X went down. Glee just plain became irrelevant like a puff of smoke. Eddie, you can do it! Not cure your addiction completely, but just control it…and find happiness with Andi!"

"So how do I do it, Steven?" Eddie was pleading almost as tears rolled down his cheeks. "I need your help…"

"No, you really don't," Steven answered. "You now have it within you. You now have grace in your heart. You've been washed by the blood of the Lamb…and have the good Lord and Jesus Christ in your heart, Eddie! You are just now recognizing it in your own heart."

Eddie was humbled. "I know now that the good Lord's grace is in my heart and has saved me many times in the past, without me even knowing it. I see that now, and I saw the good Lord catch my attention as I lay in an upside-down car in the desert."

"That's the start of the rest of your life, Eddie." Steven put his arm around his friend. "Let me quote John 14:6 for you: 'Thomas asked: Lord, we don't know where you are going, so how can we know the way? And Jesus answered: I am the way and the truth and the life. No one comes to the Father except through me.'"

Eddie was crying. Steven was also. The two friends stopped in the desert and hugged. Rommel, sitting on his haunches nearby, cocked his massive head to one side. The dog was actually smiling…

Steven and Eddie were now riding again side by side after a good run, both horses now just resting, when Eddie looked at Steven, smiling broadly.

Steven raised his eyebrows. He knew something funny was coming. "Tell me, Ed…"

"You know, Steven?" Eddie began. "Yesterday, after I mowed my lawn, I sat down and had a nice cold beer…"

Steven shook his head, still smiling. He hadn't heard this one. "The day was really quite beautiful, and the drink facilitated some deep thinking. Andi walked by and asked me what I was doing, and I said 'nothing.' The reason I said 'nothing' instead of saying 'just thinking' is because she then would have asked 'about what?' At that point I would have had to explain that men are deep thinkers about various topics, which would lead to other questions. I was really pondering an age-old question: Is giving birth more painful than getting kicked in the nuts, but how could we really 'know'? Well, after another beer, and some more heavy deductive thinking, I have come up with an answer to that question. Getting kicked in the nuts is more painful than having a baby, and even though I obviously couldn't really 'know,' here is the reason for my conclusion."

Steven complied, playing the straight man. "And your conclusion is?"

Eddie continued, "A year or so after giving birth, a woman will often say, 'It might be nice to have another child.' On the other hand, you never hear a guy say, 'You know, I think I would like another kick in the nuts.' I rest my case. It was time for another beer, and then maybe a nap in that hammock."

Steven laughed out loud. "Good one, Ed! I hadn't heard that one, but it really makes a lot of sense. Speaking of Andi, you've got a wonderful, goodhearted, gorgeous wife there, and you should thank the Lord every day that she's your…what, fifth wife?" Steven continued, "If you straighten yourself out, Eddie, you'll be a happy man! In my case, I've had several bad relationships, and am not happy, so I became a philosopher."

It was Eddie's turn to laugh out loud, which he did so raucously that its echo could probably be heard back at the compound, a genuine laugh probably resulting from the relief their conversation brought, Steven thought. Then Eddie turned serious and looked directly at his friend and said, "Steven, any decisions after our meeting?"

"Eddie, I've decided, after hearing all the evidence and seeing all the documents, that the president and his attorney general, all his czars and Muslim nut jobs in his cabinet, Defense Department, Education Department, Interior Department, and Homeland Security, should be rounded up and shot…no I'm joking…but all at least made party defendants in both our civil suit and criminal prosecution against all the Alvarado defendants with collateral criminal indictments filed and state criminal warrants issued for their arrests in Texas."

"You've given this a lot of thought, haven't you, buddy?" Eddie said.

"Yessir." Steven was calm. "I have also talked to my prosecution team… and Ernie Martinez, at length, over the last week…"

"And?" Eddie was smiling.

"All agree it's the only way we can save our country…the country we all love."

Eddie was solemn. "You realize the dangers?"

"I do."

"Go see the governor, Steven! You gotta be in every top-secret loop, and he knows you're going. I've called him already to let him know that you're going. Just you, okay?"

"I will."

- 28 -

The secret burner cell phone was vibrating in the pocket of Jason Warren's hoodie as he worked out at the west side El Paso's Gold's Gym, lifting weights in the main hall of the gym.

Jason pulled the cell phone out of his pocket and clicked it on. "Yes?"

The now familiar clipped voice said, "Good afternoon, Mr. Warren. Don't say anything; just walk out to your car in the parking lot right now." Jason did as he was told and, holding the phone to his ear, walked outside to where his car was parked.

Once at his snow-white Porsche, he looked all around, clicked the door open, sat on the driver's seat, and said, "I'm there."

The voice said, "There is another package on your passenger seat next to you and another burner cell phone. Follow the directions explicitly."

The line went dead.

Jason looked next to him. Saw another package just like the first one he received from the young Asian on the street. He picked it up to examine it; it was an identical brown wrapped package. He knew that he had been watched and that his car was entered and relocked as he specifically remembered locking it before going into the gym.

He again took out his small Swiss army knife from the glove compartment and slit open the package. Another note on top. He unfolded it and read,

"Mr. Warren, this new burner phone is our final link. You will receive your final instructions shortly. The cash is your next installment. Again, it is unmarked and completely sanitary."

Jason laid the note down, took out crumpled tissue again, but this time there were *four* separate packages. He already knew that this installment was another $25,000 total. He smiled to himself thinking of the final installment he was now planning of one million to have wired into his new secret Cayman Island account that would receive the wire transfer, an account Jason had opened after he found out the full extent of the caller's request for his unique services.

It was very late. Jason was in his office staring out at the spectacular view outside with his own computer monitors and keyboard right in front of him.

In the "Star Wars" computer control center, right outside his office, all the cubicles were deserted. The huge dynamic map wall board monitor had blinking lights like a giant pinball machine as always, flashing as the grid electrical current flowed to millions of customer terminals.

Jason was expecting another call on his private line. It was late, almost eleven o'clock, Mountain Standard Time. He had the burner cell phone in his pocket and had been instructed to be in his office at precisely eleven to accept his final instructions. He was looking out on the magnificent nighttime view from his office, not really seeing the electrical light show going on right outside as he was distracted by what he was planning to demand, when suddenly the burner cell phone in his pocket vibrated.

Jason, startled out of his thoughts, took the phone out and answered, "Yes?"

"Good evening, Mr. Warren, are you ready for your final instructions for the conduct of our test project?" the now familiar clipped-speech voice said in formal English.

"Yessir," Jason answered. He swallowed nervously and added, "Are *you* ready for *your* final instructions?" his voice cracking.

The voice was silent.

"Are you still there?" Jason asked. He held his breath momentarily.

"Yes, Mr. Warren. I am still here." The voice paused a beat, then continued. "But first, after our last conversation about our test project and what it entailed, you were going to tell me exactly how you would do it, Mr. Warren."

Jason exhaled and looked at his own reflection in glass to the dark outside. "With just a few focused keystrokes I can shut down the entire 2,500-square-mile area by changing settings in ways that will trigger cascading blackouts of the entire area, that I myself control from my desk. I have the *back-door* code to our remote terminal unit that's right in our control center, which is right outside my office, and I can command it to trip and reset all the breakers. That, sir, would incapacitate all our substations that control all the electricity distribution points for the entire area where high-line voltage electricity is transformed for local use by changing the settings on substations' programmable circuit breakers by lowering the settings from 500 amperes to 200 amperes on some breakers, while raising others to 900 amperes."

"But…but what would that do?" the speaker asked.

Jason continued to watch his own reflection in the glass. "Normal electrical power usage could trip the 200-amp breakers and take those lines out of service, diverting power and overloading neighboring lines." He was especially proud of his secret "back door" as it was his key to the million-dollar final installment he would demand for the service he would perform.

The speaker feigned confusion. "But how specifically will that carry out the desired effect of our test project?"

"As you might know," Jason answered, full of himself, "line voltage refers to the voltage that is available in standard residential or commercial wall outlets—"

"I know all that," the voice interrupted rather sarcastically, Jason thought, as the caller continued, "but what has that to do with our test project?"

"It's got everything to do with the test project you're paying me for," Jason said, oblivious to the ramifications of a test and money he was betraying his country for. "In the United States, this voltage is almost always in the neighborhood of 120 VAC, though it's commonly referred to as 110 VAC or 117 VAC…in other parts of the world, that may be lower or higher…"

"I've got all that, Mr. Warren! But how is that relevant to our transaction?"

Jason Warren couldn't contain himself. "Well, in Europe, line voltage is called main voltage or just plain mains…and line voltage, let me tell you, kills!" Jason paused for effect and drama, mesmerized by the sound of his own voice and his reflection in the window glass. "In real-world projects, line voltage is absolutely necessary, while for all others just plain batteries, that will wear out, will do just fine." Jason paused, proud of his own blinders, as he continued, "Batteries, of course, wear out and are the lifeblood of most electronic components of the computer system I've designed and now completely control…"

The voice cut him off. "All that is just great, Mr. Warren! I just want our test project to be successful, and that's what I hired you for! Do you understand me?" The voice was complete ice.

An oblivious Jason Warren rambled on, "Generators make electrical power and converters convert to 120 VAC line voltage to more useful 5 VAC. Transformers take line voltage down so it's useful to residential and retail customers," he finally finished.

The voice was finished as well. "Let us get right to our test project, Mr. Warren! Describe the 'back door' to the computer system that you yourself created."

Sensing that the speaker was getting annoyed with him, Jason placated, "With their breakers set at 900 amps—too high to trip—the overloads would cause transformers and other critical equipment to melt down, requiring major repairs that would prolong a blackout."

The speaker remained silent, so Jason continued, "There are a plethora of intelligent electrical devices going into substations and power stations all over the United States. What's to keep somebody from accessing those devices and changing the settings?"

"And how is that relevant to our test project, Mr. Warren?" the voice asked in a hushed icy voice.

The moment that Jason Warren had been waiting for was upon him. "Some of the most technically advanced relays, made by companies like Schweitzer Engineering, General Electric, and Siemens, can be programmed over a telephone modem connection after typing a simple eight-digit password!"

"Yes, we know about General Electric Corporation…and well know that hackers have very little trouble cracking an eight-digit password and finding substation phone lines that connect to these relays. It can be done with so-called 'war dialers,' simple PC programs that dial consecutive phone numbers looking for modems." The voice paused again. "That still does not answer my question. Therefore, I ask you again…how will you get the desired effect of our test project?"

Jason sighed audibly. "Try to understand that developing a functional exploit, getting it placed on the exact part of the network that it needs to be on to have the desired effect, i.e. specific programmable logic controllers that run the utility's machinery, then keeping it hidden on that network over a period of months or years while security teams try to hunt it down, and doing all of this at the same time on hundreds of networks is extremely difficult. To put it into perspective, it would be like trying to rob a hundred different banks at the exact same time," Jason said, very proud of his clever analogy. "As you might know, all our electrical grids are monitored and supervised by supervisory control and data acquisition systems having software and hardware elements that allow our company to control electrical line voltage locally or at remote locations; the monitors gather and process real-time data."

"Yes, Mr. Warren, I know all about SCADA systems of high-level supervisory management…"

Jason interrupted the speaker. "That's my point exactly! My 'back door' completely bypasses the control system architecture that I myself created, and my eight-digit password will allow you in the back door where your test project can be accomplished."

"So what are your terms for the eight-digit password?" the speaker asked impatiently.

"One million US dollars wired into an account, the number of which I will text to you. Then, upon receipt of the wire transfer confirmation, and only then, will I text the eight-digit password for your use." He did not tell the speaker that immediately after its single use, his "back door" to the entire system would erase itself automatically.

The voice again: "And how will we know that the eight-digit password is not a fake number?"

"You won't! You'll just have to trust that it gives you access to the entire system to conduct your test project."

"Mr. Warren, listen very carefully," the voice said in clipped English. "I know where you live…I know all about your sweet little daughter Michelle and your son Jacob." The caller paused momentarily. "And I even know all about your nurse wife, Jillian!"

"Are you threatening me?"

"No, Mr. Warren, I am not," the voice said. "Just a bit more persuasion if the test turned out badly. . . or not at all."

"The test will be a total success," Jason blurted. "I have programmed the system, have reprogrammed the back door to it, and will text the code to you upon receipt of our agreed upon amount by wire transfer in the account number I will also text to you. I'll specify that account number on the text message as well. Once I have confirmation of the wire transfer, I will text you the password to the back door of the system."

"Very well, Mr. Warren. Your instructions are understood." The speaker paused. "You will be contacted for the last time on this phone, forty-eight hours precisely before when you should text the eight-digit password."

Jason Warren, now emboldened, repeated himself: "At that time, I will text you the eight-digit code and you *will* wire transfer the money, my money, into the account whose number I will text to you as well! Then and only then, and upon receipt of payment wire transfer receipt confirmation, will I give you that password! Do you understand?" Somewhat incoherent now with excitement, he smiled at his own image in the plate-glass window of his office.

"Was the amount you received already satisfactory?" the speaker asked, redirecting Jason to the test project again.

"It was, but I need more. I'm going to protect my children."

"Your son's complete college education will be taken care of if the test is successful."

"It will be!" Jason finished and clicked off.

The line went dead.

– 29 –

The governor of Texas, the governor's chief of staff, and Steven Vandorol were in a small private conference room at the governor's mansion in Austin, Texas. Steven had reviewed the evidence in detail, both witness testimony and documentary, and concluded by making the same recommendation to the governor that he had made to Ernie Martinez and Eddie Egen.

"Governor, especially in view of last month's Islamist terrorist attack of people in a retirement party and twenty-seven people killed…" Steven paused then continued, "You've got to close the border into Mexico, especially to Muslims, all Muslims. Just round them up like the leading presidential candidate is telling the American people he will do if he is elected."

"I agree with him. As a matter of fact, we really need to deport all radical Muslims, or round them up and put them in concentration camps…just like we did with Germans, Italians, and Japanese during World War II, by executive order of President Roosevelt." The governor paused, thought for several seconds, then continued, "General Nicholas and Eddie Egen both called me about you, Steven."

"Yes, governor, I know. Eddie told me that he did. What do you want me to do?" Steven asked.

"Nothing said today in this room leaves here." The governor looked directly at Steven. "I'm counting on your absolute discretion about what I'm about to tell you. Both General Nicholas and Eddie Egen cleared you to know…"

"Governor, you can count on me!" Steven said.

"I know I can." The governor was solemn. "There is a core within the Pentagon, State Department, CIA, and FBI that will take over Washington, DC, and the federal government on the day after election night."

Steven was stunned, swallowed, but said nothing as the governor continued, "The four joint chiefs, Army, Marine Corps, Navy, and Air Force, will be the joint military leadership that, after the takeover of Washington,

190

will install the winning candidate, swearing him or her to the Constitution of the United States of America as every president in our history has been."

Steven said nothing.

The governor continued. "All military bases will go on lockdown, just as during 9/11, including Fort Bliss."

Steven still said nothing.

"And all military bases will be on high alert." The governor was perspiring, dabbed his forehead with his hand, and continued. "The border with Mexico will be closed completely by me, and the governors of Arizona and New Mexico will close their borders as well, and the borders will be secured by all three National Guards."

Steven still said nothing but thought about California.

"The California-Mexico border will be closed and secured by 3rd Cavalry, leaving Ft. Bliss twenty-four hours before election eve on November 7, with 3rd Apache Helicopter Group leaving Biggs Field twelve hours later."

Steven thought about Captain G. Jack Reacher, his good friend. *I'll say a prayer for him,* he thought as the governor continued. "The FBI will be closing all mosques nationwide and arresting all radical Muslims on their terror lists, and our insiders with the Canadian government will shut down the US-Canada border, with Canadian Mounted Police securing all critical border crossings. Any questions so far?"

Steven was ready. "What about the mainstream media and the internet?"

"Good question, Steven. All radio and television will be satellite blocked, and internet servers will also be blocked. Only secure military communication will be open, and the New York, Chicago, Los Angeles, and Washington, DC, electrical power grids will be interrupted for forty-eight hours."

Steven was awed. "So, what do you want me to do?"

"Just keep on what you're doing," the governor answered. "We are counting on your special prosecution and indictment to rally the American people to support the rule of law."

"What guarantee is there that the joint chiefs' military leadership will not remain in power after the takeover and refuse to install the legitimately elected president?"

The governor said, "The grace of God and our Lord and Savior Jesus Christ."

It was Steven's turn to say, "Good answer, governor," who continued, "Did you see the last State of the Union speech, Steven?"

"No, I didn't. I had to spend some time organizing my sock drawer," Steven joked. "It was a real mess…like our country."

"Well, it was a joke…on us, our country, and the vast majority of the silent majority," the governor said, laughing also. "It was like a bunch of the Walking Dead with pasted-on masks listening to the Muslim court jester lie through his teeth and all the dead nodding in agreement."

"It's kind of like the naked emperor, the emperor with no clothes," Steven agreed. "And nobody to yell out that the guy is naked! So, who is going to lead this military takeover?"

"Likely the chairman of the joint chiefs of staff." The governor paused, thoughtful. "Steven, you are now one of only about fifty people in the country privy to this, but former General Petraeus comes out of retirement and becomes chairman of the joint chiefs of staff."

"Wow!" Steven was almost dazed. "I'm both honored that you told me and awed by the responsibility of knowing. Thank you."

"You're welcome, Steven." The governor smiled. "You are at the spear point of this revolution and civil war against our federal government in DC, and from all I know about you now, you are the right man at the right time in our nation's history."

"Thank you again, governor. But I've survived only by the grace of the good Lord and all the many angels He designated to help me survive." Steven paused, tearing up.

"We're all in the good Lord's hands, Steven. God's grace is sufficient for us anywhere His providence places us."

Quoting 1 Thessalonians 5:18, Steven finished, "In everything give thanks, for this is the will of God. If the good Lord brings me to this, He will take me through it!"

"Well put," the governor said. "Our faith in God will carry us through this. Do you have any questions?"

"Onward and upward," Steven said. "Now I know why the president is trying to destroy General Petraeus by stripping him of all military benefits. Do you think they have any hint of the takeover?"

The governor laughed. "I don't think so, for two reasons: first, like most politicians in Washington, including most Republicans, are all clueless as to what's happening in this country…and so is all the rest of our world, while our Muslim-planted president is intentionally 'transforming' our country like he promised, by the way, with all that hope and change crap." The governor paused. "Second, and more important, we have insiders at the FBI and CIA who are a part of the takeover."

Steven thought about Courtney Wellington but said, "Can Petraeus be trusted to ultimately turn over the governing to the democratically elected president, which may be the Republicans' Trump, Cruz, or Rubio?"

"I think so. He does have many in the FBI and CIA and most active and retired military right behind him. They can't stand the Muslim puppet either, having singlehandedly gutted the military by forcing retirement on over two thousand top-echelon line officers nationwide."

"Governor, do you think the general was compromised with the American people by the corrupt media that reported that he shared classified information with his mistress biographer, by sharing it in emails, left in the draft folder of a joint Gmail account?"

"No, I really don't," the governor said. "After all, as Jesus Christ said, 'Know them by their fruits.'"

Steven added, "And Petraeus is a moral man and the most decorated man of our time, and Christ also said for us failed humans to be forgiving."

The governor finished, "Right, Steven, and the American people will also."

"With the good Lord's grace?" Steven said.

"With the good Lord's grace!"

And on principles and fruits, not on love of materials, money and power. On the basis of John 14:6 where Christ is the way and the life and no one gets to the Father except through Him, Steven thought, but said, "May God help us all." He sat back and looked at the governor.

The governor sat for a long time, thinking. Steven saw that he was in turmoil internally, as he finished as well, "Steven, thank you for your clear analysis and recommendations. I will consider it all carefully. You talk with Mike only, and then I will let you know, through Mike's personal call within the next few days...and this is the last time we'll, you and I, will talk about this, okay?" The governor rose from his chair and came toward Steven, hand extended.

Steven nodded and shook the governor's hand.

"Well, Steven, as an Oklahoma Law School grad, but now an adopted Texas son, who are you rooting for in tomorrow's game in the Cotton Bowl?"

Steven broke into a broad smile and said, "That's my secret."

- 30 -

"I'll have the lobster and steak combination, the steak medium rare, Caesar salad, and another bottle of Dom Perignon," said General Wang Xiangsui, major general in the People's Army of Communist China, and aka Mr. Horohito Hayakawa, Japanese businessman, Toyota Motors US executive from San Francisco, to the white-coated waiter at the Dome Grill Restaurant and the main dining room of the elegant Camino Real Hotel in downtown El Paso.

Built in 1912, the marvelous hotel was an El Paso landmark located in the heart of the city's revitalized downtown area, adjacent to the convention center and the Plaza Theater.

"Very good, Mr. Hayakawa," the waiter replied, picking up the menu. "And what are you having for lunch, Mr. Powell?"

Powell put down his menu. "I'll have the same...and coffee, black."

"Yessir." The waiter picked up his menu and left.

The general looked directly at Ward. "Hung over, Powell?" He sipped his champagne daintily. He knew Powell very well.

He looks like a giant toad, Ward thought, but only nodded. He wasn't about to tell the general that he had spent the last two days right up on the seventeenth floor of this same hotel in bed with his El Paso contact.

"So, you made contact with your harlot?" General Xiangsui knew all the players very well. His intelligence had to be much better than the KGB's, or anyone else's for that matter, but especially better than that of the United States. For now, General Xiangsui would follow the old American Mafia adage that you have to keep your friends close and your enemies closer.

"She almost killed me," Ward admitted with a sly smile. He swallowed then continued. "I know her well. Have known her since I was in DC." He didn't share the fact that she was still upstairs on the top floor of the hotel.

"I know" was all the general said. "Tell me about the rest."

The waiter pushed the salad cart to their table and began making the salad.

Both remained silent while the waiter prepared the Caesar salad. He finished, gave them both their salads, and said, "Enjoy...gentlemen," then pushed the cart away.

"The strike team and reinforcements from Canada are now in place in safe houses in Canutillo and downtown El Paso." Powell was proud, as if he had done it all himself.

General Xiangsui noticed. "And what about the El Paso faction that was here already?" He knew the answer to that as well.

Ward said, "They screwed up big-time! First they messed up the killing of El Paso Police Chief Eddie Egen..."

Xiangsui was eating his salad, nodding. "I know...continue, Mr. Powell."

"...and then they screwed up killing Vandorol when he was on his early morning run and his dog woke up the whole neighborhood barking."

Xiangsui interrupted again. "I know about that one as well!"

Ward thought, *then why did you ask, you sloppy fat pig?* but said, "Colonel Liang said that you would deal most harshly with the offenders."

"I will," the general said. "What about the rest of them here in El Paso?"

"Colonel Lemev's got them handled...at arm's length...not telling them anything...specifically not telling anything to the stupid Muslims."

"Mr. Powell, don't underestimate them. They're vicious and ruthless," Xiangsui said, screwing up his mouth as if the Caesar salad had urine in it. He already marked all of them for death as soon as the El Paso mission in the takeover was complete.

"I won't. Colonel Lemev isn't either. He agrees with your buddy Liang about the mission entirely." Ward was finished.

Xiangsui wasn't. "Liang is not my buddy, Mr. Powell. You better show him some respect." He daintily ate his salad.

Ward swallowed. "I was just kidding." He looked down and got a forkful of salad.

General Xiangsui knew Ward Powell very well. "This is not a vacation! Colonel Liang is our ablest intelligence officer, and he would just as soon kill you than look at you."

It was Ward's turn. "I know" was all he said.

"So what's the plan?" The general knew the answer, already having talked to his co-author at length, even telling his co-author and dear friend, Qiao Liang, about the year of the horse surprise. He just wanted to know what Ward had to say.

Ward answered, "The first step is to kill Steven Vandorol...and I'd like for you, general, to let me get Colonel Liang to lead the strike team...on an assault on his home on Golden Hill Terrace." *Granted,* Ward thought, *it's going to really piss Lemev off...but I need to keep Lemev off balance, make him my confidant, then jerk the rug out from under him by killing him.* "Then we're killing all the others on the special prosecution team including Egen."

"Granted." The general ate some more of his salad, paused, and continued. "What do we know about their secret witnesses?"

"I think they are somewhere in New Mexico, general," Ward answered, frowning.

The general very deliberately put his fork down. "That's all you have, Mr. Powell? You guys had twenty-four men, three Muslim plants, a group of cartel gunmen, several insiders...in both the ranch and the prosecution team...and you tell me 'somewhere in New Mexico'?"

Ward said nothing.

"Get the Alvarados on it, Mr. Powell!" the general exclaimed. "Father and son, they have all the corruption and sleaze in DC, Juarez, Mexico City, and El Paso right on their personal payroll!" The general wasn't finished. "It's just like in DC... where they are all on somebody's payroll." He paused, took a bite of his salad, and continued. "After all, Ricardo is the leader of the Juarez drug cartel, one of the biggest in Mexico...*El Chapo* they call him...is responsible for almost 40 percent of the drug traffic coming across the southern border to satisfy America's insatiable appetite for drugs..." The general was chuckling. "America is fast becoming a nation of addicts!"

Ward already knew about the Alvarados, especially drug lord Ricardo Alvarado now and before in DC. "You mean like the Clinton Foundation Mafia have your communist China on your payroll with national secrets?"

Ward thought he would impress the general with his knowledge of world politics.

The general wasn't impressed. "Mr. Powell, you're full of it…as the old American saying goes. We Chinese own America by virtue of its wasted, bloated big government ways…we'll be foreclosing very soon… it's all about the money—access to it, power over it, and for Washington, DC, politicians, getting personally wealthy. It's the way of humanity, has been since the beginning of time…and we, the kings of the East…as is prophesied in the Christian Bible… we Chinese will own it all. I want Vandorol, his team, anybody associated with him, anyone he cares about… all eliminated right now…no more excuses! But be careful with Vandorol; he's getting a tremendous amount of public support in Texas and nationally as a conservative media spokesman, and he has been the ultimate survivor through Germany after World War II, Brazil, United States, and even Japan…where his aunt and uncle—"

"I know all about them," Ward interrupted, smiling smugly.

"Don't interrupt me again, Mr. Powell!" Properly chastised, Ward looked down at his food, and the general continued, "…took young Vandorol on a tour of duty. So, he even has an Asian perspective…as such he could be a dangerous adversary. Don't take him for granted or not seriously."

Ward was nodding, eyes blank, not really listening.

The general noticed. *His monstrous hubris and addiction give him a completely closed mind*, he thought to himself.

The general reached to the chair opposite Ward and pulled out two folded newspapers, both the *El Paso Herald-Chronicle* and Sunday *Dallas Morning Clarion*, handed them to Ward, and with an evil grin on his fat face said, "Here, read about the new conservative superhero, Mr. Powell… when he was a big shot in the Sunbelt before he killed us in DC. I guess you missed it?"

Ward blushed noticeably. He had missed three days of national news while in bed with his El Paso contact. He unfolded the *El Paso Herald-Chronicle* first and kept the *Dallas Morning Clarion* in his lap while he read…

El Paso Herald-Chronicle

Volume 113, Issue 282 Sunday, November 15, 2015   35¢

VANDOROL NOVEL DETAILS RISE, FALL OF OIL AND REAL ESTATE EMPIRE

Steven Vandorol enjoyed all the luxuries that an oil and real estate rich economy could give. He drove Lamborghini and Ferrari sports cars, flew about in a private Lear jet, made mega-million real estate and oil and gas deals in his plush suite of offices and lived in a Sunbelt mansion.

Vandorol began his own law firm in the early 2000's—specializing in real estate law and was quickly recognized as one of the best real estate lawyers in the state. Less than seven years after opening his firm, Vandorol was lead counsel in more than $2 billion worth of real estate transactions and represented almost 50 Oklahoma, Colorado and Texas banks, four real estate mortgage companies, a mortgage banking investment concern, five regional insurance companies and numerous venture capital corporations.

Vandorol's success gave him a lifestyle most people only dream about. However, that dream faded as his investments turned sour and he found himself caught up in a whirlpool of litigation and bad banking and real estate deals.

From January to November 2005, in addition to practicing law, Vandorol was the interim chief executive officer of a major venture capital corporation conducting business in Colorado, Oklahoma, Texas, Florida and Georgia. In the late fall, an over $100 million lawsuit was filed, the first of many naming Vandorol as co-defendant, stopping his real estate empire "dead in the water."

A few weeks later, a major client bank was declared insolvent, starting an international toppling of financial dominoes that has not yet fully played out.

Even though the suit was dismissed in December 2007, Vandorol remained a defendant in other litigation. He was a victim of the economic bust that sparked the worst economic decline since the Great Depression.

His story, told through the eyes of a fictionalized character, is at the heart of his recently released novel. The thick paperback book is currently enjoying Southwest and national popularity.

Despite the central theme of the novel, Vandorol is quick to point out, *Sunbelt* is not another "boom and bust" book," the author said.

"We've had plenty of books that deal with the oil-and-gas boom and crash. But they totally ignored the even greater real estate crash that happened after the energy crash. Half of the story remained untold—real estate wasn't even touched on," said Vandorol.

Until now.

The main character of the novel is an attorney—a man who lived life much like Vandorol once did. The story traces his life—in the grip of forces beyond his control—as he falls from multimillionaire status to bankruptcy. The book details from an insider's point of view the booming real estate industry and its cataclysmic fall as a result of the mortgage securities debacle initially caused by the Clinton administration. That cataclysmic drop forced banks to make substandard mortgage loans that was compounded by Wall Street speculation in mortgage securities, which then caused the great "fake" recession of 2006, vaulted Obama to the presidency and kept him there for a second term, handily defeating the Republican Romney in 2012. The book was written while Vandorol practiced law in Washington, DC.

But the novel probes even deeper, exploring the psychology of the event through the eyes and minds of its characters.

"It's about being caught up in a lot of things and having the world fall down around your head," said Vandorol. "Writing the novel was a way for me to put it all down and into perspective. It was a way for me to flush the hurt and pain from my system."

He called writing the novel "therapy."

Currently, Vandorol practices law here in El Paso and leads the special prosecution team in Case No. 2015-1234 now pending in the District Court of El Paso County, 65th Judicial District, State of Texas, where the Alvarados, father Alberto and son Ricardo, El Paso Power & Electric Company, Kemper & Smith, El Paso attorneys, Washington, DC, law firm Henderson & Lane, Attorneys, and other defendants, both named and unnamed co-conspirators. The investigations resulted in Texas state indictments last June by a special grand jury called by Chief District Judge Kathy Carbon, at the joint request of the governors of Texas, New Mexico, Arizona and Oklahoma.

The indictment has national implications, District Attorney Ernesto Martinez said, and involves vast corruption at the highest levels of our federal government in Washington, D.C., Denver, New York and Los Angeles.

Vandorol came to know intimately the insider world of Washington, DC, where he practiced law with the K Street law firm Henderson & Lane one of the defendants.

"I was in Washington, DC, in the belly of the beast after leaving the Sunbelt's oil and real estate booms and big crash and recession that followed, and was working for Henderson & Lane, which specializes in political lobbying. Washington is the center of politics and power in the entire world," said Vandorol. "Unfortunately, like everything else in the world, that center has been corrupted by greed, power and evil. Writing the book was a time-consuming and gut-wrenching process. A slow and painful one, it was my therapy, full of personal blood, sweat and tears."

Once the story was written down, Vandorol said, "then it is separated [from me] and I can put it behind me and learn from that."

Ward Powell folded the paper and looked directly in the general's eyes. "So, the conservative superhero is an author just like you and your *buddy* Liang, right?" Powell had a smug look on his face. He took the folded Sunday *Dallas Morning Chronicle*, tucked it under his arm, and said, "I'll read this crap later...thanks for dinner, general," and moved toward the door of the Dome Grill, smiling.

The general's voice was ice. "The United States is at risk of cyber-attacks which we Chinese have perfected, and as I wrote in *my* book."

Ward stopped, swallowed nervously, and sat right back down as the general continued. "All critical infrastructure networks including the electric power grids, utilities, oil and gas refineries and pipelines, water treatment plants, and transportation networks are vulnerable to cyber-attacks and have already been prioritized at the highest levels of our government by the chairman himself." There was an ominous tone in his clipped enunciation. "Destroy nine interconnection substations and a transformer manufacturer and the entire US electrical grid would be down for at least eighteen months, probably longer. That lengthy outage would be possible for several reasons, including that only a handful of US factories build transformers, including General Electric Corporation, which is completely dependent on our Chinese markets for its very survival," the general finished with palpable pride and broad ear-to-ear smile on his fat face

Ward was looking at the general with a blank stare as he thought, *I don't care about all that crap*, but managed, "What's the main short-term priority? For our purposes right now."

The general smiled. "We're working on a New Year's Year of the Horse surprise."

The general again looked like Jabba the Hutt who had just swallowed a lizard, Ward thought, but said, "It'll be the year of the horse on the Chinese zodiac calendar…"

"Correct, Powell, and it symbolizes the five elements, which are fire, earth, water, metal, and wood, and we will cover America with that fire." The general paused a moment, smiled with his fat jowls raising his eyebrows. "And I've subverted a fool American to do just that and who is now irrelevant and expendable collateral damage, as is his entire family, as the Americans are fond of saying."

The general continued, "With a few focused keystrokes, our hackers could shut the computer networks down—or change the settings in ways that might trigger cascading blackouts, even bypassing SCADA systems entirely. After all, we in the military have been actively involved in stealing American dual-use technologies, as well as smuggling restricted materials through Hong Kong, Taiwan, and other trans-shipment centers, into our China." The general chuckled. "President Clinton even illegally authorized the transfer of America's most guarded ballistic missile technology, the Chinagate Scandal, in return for over ten million in contributions to his campaign and foundation."

Ward Powell had a blank look on his face. "What do you want me to do, general?"

"I've got a little job for your team, Mr. Powell," General Xiangsui answered. "Get your driver Uri on it or anyone else you can trust to do it well." The general paused. "I'll give you their names in the next few days with details. I want no traces…or evidence. Got it?"

"Yes, general," Powell answered. He was already thinking of her. . .

31

After record heat, cold front should blow in

The Dallas Morning Clarion

Dallas' Leading Newspaper $3.00 Dallas, Texas
Sunday, November 15, 2015

NEW AMERICAN REFORMATION LED BY TEXAS SECOND AMERICAN CIVIL WAR

UPI—Dallas. Texas spiritual leaders believe God's grand plan for Texas is to lead the New American Apostolic Reformation and Second American Civil War.

"Our spiritual leaders call Texas 'The Prophet State,'" a former Texas governor said to a capacity crowd of over 250,000 Christians and Tea Party faithful during the Restoration of Love conference amassed at AT&T Stadium in Arlington this past weekend in Dallas.

The former governor asked God for "wisdom, guidance, strength and courage to repel the cancer of evil that is destroying our great nation from within and to bless this great state in the coming Second American Civil War." Thunderous applause resounded as the crowd raised their hands skyward.

"This Washington administration and progressives in both political parties, allied with Islamist radical terrorists, worldwide communists, Marxist and socialist extremists, have this generation in a demonic stronghold of evil," the former governor said.

"That the Texas Army of God was joined by the United States of America, a coalition of states which would reassert the Constitution as intended by our founding fathers," former Governor Perry continued as the capacity crowd fell completely silent...

"We the people of the Reformed United States, in order to form a more perfect union, establish justice, insure states' rights tranquility, provide for the common defense, promote the security of our borders and secure the blessings of liberty to ourselves and our children, do ordain and establish this Constitution for the Reformed United States of America, the Constitution of the United States of America as ordained and established by our founding fathers after the Constitutional Convention held in Philadelphia, Pennsylvania, and presided by George Washington, our great founding father, so help us Lord and His Son, Jesus Christ. Amen."

In a rousing speech interrupted by numerous standing ovations, the former governor detailed those responsible for the "evil" encompassing this nation and the world, and said the current president and his administration have committed treason and betrayed the people of the United States by: opening our borders to Muslim terrorists, giving nuclear weapons to Iran and betraying our sole ally in the Middle East, the State of Israel.

———

The rest of his speech is printed fully and verbatim, as follows:

"We have an administration and State Department that sent a known homosexual to a rabid Muslim snake pit of Libya, where Shi'ite Muslims summarily behead homosexuals, all without any security whatsoever, and then blamed an anti-Muslim video on YouTube, which hardly anyone has seen, to let, or abet, or intentionally conspire with, the Muslim world to catch it on fire, when even the Libyan president himself admitted that the attack was a pre-planned terrorist attack by Muslim terrorists.

"An administration that has neutered our military and rendered our intelligence community impotent, and intentionally continues to gut it and conspires with Muslims against our allies.

"The Muslim Brotherhood the president put in power in Egypt salivates for the blood of Americans and war with Israel. Egypt has since ousted Morsi and is expelling Muslim radicals at every opportunity. The first thing the new Egyptian military dictatorship did was get rid of Morsi and outlaw the Muslim Brotherhood. The military dictatorship then took over the billions of military hardware, tanks and fighter jets previously sent to radical Muslim Morsi.

"The people we put in power in Libya won't or can't confront the Islamists who butcher US diplomats in the streets. For the civilized world, the Arab Spring is turning into a season of hell.

"The president steadfastly refuses to create a redline, the crossing of which would bring military retaliation against Iran. The Mullah-ocracy is just a few months away from getting nuclear weapons. Our Cairo embassy apologizes to the flag-burning mob for a video that offends Muslim sensibilities that no one saw.

"The president, a Muslim himself, is going to declare himself dictator and will continue living in the White House as America dies, or in Washington, DC, even after the national elections in November.

"That the president is committed to flooding the country with illegal aliens to dilute our national character. That his order to end the deportation of illegals under thirty is just the first stage of an undeclared war on our borders: Get them in. Get them on public assistance. Get them voting Democratic Party.

"That the president sympathizes with Islamists and will do nothing to stop their march to power throughout the Muslim world, and believes we brought 9/11 on ourselves, that the Muslim Brotherhood is a force for progress in the world and that Israel, a sovereign nation which he truly despises, must be eliminated by a one-state solution where Jews will be a minority.

"That this is a president whose rage was fueled by his associations—Frank Marshall Davis, Rev. Jeremiah Wright, Bill Ayers, Bernadine Dohrn, Rashid Khalidi, Edward Said, Derrick Bell, Fr. Michael Pflieger, Van Jones, MoveOn.org, Code Pink, ACORN, Occupy Wall Street and Sol Elinsky, the one who wrote the Bible of the progressives, 'Rules of Radicals,' which is dedicated to Lucifer. And, last but not least, former Nazi concentration camp guard during World War II, Hungarian-American George Soros.

"When the truth is eventually told, the chronicles of the president's years will represent the most sordid in American history and symbolize a pivot point when self-serving politicians collaborated with a compliant press to trigger the fall of the American republic.

"If they win, the American people should be prepared for economic collapse, a full assault on constitutional rights, societal fragmentation and civil war.

"There is a criminal in the White House who is bent on a radical transformation of the country and must be removed from office if the United States is to survive.

"But representative government will not return to America simply by defeating the president. It will only return when ordinary Americans feel empowered by their political institutions, not oppressed by them.

"I believe it's time we stand up for what we believe.

"Fellow Americans must support the people of the Reformed United States, now comprised of the states of Texas, Arizona, New Mexico, Oklahoma, Arizona, Colorado, Missouri, Arkansas and Louisiana, and the joint indictment led by Texas filed in El Paso County District Court and executed prior to the November general election.

"In God we trust."

32

In the elegant lobby of the El Paso Camino Real Hotel, Ward finished reading the Sunday *Dallas Morning News* article, refolded the paper, and noisily ripped the several pages in half, saying out loud, "What a pile of crap." When he looked around, he saw an old couple leaving that were staring at him. Ward glared in their direction as they hurried out the massive circular doorway to his obscene gesture following them.

Ward slammed the torn newspaper into the lobby trash and walked over to a corner easy chair grouping, looked all round—the lobby was empty, even the front desk was unmanned—took out his cell phone, sat down, and dialed. Putting the phone to his ear, he said, "What are you doing right now?" Listened, his smile widening.

"Nah, I'm way too tired…"

Listened…

"Yeah, I thought this place would be better than the Artesian when I found out the fat gay general was staying right here as well." Ward paused a moment. "Yeah, I'm a funny guy… Hey, seriously, I've got a couple of little jobs for you." He listened again, said, "I need the plans and specifications for Vandorol's house up on Golden Hill Terrace." He paused, listened again.

"I don't care where you get them from. Just get them, okay? And get them to his law office as well while you're at it. You could probably get them from the county clerks…"

Listened again then said, "I'm busy with all these guys for a few days," Ward lied. "How about next weekend?" A few beats later he said, "Okay, we'll stay at the Artesian…they have mirrors above the four-poster beds…"

Ward was listening, smiling again. "That's going to happen before Thanksgiving…I almost forgot, you distracted me. Listen, I got a second little job for you." He paused. "No, not that kind of job," he said, almost giggling. "Stop! This is another job that's right up your alley as a professional." He was still grinning like a teenager. "No, seriously, I'll text you names and addresses later, okay? … You got it! I don't care how. No traces, no evidence anywhere. Nothing!"

He clicked off, still smiling like Lucifer himself.

The line went dead.

She walked out to Mesa Street. Her car was parked at a meter two blocks away. The sun was burning hot, the street deserted. Car windows up of cars driving by. She walked to the stoplight. It was red. She waited patiently, glancing all round. The light turned green. She walked across leisurely and reached her car, got in, and let the windows down, turned the air conditioner on full blast, let it run for a few minutes, still looking around, still deserted, looked in her rearview mirror, no cars coming either way, slowly pulled away into the street, and drove north on Mesa Street at the speed limit.

———

Spetsnaz Colonel Stanislav Lemev checked the luminous dial on his watch. It was almost 3 am Saturday, November 22, 2015, a week before Thanksgiving, the very best time for a hit. Russian commando lore had developed that three o'clock was the best time during the night for a hit, as targets were in the deepest level of their slumber, the dreamless alpha REM sleep. A time of total incapacity. The best time to kill and eliminate Steven Vandorol.

It was a moonless sky over Scenic Drive and Golden Hill Terrace, yet the brilliant star-filled sky competed with the bright lights of downtown El Paso and Juarez, stretching into the horizon, a carpet of sparkling jewels lying on a jet-black carpet.

The November night air was crisp and cool. A wonderful cool East Texas November night. "A good night for a killing," well-tanned Colonel Lemev said out loud to the Syrian Muhammad Abu, sitting in back next to him as their car pulled into the deserted parking lot of Sierra Medical Center, right across from Steven's house, on Golden Hill Terrace. Ward Powell was driving, and Uri Gagarin sat in the front with an Uzi in his lap.

Huge Colonel Qiao Liang, ninja assassin and leader of tonight's execution, sat in the back in silence, crowding the other two. All wore black nylon sweats, hoodies, and black running shoes. Their black Suburban was bulletproof and had been fitted with additional armor plates back in Anchorage and had New Mexico license plates, fake and untraceable.

The planning for the hit on Vandorol and his home had taken a week at their safe house in Sunland Park. The surveillance had been done by the two locals following Steven who knew El Paso, they told Colonel Lemev, like the back of their hands. The two, using local maps, had planned the first hit on Vandorol and his dog Rommel, also likely collateral damage, that failed miserably when Rommel woke the entire neighborhood. The two also had failed in the attempt on Police Chief Eddie Egen as he returned from out of town. Ward Powell had a floor plan for Steven's home from his secret El Paso contact, he told them all. The locals had stopped sight surveillance of Steven's whereabouts, as his daily schedule of morning run with his dog, to courthouse downtown, to his office for lunch with Ray, then back to his office, usually until six, then to home, had not varied even slightly. *The assassination was not going to fail this time,* Lemev thought. This was going to be a Russian success he could report to his superiors, and the additional US dollars from DC and the Alvarados just a bonus.

Lemev was disappointed that Liang had been put in charge of the initial hit on Vandorol's home by the general and Ward Powell; he wanted to perform the hit personally. The great Steven Vandorol, the now conservative media star he had read about in the local and national media, would take three rounds in the forehead while on his knees, begging for mercy, the colonel fantasized. He himself would go through the garage after it exploded, while Colonel Liang would blast through the north door simultaneously. Yuri and Abu would be at the front door with hand-held grenade launcher and go through the front plate glass after it exploded. It would all be over in five minutes, and the message would be loud and clear to the sleeping giant being subverted from within—the United States of America, or Big Satan, as the radical Muslims were always ranting.

In recent developments, more support and money flowed in for the assassination team from a strange and unknown source, although Ward Powell was strutting around like a peacock as if he himself had been responsible for it. Regardless, Ward promised Lemev that if the hit was successful, Powell and Lemev would be millionaires living in Baja, California, with all the booze, women, food, and money they could imagine. When Lemev had questioned Powell, he just smiled and said their source had more money than the Saudi king, whom they both characterized as just another Muslim pedophile. Ward made Lemev feel a lot better about Colonel Liang being in charge of the assault on Vandorol's house, especially since Liang granted Lemev's wish to personally kill Vandorol and make him beg for his life. Lemev was already salivating, looking forward to the celebration Ward promised after the killing, involving at least five girls for each as "refreshments."

The minute hand hit 3 am, the colonel hit the cell phone detonator, and three simultaneous explosions rocked Scenic Drive and Golden Hill Terrace like an earthquake.

The north garage door disintegrated, and the colonel rushed in, pistol with silencer attached held straight ahead. The garage on that side was empty, and Steven's Taurus was parked on the other side. The colonel's first thought: *The dog is with Steven in the bedroom.* He heard the glass shattering and wood splintering the north door of the house as Colonel Liang came through. The plate glass in the front of the house exploded as well from the grenade Uri had fired.

The noise was tremendous and the chaos complete on a dark and sleeping Golden Hill Terrace. The black smoke filtered through the ducts…

I should have come through the back by the bedroom, Lemev thought as he met Yuri and Abu crashing through the front, guns drawn, while Colonel Liang came through on the north side.

"No dog in the back!" Yuri shouted, meeting Lemev coming in from the garage and Abu through the front.

Empty.

No dog.

No Steven.

From the living room, Lemev saw Liang at the bedroom doors having come through the exploded back door. He was pointing his gun. Hesitated, turned to the other bedroom. Paused, as Lemev and Yuri met him at both doors.

Empty. No dog. No Steven.

The beds in both rooms were made and the rooms immaculate.

"*Der'mo*!" the colonel exclaimed. "The Vandorol *sukin syn* and his stupid dog are gone!" To the Syrian, "Abu, open the front doors to let us all out…I'll take both bedrooms; look through the rest of the house and garage quickly. We gotta get out quick."

The colonel looked in the closet, pulled out drawers and dumped them on the floor, while Liang did the same in the other bedroom.

The colonel found a shotgun, grabbed it, and yelled, "Get all the weapons you find…and hurry!"

"Let's go," Lemev yelled, going out the side door, followed by Liang, Abu, and Yuri last. Shadows hit Scenic Drive, turned left and up toward the side street twenty yards away. Down the street they ran to the black Suburban in the deserted parking lot. All four got in quickly, and the Suburban eased down the street toward a dark Piedras Avenue, knowing that emergency vehicles would come up Scenic Drive from the fire station by the Sierra Medical Center.

Powell goosed the car, and it shot down to Piedras Avenue. "What the hell happened?" he asked.

Lemev answered, "Nothing. No Steven Vandorol. No dog. Nothing!" He paused, breathing hard. "We blew up two doors, a plate-glass window, and demolished a garage!" Paused again, then continued, "We're not going to hear the end of this, another major screw-up!"

Piedras Avenue was deserted at 3:15 am as they pulled into the back of a two-story building, the first floor of which was the La Cocina Restaurant on

Rio Grande Avenue where three other vehicles were inconspicuously parked. The apartment above the restaurant was their second safe house, ideally close to the Fort Bliss entrance and downtown El Paso.

All four got out, into the back entrance to the upstairs, as sirens screamed and wailed on Scenic Drive and Golden Hill Terrace.

33

Big Bend National Park, Texas, is remotely located in the heart of the Chihuahua Desert where the Rio Grande is the quintessential desert river rafting experience. Located in southwest Texas on the Mexican border, the Rio Grande is an ideal river rafting destination during the fall, winter, and spring when it is too cold in other parts of the United States to go river rafting.

It was the perfect time during the week before Thanksgiving when temperatures went from the high 80s during the day to a cool 60s during the night. Perfect Texas desert and mountain weather.

The Rio Grande's banks were painted with a spectacular rainbow of colors by wildflowers, and Big Bend rafting parties floated on Class l-lll rapids through magnificent canyons and spectacular vistas.

It was late afternoon in Santa Elena Canyon, the most photographed canyon in Big Bend. The Sierra Ponce cliffs were high limestone walls that jutted straight up from the Rio Grande and created a majestic almost reverent canyon atmosphere—truly a cathedral to the good Lord's magnificent and absolute power over the world.

"The good Lord has sure blessed the United States and especially the great State of Texas, right, Eddie, my friend?" Steven said to Eddie and his wife, Andi, and Steven's two kids, Josef and Karina, both spending their week before Thanksgiving with their father in El Paso.

After Eddie was run off the road and almost killed by persons unknown, and Steven and Eddie's conversation during their desert ride after the ranch meeting, Eddie seemed to get a new lease on life, Steven thought. First, he had apologized to Andi for his part in the breakdown of their relationship, confessed all his most recent philandering, admitted to her, and to himself, that he had a sexual addiction, and scheduled counseling with a good Christian therapist. Sensing contrition, she had forgiven him. Complete rehabilitation would take time, as both agreed to work on their own parts in the breakdown of their marriage.

Also, whenever possible, Steven and Eddie prayed together, and Steven continued encouraging Eddie as his best friend. Just being there and listening helped immensely, Eddie had said to Steven. Eddie was grateful for that friendship, he told Steven numerous times, and Steven was grateful for the great friendship as well, now hopefully untainted by prior layers of evil for both.

Andi asked for forgiveness herself for her part in their breakdown and promised to seek counseling herself. Since she was a staunch Catholic, had been all her life because of her parents, her tyrannical father especially, she questioned dogma and the Catholic religion's emphasis on ritual rather than true faith in Jesus Christ, yet still kept the divorce pending, just in case he backslid into old toxic patterns, Eddie told Steven before they left El Paso.

Eddie and Andi Egen, being avid whitewater rafters, had scheduled a pre-Thanksgiving rafting trip to Big Bend as an opportunity to reconnect with each other. To express gratitude to his friend for his counsel, help, and friendship, Eddie invited Steven and his dog Rommel to come along as well. As Eddie and Andi knew that Steven's son and daughter in Oklahoma were to have a week off for Thanksgiving, they called the kids' trustee, Robert Bailey, who arranged everything with Marianne, Steven's ex-wife and the kids' mother, purchased airline tickets, and surprised Steven with his two kids arriving in El Paso late in the evening. Steven was overjoyed. It had been more than two months since he had spent the weekend in Oklahoma with them.

"You're so right, Steven, and the good Lord sure has blessed us, me and Andi, and you, my friend, with these two great kids." Eddie looked at the two kids sitting by the fire.

Josef, Steven's shy fifteen-year-old, was named after Steven's older brother. Their names were both spelled in the Hungarian tradition, with an *F* not *ph*. He looked embarrassed but smiled nevertheless. A strapping six-foot-two, he resembled his father and uncle, Steven's brother Joey, whom Steven hadn't seen since he was a teenager in Brazil. He wore jeans and a T-shirt that had "Basketball Is My Life" on the front in bold gold lettering. He didn't say anything, just continued smiling. Just like his own older brother had been of Steven, Joey was extremely protective of his little sister, Karina.

Rommel had immediately bonded with Karina as a puppy previously in El Paso when she had visited before and had not left her side since her arrival this time. Karina was a beautiful young girl now, with her father's brown eyes, long eyelashes, long auburn hair, and high forehead. While Josef looked somewhat like his dad, Karina was his clone, a female Steven Vandorol. His son was a superb basketball player while his daughter, at thirteen, was already a great swimmer and athlete.

"Rommel is blessed too, Uncle Eddie. Right?" Karina exclaimed, stroking Rommel's huge head, which was bigger than hers. She was grinning at the dog and Uncle Eddie, large brown eyes twinkling.

Eddie nodded. "He sure is, honey, but it's you two kids that are really blessed by the Lord to have a father like yours. He would take a bullet for you guys any time."

Steven's turn to be a little embarrassed. "Well, Eddie and Andi, as I've always told them, Josef and Karina have been the only consistent joys in my entire life." Steven paused. He had tears in his eyes but smiled. "We better talk about something else before we all have a good cry together."

Andi stood up. "Why don't we all go for a walk along the bank and watch the sunset from around that bend."

Andi was a cute petite woman. A short five foot, well-tanned, with flashing black eyes and jet-black hair in a ponytail down to her waist, she was of Italian descent, a tiny Gina Lollobrigida or a tinier Sophia Loren. "You too, Rommel," she said as Rommel's ears perked up; he barked loud and looked to Steven for instruction.

Steven smiled. "Yeah, you too, Rommel, but stay close to Josef and Karina."

Rommel looked from Karina to Josef and barked again as they all started their walk.

"I swear that dog understands you, Steven," Eddie chuckled and put his arm around Andi as they walked down the shoreline.

Steven put his arms around both his kids. "Rommel and I talk all the time. Sometimes he even answers…"

Laughter by all as they left their camp, one of about fifteen other camps of the other rafting groups scattered along the banks of the Rio Grande near their own camp. Up and down the banks, campfires lit the canyon as the setting sun cast long shadows on the cooling canyon floor. Tents, canoes, and rafts dotted the banks as well, lending a warm festive glow to the whole shoreline. The scent of thousands of wildflowers in all colors of the rainbow filled their senses.

With water gently lapping their bare feet, they all ambled in a tight little group along the embankment toward the bend in the river where they could better see the sunset. Steven, with his arms still around his kids and Rommel right by Karina, looked back just in time to see Eddie and Andi kissing. Karina looked back also, as did Josef.

Eddie finished kissing Andi and looked up. "So, we have an audience?" He and Andi were both grinning, their eyes sparkling.

"Yep, even Rommel." Steven laughed and hugged both his kids.

"I love you, Dad," Karina said spontaneously, and Josef followed: "Me too, Dad."

That was less embarrassing to a teenager, Steven thought about his son and walked along holding them both.

They all rounded the bend and saw the high limestone walls jutting up from the water to their right and the deep blue Madera and Carmen Mountains to the left.

In between in a cloudless sky, the yellow-orange sun was just setting. Another spectacular Texas sunset, the colors magnificent—oranges, reds, and yellows all sparkling on billowing clouds in the darkening neon blue sky shining on colorful layers of limestone, sandstone, mudstone, and crystalline rocks formed two billion years ago.

Five people and a dog stood in awed silence and watched the magnificent Texas sunset.

After a while, and whispering from behind, Eddie said, "Thank you, Steven."

Josef and Karina were both listening.

Steven turned back. "You are most welcome, Eddie, my friend."

As they were walking back, Steven with his arms around both kids and Rommel still sticking to Karina, Josef looked over to his dad and said, "What was Eddie thanking you for, Dad?"

"Well, I'll tell you, son." Steven paused. "And I'll tell you both honestly, as you're not little kids anymore like you were when your mother and I got a divorce, okay?"

Both were nodding. Even Rommel's ears perked up. Steven smiled and thought, *that silly dog understands me*, as he began, "I've been helping Eddie with his relationship with Andi. They were having some serious problems in their marriage."

Both kids were looking at their father intently. Both were listening and said nothing.

"You kids remember my first law partner and mentor, George Miller, right?" They nodded, so Steven continued. "Well, George told me when he assigned me to handle my first divorce case as a young lawyer to always remember that the buildup and breakdown of every relationship is always 50/50!"

Both looked a little puzzled.

Steven noticed as they kept walking slowly by their dad's side.

Josef spoke first, frowning. "What's that mean, Dad? I really don't understand." He had anger issues about Steven's divorce from their mom that had resulted in some distance between them.

Steven answered, "It means, son, that two people, a man and a woman, start a relationship, they start building it up...together...and when the relationship breaks up...by divorce, it does because both...together contribute to that breakup equally...50/50. Does that make sense, bud?"

Josef was nodding. He got it. Karina did as well. Even Rommel seemed to get it, cocking his head toward them—and smiling again.

34

"Steven, you don't know how glad I am to see you," Ernesto Martinez said to Steven, sitting at the head of the massive table in the district attorney's large conference room. To his right, Steven, Eddie, and Ray. To his left, North, Beth Barker, and Ed's intelligence chief, Texas Ranger Officer Lucas Davenport and Lieutenant Milo Sturgis.

"I'm glad to see you too, Ernie." Steven smiled at Ernie. "So, who trashed my house?"

After spending all of Thanksgiving week in Big Bend, Steven, his children, Eddie, and Andi all returned to El Paso to Ed's ranch late Saturday, November 28, for a post-Thanksgiving dinner. Since it was late, and Josef and Karina had a Sunday morning flight back to Tulsa, Steven and his kids stayed overnight at Ed's ranch. After a tearful farewell and watching their flight leave from El Paso International Airport, Steven went home to change into jeans and boots to return to the ranch for a later horseback ride after church services with the Egens. It was only then that Steven came upon his home marked off with yellow tape as a crime scene. Steven immediately called Ed and found out he had just talked to Lieutenant Milo Sturgis, who brought him up to date about the apparent attempt on Steven's life and the destruction of his house in their absence from El Paso.

Eddie answered for Ernie. "It all happened Saturday morning around 3:15 am." Ed paused and looked at his investigator, Milo, who nodded. "It was apparently four people from the evidence...there wasn't much. One explosion blew out the garage doors, another the north door, and a third, a grenade launched through the plate glass in the front. It all happened simultaneously. A fourth guy was also at the front door."

"Professionals?" Steven asked.

"Definitely," Lieutenant Sturgis answered. "They tore up your house in minutes. No fingerprints or footprints. Nothing. The simultaneous explosions were approximately 3:05, give or take, a neighbor said, who called 911 at 3:10 and emergency vehicles, El Paso PD's, arrived at 3:20 and fire engines at 3:30…and a local terrorist crime news blackout went into effect…"

Eddie interrupted, "Steven, I hate to tell you, but the hand grenade was made in China and the tactics appear Russian Spetsnaz commando MO. It looks like a well-planned, well-organized assassination hit." Eddie paused. "The Alvarados probably hired out-of-work Russian mercenaries for the hit on you."

Steven smiled. "I sure didn't know the Ruskies were that pissed off. I thought I just pissed the Chinese off in DC. I thought I did a good job for my then clients, the Alvarados."

All chuckled, but Ernie said, "Steven, this is serious…the good Lord was taking care of you. Chief, what about security for Steven…and the rest of the prosecution team?"

"The good Lord *and* Ed and Andi." Steven put his hand on his friend. "Thank you, Eddie." Steven turned from his friend to his boss. "I know this is serious, Ernie, and scary. But I'm not going to cower to these killers, whoever they are. You hired me to do a job, and I'm going to do it." Steven looked at Lieutenant Sturgis. "Thank you also, lieutenant, for securing my house, fixing the doors and glass. They did a really good job in just a couple of days. Thanks again."

"You're welcome, Steven," Lieutenant Sturgis answered. "Can we help you with anything else?"

"No thanks, Milo. I pretty well have the inside back in shape. Ray helped a bunch. Thanks, Ray."

"You bet, Steven. Glad to help…anytime. Sorry about them taking all your weapons. We'll get you rearmed."

Steven smiled. "I'm really pissed about them taking the shotgun you gave me for Christmas last year, Ray!" He paused a beat, thinking. "They didn't find the two vintage WWII German lugers G Jack gave me…"

Ernie Martinez again looked at Chief Egen. "Chief, what about protection for Steven?"

Eddie said, "We're on it, boss. Steven's house and office are now under 24/7 surveillance, and we're following Steven around…two shifts…"

Steven interrupted both. "And I'm under surveillance 24/7 by the good Lord and my Savior, Jesus Christ, and the angels of our Lord, forever. John 14:6 says it all, right, Eddie?"

Eddie replied immediately, "Right!"

"Amen!" Ernesto Martinez finished. "So how is the search for legal help going, Steven? Any prospects?" Ernie was changing the subject.

Steven frowned. "Not yet. I interviewed three prospects; you sent me one, John Clarke, but they were all way too inexperienced."

Beth interjected, "Steven, I've got someone I'd like to talk to you about."

"Okay. Good. Tell me over lunch. North, Ray, Ed, you know we're having lunch at Cafe Central again, right?"

"I'll have to take a raincheck," Eddie said. "Been gone a whole week, so I've got a lot to catch up on." One of which was catching up on his marriage to Andi, Steven knew.

"That's okay, Eddie." Steven nodded at his friend. "Call me later."

"How's the case prep going?" Ernie asked Steven but looking directly at Beth.

As usual, Steven was calm. "North, Beth, and I have started to review the twenty-some boxes of evidence before we review all the witnesses again and start to prepare the amended or superseding indictment. Eddie and Major Reacher have also been really helpful…"

"What's Major Reacher doing for you? I thought he was a captain?" Ernie asked.

Steven answered, "No, he's a major now…and in charge of Apache Helicopter Battalion 509 and is our liaison with General Nicholas at Bliss and Briggs Army Airfield."

"Okay, that's great," Ernie answered. "How about our witnesses, Ed? Are they all secure?"

Eddie answered immediately, "Definitely. Only Lieutenant Davenport, Milo, and I know where...and their security is in my senior trusted guys' hands."

"Ernie, are we gonna get some more legal help?" Steven asked. "You gave me two investigators, and Ray has been working with them."

"Yes, I've assigned Jack Parlance and Rudy Acosta to help you guys," Ernie said, looking directly at Beth.

Beth interrupted, "Jack is a little weak, but Rudy is a good man."

"Thank you for the critique, Ms. Barker," Ernie said, eyebrows raised, and Steven noticed the slight tension between the two, thought, *Sounds like a little sexual drama...*

Beth got the message. "Sorry." She looked at Steven, who remained placid. No expression. It wasn't his deal.

Steven said to his boss, "We have to have the amended superseding indictment filed by the end of January to make the August trial date, Judge Carbon told me. So, trial preparation will start in earnest in January. Hopefully, I can have someone hired in December or January to help with my practice. I've prayed about it, and I'll keep looking."

"I'll help all I can," Ernie said. "And you be careful, Steven, okay?" Ernesto looked at Steven, rising from his chair signaling the meeting's end.

"Always." Steven rose as well. The meeting was over.

Ernesto wasn't finished. "Ed, let's give Steven 24/7, okay?"

"You've got it, Patron," Eddie answered immediately. "Davenport, the Rangers and I are all on it!"

"Me too," Ray finished as all rose from their chairs...

On the way out of the conference room, Steven turned to Ray walking beside him. "Ray, I just remembered something I've been meaning to talk to you about..."

Ray looked at Steven. "What's that?"

North and Beth were coming behind Ray, walking out as well. Eddie remained behind still talking with Ernie, Sturgis, and Milo.

Steven saw North and Beth following Ray and looked back at Ray. "Not right now; let's talk outside."

Beth breezed by both Steven and Ray, looked sharply at Steven. "Excuse me, guys." She turned left to go to her office.

Ray noticed. "Did you see that look?"

Steven nodded. "Yes, what do you think that was all about, Ray?"

"I don't know. Maybe she's got the hots for you, buddy." Ray smiled impishly and then continued. "What did you want to talk about, Steven?"

They watched Beth walk down the hall to her office; she went inside and closed the door.

Ray, still smiling, said, "She does have a nice rearview, don't cha think?"

"No comment," Steven said. "Remember when we rode horses that Saturday morning when we had our meeting with General Nicholas?"

"Yeah, it was great."

"Well, when you, Eddie, and I rode back in, Jesus Chavez was handling our horses, and he was really trying to avoid you, Ray. Did you notice?"

Ray thought a moment. "I sure did."

"And you looked at him really hard; I noticed that as well. Why was that?"

Ray looked straight at Steven. "Jesus Chavez was higher than a kite on drugs, cocaine! I could see it in his eyes and manner…"

"Yeah?" Steven was surprised. "He's been working for Eddie for ten years now, and his father was a Texas Ranger, now retired…"

"Yeah, I know…he's still a macho little mojo…we got to be careful…"

"Okay, can you keep an eye on him?" Steven asked.

"I surely will…very carefully."

"You were really quiet during the meeting, North. You all right?" Steven asked North sitting directly across from him at Cafe Central again, with Ray sitting to Steven's right and Beth to his left. He was having his favorite green chile and sour cream soup again, eating with real gusto, as always.

North answered, "Yeah, I'm fine. I'm just pissed at what happened to your home, Steven...and what could've happened to you." North paused and looking directly at Steven. "I'm really sorry."

"Thanks, North. I appreciate your concern," Steven said. "But I'm really okay with this. Stuff happens, and like Ed said to me: everything in R.O.W., that's the Rest of the World, will always disappoint you. I've got my Lord, my kids, my friends..." Steven looked around the table and continued, "...my dog Rommel and horse Pegasus...so essentially I'm bulletproof...as my friend Courtney Wellington once said, 'With the good Lord in your heart, all one needs is something to do, someone to love, and something to look forward to'....so I'm really good."

Beth raised her martini. "Here, here, a toast to Steven. May he continue to have all three." She downed her second lunch martini. The waiter replaced it with another immediately.

"Thanks, Beth," Steven said, and wondered about her tone. Rather than a compliment, the toast had sounded more like an insult.

Steven finished his soup. "North, I've decided that you'll be first chair for the trial." He glanced at Beth, whose face fell. "Beth, I want you to take the lead in examining our witnesses, okay?"

Beth wasn't thrilled. "Okay, Steven, if that's what you want." She returned to her soup, head down, concentrating.

Steven continued, "I'll handle the cross-examination of the defense witnesses and the direct on witness A and B, two of the best witnesses to all the corruption and treason that we have stashed." Steven paused a beat. "Their testimony alone will bring down the current administration, the president, former attorney general of the United States, former secretary of state, and the leading androgynous Democratic presidential candidate."

North laughed. Beth didn't. She was scowling, eating her soup without looking up, Steven noticed.

"The two new guys, Jack and Rudy, will back you two, respectively. North, you okay with that?"

North nodded. "Jack's okay. I think Beth's a little too hard on him...I don't know why."

North looked at Beth, who changed the subject. "Steven, like I said during the meeting, I do have a candidate to help you with your law practice while you're the big *conservative media big deal.*" She was smiling brightly.

Steven noticed the slight top spin in her voice. "Good, who is it?" He kept looking directly into her eyes.

Beth broke eye contact, glanced out the window. "His name is Ward Powell." She paused a beat. "I don't know him very well, I just met him...we were introduced at the bar luncheon last month. He's just come to El Paso from Chicago...or is it from Alaska..." She was looking up at the ceiling.

"Why did he come to El Paso?" Steven asked, a bad feeling in his gut.

"I don't know, but he sounds good...and is a real handsome guy," Beth answered, downing her third martini.

"Fine, I'll talk to him." Steven paused. "Where can I find him?"

Beth shrugged. "I don't know that either. You might check with the Bar Association. They'll know."

"Okay, thanks. I will." Steven was finished. "Hey, North, do you know anything about this Ward Powell?"

North Anderson shook his head. "No, I sure don't."

"Check him out, will you?" Steven asked. Beth cringed slightly, and Steven noticed. "Ray, would you run a background check on this Ward Powell guy as well?"

Ray nodded, continued eating.

Beth, changing the subject again, said to North, "About Jack Parlance, I'm okay with him. I just don't like his ego." She looked at Steven. "Just keep him out of my way, okay?"

North nodded.

Steven said, "Okay, I'm glad that's settled. Jack Parlance will back you, North, and Rudy Acosta will back Beth." He rose. "Are we done here?"

They all rose and started out, North first, Steven and Ray next, and Beth, putting on lipstick, lingered back. "Steven, can I see you just a second?"

Steven turned back. "Yes?" She was motioning for him to come back.

"Go ahead, Ray, I'll catch up with you," Steven said and turned back to the table.

Beth gestured for him to sit. Steven did. "What's up?"

"I feel bad about what happened, Steven. Can I take you to dinner this week?" Beth was smiling and placed her hand on Steven's.

"Beth, you don't have to do that. I'm fine, really..."

"I know you are, and I admire you for it, but I'd really like to, please?" She was almost pleading.

Steven softened. "Well, if you insist. When?"

"Friday night okay?"

"Sure."

"Great, I'm driving. I'll pick you up at 7:30?"

– 35 –

"Come on in, Ms. Barker. Very nice to see you this evening." Steven was smiling warmly as he held the front door open for a beautiful Beth Barker.

She looked very glamorous this particular evening in her cocktail dress rather than business suit, in which Steven had seen her before. Her face and blue eyes sparkled above a dimpled smile, below high cheekbones and a narrow, straight nose, flawed only by a small scar on one side, Steven noticed again. Her black silk dress hung perfectly on her well-shaped frame. The low-cut dress exposed beautiful cleavage, which clearly showed she wasn't wearing a bra. She also wore very thin-strap black sandals revealing her perfect bare feet and manicured toenails. Steven almost gasped at this vision but concealed his feelings well. He felt warm all over. Beth was breathtaking.

"Thank you, it's good to see you too, Mr. Vandorol," she said as she breezed by, giving Steven a peck on his cheek.

Steven closed the door. "Can I take your jacket?"

She paused, handed him her exquisite black leather jacket. Steven hung it in the hall closet. "Can I get you some wine?" Steven walked ahead and into the kitchen where there were two bottles of wine.

"You may." She was smiling and following Steven.

"White or red?"

"Red's good."

Steven poured her a glass of Chianti, picked up his own, and led her into his living room with Rommel sitting regally by the couch.

"Rommel, meet Ms. Beth Barker."

Rommel woofed.

"Wow," Beth exclaimed. "What a handsome dog!" She walked over to Rommel but looked at Steven tentatively. "Can I pet him?"

"Let him smell the back of your hand first."

She cautiously extended her hand to Rommel. The dog slowly smelled her hand and rose to upright. Rommel was huge; Beth was small in comparison.

227

Rommel came to her waist. Beth carefully petted his enormous head. "Wow, he is a handsome…monster."

"Pat his side, Beth, and he'll love you forever," Steven laughed. "Have a seat; we'll watch the sunset."

Beth petted Rommel's massive side and sat down in a leather wingback chair. Rommel walked away slowly and sat down right beside Steven, who thought, *Rommel doesn't like her.*

Steven stroked his huge head. "Look at that sunset, Beth. Isn't it spectacular?" Steven looked out into the El Paso sky, sun now setting, millions of twinkling stars and the El Paso-Juarez border below stretching into eternity.

"You have the best view in El Paso," Beth said.

"On Scenic Drive at least," Steven answered, still smiling. "I'm glad Ed's guys got the windows all fixed." He sipped his Chianti and was sitting in the other wingback chair. Rommel lying beside him, head down, snout on his extended front two paws, was watching Beth intently. "We sit here often and watch the sunsets, Rommel and I."

The view of the sunset was a technicolor spectacular. Steven was still warm in Beth's presence. Felt a little awkward yet was strangely excited.

Beth spoke first. "Well, did you check out Ward Powell, that attorney lead I gave you?"

"Ray was really busy this past week, but he's starting a background check on him," he answered.

Right out of the blue, Beth asked, "Steven, are you happy?" She looked directly into his eyes.

Steven locked eyes with her, smiled, and raised his eyebrows. Took a sip of his wine and said, "Happy? Yes, to a certain extent, I have my God, my kids and friends. I do have serenity and peace of mind at this point in my life, and that's enough for now."

Beth looked puzzled by Steven's answer but asked, "Are you dating anyone?" Her eyes were sparkling.

"Not really. I've had dates occasionally. Frankly, I've been living on the beach, so to speak, no entanglements, and I like it that way." Steven looked directly into her captivating eyes and said, "I'll not settle for anything less than a 1-2-3-4 relationship."

"So, what's a 1-2-3-4 relationship, and is there one in your future?" Beth was smiling, eyebrows raised in anticipation.

Steven was again feeling a bit uncomfortable as to where the conversation was headed. "I'll answer both questions over dinner; how is that? I'm hungry."

———

"True intimacy between a man and a woman can only happen on a 1-2-3-4 basis," Steven said to Beth. "And between a man and a woman conditional love was established by Adam and Eve in Paradise. Unconditional love exists only in blood relationships as was also established by the good Lord after Adam and Eve's fall from grace."

Steven and Beth were sitting directly across from each other at a cozy table by the fireplace in a secluded corner of the Dome Restaurant, in the Camino Real Hotel just a few blocks from the courthouse.

In view of the recent trauma and destruction of Steven's garage, Beth had picked this restaurant for the security, since it was so close to the courthouse, and she had parked in the secure hotel parking. She had insisted on driving.

It was a chilly and clear December evening outside, but inside the fireplace embers radiated warmth to the glow of many lit candles around the main dining area, sparsely occupied, soft piano music playing in the background, and a slight fragrance of garlic added to the warm atmosphere.

Beth was on her third glass of wine, Steven, his second. A slight smile was dancing on her lips. She raised her perfect eyebrows. "That all sounds pretty biblical, Steven. What do Adam and Eve have to do with 1-2-3-4 relationships?" Her tone sounded a little cynical.

"Absolutely everything." Steven kept direct eye contact. "As my first law partner, George Miller, said to me when I handled my first divorce: 'Steven, never forget who offered who the apple in Paradise.'" Steven picked up his glass of wine and sipped.

He was still uncomfortable. Beth's seductiveness had unnerved him considerably. He was having a hard time maintaining his composure and disguising his emotions. It had been over five years since the Washington debacle with Glee Robinson, his last serious relationship, and abstinence had not been cure-all but vigilantly holding the line on Steven's own sexual addiction had.

"So, we women are at fault for ensnaring you gullible males of the species? That's kind of a religion of sexism, isn't it?" Her slight smile had turned to a sneer, enhancing Steven's discomfort.

"No, it isn't," Steven said, emphatic. "George also said that the ultimate in maturity for us males is to transfer the thinking process from between our legs to between our ears." Steven smiled brightly, his anxiety easing. Saying his true feelings and telling the truth always made him feel better these last few years in El Paso.

Beth softened. "I guess that's true for us females also. I'm sorry I overreacted. Tell me about 1-2-3-4 relationships..." She picked up her glass and held it, locking eyes again.

Wow, Steven thought. *She is gorgeous. I've got to focus.* He also picked up his glass and slowly sipped his Chianti.

"It's not my original theory...my good friend Courtney Wellington told me the theory first." Steven paused and smiled, thinking of Courtney and Arlene. "Courtney and his wife, Arlene, of Washington, DC, are my role models of a 1-2-3-4 relationship that I want and hope the good Lord will, in His timing and grace, provide for me." His eyes clouded up.

Beth noticed. "You really went through a lot in DC, didn't you, Steven?"

She seemed sincere, Steven thought as he answered, "Yes, I did. And the good Lord and the Wellingtons helped me through...but we digress." Steven wanted to change the subject back and away from the searing anguish of corrupt and evil DC. "One, two, three, four starts with one, the self with the good Lord and Jesus Christ in your heart, that's the one."

Beth was listening.

"I guess that's one, the self," Steven said. "For without the self being alive and surviving, there is nothing. It's both the physical and spiritual self. For where is God but, in my being, in my soul, and in my heart. And in divine guidance in our freedom of choice and grace." Steven wiped his eyes.

Awareness had turned to understanding for Steven as he refocused and said, "I guess there are only two important aspects of life on this planet, and I know one of the two is survival, in our jobs, and the satisfaction of doing it well, and that's got to lead to peace of mind and serenity." He looked directly into Beth's hazel eyes and sensed her increased anxiety, so he continued.

"The other of the two?" Steven had asked himself before, as he had then been talking to his own soul. His own spiritual leader. His spiritual self, as Steven had figured it all out, so he continued to Beth, "It's that intimacy that I have thought about so often, and it must be there on levels, and in good relationships between good people, the ultimate being between a man and a woman. Something I never had but have previously thought about a thousand times. That's it, that's the other of the two, and the only important aspects of life on this planet. The intimacy of various relationships on various levels, especially with a soul mate, which leads to that elusive concept of happiness."

I remember being happy, Steven thought. *With Helena. With my brother Joey. With my children. With Marianne. With Marianne? Yes, with Marianne, before I destroyed…or we destroyed…by each of our 50/50 responsibility in that particular breakdown, and in DC with Courtney and Arlene and my friend Vanessa Moore, and with my friends in the now, Eddie and Andi, Ray, and G. Jack Reacher.* Steven continued, "The intimacy of relationships leads to happiness, survival. That's the two," Steven said to Beth.

"I've now got one and two. One is the self, and two is the only two aspects of life on this planet for the self. Survival and intimacy. Certainly, there's nothing in third position," Steven said. Beth was getting very anxious, flustered even, he noticed.

Beth interrupted. "How does one get both of the two, survival *and* intimacy?" She was frowning, eyes blank.

After a long pause, Steven said, "The ultimate of human freedoms is the freedom of choice. It is a matter of choice. After all, we do have the God-given capacity to think. I've made a personal choice for survival, and with the good Lord's grace, I've made a personal choice for that intimacy, whenever it will come my way, and put it completely in the good Lord's hands."

Beth was still not getting it. It seemed to Steven that she had a blind spot as to what he was saying. Or she was deaf to it.

Beth was staring at Steven as if he were talking in a foreign language.

Steven continued anyway. "The three is the 'how' to get intimacy, to have intimacy, especially the top-of-the-line intimacy between a man and a woman. Of my lifetime search, at least." He paused, thinking. "There are three ingredients to the 'how' of intimacy…"

Courtney's words drifted in his mind as Steven thought about the cake baking analogy and continued to talk. "Commonality is certainly an important ingredient. Not just the superficial stuff, but the lasting ones, like heritage, background, values, ethics, and morals. Commonality examples abound. Family strength. Personal strength and courage. It's a commonality in values, and morals, and even the commonality of layers. Commonality of feelings, instincts, and spiritual abilities. Commonality in strength, courage, and street smarts. All-important ingredients," Steven said. "It makes sense. It explains the futility of interracial connections."

That got Beth's attention She was married to a Mexican man, Antonio Montes, considerably younger than she was. Her boy-toy Mexican sonny boy, as Steven remembered, and then continued. "The futility of religious boundaries and cultural values. The lack of success is staggering once the lust has played itself out. The end of those relationships is always predictable."

Beth flushed, embarrassed. She looked away.

"What else…?" Again, Steven continued anyway. "I guess all important after commonality in the connection, and inherent in the connection, is some sort of a sharing process between a man and a woman. That's the constant sharing and continued sharing of positive and negative. Not just the good. Not just the bad. But the good, bad, and ugly, and the truth, all on a continuing basis. Not on a schedule, but the spontaneous and continuing sharing of the good, bad, and ugly as they develop."

By now Steven was talking to himself. "The three to get intimacy, I now know is commonality, sharing, and love."

Beth seemed to be in a trance, not listening at all. Steven thought, *I'm just blah, blah, blahing…* but continued anyway. "And love? Well, I am going to define it for you, Beth, as I believe in it, always have, even though I don't know why." He was attempting the impossible. *Since the beginning of time, those who attempted to define love have all failed. Poets, writers, philosophers have all failed in defining love,* Steven thought. "If it is a progression, it is an upward progression. Love has to have four parts!" *Yes, that's the four,* he thought and smiled, as he was barely scratching the surface now. "What's the four?" Once again, divine guidance.

"I have it. Love is defined in *four* parts. That's the four."

Beth still wasn't listening…to anything, as Steven continued to what was in his heart. "Certainly, in most cases the initial connection is the sexual attractiveness. Yes, that is a part of it. But there's got to be more. Much more." Steven looked directly at Beth, and she focused somewhere behind him into outer space. "So, I guess the first of four is passion. However, without more, it's nothing but lust. It is passion that is the first ingredient of love, which in itself is much more than the sexual. We are sexual beings on this planet, relying on the act itself for the propagation and carrying on of the species. The sexual is inherent to all forms of life on this planet, and especially in ours, who have the freedom of choice. I do think it's more than just the act of sex or of sexual attraction. It is a sense of excitement. Of pride. Of excitement mixed with pride. A sense of excitement about the intimate connection with that other person." *The feeling is more important than the act; I heard that in a movie,* Steven remembered. "The feeling of passion, tenderness, and affection flowing back and forth between a man and a woman in a lifetime committed relationship!"

Beth looked at Steven with hooded eyes. Suddenly, she had become irrelevant to him, as had Glee Robinson back in Washington, DC, and as had all the fleeting and meaningless hookups of days gone by.

Once again, the whispers in his ear... Steven said, "Next is tenderness. The acceptance of one's own and the other's humanity. That the person does all the very same things I do myself, and tenderness is an acceptance of them...

"We all have bad days, good days, good health, bad health, we get tired and have different moods. We all get sick, make mistakes, and have triumphs and disappointments. True tenderness is an acceptance of all of them unconditionally. Of a touch. A caress. A kiss. A hug. The taking of another's face in your hands and saying, 'It's going to be all right.' Giving that other a break. Of understanding."

Steven smiled, still thinking of Courtney's cake, but said, "And I think I got the third of the four. It's the cement that binds. It's that commitment to the other in the connection. A commitment over time. So many just mouth 'till death do us part,' without thinking of its meaning. Certainly, that is a part of the ultimate of human freedoms, the freedom of choice.

"So, what's the fourth of four?" Beth asked, apparently back from outer space. She had blinders on, but she wasn't stupid.

There's a fourth of the four, Steven thought, and in response to his own question, a whisper again, said out loud, "It's in me. With the self, once again, the cornerstone of the definition of love has to be self-love. For if one does not love oneself first, one certainly cannot really love another." Steven thought back to all the times of self-loathing...

Beth didn't get that one either. She was staring at him, eyes shining. "Steven Vandorol, do you find me attractive?"

Steven smiled back. She apparently had her shoes off, because he felt her bare foot on his leg moving softly, slowly up his shin. It felt like a butterfly dancing on his lower leg. It was intensely sensual—and very disturbing to Steven. "Beth, you know I do," he answered, once again regaining his composure. "You are a beautiful woman, no question..."

Her eyes twinkled from the fire in the fireplace. "Do you think you and I could have such a 1-2-3-4 relationship, Steven?" She rested her bare foot on his knee. It sent a slight electric shock up his leg. Steven grabbed her soft bare foot under the table with his right hand. He felt the silky softness. A very disturbing yet sensuous feeling of softness.

"Why, Mrs. Barker, you are a married woman. What are you suggesting?

"Oh, you know, Steven...life is too short, and we could have a lot of fun together, don't you think?"

"And what would we do, Mrs. Barker?" Steven was baiting Beth.

"This is a great hotel, Mr. Vandorol!" Beth said, eyes dancing, eyebrows raising. "We could get a room at the top... How's that?"

"Beth," Steven said calmly. "You have not been listening. I hope this does not affect our working relationship, but no thank you." Steven released her foot.

She downed her glass, rose abruptly, grabbed her purse, and quickly walked out of the restaurant.

"I guess I'll have to take a cab home," Steven said out loud to no one in particular.

"Your hit team consists of a bunch of incompetents," Gravelly Voice said on the speakerphone. "Your intelligence was lousy, Colonel Lemev."

Lemev was silent. There was nothing he could say. At this point, silence was best, he thought. He didn't say that surveillance on Steven had been based on the assumption that Steven's daily habits would not change. *How were they supposed to guess that Steven's children would come to El Paso for Thanksgiving and that they would all spend an entire week in Big Bend rafting, at Ed Eggen's expense?* Lemev frowned at the cell phone…and at his communist Chinese colleague sitting beside him whom the unknown communist Chinese observer Gravelly Voice knew absolutely nothing about, but still said, "Security has doubled on the Egen Ranch, and Steven has two officers with him at all times. It's going to be hard to get at him."

"Then kill his stupid dog and take out the next target, Ed Egen!" Gravelly Voice was calmer now. "No more excuses, colonel. Just get it done…we don't care how, understand?"

Lemev finally spoke again. "I understand. We will try to corrupt someone on the inside to betray Steven and feed us information."

Gravelly Voice, with sarcasm, said, "And how do you plan to do just that, colonel?"

"With the Big Three here in America: money, drugs, and sex," the colonel answered. *Colonel Liang has the computer know-how to get everyone's weaknesses explored,* Lemev thought, looked at Colonel Liang, smiled, and was surprised that he was actually smiling back.

"Have you got any likely candidates yet?" Gravelly Voice asked.

"We're working on a short list… We'll let you know when you've got good news. You probably need some good news in the cesspool you're in." Lemev could not resist the last little dig.

"Our contact in Juarez has upped the stakes in spite of your incompetence," Gravelly Voice said, ignoring the verbal dig.

Lemev was now *really* interested again. "Oh yeah?" Lemev could always use more money for his and Ward Powell's extracurricular activities and retirement as multimillionaires. "What's in it for our team?"

"Your entire team will be rewarded with more money than they have ever seen, all twelve members, especially you, colonel, in spite of all the incompetence. The administration must have the prosecution team eliminated, especially Vandorol, and see the indictment disappear before the American people unite behind the Republican candidate and make this administration...and our party...totally irrelevant!" Gravelly Voice was finished.

Lemev was not. "It's going to be much harder now that Vandorol's got 24/7 security..."

"I don't care what it takes or how much money it takes, just get it done," Gravelly Voice snapped, and the line went dead.

———

Colonel Stanislav Lemev, professional soldier and Spetsnaz full colonel, Russian veteran of Afghanistan and Syria, undercover KGB veteran of Crimea and Kinston takeovers, Hero of Russia, decorated by Premier Vladimir Putin himself, was laughing like an oversexed adolescent. He was now talking about "arrogant Gravelly Voice," as he called the White House's Muslim stooge that already made him a multimillionaire. "What a royal pain." Lemev paused, looking directly at Ward Powell sitting opposite him drinking tequila, then continued, "That stupid Muslim is really going to squeal when we castrate him and the president!"

After Gravelly Voice's tongue lashing at the safe house earlier, Colonel Lemev and Ward adjourned to Juarez for some "play time" with their favorite prostitutes and were waiting at the bar of Juarez's best brothel, The Chica Chingado, drinking Stolichnaya vodka and Hornitos tequila, the best in two countries. They were waiting for their four favorite girls to come to work...

While waiting for the pros, Lemev asked, "So who's your secret plant in the El Paso special prosecution, Ward?"

"She's gorgeous and classy, my colonel!" Ward said, being coy and evasive. The only other person who knew about her was his other sidekick, Uri Gagarin.

Lemev screwed up his mouth into an ugly snarl. "And you gonna tell me, Ward, aren't you? After all, I am now your best buddy, right?"

Lemev is actually begging, Ward thought, but said, "Yes, you are my favorite pal!" Ward paused and with evil grin said, "To hell with you, Colonel Lemev. I don't have to tell you anything! All I'm going to tell you is that she'd betray Vandorol in a heartbeat."

- 37 -

Steven was in his office late. The sun had set and the lights in Juarez were sparkling in the pitch-black darkness. Ray and Christina were in their offices working, as was the new paralegal, Marcy. Soft classical music mellowed the subdued working atmosphere.

Steven was tired. Exhausted. After the Thanksgiving weeklong rafting trip to Big Bend, the aftermath of the violation of his El Paso oasis, and the temptation by Beth Barker, playing catch-up with his law practice had been the order. The trip had been relaxing and exhilarating for Steven, especially since he thought he had repaired the chasm between father and son. The emotional intimacy with his two precious kids, "the two and only consistent joys," had renewed him spiritually and was, to Steven, priceless. Eddie and Andi's renewed marriage was a collateral benefit. The blowup of his home in his absence had been totally incidental to the good Lord's mysterious ways, and a full evidence of His grace, Steven thought.

Since the trip, Steven, Ray, Christina, and new hire Marcy had worked fifteen-hour days, working with existing clients and new clients, mainly soldiers and referrals from Fort Bliss. Steven was on a treadmill-of-a-morning run with Rommel routine, which he had maintained since his DC friend Vanessa Moore suggested it to him during his worst of times, practicing in that cesspool, working long days and returning home at night. The only difference was that his home was now under twenty-four-hour surveillance from two garage apartments, one next door on Golden Hill Terrace, and the other across the street on Scenic Drive across from his office, in addition to two unmarked police cars following him around everywhere while he was awake.

Steven was tired. Exhausted. The former workaholic was rearing its ugly head again. *I've got to watch it,* Steven thought. The therapeutic cycle of awareness, understanding, and decision not to regress back into the escape from lack of emotional intimacy to the escapism and distraction of workaholism meant focus and vigilance on his part. He prayed to the Lord for guidance at each such instance, all in the practice, practice, practice portion of the therapeutic cycle to gain a higher level of freedom from his past layers of evil.

Steven picked up his phone and punched in a DC number.

A sweet voice answered. "Hello?"

"Hi, Arlene. Merry Christmas." Steven was smiling. Just hearing her sweet, gentle voice calmed and renewed him once again, as it always did.

"Well, Steven, my surrogate son in El Paso...Merry Christmas to you," Arlene answered sweetly. "How are your kids?"

"Just great, Arlene!" Steven answered. "They were with me in Texas for a whole week over Thanksgiving." Steven felt himself calming even more just talking about his kids to Arlene.

"Oh, yes?" Arlene exclaimed brightly, her voice warm with affection. "Tell me all about it..."

"Yes, they came down from Oklahoma on the Thursday of the week before Thanksgiving, and Eddie Egen had a surprise for all three of us. A raft trip in Big Bend National Park."

"That's in far southwest Texas, isn't it?"

"Yes, the Rio Grande runs right through and borders the Chihuahuan Desert in Mexico. Arlene, I'm telling you it's spectacular, and the sunsets are awesome."

Arlene knew what was important. "Did you enjoy your kids?"

"Oh, you know I did." Steven was still grinning. "They were great... and we had some good conversations...especially with Karina, who is just like her old dad, as you know." Steven paused a beat. "And with my son, Josef, I think we repaired that distance that developed after the divorce from Marianne." He paused again. "Time will tell. I've prayed about it...a lot." Steven was tearing up, but said, "I think I repaired some old hurts as a result of the divorce. They are older and smarter now, and Karina told me it was the best thing that we divorced. It made them both stronger, they said, and they both forgave me. They actually said so, Arlene." Steven wiped his eyes.

"That's really good, Steven," Arlene said. "I know you fretted a lot about that and had a lot of guilt over the divorce. I could see that while you were in DC... So, you got some closure this time?"

"Yes, ma'am, I did. In DC I saw myself, who I was, and now I also see myself as a father, who I am as a father and a parent."

"So, when did they go back to Oklahoma?" Arlene asked.

"The Sunday after Thanksgiving."

"Are you seeing them for Christmas?"

"No, their trustee, Robert Bailey, you remember Bob?"

"Yes, I do. Your friend and lawyer in Oklahoma."

"Yes, Bob and his wife and their kids, all teenagers now, are taking them to Crested Butte skiing for ten days. It's all about teenagers hanging out and pizza, as you and Courtney well know about your own grandkids..."

"Gosh, yes. They'll have a lot of fun. So, you'll be by yourself Christmas?"

"Yeah, me and my dog," Steven said. "I'll probably go over to Eddie and Andi's now that they are back together."

"I'm glad to hear about Ed and Andi. They are your good friends. Hey, Steven, I just had a thought. Why don't you come to Washington and spend Christmas with us? You are part of our family."

"Oh, Arlene, that's so sweet of you, and I really appreciate the invitation." Steven paused, thinking. "But my boat here in El Paso is just really loaded with the special prosecution and all, and trying to find a lawyer to help in my practice...it's been brutal. But really, I so appreciate you and Courtney. Thank you for everything."

"You're most welcome, Steven. Try not to work so hard, take it easy on Eddie's ranch, and take out some time just for yourself, okay?"

"Oh, I will. I'm working out. Riding my horse regularly, and I've got Rommel."

Arlene was silent, listening. "So, you're, all right?" She paused. "Are you seeing anyone?"

"No, I'm not," Steven answered. "I've had some dates, one recent snafu, but nothing regular." Steven had discussed his addiction with Courtney and

Arlene and that abstinence was his solution. "It's a lot of practice, practice, and practice on that particular issue of the therapeutic cycle."

"Like I've told you before, Steven, it'll come. You're a good person," Arlene said. "And the good Lord works in mysterious ways."

"Yes, Arlene, I know that very well now. And as Courtney has said, the good Lord has His own timing. How is Courtney?" Steven asked.

"Well, he is right here. He's been patiently listening to our conversation. Here he is..."

After a short pause, Steven heard, "Hello, Steven. Merry Christmas, son!" Courtney was smiling, Steven could tell. "So, the kids had a great time in El Paso and Big Bend?"

"Yes, they did," Steven said. "But something else happened that I didn't tell Arlene about. I didn't want her to worry. You go ahead and tell her if you want to, okay?"

"I'm listening" Courtney said.

"On Friday morning, after we left for Big Bend, a four-man hit team almost blew up my house, breaking in. Extensive damage, windows, front, and back doors. Garage door disappeared. The explosives were Chinese, the hand-fired grenade Russian."

Courtney was silent.

"I was just talking with Arlene about the good Lord and His mysterious ways. I've thanked God on my knees that my kids and I weren't home. And Eddie and Andi Egen, of course." Steven paused, wiped his eyes, and continued. "Anyway, the good Lord was watching over us. I'm so grateful."

"But, Steven, listen to me, the good Lord is watching out for you because you are making good choices in your life and doing the right thing in all cases. You are taking an active part in your own salvation. You are a good person, and the good Lord sees your goodness and faith." Courtney paused, gave Steven a few moments, and continued, changing the subject. "So, you can't join us for Christmas?"

"No, I'm so sorry, but like I told Arlene, with the special prosecution trial set for August, and trying to hire a lawyer to help with my private practice in the meantime, I may not even get any rest..."

"Have you found any leads for lawyers?" Courtney asked.

"I've interviewed a couple, but nothing solid yet." Steven paused. "There is not the large pool of legal talent here in El Paso as there was in DC, Courtney. Maybe my expectations are too high."

"The large majority of lawyers in DC are just like what Shakespeare said in Henry VI, and I quote, 'Every five hundred years, the first thing we do, let's kill all the lawyers...'"

Steven laughed. "Yeah, all the John Edward and Bill Clinton lookalike contest winners..."

It was Courtney's turn to laugh. "Yeah, most of them are greedy amoral hacks, but you did make some real friends in Washington, right?"

"Yes, I did. I still think about Vanessa Moore a lot. She became a true friend, and I really liked her very much." Steven paused, remembering. "I always think about her and I having bagels with cream cheese and bacon in the mornings." He warmed with a strange but good feeling all over as he thought about Vanessa. Steven really missed her a lot, he suddenly realized.

Courtney was silent.

"And like I've told you before, Vanessa encouraged me to run regularly during my worst times. That really helped a lot as well," Steven said. "It was like therapy in the corruption, chaos, and sleaze of Washington, Courtney."

"I remember. She was very supportive, even to her detriment with the other partners at Henderson Lane," Courtney mused.

"Yes, including her fool husband, Dudley Moore." Steven thought a moment. "I could never tell why they stayed married."

"Well, we all have our issues, right, Steven?" Courtney asked.

"Courtney, you still there?" Steven asked.

Courtney answered, "Steven, I heard..." He paused a beat then continued. "I heard that Vanessa and Dudley got a divorce."

Steven was aghast. "Re...really?"

"Yes, really."

"She still in DC?"

Courtney hesitated. "I don't really know…but their divorce was common knowledge in DC legal circles. Call her, Steven. You two were great friends. Call her!" Courtney repeated.

"During my toughest times there…" Steven interrupted.

"Yes, and you worked so well together. Call her!" Courtney said a third time. "She could be available to work with you. You really need the help, don't you, Steven? But be careful…"

"I sure do, Courtney." Steven was now smiling brightly. "I'll call Vanessa."

"Arlene and I will say a prayer for you. Steven, the good Lord's grace saved you once again, but you have to be really careful and extremely vigilant of R.O.W., the rest of the world, as you say!" Courtney paused again as Steven thought of the now 24/7 surveillance and protection. "But my CIA contacts tell me that you have a bull's-eye on your back! Since you've got all that media attention, you've become a conservative star, especially in view of the voting public, the American people. But there are lots and lots of other rumors…about Russians and communist Chinese…and Muslim terrorism… lots of internet and social media chatter as well. Just please, please be careful for yourself, your kids, and your friends."

"Courtney, I appreciate that, and I especially appreciate yours and Arlene's friendship and love. Thank you so much for everything. I was a bit down before, but I feel so much better just talking to you and Arlene."

"You're most welcome. Steven, you are a good person, like Arlene says, and that's the truth. Always remember the power of prayer and that the good Lord works in mysterious ways."

Steven hung up the phone and thought, *Courtney and I sure talked a lot about Vanessa Moore…* Steven paused, now grinning like a teenager, and said out loud, "I'm going to call Vanessa!"

38

Steven Vandorol was in the belly of the beast…alone.

Cloudcroft, New Mexico. The Lodge at Cloudcroft. Saturday, December 19, 2015, anno Domini.

On last Thursday evening, Steven had been working at his office when Chris buzzed him and said that a Ricardo Alvarado was on the phone and that the call was personal. When Steven answered, Ricardo, without any preliminaries, merely said, "We need to meet, Steven."

Steven said, "Where?"

Ricardo answered, "The Lodge at Cloudcroft, Saturday, be there!" and hung up.

First, Steven discussed the conversation with Ray, who said he shouldn't go and that it was a setup…a trap. Steven then discussed with Eddie and Ernie, both said he shouldn't go, that it was a setup…a trap. Eddie was adamant about Steven not meeting "El Chapo" Alvarado without cover or security.

Steven went to Cloudcroft, New Mexico, alone and well-armed, anyway.

He was stirring his vodka martini with an olive on a little plastic sword in the deserted bar area of the Lodge. Even the bartender left after serving his drink.

Steven wore a navy blazer over a long-sleeved button-down collar shirt, jeans and boots, and holstered Glock, round already chambered, on his belt in the small of his back.

Steven took a sip of his drink and remembered his very first trip to El Paso and Cloudcroft, with his then best friend in the whole wide world, Martin L. King, almost eight years ago.

Martin King, King of the World and King of Washington, DC, had introduced Steven Vandorol to the Alvarados, father Alberto and son Ricardo, when Steven was "of counsel" at Henderson Lane on K Street in DC. Steven proceeded to represent both men, making millions in attorney fees for the law firm.

Almost eight years ago, Steven and Martin had then come to El Paso together from DC, Steven to close a major shopping center real estate deal for his then clients, the Alvarados. At that time Martin had come along on some vague *other business* that Steven never did quite understand so the two could "recharge" their batteries after the turmoil and chaos that was then Washington, DC.

After Steven completed that real estate transaction for the Alvarados, Martin convinced him to go up to Cloudcroft, New Mexico, with him, ostensibly to "recharge" their respective batteries after a couple of very hectic and chaotic DC months. Steven had been really depressed, angry, and exhausted back then, as he well remembered.

Steven remembered the first drive from El Paso up to Cloudcroft with Martin King, just like it had been yesterday…

Martin noticed that Steven was really down. "You're looking good, Steven," Martin said. "You're having fun, aren't you?"

"Hey, it was not the closing, let me tell you. I really liked El Paso, and I really like this." Steven pointed outside.

"This crappy desert wasteland?" Martin asked.

"It's peaceful. It's great, and I'll tell you what, I haven't been this comfortable in a place for a real long time, if ever."

"Hey, you are relaxed. Don't get too used to it. We got big deals still to do back in DC. Why do you think you're so relaxed?" Martin stared at Steven, both sitting in the back seat of the limousine the Alvarados provided, complete with driver and bodyguard.

Steven paused a moment, then continued. "You know, I thought about it, and I like the people. They are really cool. Being fluent in Spanish helps, but I mainly think it's the early Brazilian experience. I used to live in places like they have in Juarez."

"That would make sense," Martin said, and seemed to want to change the subject. "Well, what did you think of the family spread?" Martin was talking about the Alvarado mansion in Juarez, Mexico, where Steven and Martin had dinner after the shopping center deal closing.

"I can't believe it," Steven replied. "They are old-line rich, aren't they?"

"You better believe it," Martin indicated. "They go a long way back. They are powerful. They're landowners, and they got a lot of pull."

"Yeah, I like the old man even better than Ricardo. And I like him a lot."

"Oh, yeah. They're the classic example." Martin was smiling broadly.

"Martin, quit the crap. I don't want to hear it right now." Martin had mentioned his Mijo theory about Mexicans generally.

Okay, suit yourself!" Martin smiled. "Your accommodations were okay?"

"Oh yeah, I had a wing to myself. Just like you did."

Steven thought back to the elegant house with its ornate but still garish trim that was the hacienda of the Patron on a hill above Juarez, in an exclusive section. The old man had insisted they stay at the house, dismissing the ranch as being inappropriate.

It was a huge mansion. A mansion among squalor, as they were driven to it by huge tough-looking bodyguards. Steven and Martin passed places not unlike those Steven had lived in during his childhood in Brazil. While Martin had vented distaste, they had calmed Steven even further. He had told the truth. He had not been so comfortable in a long time.

The villa had four stories and resembled a French chateau. They were treated like royalty by the cadre of maids, butlers, waiters, drivers, and bodyguards. Steven was impressed. Martin had seen it before. Apparently, he was like a favorite returning guest, as all the help knew him. Dr. King was a king among all his subjects. Both had upstairs suites to themselves and met for dinner at a huge dining table, dressed in tuxedos. The old man sat at the head, and his sons, Ricardo Alvarado most prominent, and their wives to his right and left. The family matriarch was not in attendance.

It had been a marvelous dinner party. Steven had enjoyed himself immensely. Once again, the King had an audience. Steven didn't understand why Martin came to El Paso, and when he asked Martin, he had dismissed Steven's questions with vague statements about the free trade agreement, and lobbying efforts, financed by the old man, about which, of course, Martin didn't want to *complain. Huge bucks. There was more to it, Steven thought, but dismissed it, as his batteries were in fact recharging.*

"Can't believe that house, that mansion," Steven exclaimed.

"You should see their residence on the American side."

"What?"

"That's right. They got a pretty big one in El Paso as well, on the west side, of course. The old man does, and all the sons do too."

"You mean they have two residences each?"

"Why do you even ask? Don't you think that's the American way?" Martin was again smiling. "That was pretty nice of them to make this limousine and the two up front available to us." Martin inclined his head at the burly driver and bodyguard sitting up front, neither of which had apparently smiled in their entire lives.

Steven asked, "Do you think the protection is necessary, Martin?" Steven knew they were carrying guns and wondered at the necessity.

"Hey, it pays to be cautious and safe, and why not?"

"Oh, what is on the schedule, Martin?"

"We're just going to be cooling out. We got a dinner party at seven. We will be getting there about noon, so we got lots of time to chill, look around, and enjoy."

Steven just wanted solitude. "Martin, can we take a breather from women?"

"Hey. You do what you want, and I do what I want." Martin smiled lecherously.

"You already have someone lined up?" Steven knew that he probably did.

"Ready and waiting."

"I hope she doesn't have a sister." Steven was in earnest and not up for sexual acrobatics.

"She don't. Suit yourself, Steven. I know you want to recharge your batteries." Martin was grinning from ear to ear, as if he had in fact swallowed a mouse. "But that doesn't keep me from doing my thang, as you know."

"I wouldn't consider it, Martin." Steven was grinning also. Martin was consistent all the time in doing his "thang."

Later that same day, Steven was stirring his vodka martini with an olive on a little plastic sword, in the bar area of the Lodge at Cloudcroft.

The limo had dropped them off in the circular driveway outside the door of yet another chateau among the expanse of trees, just inside the town of Cloudcroft, New Mexico. The place was gorgeous. The wood floor creaked as they had walked into the registration area. They had walked past registration without stopping, except that it was Dr. King this, Dr. King that. They had obviously been expected and were ushered to their rooms by the bodyguards.

Steven, at Martin's behest, had packed light. He was in sport coat and slacks, had two extra changes, and some jeans and boots, all at Martin's insistence. The immense fireplace in the lobby had been roaring. It had been very cool, and Steven understood that Cloudcroft was a haven from the hot El Paso days during the summer. It was even better now in the fall.

He really liked his room. It was tiny. Almost cubical. Rustic. He had kicked off his shoes and laid on the bed to rest. The bed was high off the floor and very comfortable. Turn-of-the-century lamps and decorations. Wood-burning fireplace.

Steven Vandorol was very much at peace with himself. After a short rest, he had ambled down to the bar.

It was early afternoon, and he was having his favorite drink. Steven was alone. Only Steven and the bartender, who walked in and out at times, were in the bar.

Steven was sitting at a table next to the restaurant, which was also empty. Steven had looked and seen one long table, seating sixteen, already prepared, among all the regular tables. He had assumed it would be for their dinner party later. He was looking around enjoying the calm.

As he looked to the front, he saw a woman walk in. Steven swallowed hard. He could not believe his eyes.

"Vicki," he exclaimed, getting up from his chair as a tiny beautiful woman with dark short-cropped hair broke into a smile, her sparkling brown eyes widening.

She was equally surprised, smiling as well. "Steven, what in the world…"

Steven went to her in a rush and enthusiastically hugged her, much to the surprise of the hostess, now standing beside her.

"What...?" they both stammered almost in unison.

"Vicki, I just can't believe it," Steven said, holding her.

"I go by Victoria, my given name, now." She drew back just a little.

"Well, excuse me, Victoria. I can't believe it." Steven was still stammering. "What are you doing here?" He held her by the waist, and she held his. "What are you doing here?" he repeated. She continued to hold Steven.

"Why don't we sit down, have a drink, and talk about it?" Steven left his right arm around her tiny waist and turned.

"That sounds great," she said as Steven led her to his table, his arm still around her waist, and hers around his. Steven held out her chair. She sat down. She was radiant. Her dark hair stylish and close cropped. Victoria was now a beautiful woman, not the little high school girl he remembered from Lawton High School in Lawton, Oklahoma.

"I just can't believe it. It was 1987. Wasn't it?" Steven was grinning like a high school boy as he sat down opposite her. "Well... Hey, you first. tell me."

"I live in Albuquerque, Steven," she said, smiling.

Steven blurted, "You married?"

"Not anymore. I'm a three-time loser, Steven, and it's all your fault."

"What do you mean?" He looked into her beautiful eyes.

Victoria looked away. "If we had married, as high school sweethearts, I wouldn't have had to marry three jerks."

Steven laughed but persisted, "Are you here with someone?"

She shook her head. "No, I'm not. This is where I come alone. It's a favorite spot in New Mexico. How about you. It's my turn. Are you married?"

"Not anymore." Steven heard a certain sadness in his own voice.

"And are you here with someone?" She ignored the slight sadness.

"Yes, I am," Steven replied, and as her eyes turned downcast slightly, he continued. "He is big, black, and beautiful, and his name is Martin King. I will introduce you. He is a client and my very best friend..."

Victoria's eyes brightened again. "I really am glad to see you. It's been such a long time.

We are getting old."

"Not you," Steven complimented her.

Instantly, they were a couple of high school seniors again. As was the case when they were just kids, they had connected again immediately as adults. The excitement was electric, and both felt it.

"Can we have dinner?" Steven felt like kissing her.

"Sure." Pouting full lips. "Here?"

"Yes. It's Martin's deal. He's having a dinner party right here at seven. I want you to join me."

"But, Steven. It's a dinner party."

"It's nothing formal, and probably everybody is going to have a date except me." Steven reached across and gently squeezed her very soft small hands.

"Are you sure it will be all right?" She gently squeezed back.

"Of course. I can't wait for you to meet Martin."

"Who is he?"

Without hesitation, Steven repeated, "He is my friend. My very best friend in the world." A puzzled look passed her face, and Steven added, "He is also a client, and I am the general counsel for his lobbying group."

"So, you're a lawyer?" Victoria frowned. "I wish I had been able to catch you back then."

Steven grinned. "I wish I would have let you."

"Do you think anything would have really been different?"

Victoria now had a sad smile, as two high school kids, holding hands, talked away the afternoon.

This is really weird, Steven thought, sitting in a dining room full of zombies. No one seemed to know each other, even at their table of sixteen, yet they appeared to have been together for a long time. Figures in a House of Wax. They all seemed sorely out of place. Hawks, in tight-fitting clothing, with bulges under their arms, attempting to act normal and look inconspicuous, stood at all the entrances. Steven dismissed the uneasiness quickly, for next to him sat his high school girlfriend, Victoria. She had been impressed with Martin and vice versa.

At the head of the table was Martin, once again at center stage. A stunning Eurasian woman sat to Martin's left. Martin's date. Next to Martin's date, old man Alvarado, still looking ridiculous, and the kid, Ricardo Alvarado, with his wife, the beautiful Brazilian Carmen. A very young big-breasted teenager with too much makeup and in expensive, too-tight fitting clothes, obviously the patriarch's date. Steven guessed she was the substitute for the ugly broken-down old Mexican woman, the family matriarch, in obvious distress, that Steven had met back in El Paso. The patriarch, their host, along with Martin, the three women, and Ricardo, with his lush ponytail, all seemed strangely out of place.

The mysterious Korean, Dr. Chan, the surprise star guest to Steven, sat to Martin's right, another Korean next to him, two more across. When introduced, Steven didn't get any of their names. Four more hawks, in tight fitting yet expensive garish clothing, all with bulges, filled the other seats.

Steven and Victoria were the only bystanders at this dinner party. Martin had been enthusiastic and very interested about the coincidence with Victoria and jokingly reminded Steven about the "no date pledge" for the evening. "See what I mean, Steven," Martin had said, "things never turn out like you expect, and this time I think it definitely turned out in your favor."

Steven had to agree that it was quite a coincidence, yet it made him uneasy as he thought of Glee. But since things had taken a wrong turn there, "What the hell," he thought once again when faced with "women decisions."

The conversation at their table became more and more animated, as expensive wine flowed freely. On the end, opposite of Martin, Steven, with Victoria to his right, seemed miles away from the rest. Steven was glad that Martin was again on center stage, not including him, leaving him alone to recharge his batteries.

Steven and Victoria had a wonderful afternoon of conversation. He had caught her up on himself, with many exceptions, and Victoria had talked much about herself. Of her three marriages all ending in disaster, only the first one had any sustaining length, having resulted in two boys, now teenagers, who were her life. They had agreed that their personal lives had many parallels. She had gone *from the Sunbelt to the East Coast in her first marriage, to the Midwest in the second, back to the Sunbelt in the third, then to Albuquerque alone, with her sons, and settled.*

Steven, remembering their afternoon conversation, said, "We haven't had much success in relationships, Victoria."

"Like I said, Steven, I should never have let you go, back in '87." Victoria was radiant.

"We were just kids then. We really knew nothing." Steven raised his eyebrows. "But we checked each other out pretty carefully, as I recall."

She smiled. "For about seventeen months. Then you went away to college. I wanted you to go to the same place I was going, but no, you had to be Mr. Independent and go to West Point."

They had held hands all afternoon, like two school kids. Steven and Victoria were still holding hands under the linen tablecloth. Discreetly yet firmly. Steven knew what was in store. A perfect opportunity. Yet he was reluctant to ask.

"You went to the university, and I went to West Point." He shook his head. "Just like a couple of kids."

"You're right. We were just kids. Neither of us knew any better." Victoria squeezed his hand.

Steven squeezed back. "We probably would have married and divorced, after having a bunch of kids, anyway."

"But why does it have to happen that way, Steven. I don't understand." She really didn't seem to, Steven thought.

"I'm starting to," Steven said, looking at Martin, who had almost everyone hypnotized.

Only the mysterious Korean Dr. Chan remained aloof and unsmiling. There seemed to be some forced performance by Martin. He was trying to please a little too much...seemed a little uneasy. A little off balance. This was a side of Martin that Steven had not seen before. Steven once again dismissed it. He was too busy with Victoria.

The din quieted only for a time as the sumptuous food arrived and everyone began eating. Soon the gesturing, laughing, and conversation began again and continued for a time. As the evening wore on, the tone lowered again. Only when Ricardo engaged Victoria in idle conversation did Steven have a chance to observe the others and catch Martin's eye, who winked at him, imperceptibly to all except Steven. It was as if Martin knew what the evening held in store for Steven and Victoria.

"That was a great dinner," Victoria said to Steven as Ricardo kissed Carmen on her neck, signaling that their conversation was over. Victoria looked at Steven and mouthed, "What a fool," and rolled her eyes toward Ricardo Alvarado.

Steven smiled and squeezed her hand again.

The dinner party was breaking up. Steven couldn't tell whether Dr. Chan or Martin had been first to rise, but they were both now standing, signaling the end of the party. Steven was relieved. He was ready for his own festivities but held back, so as not to appear too eager. Martin would be merciless. Slowly they were drifting out. When Steven felt comfortable, he seized the opportunity and, still holding Victoria's hand, walked out.

As they passed Martin, the two shook hands warmly, as if Martin was in a receiving line. It was Martin's way of communicating with Steven. "Dr. Chan and I are going to have a nightcap. You silly kids go on," Martin said, winking at Steven. "Recharge those batteries."

Steven looked at Victoria, and she wore a dazzling smile.

The two walked hand-in-hand from the restaurant into the lobby, with the roaring fire in the fireplace. They walked down the hall, past the jewelry shop on the right, gift shop on the left, and on down the four steps into the room wing, the head of the stairs up in front. As they reached the stairs, Steven went left and she to the right. Steven just smiled, which she returned, as their fingers remained laced to the last moment. Both knew the evening was not over.

There was a soft knock on the door, which Steven knew would be coming. He quickly opened the door. She looked dazzling. Victoria stood at the door wearing only a loose-fitting silk kimono and a bright smile. He held out his left hand. She took it. He drew her into the dark room lit only by burning red embers in the fireplace, and, as she came in, he slid his right hand around her waist, felt the softness, covered only by silk, and drew her into the room completely. She seemed to melt into the room. He kicked the door closed behind her. They were school children no more.

With a whooshing sound, the robe dropped to the floor...

Steven refocused on his own image in the mirror, took another sip of his drink, and remembered how Martin had gone to great lengths and much expense to find Victoria from his high school days to keep Steven enslaved and in his spider's web...

Suddenly, jarred out of his thoughts and feeling dirty all over again, in the mirror behind the bar, Steven saw Ricardo Alvarado walk in, lush black ponytail swinging.

Steven kept looking straight ahead as Ricardo sat down on the barstool beside him. "Hello, Steven Vandorol." Ricardo smiled and, not waiting for a reply, addressed the bartender, who had returned to the bar unnoticed by Steven. "Pablo, Hornitos tequila por favor!"

Ricardo Alvarado was still a handsome man, maybe five-foot-three, 150 pounds, jet-black hair, lush ponytail down to his waist, dressed in very tight designer jeans, starched snow-white shirt, massive gold Rolex on one wrist, heavy gold bracelet on the other, five-carat diamond pinkie rings on both hands.

His shirt was open in the front almost down to his waist, revealing a rug of curly black hair and three massive gold chains, one with a three-inch gold crucifix inlayed with diamonds.

Ricardo had the emaciated face of a probable alcoholic or drug addict, and looked almost like the dead cartel drug lord Pablo Escobar, while almost ten years ago when Steven last saw him here in Cloudcroft, Ricardo looked like a young Robert Blake, the actor of *In Cold Blood*, the movie, Steven thought. Now he was just a wasted old man trying to remain an adolescent Don Juan, despite the ravages of time and high living on drugs, sex, and rock and roll.

Still watching him in the mirror, Steven said, "What do you want, Ricardo?"

Always glib, Ricardo was speechless as he stammered, "Huh...er... wha..."

255

Steven, still watching in the mirror, repeated, "I said…*what* do you want?"

"What? No hello? No how are you, Ricardo? No how's tricks, Ricardo…?"

"I'm not repeating myself!"

"Okay, Steven, you win!" Ricardo paused. "I wanted to talk to you in person. Are you wired?" Ricardo downed the tequila, turned the shot glass over, and slammed it on the bar. "Nice boots. Alligator?"

Steven: "Are you?"

Ricardo stammered again, "Uh…er…you win again!"

"Are we playing a game here?" Steven was still looking in the mirror at him.

"Okay. Okay. No game here…" Ricardo paused as the bartender put another shot of tequila down on the bar, with lime wedges and salt. Ricardo put salt on his knuckle, touched it to his lips, downed the shot, bit on the lime, slammed the glass upside down, and said "Una otra" to the bartender.

The bartender put another shot in front of him.

Steven, still looking straight ahead, watching the little ceremony in the mirror, answered, "No, sea turtle." He paused and continued, "Ricardo, you're still the same obnoxious *mijo* you were almost ten years ago when I last saw you here in Cloudcroft."

"Our family, my father and I, made you a lot of money…" Ricardo was off balance, almost pleading.

"Wait a second, Ricardo." Steven paused then continued. "Do you have a contract out on me?" Steven noticed that several people were now at various tables in the bar area, about a dozen or so. He continued looking straight ahead.

Ricardo Alvarado was stunned, "Er…er…no, Steven. No…"

"But your old man does, right?"

Ricardo was shaking his head no, trying to regain his composure. "There's twenty million on deposit for you, Steven, in a Juarez bank."

"Dollars or pesos?"

"Dollars."

"And all I gotta do is go across the border to get it?" Steven knew that would be a clear violation of federal statutes and that he could lose his license to practice law.

"No, Steven, if you withdraw from the prosecution, I'll personally bring it to you!" Ricardo had regained his composure and was now smiling broadly, as he glanced in the mirror at someone now seated at a table behind him, raised his eyebrows, and closed and opened his eyes, an apparent signal.

Steven noticed and, still looking straight ahead, said, "Did you hire the Russian mafia to do it...or was it Spetznaʒ, Ruski commandos that were out of work?" Steven was smiling broadly now as he got off the barstool and headed for the lobby.

Ricardo yelled after him, "Steven, where are you going..."

Steven, almost to the door, turned and said, "Ricardo, once just a delivery boy...always just a delivery boy... Feliz Navidad, Madre Chingado..." and he walked out the door.

Exactly 108 miles away, in the safe house on Rio Grande Avenue in El Paso above the La Cocina Restaurant, Ward Powell's burner cell phone vibrated in his pocket. He was alone. The general had called a meeting of the strike team and was meeting with them at the Sunland Park safe house to plan for the New Year's Year of the Horse surprise. Ward's presence was not required. Anyway, he had a hot date lined up at the Artesian...

Ward took out his phone, clicked on, and said, "How's your surveillance and plan going?" Listened several seconds, then said, "Remember, no traces...or witnesses or evidence, no nothing, right?" Listened again. "Good, you've got it handled!" Paused a beat and said, "How about the floor plans for his office?" Listened again and said, "Good deal! I'll get them from you tonight..." Listened again and started grinning like a teenager. "Your motor already running hot?" Listened, paused, swallowed, then, still smiling, said, "Room 404, Artesian, be there!" and clicked off.

39

Steven was driving up Scenic Drive before going to lunch downtown and thought he would check on Rommel, to make sure he had enough food.

The closer Steven got to his house, the worse he felt. His stomach was queasy. A real bad feeling. Steven sped up as he rounded Sierra Medical Center up Scenic Drive and turned on Golden Hill Terrace into his driveway. Touched the garage opener, but the garage wouldn't open.

What the. . . Steven thought. The door opener had not been reset after the destruction of his garage door. He jumped out of his car and left the car door open, ran up to the front. Unlocked the front gate, then the front door, opened, and yelled, "Rommel!"

No Rommel.

Rushed into the kitchen. "Rommel!" Steven yelled again.

Into the garage, to Rommel's house, looked.

No Rommel.

Rushed out back to the patio, froze. Rommel was lying in the grass, and Steven saw blood. Lots of blood. Rommel was covered in blood, the bright red liquid pooling around him.

"Oh my God!" he shouted, running to his dog. Rommel raised his head and moaned softly. Steven kneeled down, whispered, "Hold on, boy," as he took off his sport coat and laid it on Rommel. Ripped off his shirt and held it near his neck where blood was flowing and pressed it tight. Pulled his cell phone out, dialed 911...it was ringing.

"This is 911. What's your emergency?"

"This is Judge Steven Vandorol, the address is 4444 Golden Hill Terrace on Scenic Drive, right next to Sierra Medical Center. Someone shot my dog, Rommel, probably from a high-powered rifle from the Scenic Point above my house. The dog is still alive but is bleeding badly! Please...please send an ambulance and contact Chief Eddie Egen also, immediately. Please, got all that?"

"Yessir, judge. Standby..."

Steven touched his cell phone off, pocketed it, and held his pressed hand on the wound. "Take it easy, boy, I love you, Rommel, hold on boy, hold on..." Steven paused, looked upward. "Please...please, Lord, don't let my dog die..."

Steven cried.

Rommel moaned again, brown eyes wide. He twitched as Steven rubbed his massive head tenderly.

Steven heard sirens.

"Hold on, my friend. I'm going to open the garage door. I'll be right back."

Steven went back in the house, through the kitchen into the garage, hit the button, and the garage door started up. He followed the door opening out, ducking his head, jumped in his car, and drove it up the street in front. Left the door open and ran back through the garage as sirens wailed close behind.

Steven was back to Rommel in a flash, kneeled down. "You'll be okay, boy, just hold on. Help is coming." He pressed on the wound. "Please, Lord, not my dog, please. Don't let him die. Please let him live! Please..."

The siren screaming was out in front, Steven could hear. It stopped abruptly. Doors opening, closing, gurney swinging open, paramedics running as a police officer burst in, saying "Judge!"

"Right here. I'm holding my shirt on the wound," Steven said as the gurney came out with two EMTs. Rommel looked up at Steven and whined softly.

"You'll be fine, boy."

The EMT kneeled down. "Judge, you can let go, we've got 'im." He was calm, calming both Steven and Rommel.

Steven stood, glanced at the officer's name plate. "Did you call Chief Egen?"

"Yes, judge, he's on his way."

"Good. I think the shot came from Scenic Point."

"Yeah...the chief already sent the crime scene guys up there."

Steven took a strong, deep breath, exhaled. The adrenaline was kicking in big-time. Steven was shaking, tensing up...

The EMTs had Rommel up on the gurney. "We've sedated your dog, judge. He's lost some blood, but we think he'll be okay. It's lucky you found him early."

"I don't think luck had anything to do with it," Steven replied. "Can I go with him to the hospital?"

"Not necessary, judge. It's better if you didn't. We'll take good care of him for you."

Steven was calming further. "I'll follow you to Providence. My dog needs a private room, okay?" Steven got in his car.

"We've got it, judge."

———

The EMTs wheeled Rommel into Emergency at Providence Hospital, just as Eddie Egen drove up, got out of his cruiser, and walked up to Steven getting out of his car.

"Steven, how are you?" Eddie asked, eyes wide. "I've sent a unit up to Scenic Point." He hugged Steven.

Steven hugged him back. "I'm okay. Thanks for coming so fast."

Ed looked around up high toward the Franklin Mountains. Extended his arm toward the north and held it.

"You're right, Steven! There's a direct line up to Scenic Point. Look."

Steven looked up, and sure enough the crime scene crew was already up there. An officer was waving.

Steven waved back and motioned for them to come down after they were through. "They probably won't find anything."

"I agree. They're professionals," Ed said. "I'm really sorry, Steven."

Steven nodded. "Thanks, Ed! They said Rommel would probably live..." He was tearing up again...

"Also, Steven, this was another professional well-timed deal. The officer following you, Jack Turner, got sideswiped by a 2003 black Taurus, smoked windows, no license plate, just as he turned up Scenic Drive..." Eddie was almost breathless.

"Is Turner all right?" Steven asked.

"Yeah, he's fine. Just shaken up. Pissed. How's Rommel, that sweet dog?"

"Rommel will be okay," Steven repeated, wiping his eyes. "Ed, I had a premonition. That's why I stopped by. I was on the way downtown for lunch with North."

"Wow, Steven. A shiver just ran down my back. That's pretty amazing..."

"No, that's divine guidance and grace."

Steven sat outside in the back of his house on Scenic Drive, the entire universe of El Paso and Juarez sparkling right before his eyes. Rommel sat quietly with his head on his forelegs at his side. Steven marveled at the beauty and splendor beneath him and gently stroked Rommel's head.

Rommel had fully recovered. Had the best care, a private room at Sierra Medical and a private nurse. Only a small shaved spot on his neck with bandage remained. Steven, the ultimate survivor, helped his dog survive as well, by the grace of God, in answer to Steven's prayer.

Steven was peaceful. Steven was serene. Steven was lonely on Christmas Eve. It had been a long and stressful week.

His children, Josef and Karina, were probably already asleep in Crested Butte, where they had joined their "uncle" Bob, Robert Bailey, and his family for a weeklong skiing vacation. It was the first Christmas since he had left DC that Steven had been unable to spend with them. He really missed his two kids.

Both had called earlier to wish their dad a Merry Christmas.

He looked out on the beautiful scene before him and thought back to that time long before when the two most consistent joys of his life—his kids—had saved his life. He also remembered the horror of a certain bridge abutment that day in the Sunbelt when the end was in sight…

Steven, on automatic pilot, jolted by a demand to appear in person, walked up the stairs at Century Bank Oklahoma in Oklahoma City—a major bank client—to Kern McIlvaney's office, where he had been ordered to appear. A strange haze still hung over the ground, dreamlike. He arrived to the stern look of the receptionist.

"Here to see Kern," Steven said.

Without a word, she rose and went back.

Steven glanced in the mirror. He was, as usual, impeccably dressed in a light-brown houndstooth, tailor-made suit. His eyes hooked onto his trademark: a white silk pocket square that had both a haphazard and razor-sharp look all at the same time. Tailored white cotton shirt with monogram on the sleeve in black Old English, SJV, half hidden by his suit coat sleeve. A matching silk red tie, perfectly knotted at the apex.

His eyes wandered to his face. Chiseled from granite. Clean shaven. Flawless skin. Hungarian dark. Wide forehead. Receding hairline. Prominent equine nose, nostrils flaring slightly. Also Hungarian. High cheekbones accenting large brown piercing eyes, with just a hint of slant, evident in the race coming from the Mongol and Hun hordes beginning the Hungarian bloodlines. His gaze reflected his soul. Sometimes fierce. Sometimes tender. Always sensitive. Always observing. Never clear, nor serene. Perfect window to his troubled soul. Gold Ralph Lauren wire-rimmed glasses shrouding the brown eyes. Sensual lips which, on a resting face, displayed an elusive sadness and, when unsmiling, a grim, almost ruthless determination. Hair perfect. Brown silk with a hint of sideburns, razor edged. Steven thought to himself, That's not me at all. I am scared.

"He will see you now." The woman, returning to the reception room, interrupted Steven's thoughts.

He walked past her scowl into Kern's office.

Kern was sitting to the left, in a couch and easy chair grouping, in the corner of his office. The sun was streaming in. Almost blinding. Throwing shadows over a myriad of plants in front of the glass picture window. The room had an aura of the jungle. A jungle in a nightmare. Steven's private nightmare. The black panther sat in the jungle. Menacing. Snarling.

"Sit down." Kern pointed to the easy chair. Steven knew what the topic of conversation would be. "The $800,000 Capital Financial debt has been past due and outstanding for long enough." Steven knew. He didn't have to say anything, as Kern continued, "I gave you the stock back on a trust receipt, and you have cheated me."

Steven started to protest but thought better of it. Said nothing.

"I want my money, and I want it by five o'clock today. If the money is not here by five o'clock, or the stock instead, I will be immediately filing a lawsuit against Capital Financial, and you as the guarantor. If the stock is not here, I'm calling the FBI." Kern was so angry that his voice shook. "This conversation is over."

Kern got up and stood glaring at Steven, rising awkwardly from the easy chair.

Steven was in a daze. A dreamlike state. He mechanically rose to his feet and walked out the door. Down the stairs. Still the haze. Still the fog. Got into his sleek silver Ferrari with the silver Australian sheepskin custom interior...

Consciousness suddenly returned. Steven looked out the front windshield. His eyes were desperately trying to focus. He blinked. Then again. He was on the interstate heading east. Telephone poles, trees, bushes, cars, fence, cows, all flashed by at terrific speeds. Only Steven was motionless.

Why is it so foggy? *he thought.* God...they...everything...flying by me awful fast.

Steven glanced at the tachometer. Unknowingly smiled. The needle was vibrating, already past the red line: 8500 RPM, 190 mph. A daydream. The sun was bright. Brilliant. Beautiful. Steven was floating in a brilliant haze.

He looked up and out the windshield.

Suddenly, a concrete bridge abutment was heading straight for the front of the car like a rocket. A cannon shot heading toward his face. A split second. An eternity...slow motion...

His mind was a screen. An old-time movie. He sat in the dark theater. He was all alone in the theater. The screen bright, bathed in brilliant light. The frames were flashing in slow motion. Hazy. Foggy. Slow. He watched the silent movie, faint piano music in the far distance. Pictures flashed in succession. His son. "My son." Smiling, laughing, playing. "My daughter. My little girl." The sweet, innocent face of his daughter, looking at a flower. A pause. An eternity. As he saw that last still frame, that precious face, his right hand jerked onto the steering wheel. Hard.

The concrete abutment flashed by the left side of the car. He drew to the right as the abutment grazed his left sleeve. Both past and future vanished. His foot came off the accelerator—170, 160, 80...

The car stopped. He was by the side of the highway. He laid his forehead on his forearm, gripping the steering wheel, as tears dropped onto his drenched, tailor-made suit. Steven Vandorol lived that day in the Sunbelt. For his two children who had no choice.

His two precious kids were now older, well-protected and thriving, but still Steven had pangs of guilt over the time he had missed when he had not been there for them or seen himself fully.

He was much better now, having survived by the grace of God when he had thought it was because of his two kids. Then in DC he walked through that valley of evil, corruption, and sleaze and survived again by the grace of God.

Steven was now serene but still very lonely on this Christmas Eve 2015, anno Domini, the year of the Lord…

On his stereo, Lee Greenwood's CD *God Bless the USA*, Steven's favorite, played soft, and "O Holy Night" was just starting.

Steven took a sip of his wine, stroked Rommel's massive head, and listened to the words:

> *O holy night!*
> *The stars are brightly shining,*
> *It is the night of our dear savior's birth.*
> *Long lay the world in sin and error pining.*
> *Till He appeared and the soul felt its worth.*

A thrill of hope, the weary world rejoices,
For yonder breaks a new and glorious morn.
Fall on your knees!

At its beautiful crescendo and the words

Fall on your knees!
O hear the angel voices…

tears streamed down his face, and Steven went to his knees by his dog's side…and prayed.

He prayed for the continued safety and wellbeing of his children, and the strengthening of his faith. Steven prayed for guidance to make the right choices and for the protection by the good Lord and Jesus Christ of his faith, his family, and his friends.

As he heard the whispers of divine guidance, his tears washed away the loneliness.

"Well, Rommel, I think it's time we got some sleep."

Rommel looked up, tilted his huge head to one side, and Steven thought he actually smiled again…

- 40 -

Steven Vandorol was vigilant driving to the office the day after Christmas, thinking about the evil pervading the nation. He was even more vigilant these days since the destruction of his garage door and the wounding of his dog. He recognized that previously, in DC, his main opponents had been neurosis and psychological pathology, corruption and sleaze, but now it was abject evil, he thought.

Steven remembered Arlene Wellington's words during his worst time in DC: "If you have goodness, truth, beauty, and love in your heart, and you couple that with a good sense of humor, you can face anything, for those are the weapons of angels." Steven had focused especially on the weapons of angels, the sword of righteousness of the archangel Gabriel, in shearing layers of evil out of his own heart, mind, and soul, all with the grace of God.

Steven also remembered when Courtney said, "The farther backward you can look, the farther forward you're likely to see." Steven was right between the past and the future. *In a pause mode, I guess…and looking to the future, hopefully fully armed with the weapons of angels,* he thought.

Steven was focused and calm. On the side of angels, and with the Lord Jesus Christ in his heart, he focused on the coming war between good and evil as a professional warrior at the sword point, as Ernie Martinez had said.

Steven was also surviving and doing it well. Peace of mind brought serenity. He left ultimate emotional intimacy for himself, as between a man and a woman, to the good Lord and His mysterious ways—and the good Lord's timing.

He had studied law and practiced it a long time before seeing himself fully. The lawyer in him had not been suffocated; neither had the artist. Steven had always been the ultimate survival warrior that he always had to be. He always thought he had survived because of his layers of evil, when in fact he had survived by the grace of God, and in spite of those layers.

There is no honor in sending people to die for something you won't even fight for yourself. Steven would not ask anyone to do anything he wouldn't do himself.

These thoughts went through his mind as he drove north on Mesa toward his office the day after Christmas. The El Paso sky was cloudless, and the sun sparkled and shone bright in the Texas sky. It was a cool dry day in the Sun City.

Christmas without his two kids had been peaceful. Steven and Rommel had a quiet and calm Christmas Eve alone and an even calmer Christmas Day. Steven and Rommel joined Eddie and Andi, Ray and his wife, Jessie, on the ranch, and they all even enjoyed a late evening ride. Ray presented Steven with another Persuader pump-action shotgun for his Christmas gift. Except for his two kids and the Wellingtons, Steven had been with loved ones on Christmas Day right there in El Paso.

Steven would be alone at his office today. He had given Christina and Marcie the entire week off between Christmas and New Year.

He glanced in his rearview mirror. No traffic behind him. Traffic was light on North Mesa Street. UTEP at Christmastime was deserted, though the Sun Bowl classic on New Year's Day would bring them back in droves. Oklahoma would be playing Stanford for a national ranking…

Out of the corner of his eye, Steven saw another black SUV with dark windshield at Kearbey and North Mesa. As he passed that intersection, he glanced at its license plate, XEL 210, and made a mental note. He pulled into the gas station just ahead. Got out and looked around. The car was gone.

Steven filled up his car, carefully looking around. He caught a glimpse of the black SUV again on Stanton Street driving with other traffic north on Mesa Street.

There may be more than just one, Steven thought as he pulled back onto Kearbey Street leading to his office.

Traffic was still light as he pulled onto Sun Bowl Drive. It was deserted. Drove past his office building to the end of the block, turned around, and drove into the driveway and back to the parking lot. It was also deserted.

Got out. Looked around and pulled out his Glock. Took off the safety and checked the clip. Back in. Chambered a round. Locked and loaded.

Steven walked up and around to the side door. Used his card to open it, went in by the elevator, and walked upstairs to the second floor. He was cautious as he approached his office's entrance, his steps muffled by the deep-pile carpet.

At the front door, Steven had a bad feeling, the hair tingled on the back of his neck, got down on all fours and put his head on the carpet sideways. Peered under the door. There was a wire leading up on the inside door. He slowly got up and walked several steps away. Got his cell phone out, clicked to Ed's number, pressed. It was ringing...

Ed answered immediately. "Hello, Steven, what's up?"

"Ed, I'm at my office, and I looked under the door, and there's a wire going up from the floor on the inside of the door—"

"Don't touch anything on the door! I'm contacting the unit that was following you around today right now. Stand by!"

"Gotcha. Bye."

The unit arrived first. Steven let two officers in downstairs who then confirmed the wire and called the bomb squad. The bomb squad, using penlight cameras, managed to find the proper connection and cut the hot wire connection to disarm the explosive. Steven opened the door, and the officers peeled off an adhesive plastic charge from the door jamb, Russian markings. The entire second floor, and Steven, they said, would have been history had he opened the suite door. Eddie Egen and Lieutenant Samson arrived next and helped sweep the entire office, all clear.

Steven made a pot of coffee, and the two were in Steven's back office, enjoying steaming mugs.

Eddie spoke first. "Steven, you were lucky...err...yeah, yeah, I know...the good Lord and His mysterious ways, right?"

Steven was smiling. "Divine guidance. You've got it." He paused. "Also, vigilance paid off! Do you think it's the same bunch that almost torched my house?"

"Yeah, probably. These are professionals, probably Staci, or Spetsnaʒ, by all indications." Eddie swallowed then continued. "Russian markings on the detonator…"

"That's all Cold War stuff," Steven mused. "By the way, the plate on the first black SUV was XEL 210…Texas plate."

"Got it," Ed said. Dialed on his cell, paused. "George, Egen…check license plate XEL 210 Texas plates, okay?"

Eddie clicked off. "The Ruskies never stopped. They are behind all the turmoil in the world. They're behind Iran, Syria, all the Muslim Caliphate cancer…" He took a sip of his coffee, paused, and continued, "When President Reagan blew up the Soviet Union, Russia became a nation of thugs, and a lot of the military became mercenaries and hired killers."

"And the Chinese?" Steven asked. "They almost succeeded in DC five years ago." He took a sip of his coffee.

"Hey, Steven, you really love your coffee, don't you?" Eddie Egen asked, taking a sip from his own mug.

"I sure do. Let's get a refill, okay?"

They got up and walked out to the reception area. Pouring coffee for himself, Eddie said, "I don't understand how you drink so much coffee." He was smiling broadly.

Steven poured himself coffee as well and answered, "Law of gravity. If you tip it up, it comes right out. You can't help but drink it!"

Eddie laughed. "Your heart must be thumping all the time."

Steven smiled. "Better than the alternative," he said as he walked back to his office, Eddie following right behind.

Both sat back down, and Eddie took a sip of his coffee, smiling in satisfaction. "Ah, it *is* great coffee! I can tell why you drink so much…it's like gourmet stuff. Where do you get it from?"

Steven took a sip from his own cup and said, "I order it on Amazon. It's the best coffee from Brazil, a private reserve Brazil Santos Bourbon coffee…I drink it at home as well…glad you like it."

"Expensive?"

"Nope," Steven answered. "The Cowboy Blend is about twenty bucks for a 12-ounce foil pack."

Eddie took another sip and returned to their conversation about the Chinese. "Thanks to *you* they didn't succeed in DC. Hey Steven, the Chinese can't stand the Ruskies, but they hate us worse. I think all the players, the Chinese, the Ruskies…and Muslim radicals, are all joined together in this brand-new world war in which America is at the top."

Steven nodded. "What's that commie saying? The enemy of my enemy is my friend…"

"Or the gangster saying about 'hold your friends close, but your enemies closer.'" Eddie paused, smiling. "…So, they won't punch you in the gut."

Steven laughed. "Yeah, like 'El Chapo, Ricardo Alvarado,' that's why I went to Cloudcroft!" Steven had told Eddie all about the meeting in Cloudcroft and the twenty million bribe offer.

"Yeah, Steven," Eddie said. "The good Lord's grace again, right? You were fortunate. He probably coulda had you killed." Eddie was serious.

"I was vigilant!" Steven answered. "And there were too many people around at the lodge." He paused, thinking. "Ricardo Alvarado may be a real *mijo*, but he didn't get to be a drug lord by being stupid."

"Yeah, you're right," Eddie said. "So, how's the search for another lawyer going? Any leads?"

Steven smiled. "Yes, good news. You remember I told you about Vanessa Moore in Washington, DC?"

"Yes, I do," Eddie said. "Wasn't she your friend and colleague, co-worker at Henderson Lane?"

"That's right. She also was there for me during my toughest times." Steven paused a beat. "She's the one who encouraged me to keep running, which I still do, as you know, regularly…"

"So, what about her?" Eddie asked, smiling.

"Well, I called her. She's now divorced, and she's coming out to El Paso the first week in January to see if she wants to work with me."

"That's really great, Steven."

The outside line rang.

"Ed, I'm here by myself today, let me get it." Steven picked up the phone. "Law office, may I help you?" Listened, "Well, hello, Judge Carbon, Merry Christmas to you." Steven paused, listened, "How are *you*? Listened, "I'm really well…sitting here having coffee with the Chief! How are you?"

Steven took another sip of his coffee, moments passed, and his smile broadened. He motioned a thumbs-up to Eddie. "Well, thank you, judge. And happy New Year to you as well. I would be delighted. I was going to spend New Year's Eve with my dog." Steven winked at Eddie, sitting across from him. "Shall we meet at Cafe Central…seven o'clock?"

Steven listened again. Continued smiling, then, "That's even better…I'll have cocktails all ready. Great, I'll see you then…thank you." Steven hung up the phone, grinning from ear to ear. "The good Lord works in mysterious ways. Ed, I've got a date for New Year's Eve…"

- 41 -

She was parked on the corner of Wilmot and Parkland in the Walmart Super Center parking lot, which was packed with almost a thousand cars of all shapes, sizes, and colors, but mostly white—the norm in El Paso as protection against the burning El Paso sun. It was early afternoon, people coming and going, shopping for New Year's Day festivities and football-watching parties. Her targets were in a neighborhood three blocks away. She had scouted the home, the neighborhood near Coronado High School, in the evenings several times and was ready to carry out her assignment. She was a professional who did all her jobs very well. She enjoyed her work immensely and derived great satisfaction from it. She was a killer.

She was parked in a nondescript white Nissan Sentra, dark windows, engine idling, air conditioning on full blast, and right in the middle of the lot next to cars almost identical to hers. She glanced at the car's digital clock, 1:10 pm…the target's neighborhood would be deserted. It was time. She had allotted one hour for her job. She was a very thorough professional…

She turned off the engine, stepped out of the car, locked the doors, and started walking toward Wilmot Street.

She could have easily passed for a high school senior, although a gorgeous one, for sure, she thought to herself. Long dark hair in a ponytail to mid-back, mirror Cartier sunglasses, large lenses hiding most of her face, all covered with a Dallas Cowboys hat and no makeup whatsoever, except for lip gloss. She wore a Coronado High School red football jersey, sweatpants, and black Nike running shoes. A 9mm Beretta M9 with silencer was tucked in the small of her back on a belt, all hidden by the jersey, and she carried a North Face backpack containing a nylon face mask, lip gloss, gloves, and two extra clips. She was ready.

The sun was straight up in the sky, brilliant and white hot. Glaring and oppressive yet a cool 70's in the shade. Nothing else was even marginally visible.

She slowly walked across the burning hot parking lot, passing cars radiating and reflecting the hot sun, and smelling the acrid odor of hot asphalt and gasoline. She seemed to be walking in a Sun City hell until she reached Wilmot Street. Looked both ways, no cars coming, and walked across to Parkland Street. She moved slowly down the street to the right and continued down the block.

The streets had large homes, long driveways, large landscaped lawns, rock gardens with desert plants, and silvery rock that was the norm in El Paso residential areas. Cacti landscaping with mesquite and acacia trees. All was deserted, except for an occasional tricycle or kid's toys lying in the driveways. The homes were mostly white-and-gray stucco with large windows, thick drapes, and boxlike sun-reflecting awnings. Prevalent Spanish modern architecture.

No one was braving the oppressive midday sun as she casually walked down that block, turned up on Vista del Sol Street, and walked to number 1055, her final destination. She stopped and looked around, scanning all the nearby homes and the entire neighborhood. The mail had already been delivered; she checked the box again anyway just to be sure. Still empty. She looked across the street. All window blinds were down. She could see the heat rising from the rooftops, the sun still almost blinding. She shaded her eyes—all deserted. All garage doors down. She was completely alone on a deserted street.

She walked to the side of the house by a cement walkway to the gate to the backyard, unlatched it, stepped in, and closed the rough cedar gate behind her. She was in the backyard, surrounded by an eight-foot rough cedar wooden fence. The backyard was large and ran the entire length of the house and had two sprawling elm trees that canopied most of the yard, lowering the temperature by 20 degrees at least. It was exquisitely landscaped with brick flower beds full of succulents and cacti, all professionally arranged.

A child's playset sat in between the trees—all redwood, with plastic slides and swings, and a wooden playhouse on top. The patio to the right was covered with a huge Sunshade retractable awning and included a massive built-in barbeque grill, two tables, chairs, and two chaise lounges, as well as a plastic kiddie pool half full of water with two plastic yellow ducks floating in the water.

She walked to the glass patio doors, which had heavy curtains drawn. She tried the sliding glass door, unlocked it, and slid it open. All dark and cool inside. She stepped in and waited. She knew there was no one home. Backing into the family den, she took out the sheer nylon mask and started to put it on, hesitated, then put it back in the backpack. She took out her gloves, put them on, and walked into the kitchen. Found a glass from the cabinet, filled it with water from the refrigerator door dispenser, opened the door, looked around, got a pear out, and sat down on the barstool. Took out the Beretta, tightened the screwed-on silencer, chambered a round, put the weapon on the counter, took a drink, bit into the pear, and waited…

At 1:30, she heard the garage door rambling open, car doors opening and closing, long pause, and the door into the den opened. "Close the garage door, Michelle," Jillian said as she stepped in, saw her standing right there, stuttered, eyes widened, terrified. "Who…?" And she shot her right between the eyes. Pop, pop. Jillian teetered for an instant and fell dead to the right, helped by her with a slight push. She heard the garage door rambling down. She also heard the little girl coming to the door, pushing it in. "Mommy, can I have a peanut butter and jelly…." The little girl saw the woman and screamed as the gun fired…pop, pop…and the child died instantly. She dragged the little girl and left her beside her mother.

Walking back to the bar, she put the Beretta on the counter and finished eating her pear, drank the rest of the water, put the glass in the sink, and waited again. Took out her cell phone, set it on the counter as well, and waited.

The cell phone rang.

"Yes." She listened, clicked off, and continued to wait, looking around, enjoying the cool air conditioning.

In fifteen minutes, she heard the garage door opening again and the distinct purring of the Porsche driving in. She got off the stool, picked up the Beretta, slowly walked to the door, stood with her back against the wall, and waited.

The door opened. "Michelle my belle, Daddy's home!" Jason Warren yelled as he stepped into the kitchen, a wide smile on his face, eyes wide open.

And she shot him right between the eyes; one muffled pop and Jason Warren died with his eyes wide open, stood for a second, and collapsed straight down as if his legs disappeared from under him.

She watched the blood pool out for a few seconds, raised the gun again, and shot him in the chest twice…pop, pop…the muzzle stayed open…gun was empty.

She picked up the shell casings, put them in her pocket, reloaded, chambered a round, and put the weapon in her belt in the small of her back. Stepped over a dead Jason Warren and out into the garage, pressed the door button, and the door rambled down shut. She came back in, closed and locked the inside door. touched up her lip gloss, eased out through the curtain, and went out the same way she came in. Walked to the side and out the back gate and closed it behind her. Took her gloves off, put them in her bag. Walked down the driveway back to the street and looked around again, turned left on the still deserted street, and in the oppressive heat walked slowly back to her car, smiling like a teenage cheerleader walking to Walmart…

"Come on in, judge. Really nice to see you this fine El Paso evening." Steven was smiling warmly as he held the front door open for Judge Kathy Carbon, 168th District Court, Chief Judge, the second beautiful woman to cross his threshold this December.

Kathy Carbon looked stunning on this New Year's Eve. She was a tiny four-foot-ten, Steven guessed, less than a hundred pounds. Black shiny hair speckled with gray. Perfect makeup, high cheekbones, a tiny nose, small mouth, rosebud lips. Steven knew her very well professionally, had practiced in her court hundreds of times, and she had even appointed Steven to the Municipal Bench when there had been an opening. She was also instrumental in recommending Steven to the district attorney for heading the special prosecution. Kathy and Steven had become good friends, professionally. And Steven admired and liked her very much.

"Thank you, Mr. Vandorol, but tonight I am a civilian. Please call me Kathy...Steven," she said as she hugged him warmly.

Steven hugged her right back. "I guess then I can say, Kathy, you look positively gorgeous this evening. Happy New Year."

"Thank you, Steven. Happy New Year to you too. You look very nice yourself."

Steven had on a white shirt, paisley tie perfectly knotted, tan slacks with a razor-sharp pleat, and his favorite maroon sea turtle boots, shined to a high gloss.

"Nice boots! I've seen them before in my court." She smiled coyly. "I couldn't compliment you on them in court."

Steven laughed. "Yes, they are my favorites!"

"Alligator?" Kathy asked.

"Sea turtle. El Paso's own Tony Lamas!"

She entered; Steven closed the front door. "Can I take your jacket?"

"Sure, thanks," she said as she shrugged off her coat and handed it to Steven, who laid it across the back of the sofa. "What a gorgeous view!" She paused before the plate-glass window then looked around. "And you have a very nice place also, by the way."

"Thank you, Kathy." Steven had her elbow. "It's my oasis…my favorite place in the world. Can I get you some wine?"

Rommel was again sitting by the couch watching the slight beautiful woman intently, ears standing tall.

"That would be grand," she said as she nonchalantly walked up to Rommel lying on the couch and patted his head. Rommel was almost purring.

"Well, that's interesting," Steven said.

"What is?" Kathy asked, still stroking Rommel's head.

"Rommel is sure not shy tonight!" Steven answered. "He usually takes his time in warming up to people." He poured two glasses of Chianti, walked back in, and handed a glass to Kathy. "Chianti okay?"

"Perfect." Kathy took the glass and sat down on the couch right next to Rommel's huge head. She raised her glass. "Happy New Year again."

Steven raised his glass. "And to you, Kathy," he said as Rommel laid his huge snout right in his guest's lap. Steven laughed. "Rommel…"

"He's fine," Kathy said as she patted his huge head. "He's a beautiful dog, Steven." She paused a moment and took a sip of her wine. "Ernie told me…in confidence…about the attack on your home. Are you all right?" She locked eyes with him.

Steven sat down in the wingback chair. "Yep, I got my dog and my oasis. I'm fine! Eddie's got me 24/7 security. We're being watched, as we speak." He took a drink. "Thank you for the invitation. I've been looking forward to our date. Are you okay with it?"

"You mean going public with your friendship?" She smiled at Steven. "I'll answer that…no problem whatsoever. You're a goodlooking guy, Steven, and a darn fine lawyer as well. No, no problem at all."

"Thank you, Kathy. You're a dear. A very beautiful dear." Steven was smiling warmly. "What's your future look like?"

"I'm in my own oasis." She smiled at Steven and raised her glass again. "Here's to each of us finding our dream…"

Steven raised his glass also. "Happiness is like a butterfly. You can chase it and chase it and never catch it. But when you sit down to take a rest, it alights on your shoulder."

"Amen." Judge Kathy Carbon clicked her glass with her friend, Steven Vandorol, took a sip, paused a moment, and said, "How is the amended indictment coming along?"

Steven took a sip of his wine and cleared his throat. "I'm working on it when I can." He paused. "It's been tough in November and December, but I've kind of caught up. I'm still looking to hire an experienced young lawyer to help me with my practice so I can devote full time to the special prosecution."

Steven paused again and said, "I'll have the amended or superseding indictment ready for filing in early July." Now smiling, he added, "And there's good news as well. A lawyer in DC that I worked with there…she's still a good friend…is coming to El Paso next week in to check out El Paso and maybe work with me."

"That's great, Steven! I can then call for the secret and closed grand jury to be empaneled." Kathy paused, thought, and continued, "And after you present your entire case, and the grand jury issues and certifies the true bill of indictment—"

Steven interrupted, "You can issue warrants for the arrest of all the criminals…"

———

At home alone after dropping Judge Carbon off after dinner at Cafe Central and a subdued New Year's Eve party, Steven sat in the dark drinking a glass of Courvoisier, stroking Rommel's head, his large black eyes shining in the brilliance of lights streaming into the room. Before the two lay the El Paso-Juarez panorama of a billion sparkling jewels, all lying on a jet-black velvet ocean before an infinite sky, shimmering, blinking, pulsating, and piercing the blackness of the nighttime void.

As he marveled at the spectacle outside, Steven walked out onto the panoramic balcony where the entire world of El Paso and Juarez stretched into eternity before him. Rommel followed and sat down beside him. Both man and dog marveled at the light show below and gazed into the black void above. The two were all alone in the magnificent outdoor "theater of God"—as if an immense outdoor IMAX screen lay before them in all its technicolor glory.

Steven and Rommel gazed in complete wonderment and awe at God's nighttime creation. The sky above the magnificent panorama of brilliant lights and sparkling colors was a black void standing out in silent contrast.

Steven was thoughtful. Steven was pensive. Steven was serene and peaceful. *I'm in that pause moment of time directly in between the pause… in one of my favorite sayings: the farther backward you can look …pause…the farther forward you are likely to see.* He looked down at Rommel, who again cocked his head, again almost smiling back at Steven.

"So, what do you think, Rommel? What's our future like?" he said out loud to his dog, now sitting beside him looking up at him.

Rommel grunted as if answering Steven.

"You're right, Rommel, I…we have much to be thankful for. We…I have my faith in God and Jesus Christ. I have my kids and I have good friends… and you and Pegasus…" And there before all of El Paso, Texas, and Juarez Mexico, and the good Lord and Jesus Christ in his heart, Steven Vandorol kneeled, closed his eyes, clasped his hands together, bowed his head, and with Rommel beside him, prayed out loud.

"Dear Lord and Jesus Christ I love you with all my heart and soul and thank you for all that you have done for me. I'm so very grateful for all the help, all the blessings and miracles, guidance and blessed assurance. And I'm so grateful that you are there with me, and for me, guiding me, comforting me and being in my heart and soul …protecting me and comforting me with your grace, every second of every day. And I am especially grateful for my faith, for my two precious kids, Josef and Karina...my friends and my health and survival, all by your grace. Thank you, dear God, the Father, and thank you, Jesus, Christ, His Son and my Savior."

"I ask you, dear God and Jesus Christ, to please stay with me and continue to show me the way, and help me to be the best I can be, first, for you Lord and Jesus Christ, for my precious kids and future grandkids, and for my friends...my dog, Rommel and horse Pegasus."

Steven glanced at Rommel, head bowed, eyes closed, but breathing lightly, seemingly praying also...and Steven said the Lord's Prayer out loud.

"Our Father, who art in heaven, hallowed be thy name...thy kingdom come... thy will be done, on earth, as it is in heaven....give us this day our daily bread and forgive us our debts, as we forgive our debtors...and lead us not into temptation, but deliver us from evil, for thine is the kingdom and the power and the glory, forever and ever, in Jesus Christ, your Son's name, Amen..." Steven opened his eyes, rose from his knees slowly, grasped the railing with his hands, yawned again, sighed deeply, and looked into God's brilliant and he infinite sky above. Rommel stood beside him, staring at his master and best friend adoringly.

Steven looked down at Rommel, fully visible in the brilliant light show before them, and smiled. From his dog, Steven looked back out on God's giant screen and focused on the jewels of the entire universe before him and the El Paso downtown and Juarez sparkling before them.

Steven was looking directly at the giant American flag illuminating the Well Fargo Texas Bank Tower, the red, white and blue lights of the stars and stripes standing above and in the midst of downtown like a majestic beacon.

Right below, Interstate 10 was completely deserted. Only the brilliant electric lights of the spectacular light show could be seen, shimmering before his eyes into eternity, and just a few cars or other vehicles were visible in the middle of the night, their headlights like tiny fireflies moving in the distance.

Steven and Rommel were standing in awe of God's magnificent screen when suddenly a cascading wave-like rolling blackout turned all the lights out downtown, the brilliant American flag going completely dark, and it rolled out into the far distance, both to Steven's right and left, all lights going out one sparkling quadrant at a time, until there was nothing...

And in that instant of time, the Lord turned out the lights of the world. The immense screen before them went completely black, and there was only absolute darkness, silence and oppressive gloom.

. . . and El Paso died.

As Steven and Rommel stood in the pitch-black darkness enveloping both like a funeral shroud, Steven raised his arm to his face, clicked the presser on the luminous dial of his Timex calendar wristwatch, and the turquoise face showed that it was 3 am, January 1, 2016, anno Domini.

And then there was nothing. . .

–TO BE CONTINUED–

PLEASE READ:
EL PASO SUNSET, A NOVEL
BY LOUIS BODNAR

COMING SOON....

About the Author

Louis J. Bodnar, also the author of *Sunbelt*, a Novel published by Quadrangle Press in 1986, is a retired attorney currently living in Broken Arrow, Oklahoma with his wife Joan. A naturalized American citizen, he was born in Vilshofen, Germany, as his Hungarian parents fled from Budapest, Hungary at the end of World War II. Upon the death of his father, Dr. Steven Bodnar, the former Hungarian Minister of the Interior and one of the leaders  of the Hungarian National Socialist Party, Arrow Cross, and Earl of Legeney, he immigrated to Brazil with his mother and brother.

He spent eight years in Brazil with his mother Angela and older brother, Steven, three years of which he lived on a Brazilian Ranch, known as a "fazenda" and the remainder in a Sao Paulo emigrant slum known as Villa Anastacio.

In 1958, through the efforts of his Aunt Ilona, a war bride of a Jewish American soldier she met in Germany, he and his mother immigrated to the United States to join their family in South Bronx, New York City. In March of 1958, his mother died of cancer and his aunt and uncle became his guardians. As the uncle, Ted Lewis was career military in the U.S. Army, Ted's next assignment was overseas to Tokyo, Japan for three years. He attended a military dependents' high school the first two years. Thereafter Ted Lewis was assigned to Fort Sill, Lawton, Oklahoma where the Author graduated from high school.

He was then educated in the United States in Oklahoma, receiving an undergraduate degree from Oklahoma State University, a Juris Doctorate from the University of Oklahoma College of Law and was a candidate for an L.L.M. at Georgetown University Law Center in Washington, D.C. The Author practiced law since 1972 in Oklahoma, Washington D.C., and in Texas, first in El Paso and then Dallas, and is a retired attorney currently in Education working at Glenpool High School. He has a son, Joey, living in Waco, Texas, with two grandsons, Jacob and Logan, and daughter, Angela Timmons and son-in-law, Andrew and two grandchildren, Bailey and Brady, and step-son, Devin Dorney, in Tulsa, Oklahoma.

While actively practicing law in El Paso, Texas, from 1987 to 2002, he was an Associate Municipal Judge for the City of El Paso and a Special Prosecutor in the State of Texas v. Maury Kemp, el al insurance fraud case that was then the single largest insurance fraud case in Texas to that time.